THE TIGER AND THE ROSE

"Kiss me, Sebastián, kiss away the past. Embrace me; never let me go, my Tiger."

He bent his head and his mouth moved on hers, and Daniella forgot everything—the past, the present, the future. He was all that mattered.

"This is love," he whispered, "sacred and sweet. You are no longer my dark rose, but my passion, my fire."

A cloud of her hair covered them like a vibrant, clinging mantle and the roaring fire spread between their bodies, consuming them in passion's forging flame.

There was now only the luxury of lovemaking and the loving, silken caresses as their fervent bodies came together and Daniella's lithe frame arched toward him. She thought she would swoon.

"Please, *please!*" she begged, holding him as if he would disappear and never return, her mouth trembling against his own. She clung to him in absolute surrender, his strength hard and ready against her body.

"You are mine, we are one," Sebastián murmured, moving ever closer until they were consumed in love's flaming glory, and again he murmured, "I will love you always."

"Always," she repeated.

And their love stood still, captured forever like a fine-stemmed rose in glass.

Let Sonya T. Pelton
Capture Your Fantasies!

Captive Chains
(2304-9, $3.95/$4.95)

Shaina Hill had always yearned to be a teacher. Heading out for the remote area of Thunder Valley in the Washington Territory, she never dreamed her employer would be the rugged rancher Travis Cordell.

Inexperienced in the ways of the heart, Shaina was a willing and eager student when Travis took her in his tanned, powerful arms. When the virile, handsome rancher branded her with his kiss, Shaina knew she would be bound with Travis in love's *Captive Chains*.

Dakota Flame
(2700-1, $3.95/$4.95)

Angered by the death of his father at the white man's hands, Chief Wild Hawk wanted to lead his people to peace and obey the call of his dream vision: to capture the beautiful young girl who possessed the sacred talisman of the Dakota people. But Audrina Harris proved to be more of a captive than Wild Hawk had bargained for. Brave and fiery, she soon tempted him with her auburn hair and lovely fair skin. Each searing kiss and passionate embrace brought their worlds closer together. Their raging passion soon ignited into a fierce *Dakota Flame*.

Love, Hear My Heart
(2913-6, $4.50/$5.50)

Her mother wanted her to marry a wealthy socialite; her father wanted her to marry his business partner, the handsome river pilot, Sylvestre Diamond. But radiant Cassandra St. James needed to know what *she* wanted to do, so she slipped on board the *River Minx* for a trip down the Missouri River.

One moonlit night, she shared a passionate kiss with the one man she had sought to escape. The satiny kiss and powerful embrace of golden-eyed Sylvestre captured her desire, yet he knew it would be more difficult to claim the rebellious heart of his blue-eyed love.

TIGER ROSE

SONYA T. PELTON

ZEBRA BOOKS
KENSINGTON PUBLISHING CORP.

ZEBRA BOOKS

are published by

Kensington Publishing Corp.
475 Park Avenue South
New York, NY 10016

First printing: October, 1990

Printed in the United States of America

For all my faithful friends . . . my fans.
Love—
s.

Prologue

Charleston Harbor, 1719

Lucian Drake's dark, narrow face was livid with fury as he marched up and down the deck of his ship, whipping the blade of his sword viciously against his boot. "Tell me again," he raged at one of his men cowering now before the pirate leader.

"He hit me on the head in the dark, real sudden like," Frankie answered, a tremble in his voice. "Then he must've loosed the boat 'cause it's gone, Cap'n."

Lucian broke into French as he always did when angered and screamed invectives at the crew that they could not understand. He spoke their language once again. "Anyone see him take that gold out of my box?"

The scarred pirates shook their heads, earrings jangling as they passed sullen looks amongst themselves. Their shifty eyes moved, speaking without words.

Now Lucian spoke as if to himself. "How did he break open my cabin door? Ah! You idiots would not know, *certainemente*. That half-Spanish dandy . . . who is he anyway?" Not one of the pirate's mates had an answer. Then he jerked his thumb at the ship's carpenter, a lean, thin, tired man who had grown old at sea. Frankie couldn't see very well anymore and his bronzed face had lost its original savage cast, but still there was some fight left in him.

7

"I want that money back, Frankie," Lucian Drake snarled. "Kill the man if you have to, and do not capture him alive and bring him back. I wish to see the last of him. But you are to get that gold!"

One of the men was worried. "We could end up in jail if we get too rowdy, Cap'n. Look what they did to Stede Bonnet and William Kidd."

"All that has been taken care of, men. Stede Bonnet murdered and plundered." He grinned evilly. "I, my good men, am a noble defender of this coast and, like my younger brother who has just joined our Brotherhood, we are under orders from the governor. Now listen well: If you get into trouble, send word to the governor that you are Drake's men. Hear me: No drunken roistering or fighting—no wenching, either."

"Aye, Cap'n!!"

"No man has ever defied Lucian Drake and gotten away with it clean, as all of you well know."

"What's the name of the man we're lookin' for, Cap'n?"

Drake twirled the end of his mustache. "You saw him on my ship and you all know what he looks like . . . Well, don't you?"

"Uh . . . he was awful dirty, Cap'n."

"And he had lots of long, greasy hair that hung in his face. Do you know his name, Cap'n, or not?"

"I am not sure what his name is—but I do know he is the bastard son of Captain Kidd." He snarled as if he hated the name of the dead man. If memory served him right, and drink was not pickling his brain, Lucian also recalled that Kidd's bye-blow had had dealings with the Landakers of Cornwall.

"Come along with me, Frankie, I want to talk with you in the privacy of my cabin."

Once there, the door secured, Lucian poured his worries out to his old friend who listened with half an ear; besides being half blind, he was also half deaf.

Since Lucian had just lately promised the governor of the Carolinas that he would lay hands off the Landakers, he decided he did not want the man back on his ship.

There had been a bad feeling in Lucian's gut the whole while the greasy-haired individual had been on board. It drifted in and out of his mind that he had encountered that one in his lifetime once or twice before. He could be a spy, he told Frankie, possibly one of the crafty officials from the Windstar Fleet. Drake wanted to stay as far away from that bunch of agents as possible, those men who represented the vigilant fleet of company enforcers.

In a highly inebriated state, Lucian had once taken one of their merchant ships and it had almost been the downfall of his career. Among his other cocky mistakes had been the slaying of the raven-haired lord Steven Landaker, the capture and rape of Eileena Landaker, and the robbing of the Landaker townhouse.

"When shall I get away from the blasted Landakers, Frankie?" There had been a lasting feud between their families over the rights to some land in Cornwall . . . and the governor of the Carolinas had warned him to leave them be. This was going to be a difficult task for him.

"I despise the Landakers . . . and I am not sure that the man we captured was not one of them . . . or affiliated with them." He turned to his mate. "Frankie?"

Only loud snores answered the pirate Captain Lucian Drake.

Lucian had no idea how close was the man he searched for . . .

Chapter One

Fifteen men on the Dead Man's Chest—
   Yo-ho-ho, and a bottle of rum!
Drink and the devil had done for the rest—
   Yo-ho-ho, and a bottle of rum!
           —Robert Louis Stevenson

A huge silver fish jumped in the murky water, and clouds swirled across a night sky obscuring the bright stars. The man lay still, breathing heavily. Every muscle in his body ached from the strain of the struggle through the marsh. No doubt the boat he had stolen was being carried by the tide into the currents that twisted and eddied around these Carolina islands.

He licked his dry lips, thinking of roast beef. Huge slabs of crusty French bread. Dried-plum pie—

Heaven help him, but there were damp weeds full of prickly burrs under him. *El diablo!* . . . he was too tired to care. But the stink. It was like rotting fish. *That* he could not avoid.

Sebastián told himself he desperately needed to find a hiding place. It would be light soon. There were other boats plying these accursed islands, other small craft with the pirates he was trying to avoid possibly searching for him at this very moment. Drake's day was coming, he vowed.

11

He laughed, and it was a tired sound. Sebastián's coarse but ruggedly attractive features darkened to deepest gold, high cheekbones gleaming with sweat. His sculpted mouth twisted wryly.

His ship . . . He wondered where that good lady was at this moment. He was hoping his friend Juan Tomaz had taken the *Tiger* into his care after discovering his absence. He hoped the ship had not been broken to pieces in a hurricane in the Florida Channel. He was hoping for a lot. Now he needed to pray!

Sebastián did give thanks to God that Lucian Drake had not discovered his absence — not yet. When Lucian returned to his ship, the *El Draque,* he would likely be hooting drunk, but by daylight Drake would be sober again — and furious enough to send a party ashore in search of tracks, to beat down the thickets in search of him.

Sebastián knew the crew of the *El Draque* would search every waterfront *taberna* and brothel in Charleston. The city would be crawling with Drake's vermin, turned inside out by the ruffians; decent citizens would be in for a sound harassment, their privacy invaded until the bloody pirate was convinced that his quarry was not hidden in the town. For this reason Sebastián knew he had to find himself far from the comfortable allure of Charleston and with little delay — no matter how exhausted and hungry he might be. He could not avoid Charleston forever because then he would starve, but surely he could watch out for Drake and his men. He needed clothes and he was also badly in need of a cobbler, since his boots were in disrepair.

12

Oh *Dios,* he prayed for a delicious chicken leg right now . . . But he would not be choosy . . . a wing or two would serve as well. He wiped his salivating mouth on the grimy sleeve of his tattered white linen shirt. *Jesús,* he must have the odor of twenty bulls turned inside out and left to rot in the heat of the Spanish sun.

When Sebastián lay down, he dreamed of the last woman he had bedded. It seemed so long ago. Maggie. Was that her name . . . ?

Maggie. Yes. Her head looked as if it could not support the heavy tangle of blue-black hair that flowed to her supple hips. He stretched his long frame over her in her scarlet-canopied bed and felt himself becoming firm as he pressed against her wriggling hips. Her face was flushed with passion when he pressed deeply into her, moving with a slow, steady rhythm. He could feel her long fingers running over the corded muscles in his back. His tenderness fled and he took her demandingly, savage in his desire, murmuring words of lust, not love, into her ear. Sensing Maggie's release, he quickly wanted to join her. He gripped the masses of ebony hair . . . but she was fading. Gone. Sebastián awoke, bathed in the sweat of his erotic dream.

Coming to his elbows, Sebastián gazed up into the moss-hung branches. Maggie. Now he remembered the woman with the fire in her eyes and the unbridled thrust of her hips. He had known plenty of women, had used them and discarded them. None of the women he had bedded had meant anything to him, but the thought of using them suddenly seemed distasteful and he groaned, rolling over to his side, hungry not for woman but for

13

food. At this moment, he would give up all his experience with the willing tarts for one, just one, roast-beef dinner.

For food Sebastián had a packet of ship's biscuit, tough as iron to start and now soggy as mold on mildew. Two salty strips of dried meat had to suffice for nourishment. He felt in the pocket of his baggy brown breeches, finding he had only a little gold in his pouch—money he could not make use of until the *bastardo* Drake hauled anchor and took his prowling witch off to sea once again.

There were little sucking noises in the marsh as Sebastián set out to hunt high ground. Large fish slithered in the charcoal waters. He had to get out of these waters . . . *Sí*, quickly.

Sebastián had no idea in which direction to go—he had never before in his life set foot in the Carolinas. He had seen pictures and maps, but they could not aid his memory at this time.

Thin wraiths of fog twisted between the trees and beaded the hanging vines with moisture. A tall heron stood on one skinny leg. Sebastián's eyes narrowed as unseen filaments of damp cobwebs dangled in his face, clung to his skin as he walked deeper and deeper into the steamy, twilight-blue forest.

Madre de Dios! So much time had been wasted at sea aboard Drake's pirate ship, then sailing off the coast of Florida where the plate ships of Spain slipped in and out, pointing their black guns, running fleet of sail and wind away from the *El Draque*.

Drake had caught him twice now, when his guard had been down, but this last time he should have brought a little more security with him, like Juan Tomaz, his good friend—or perhaps a bit more weaponry on his person—*concealed* of course in various places. What was the matter with him lately? It was as if his mind were in another world. He would have to watch himself.

Now, in a lonely moment, Sebastián's thoughts turned to his parents. He had never known his father, the famous Captain Kidd who was the father of several children, not all of them bastards. Perhaps he was Captain Kidd's only bastard, he did not know. His beautiful mother Rebecca had been aboard the *Quedah Merchant* when Captain Kidd had seized the ship and her valuable cargo. At a port in Hispaniola, Captain Kidd heard the bad news that he had been proclaimed a pirate in England, and when he reached Boston he was immediately arrested on the Earl of Bellamont's orders and sent to London where he was hanged. *So much for knowing the man who had sired him,* Sebastián thought wryly.

Sebastián spoke aloud to himself. "Drake's mistake, when he captured me, was not in killing me first chance he got!"

Now Sebastián had escaped Lucian once again and he had to find his ship, the *Emerald Tiger,* if she had not been sunk in the Florida Channel. Ah, but first he would locate the home of the young woman Robert Drake—Lucian's younger brother—planned to wed and spirit away to the high seas. He had knowledge that she had befriended young Robert Drake years ago, and that she resided somewhere in the Carolinas.

Lucian Drake's crew had gossiped once too often of young Robert's precious treasure over their rum cups, calling her "Miss Wingate."

Miss Wingate. They had never mentioned her first name. For some reason he could not fathom, he found himself struggling to form an image of her, this young woman he had never met whose name intrigued him. Was she beautiful? Or was she a spinsterish schoolteacher type, as her name seemed to imply?

Sebastián wondered — as he felt the scars the drunken Lucian had given him — how she would look with a few of her own. Perhaps he would not give her a physical flaw but a brutal shock, as Sir Lucian had done to Eileena Landaker — a lasting scar which had rendered the lovely victim mute, unable to utter a single word for the rest of her life.

He would shave off his beard and mustache. Trim his hair to shoulder length — perhaps shorter. He knew how to pose the dandified gentleman; he'd donned the guise often enough . . .

Revenge would be sweet. Sebastián swung back the long, greasy strands of his once-tawny-gold hair, now turned to a dull, mousy brown — unwashed, smelly, and unkempt. He knew that Charleston couldn't be more than a dozen miles away. Soon, ah soon, the Drakes would fall into his neat little trap. All he needed was his crew . . . and the lure, Miss Wingate. He prayed she was indeed lovely and not the spinsterish type, for he could not enjoy his game with a woman who was less than passably attractive.

Ahead all was new, a virgin page on which he was free to write whatever fate permitted . . .

The cobbler Jeremy Case looked up from his bench, drew his waxed end through the leather between his knees, and snipped off the end with a sharp knife. With curiosity masked by a pretended indifference, he surveyed the tall man who stood before him in his shop.

Rubbing his nose with a stained forefinger Jeremy allowed his gaze to move deliberately over this stranger. He took in a well-cut broadcloth coat, velvet waistcoat embroidered in burgundy-and-gold silk, white ruffled shirt, and fine hose . . . Ah, but the boots—the wide-topped seagoing boots, totally out of fashion with the golden-haired man's outfit.

Jeremy spat and wiped his mouth with the back of his large hand. "Folks who come to Jeremy Case to be shod must fetch their own leather, mon."

Sebastián grinned lopsidedly and stepped out of the tall boots. "As you can see for yourself, I have no leather." He quirked a sandy eyebrow, his eyes glistening between long-lashed lids. "Not that I'd expect you to contrive proper footgear for me out of *these* things—but haven't you got a hide around that you could use, my good man?"

The cobbler snorted and reached for a boot. "You're a sailor, I can tell by these seagoing boots. Cobbled a many of 'em for seafaring gents of the trade."

The tall, freshly scrubbed man cleared his throat. "I have left the sea. And now, kind sir, I need boots to wear on the streets of Charleston." He emphasized his need and his haste.

Jeremy's shrewd blue eyes studied Sebastián's un-shod feet. "These here wasn't never made for the likes of you in the first place, I'll bet." Sliding from his bench, he rummaged amid the litter and disorder of a table, jerked open an unpainted, rickety cupboard, and drew forth a sheet of muslin. "Stand," he said.

"Sir?"

"Stand on the muslin," Jeremy ordered. When Sebastián complied, with a piece of charcoal the cobbler drew a pattern of his feet.

"So . . ." Jeremy drawled. "Surprised me, you did. You have been a sailor for some time. Sailors got splayed feet; going barefoot and wet timber splays 'em."

"How long will it take for you to make me a pair of . . . ah . . . regular boots?"

"Ain't said I'd make 'em yet, fella. Need me some buckskin, or kid's hide. I ain't got any fine leather right now. Got a calf hide, that's all. It'll cost you more if I furnish the hide for you."

Sebastián stared for a moment at his knee-high leather boots. They were far gone. He hadn't much gold left in his pockets, but he said, "I'm ready to pay. You see, I don't much care for walking the streets of Charleston in seagoing boots."

Jeremy caught the eyes of the man lingering on a fine pair of leather he'd just finished work on, just about the right size too. "Heh. If you stole those boots you could get your throat cut or your neck hung."

Sebastián's eyes narrowed. "I am not about to steal anything, sir."

"Six shillings to make you a pair of gentleman's boots." The cobbler reached for his awl. "Take it or leave it, mon."

"I will take it. You must do a good job."

Now Jeremy studied the man's long dark fingers, which looked strong enough to kill. "What about these old boots?" he asked.

"I think I'll keep them, thank you." As soon as possible he was going to sink them in the bay with everything else that could be traced to his brief career aboard the pirate ship.

Yesterday — his wardrobe furnished by a plantation slave who liked the sound of jingling coins — Sebastián had come downriver on a barge, rowed by Negroes accompanied by half-wild hogs headed to market. The high-topped pirate boots had served him well during his search for lodgings along the muddy streets of Charleston. He got a room finally in the house of a tanner, giving his name as Lord Steven Landaker. It was a small room on the third floor, but the bed was clean and the house respectable. Luck had been with him. He'd been able to purchase two black wigs, curly and long, from an aged actress.

He needed a friend of consequence in town, and he had almost given up when he recalled he carried a name locked in his memory. He might as well get down to business right off. With his best gentlemanly airs, he inquired of a passing gentleman the way to the house of Mister Wingate. Surely Robert Drake's young woman had a family . . . a father . . .

Now that he had the name of the plantation — Braidwood — Sebastián only need wait until he owned a pair of fine leather boots. He had no idea how furiously the cobbler was working on them at this very moment, his eyes twinkling with the golden glint of money.

Chapter Two

Most friendship is feigning, most
loving mere folly.
— William Shakespeare

O, beware, my lord, of jealousy;
It is the green-eyed monster which doth mock
the meat it feeds on.
— William Shakespeare

Braidwood Plantation, South Carolina, 1719

The basket of bread and cheese and drink ceased
its sway and Daniella paused to breathe of the
dewy swamp roses which grew in the clearing near
the riverbank filling the air with a sweet romantic
fragrance. The gentle wind lifted remnants of fog
from the grassy earth. Within the deep folds of her
hood, the long, dark-blond lashes of her translucent gray eyes shifted.

She came to a halt once again so as not to startle
a bird, but the blue-winged creature hopped to another flat-topped rock, pecking at the spongy moss.
He cocked his eye at the human and then took to
the sky.

Daniella awaited the poignant moment when the
man would appear from the gray morning mist.
While she looked for Robert, her shoulders lifted in

a pensive shrug. Why, she wondered, after such a long period of relative tranquility, should her life be suddenly turned upside down? Her eyes clouded as she thought of the problems which now beset her.

Marriage—to a total stranger.

The blonde heard the dear, familiar voice then. "Dany!"

When Daniella Wingate pushed back the hood of her green cloak, she revealed an oval-shaped face, fragile with a natural beauty that was Dany's own. Robert secretly leered as the wind swung a waist-length chestnut-blond mane he remembered so well, especially the feel of the heavy tresses his hands now itched to delve into. He remembered, too, the provocative swaying motion of her hips.

Robert Drake studied Dany. Framed by wind-blown wisps of flaxen hair, her face was cameo pale, flawless as expensive white velvet. Her jawline still had a stubborn thrust to it. Her nose was a slim, straight line, her lips soft and natural pink. Huge, dancing gray eyes were fringed by the thickest, most golden lashes. A dark-rose gown peeked through the folds of her forest-green cloak and the hem lifted over the delicate turn of a slender ankle. Robert wondered if she would taste like honey and feel like silk . . . all over.

Daniella studied her childhood playmate. Robert looked almost like a pirate, but he could not have become one; he would never stoop to such an infamous trade. Daniella's heart was light. It seemed that ages had passed instead of only two years. Daniella went to him and he hooked an arm about her slim waist and whirled her about in a flurry of colorful garments.

"Robert . . . how I've missed you! I cannot express how very much!" she cried, tilting her head back.

"And I've also missed you, Dany." Some irritation was evident in his voice. "Do you realize that I sent a message long ago for you to meet me?"

Daniella's skirts brushed the dewy flowers along the path and her large, expressive eyes appeared somewhat wounded as she explained while, at the same time, she wondered at Robert's slightly mocking expression. She masked her mild surprise as she stared off into the distance. "I am sorry, Robert, but I could not manage to steal away at such a late hour. Father would have been worried had he discovered my absence . . ." She tossed her long, shimmering hair. "You know that yourself from past experience."

From under hooded brows, Robert studied the creamy texture of her cheeks and the glow of her wonder-filled eyes, speculating on how it would be to gaze into those lovely orbs as he made love to Daniella. "You were never so careful in the past, Dany. What has changed you?" A lock of his thick brown hair fell over his wide forehead as he stared at the exquisite sight of Daniella.

"Father has me worried, Robert. Indeed, I believe he is not all that well."

"I'm sorry to hear that," Robert remarked. Intoxicated with burning lust for Daniella but concealing it for the moment, he turned his thoughts to even more devious imaginings. It had been a long while since he'd visited a house of ill repute. Now his desire to have Daniella was stronger than ever, but he knew she'd not be easy for the taking. Daniella Wingate had been raised in a family of high moral fiber and lived under the thumb of Mistress Tilford who, with the keenest hawk eye, watched every movement that the young chit made. Someday he thought lecherously. Someday soon he would whisk Daniella away.

Hoping Robert would not continue to regard her in that most disturbing fashion, Daniella tried to think of something to say to break the tension which was building with each passing moment. For some reason—hard though it was to suppress the flickering image—she was reminded of the dream again, the one last night in which a stranger dragged her roughly against him, his mouth slashed demandingly across hers.

Reliving the dream she'd had just that morning, Daniella could again almost experience the uncontrollable trembling when she awoke from the pleasurable yet frightening dream. This was the true reason it had taken her so long to prepare herself to meet Robert. The persistent longing and unfamiliar tingles, almost a tangible force, had nagged at her long after the dream had faded away.

Now Robert took her arm. Daniella blinked out of her disturbing haze and smiled demurely as he spoke. "I returned just last evening to Charleston." He did not mention that he had just missed his brother Lucian as his ship pulled out several days before the *Raven* sailed in. "I have so much to tell you, Dany. Come and sit while we share that basket you have brought along."

Recalling the timeswept years they had spent together in their childhood, Daniella smiled reminiscently. Lucian Drake had been more than happy to send his younger and only brother Robert from his ramshackle manor in England to the comfortable Wingate household in the Colonies. Lucian had been the only guardian Robert had known; that is, until a longtime friend of the Wingate family, Alain Carstairs, had brought Robert to Braidwood. Her father, Edward Wingate, with only his motherless daughter to inherit four merchant ships, had offered encouragement to the lad, envisioning Robert as captain, but not suitor. Robert had often returned to Cornwall to visit his brother, who was always sailing off on some new venture. Daniella had never ceased to miss Robert; this last time her handsome friend had stayed away from Braidwood for a very long period.

Suddenly, and with a deep, tortured groan, Robert turned to Daniella and kissed her. It was so sudden.

When the kiss was over, Daniella was blushing furiously—even though the kiss had been gentle, even a little chaste.

"You are still delicate, aren't you," Robert stated.

Regretfully Daniella agreed. Just the year before she had given up hope of ever becoming any taller than her present height of five feet and *almost* three inches. And she was almost twenty years old, old enough to become a bride. Her father wanted her properly wed and she couldn't understand his sudden haste to this end. She believed in love, true love, believed if she was loved by a certain man, she would be truly made whole . . . but she wanted to be romanced and treated like a princess, not just a wife, barefoot and pregnant. Too, she wanted to be able to pursue her favorite pastime—singing. She also liked reading novels, romantic ones, Shakespeare, and poring over the account books of her father's shipping business.

Robert swept his arm to where the river shimmered and meandered, lying summer-blue between the shore and the distant green of the islands. "Nothing has changed, Dany! This is still our special place and you are still my girl."

For a moment, as she reached inside the basket for two shiny apples, Daniella thought that much indeed had changed in the time Robert had been away. The most significant change had come about when she had started having the dreams. What? Two, three months ago? She couldn't recall exactly, but the most exciting and frustrating dream had come to her slumbering mind last night. She had been deeply embarrassed when she awoke. Why couldn't she put the strange dreams out of her mind? Always a stranger would reach for her, snatch her roughly against him, and then ruthlessly his lips would plunder hers and she would be sent spiraling into a maelstrom of wild, bewildering sensations. There were only impressions, and she was hazily aware of touch and a tingling awareness of the senses. There were no striking features, but she could vaguely make out jeweled eyes and dark, burnished hair. She was also aware that her dream phantom was a tall and muscular man.

"Dany?" Robert brought her back to the present. "You seem so far away from me all of a sudden." His tanned brow rose quizzically.

With a guilty flush staining her cheeks, Daniella hurried to explain. "I am here, Robert—I shall always be here," she said without strong conviction.

Yet, to Daniella, at this moment, no one in the whole wide world could be handsomer than her childhood playmate. Awkwardness gone, a few years older and wiser, Robert had slipped into vigorous manhood, but his eyes still danced with the

26

same old dark mischief. He struck a theatrical pose, long taupe traveling cloak thrown open, one hand resting with casual negligence on his dagger belt; then he took hold of her soft white hands. "Our pretend stories are coming true, Dany," he said. "I've recently joined in several ventures. Remember how we use to make believe and sail away on our own ships and make our fortune and you sang like a nightingale? Do you still sing?"

"Yes," she murmured, and curiously watched his excitement grow. Oh, if only Robert were the lover in her dreams, then everything would be crowned with perfection in her life, she thought sadly. But something was sorely amiss in their friendship. He was handsome, true, but could she love him, accept him as a lifelong mate?

"I now have a ship of my own." He squared his shoulders. "She's called the *Raven!*"

Daniella smiled happily. "Oh, Robert—that is wonderful. Truly."

"Why the crestfallen look then? Aren't you happy for me?"

"Well . . ." Daniella said with a pretty pout, "I thought perhaps you'd come back to Braidwood for good." Tormented by uncertainty, she shrugged lightly, wondering at her confusion as to whether or not she truly wanted Robert.

"You mean—to stay?" Robert asked.

"Of course!" Her flounced skirts rustled beneath her cloak as she turned, her beautiful but stern visage illuminated by loving memories. "What is so wrong with that? You stayed before. I did not mean for you to stay here forever, never to leave, but Father meant for you to captain one of the Wingate ships someday." She had even thought seriously of making a gift of one of her favorite ships to him, her friend, like the merchantman *Rampant Rose,* called thus in honor of her middle name.

"You want me to captain a *trading ship,* Dany?"

"Of course. Why not?" She pursed her full, bow-shaped mouth.

"We Drakes aren't traders. We hold privateers' papers with the royal seal."

"Privateers' papers, Robert—that is like being a pirate."

"Not actually. It is like what the man called the Tiger does. Papers, Dany, from the king or the governor of the Colonies." He did not hasten to add that the Tiger was employed solely by the Windstar Fleet, was in fact part owner in that company of private sea enforcers.

Daniella's eyes flashed with recognition of the infamous appellation. "The man they call the Tiger? You know him, Robert?"

"I could say he is an acquaintance of mine, Dany."

The Tiger was no more his friend than the man in the moon was. The elusive man was head agent of the established Windstar Fleet. Obscure and secretive, the Tiger acted with such a dazzling combination of shrewdness and stealth that no one knew his actual name or countenance.

"As rumored . . ." Daniella began. "Is the Tiger really a Landaker?"

"I don't think so," Robert said, uncertain just where the Tiger actually came from. He seemed to belong to no one or nothing.

Was this man, this Tiger one of the deceased Landaker lords? Robert inwardly mused. And what of the Landaker man his brother Lucian had slain?

Some said the Landaker ghost walked the misty moors of Cornwall at midnight and stood on the rocky cliffs of Tallrock under the moon . . . A disquieting shiver rippled through Robert. It was strange that there was no one who had ever seen what the Tiger actually looked like.

"So . . ." she said with a flash of her beautiful, full-lipped smile. "You have . . . ah . . . visited the Landakers?"

"That I have," he said, his dark eyes elusive now. "There's a secret passage from the house, Dany. You should just see the hidden treasure there."

With a frown, she spread the rough linen tablecloth on the grass. "You make it sound as if you have already seen this treasure yourself," Daniella said.

"Yes, I have seen some of the booty." Robert didn't add any more to the conversation. He gallantly spread his voluminous cloak on a rocky ledge and pulled a slightly reluctant Daniella down beside him before she could spread the lunch on the tablecloth. Suddenly, after tossing his uneaten apple aside, he yanked her close. She was a little frightened of the look in his dark eyes as a furtive hand slid up from her waist and lingered dangerously close under one of her breasts.

Softly, almost menacingly, Robert murmured, "I want to kiss you, Dany."

"Robert, please . . . not now. Let's share the lunch I have prepared."

Silence reigned. She would rather sing to him, or talk as they used to, for she did not care for Robert in a passionate way. When would she know desire for a man? She wondered, and then it came to her in a sudden clear light: When she dreamed of the faceless phantom she awoke with an awareness of what strong desire must be like . . . and her dream lover was absolutely *nothing* like Robert.

"Let's get married, Dany!" He squeezed her around the waist, dark eyes delving into soft gray ones. "We can do it today!"

Suddenly Daniella's world was reeling and tipping sideways. She twisted free and leaned against the softness of mossy rock, her voice emerging so low it was difficult for Robert to hear. "I . . . I am promised," she said.

"What?!" Robert's dark eyes blazed without any spark of light. "To *whom?*" Seizing her by the arm, he leaned close and when she would not answer immediately, he snarled, "I'll kill the sneaking bastard! Just tell me who he is!"

"I . . . I truly do not know."

"You don't . . . know?"

"Father said *he* will be a . . ." She paused and hurried on. "A surprise."

While Daniella reached for the jug of lemonade, Robert swore softly and turned a mottled shade of red. Suddenly Daniella saw a young man who was neither handsome nor kind. "A surprise?" he sneered. "You want this?"

Daniella shrugged as she uncorked the jug. "I've never even seen the man. How could I want him yet?"

"Tell me what you do know then."

"There's really not much to tell, after all. Father is giving me time to think it over."

Robert grabbed a hunk of cheese and took a healthy bite. "Think it over? God's teeth, Daniella, how can you think the matter over when you've never seen the bloody hell what the man looks

30

like?" he blurted as he chewed the food in his mouth.

"Please, do not snap at me! I am confused enough as it is."

Silent and brooding, Daniella now gazed out over the river, watching the lifting sun spread across the waters in a radiating brightness. Come to think of it, it *did* strike her as odd that her father had suddenly discovered a mate for her. He wanted her to have security when he was laid to rest, this was true, so was he ill then? Was this the reason for his haste to see her wed, to make entirely certain that she would always be well cared for and loved? Her brow ruffled in a delicate frown. But who would love her on such short notice? And how could she manage the same?

"How far has this gone?"

Daniella broke apart the bread, took a portion for herself, then handed Robert the greater part. "I have not really agreed to any betrothal. And I know that a formal one, even by proxy, is almost as unbreakable as marriage itself so I have not agreed to anything like that, either."

Looking grim indeed, Robert wondered at this man whom Edward Wingate had chosen for his daughter to wed? He would hate him, whoever the intended was, and want to kill him. His hatred was so intense at the moment that he was reminded of those he despised most in the world: the Landakers. They'd been the Drakes' enemies for centuries, but he used their name to get what he wanted, influencing others who identified the name with reputable merchants and shipping. Eileena Landaker, now mute and helpless, could tell of his using *her*, too. That is, he snickered silently to himself, if she could speak. But she had lost her voice as well as her mind when he had taken her repeatedly, letting the violation sink into the darkest recesses of her mind. She was only alive because someone had helped her escape.

"You are almost twenty, Dany, and entirely old enough to decide for yourself."

"Yes, and old enough to realize that this is the way marriages are sometimes made. You are making too much of it, Robert." She laughed lightly, though hardly feeling lighthearted at all. "I am not wed *yet*."

Utterly disregarding her words, he went on to say, "I cannot understand Edward's thinking. A fond and indulgent a man as he is, you'd think he would have discussed the serious matter of marriage with his beloved daughter."

"He might turn out to be a gentleman, and handsome to boot." Daniella tipped her head in thought, her shining gold-brown hair falling silkenly over the bodice of her dark-green cloak.

"Oh Dany, be sensible! You may lose something in this dangerous game you and your father play."

"There is no game. Anyway, you fret too much. I shall lose nothing, dear friend."

Dark eyes roved hungrily over Daniella's lips and throat and taut breasts as Robert pondered the matter: *Nothing, darling, but your snow-white purity, and that's going to be mine someday!*

A river-sweetened breeze tugged at Daniella's long hair and she looked aside, away from the suddenly fiery look in Robert's eyes. At the edge of Daniella's mind was the hazy image of her betrothed, and apprehension pressed upon her. She prayed that her husband would be kind and gentle.

Silently, Daniella stood and gathered her things back into her basket. When she turned back to look for Robert she found herself alone, with only the soft-flowing river gliding by, resplendent in the afternoon sun.

Daniella sank into the snowy whiteness of her four-poster bed for one more delicious moment. Then, sliding naked from the downy covers, she stepped gracefully to the tall, diamond-paned window.

Standing there like a radiant, shimmering flame in the sunrise, flushed from her dreams, Daniella gazed out upon the morning as it awakened in vibrant hues of shot-silver and gold. In the dream, her breath had emerged in ragged gasps when once again her dream phantom had captured her lips in a pillaging kiss. His fingers had tangled in her hair as he bent her backward over his arm, driving her wild with blazing caresses that made her moan aloud with frustration. Afire all over, she had been jerked suddenly awake, fully expecting her phantom to step from the soft gray shadows — in the flesh.

Now, with the sun's rays warming her, Daniella felt shaky and fearful the dream would return the next time she slept. Afraid — and yet anticipating . . .

Taking a deep, steadying breath, she allowed her mind to clear of the vaporous dream-stuff and grasp at sober reality. "I really must be stronger," she told herself.

Humming snatches of a favorite song, Daniella briskly moved to prepare her toilette for the day. She turned her mind to safer thoughts, smiling almost shyly when her newly appointed maid came in to help her dress.

"Good morning, Miss Wingate," Bettina said cheerily as she began to brush Daniella's long silken hair. Bettina pondered all the gossip she'd been overhearing in the kitchens, but Daniella broke into her reflections briefly.

"That feels so good, Bettina," Daniella murmured. "Your hand is gentle with the brush, unlike the maid before you who used to tear through my hair and bring tears to my eyes."

Bettina did not question why Daniella had tolerated Miss Randington for so long, but it was not her place to gossip with the young mistress of Braidwood. She found the beautiful blonde to be kind and caring, unlike what Cook Vivien said when she spoke spitefully of the "mistress's airs." She had also heard that Daniella had been spoiled terribly by her father, but Bettina saw none of this in the young miss. At first, she did wonder why Edward Wingate had sired no sons. Rumor had it that Edward could have had his pick of a new wife after his bride of ten years passed away. He could have had sons to secure his fortune, but Edward had been unable to forget the memory of his lovely Elizabeth. She had left him alone, with a baby daughter to raise by himself. Ever since Elizabeth's heartbreaking demise, Edward had been without a woman. There was not another love in his life, save his daughter Daniella Rose.

From her first step, Edward had allowed Daniella to trail at his heels, from work to garden to Charleston harbor. She knew ships, inside and out, though she had not traveled far. On Alain Carstair's suggestion, Edward had also let Daniella have a playmate from the Drakes of wild Cornwall across the sea in Great Britain. He had allowed Alain to fill Daniella's head with useless teachings, such as geometry and mathematics and singing lessons, when she should have been learning from Mistress Mary Tilford about running a household. Daniella also knew, inside and out, the running of a plantation. Edward had always hated ordering field hands around and looking after dull matters like money and credit, crops and arranging for the rice and lumber to be sent downriver. Daniella loved it, and the overseer and plantation folk depended on her abilities more than they did her father's.

"It is a beautiful day, miss," Bettina remarked as she set out a creamy muslin dress with green-and-pink embroidery all over.

"Indeed it is, Bettina," she answered, whirling in the soft, summery dress.

"That will be all, Bettina," Daniella said kindly, when she was finished with her toilette. "You may go now and see to your other tasks."

Bettina bobbed a curtsy. "Thank you, miss."

Alone, wandering about the sunny room, Daniella went to gaze out the window into the sunny garden below. So far, with her father and Mistress Tilford in charge, she had gotten all she wished for, especially the Italian tutor for her singing lessons. She had been content and happy with her work, too. On the first floor of the house was a sort of office where she took care of the accounts and even received the captains of ships, the overseer of their Cooper River plantation, and the rice purchasers. Sometimes, when Mary Tilford was ailing, she even ordered the tasks of the house servants. It seemed however, that her life was about to take a new turn.

She was soon to become wife to a mysterious stranger. How would she respond to his sudden presence? she wondered as she drew a deep, unsteady breath.

She had been lonely with Robert gone for so long. He was back, true, but for how long? Her friend would never stay around to see her wedded to another, that was certain.

Madame Gilberto's class in Bristol was drawing to a close, and Daniella was singing. Madame stood with her baton in hand.

"C'est une voix, ça," Madame Gilberto said in an aside to her pupils, the tone implying that theirs were not *voices*. They felt compelled to nod with polite smiles nonetheless.

Daniella, with her distinction, her obvious talent, was queen among them. She stood now with her hands loosely clasped, her gray eyes on the treetops seen through the windows. She sang on, indifferent alike to the jealousy or admiration. The aria chosen was from an Italian opera. Daniella sang with the highly colored art of the Italian school, and her voice stunned the listeners with its brilliance and purity. They listened, breathless, to the rising cadences which led to the inevitable high note and brought forth applause.

Madame looked at Daniella. "The voice is glorious. You have rare intelligence. *Mais . . . il y a quelque chose qui manque . . . Ici."* She pointed to her heart.

Daniella frowned lightly. What did the woman mean? she wondered. Then she heard the explanation:

"Ah!" Madame said suddenly. "You must fall in love, mademoiselle. I say *un grand passion* . . . Put tears in your voice, Daniella!"

As she walked home on the shady side of the lane that led from Madame Gilberto's to her own home, she pondered the words of her teacher and her mind at once returned to Robert. Daniella was certain that when Robert's temper cooled he would come swiftly to Braidwood. So certain in fact was she that she went about happy and cheerful as usual, as if nothing out of the ordinary had happened.

Taking the rose-tangled path toward the river's edge, Daniella again comforted herself with the thought that this must be only one more of the many quarrels their hot heads had gotten them into; soon Robert and she would be fast friends again.

For now, needing time alone to refresh herself before working on the account books, Daniella walked slowly along the path. The summer day was full of sunshine and the rapturous songs of bobolink and thrush. In the fields was a gay riot of wildflowers. She began to sing with joyous passion as she walked the rose-tangled path toward the river.

"My love, your lips touch mine
with flame, with sweetness, bliss,
like a loving night wind's kiss,
and I am forever thine own—"

Her clear young voice rang out gloriously and she flung her head back with a gesture of joyful abandonment. Her song rose higher in restless, swinging measures . . .

"My love, your lips . . ."

Daniella's voice ceased suddenly as her luminous gray eyes flickered. She frowned. Had she spotted someone walking ahead of her? Perhaps she had not heard the stranger pass by while she had been singing. Or was there really someone there ahead of her? No. She shook her head. She had only imagined it, she told herself.

Her reviving walk over, Daniella returned home.

That night, she again walked by the river's edge—but this time in her dreams . . .

"Is someone there?" her dream-voice asked. "Please show yourself."

Daniella's skin prickled when a tall, broad-shouldered figure came into view with long dark cloak flowing and lifting in a cooling river-soaked breeze. Staring up into the most disturbingly male face she'd ever laid eyes upon, she murmured, "State your name, sir, and your purpose for being here on Wingate property."

"I come in friendship, m'lady and I bid you a good morning. You are indeed beautiful—a flawless rose," the deep, compelling voice answered.

Hard hands were suddenly gripping her shoulders.

"Sir—I . . . I demand you unhand me."

She stared up at him; he stood easily over six foot. "What do you think you are doing. . . ? But I remember—you were in my dreams before? Why are you haunting my sleeping hours?"

"Don't be afraid of me, Daniella Rose."

Here was the irresistible phantom of her dreams.

His deep, soft voice twined about her mind like sweetly dangerous tendrils, curling and caressing her soul, as it had before. She had been content to remain an innocent, but somehow this tall stranger seemed to pose a threat to her purity. Surprise alive in her eyes, Daniella watched his lips close in on hers. She couldn't believe what was happening, but nonetheless watched anxiously as he bent his head over hers.

"You cannot mean to . . . kiss me again. You are not real. Get out of my mind, sir, for you do not belong in my thoughts. You frighten me and . . . and I do not wish for you to intrude on my sleeping hours. You have no right. Please go, and never return. I am soon to become a married woman and—"

Long fingers slipped beneath the glossy weight of her hair and grasped her by the nape, pulling her closer, as he murmured, "Yes . . . I can invade your dreams, Daniella, and I shall do more than that. One day you will belong to me, so you may cease fighting the inevitable and meet me, beautiful rose."

"Stop!" Daniella's slumbering mind screamed while her mouth resisted the formation of the words to halt his actions, and she could not speak anyway, not now, not if she wanted to, for his lips were capturing hers, sending a shock spiraling through her senses. Then he took hold of her shoulders to pull her even closer, and the impact of his lovemaking in her dream made her struggle to surface, but it was in vain, for he held her in a viselike grip and continued to plunder her tender lips, his passionate kiss burning and bruising, his tongue undulating within her unprepared mouth.

Her cheeks flamed, her heart pounded fiercely, her knees began to shake . . .

Finally she wrenched her mouth from his. "Out! Get out of my dream, you wretched blackguard!"

Daniella was jerked awake suddenly. She jumped out of bed and ran to the mirror, seeing her silvery reflection cast by the moon outside her window. The trees shifted in a night breeze, making purplish shadows and intermittently erasing her hauntingly sweet face in the mirror. Breathing was still difficult, her pulse still erratic.

Turning to face her bed, Daniella put her hands behind her to grip the edge of the dresser, telling herself she must return to bed. She had to sleep, otherwise she was going to have circles beneath her eyes in the morning and her father or Mary would question her . . .

Drops of perspiration stood on her forehead, but finally Daniella made it to her bed and found the peaceful sleep so badly needed.

Chapter Three

Or if some time when roaming round,
   A noble wild beast greets you,
With black stripes on a yellow ground,
   Just notice if he eats you.
This simple rule may help you learn,
   The . . . Tiger to discern.

                — Wells

There was a narrow path at the side of the house leading to the kitchen gardens and stableyard. Daniella was just crossing the path to enter the aromatic kitchen where Cook Vivien, with the new maid looking on, was making a pasty of delicious red berries with golden crust. The aroma was delicious and wafted afar.

Daniella licked her lips. Raspberry was her favorite dessert filling.

"Where have you been?" Vivien, looking hot and flustered, asked Daniella.

"Out" was all Daniella offered the cook, who pursed her thin lips. Daniella looked fresh as a rose, her blond hair pulled up in back and the puffed sleeves of her magenta gown folded back tidily. Her green cloak was suddenly tossed onto a sturdy chair nearby, making the maid wince at the young woman's carelessness.

Daniella's long-fingered hands moved deftly

41

among a collection of spices and stopped at one. "Here . . ." Daniella told Vivien. "You will need this one for the red rice." She held back a mischievous grin while Vivien only conceded with a grunt as Daniella handed over the spice.

Daniella knew Vivien disliked her, but the reason was unknown to the girl. Vivien had almost gotten herself dismissed years ago for spreading wild gossip about Daniella and Robert Drake and what they did when they went to the river's edge—which had been quite innocent, in truth.

Vivien looked over her shoulder and said, "Lord Steven Landaker of London is here."

"H-here?" Daniella looked at the woman in puzzlement. "Already?"

"So you knew he was a'coming."

"Not really." Heat was stealing into her face—and it was not from the warmth of the kitchen.

Vivien's eyes, which were a pale, watery green, fastened upon Daniella's astonished face as she turned to stare at the younger woman.

"Lord Steven Landaker, your betrothed, will dine with you and your father," Vivien said snidely.

Daniella put her hand on the table to steady herself and drew a deep breath. He was going to dine with them? Here? Lord Landaker in the flesh? Her stomach began to clench tight, and a flicker of apprehension swept through her. She had to get ahold of herself!

Bettina stared in confusion from one woman to the other. Vivien sneered at the young maid. Bettina's skin was like peaches and cream and without a flaw. Her shining hair was a deep carrot shade. Bettina's eyes softened. She thought the young mistress was beautiful and could not understand Vivien's dislike of Daniella, but then, it could be that Vivien was

42

jealous; the cook had an eye for Captain Carstairs. Alain was always bringing Daniella gifts and spending a lot of time with her.

"Please sit down, mistress, and warm yourself," Bettina dared say in the presence of the domineering Vivien.

But Vivien only gave Bettina a look, then said to Daniella, "Aye, mistress, you look pinched, you do. You, Bettina, fill a bowl of broth from the kettle."

Bettina, with large bowl in hand, stood over the white-faced Daniella as if preparing to feed her.

"Thank you," Daniella woodenly answered Bettina, taking the bowl from the kind girl's hands. Bettina made her feel better, more courageous . . . for the moment.

Daniella liked the new maid who brushed her hair so gently, and smiled to let Bettina know of her affection. An impish grin appeared on pretty Bettina's mobile mouth and set Daniella's own ablaze with mirth as Vivien looked at the beautiful young mistress in astonishment that she and the recently hired maid could get on so well in the short time they had been acquainted.

At that moment Mistress Tilford breezed into the room. Spotting Daniella, she said, "Your father has been asking for you, dear."

"I know. I heard." Daniella stared at Vivien, who looked away as if slightly embarrassed.

"Where have you been out traipsing to, even before Christians are awake?" Mary Tilford wanted to know, pointedly ignoring the crotchety cook.

"I took a walk after finishing work on the books" was the soft reply. Daniella drank the spiced broth Vivien had prepared while her creamy flesh was warmed on the outside by the crackling fire. She listened to its sound one moment, soothing, shooting up the wide chimney, then changing to a hiss now and again when fat from a mutton joint turning on the spit dropped.

Daniella mused again on the dream she'd had. She could not still her inner trembling, but she cast aside any further thought of her dream-invader. It was a puzzle, one which disturbed her greatly. It would do no good to think about the dream, she thought forlornly. Someday, perhaps not too far in the future, she would learn more about the mystery man who invaded her nighttime dreams.

The window was suddenly thrown wide by Bettina to let out some of the greasy smoke. Daniella could smell the damp earth of the newly turned borders which Rolf, jack-of-all-trades, was planting. She tried not to let waves of fear roll over her, but there was no help for it.

It was time. She could tell by Mary's stance. Praying to be anywhere but where she was, Daniella craned her neck to finish off her broth and stood, her heart a wild throb in her fluttering chest as she smoothed her clammy palms down the sides of her dress.

"They are in the blue parlor," Mary politely informed Daniella, her voice lowering as they neared the door. "It is the awesome Lord Landaker who has come."

Mary watched closely as Daniella took a deep breath and swallowed, her lovely face a mask of silent consternation. "Why do you say awesome?" she asked.

Mary pressed Daniella's arm. "You will see."

Daniella's large and luminous eyes didn't even blink.

At the door, Mary busied herself tidying Daniella's dress as if she were a child in need of coddling.

"Now?" Daniella asked.

"Now," Mary answered. "And if God wills it, sweetheart, the two of you will someday become man and wife." *It better be soon,* Mary thought, *because the master is ailing and he hasn't long to live . . . though the poor miss has no knowledge of this.*

Daniella looked at Mary as the kind but stern woman gave her a little shove toward the door.

Only a moment later Daniella turned back to Mary.

"I . . . I shall go the other way."

"What?"

"I . . ." Daniella looked at Mary with wide eyes.

Then Mary understood. "Go on with you then," she said. "You cannot put it off much longer, dear heart."

Mary watched the worried young woman as she took the long way around to give herself a few more minutes' time. How exceptional was the young Daniella, Mary thought with tears burning her eyes as she thought of leaving Braidwood behind.

The parlor was at garden level so that one could enter it by a gallery. Daniella's slippers made no sound on the polished wood floor and the door was open to the warming day.

Suddenly she was inside . . .

Daniella stood there, shivering inwardly, unnoticed by her father or their guest. She tried to gather enough courage to approach. Her breaths were very shallow and her palms were becoming even moister.

At any season of the year, even winter, the light in the Blue Parlor looked as if it filtered down through a greenhouse, and Daniella had never understood why the parlor was called "blue,"—for there was only one massive chair covered in that color. Everything else was a silver green or chartreuse shade. She supposed it was because her mother Elizabeth had given it that name and it had stuck.

Daniella shifted a little and then she saw *him*.

He was seated in that same blue chair. She almost giggled. *Peacock* blue. Daniella couldn't help but study the man who was to become her husband. From this vantage point all she could see was his dark royal-colored clothing, shadowy, lowered face, and . . . perhaps he was wearing a wig, for his black hair was quite long and so very shiny and curly!

Determinedly, Daniella took a deep breath, then stepped down from the gallery. The two men stood to come forward. Lord Steven Landaker held the ruby Venice glass and her father the deep green one. Daniella found herself staring at the ruby one and the gloved fingers that held it. The gloves were a sign of wealth, and so she did not think it unusual that he wore them . . . and his boots were fine and very new.

Unaware that she held her breath, Daniella watched as, right before her eyes, beside Edward Wingate's graceful dark slimness, the younger man seemed to grow larger than life—awesome, as Mary had said. She had always thought her father to be the best-looking man in the world. Now, though, he had an equal for sure, she thought. But already she could tell that Steven Landaker was excessively concerned with his manners and appearance.

Now she studied the man who was to be her husband—if she so wished him to be. Daniella swallowed slowly as, for a hair-standing moment, she thought she detected a merry twinkle in the hooded eyes behind the long, dark lashes. And for a moment, too, his look held hers and Daniella felt imprisoned by the heat that seemed to radiate from the unfathomable dark-gray eyes. Suddenly her betrothed stood closer; in fact, *too* close for much comfort.

Her heart began to pound when his steady gaze to her lips sent thrills reverberating through her body. "My fair damsel," he murmured just above her hand.

She had to contain a giggle as the dandified Lord Landaker bowed over her hand, for she suspected that his drink must have consisted of milk instead of a stronger libation. She went one further and imagined the man tripping and spilling the milk all over her hand and dress. But neither of these, she soon was to find, was the case as he held his glass aloft in a graceful fashion.

Then Daniella was lightly frowning as she braced herself for Lord Landaker's kiss. He was motioning her to come closer. She bent forward a little in order to have her cheek reach his puckered lips and was surprised to find his breath actually smelled of her father's most potent brandy.

With a smile which Mary had taught her must greet a special guest — whatever her own feelings might be — Daniella found her voice, clear as a bell. "I bid you welcome to Braidwood, Lord Landaker, and hope you will find your stay most delightful and, ah . . . immensely enjoyable."

"Ah, simply captivating." His voice was deep and resounding, with a bit of the "airs," as the English called them. "It is her mother's smile, is it not, Edward, my good friend?"

Friend? Daniella frowned, mesmerized by the coils of silken black hair that fell gracefully over his wide shoulders. So soon? How could this be, she wondered. She had not known that Lord Steven Landaker was a friend of the family? He sounded English; looked to have some Spanish blood, perhaps. The Wingates knew of no one from England, except perhaps merchants, and she had never seen this man in her father's office, for she had cared for the accounts and met all the business partners of the Wingate Shipping Lines.

"And," his deep voice grated across Daniella's already raw nerves, "hair as radiant as sunlight on the meadow."

He could not possibly have known her mother, Daniella told herself as she thought back in time. Lord Steven Landaker must have heard about Elizabeth Wingate's famed beauty, that was all. Daniella herself thought she'd inherited little of her mother's unique appearance, though there were those who thought them almost like twins.

Daniella thought she was passable enough, but this scrutiny was becoming boring . . . She'd rather be out walking with Robert Drake than standing here on display for the *awesome* Lord Landaker. No doubt *he* was trying to decide if she would do as a wife or not.

Daniella turned her gaze toward the huge portrait of Elizabeth that hung over the mantelpiece. The painting always gave her the assurance that something perfect and unchangeable existed in this world. One day perhaps her own portrait and that of her husband might hang there . . .

Turning her eyes back to Lord Landaker, Daniella was shocked when he lifted the ruby glass in a salute meant for her and the beautiful woman in the painting. So he had not known her mother after all! Lord Landaker was crafty, Daniella told herself. He was no doubt mean and evil, too. For a few moments more, Daniella's father and the lord stared at the stunning portrait of Elizabeth, each holding his own thoughts.

"Lovely," ruminated Lord Landaker, with chin in hand, "simply lovely."

Lord Landaker's voice had dropped lower and carried a tone of elegance. Daniella did not miss the deeper pitch, and she shivered again, not liking the man's personality thus far. There was something about him she could not put her finger on . . . but then again, perhaps he would grow on her. If given time, she might grow quite fond of him.

The portrait of Elizabeth hung beside a bright window, and it was as if Daniella herself had just stepped through it from the garden. It was all done in softest green and gold hues. Sun-warmed skin. Shadowed blue-gray eyes. A gown of palest ivory. At Elizabeth's dainty feet were the bunches of yellow roses, wild ones, which Edward Wingate had long ago chosen for his seal and sign.

Lord Landaker continued to study the portrait. His eye caught lines of graceful, sweeping movement and slender height captured for a moment in time by the famous Italian artist of that day. Elizabeth might be gone, but the loveliness of the woman lived on in the woman's daughter.

Were they going to gape at it all day? Daniella wondered, having turned her back to the men studying the portrait. She felt utterly confused, almost bewildered for some unfathomable reason, but her attention was soon recalled by her father's soothing voice.

"Darling, Lord Landaker brings us very sad news."

"What could that be, Father?"

Daniella had moved closer and could feel the disturbing eyes of her intended on her again. Why did it bother her that the "awesome" man stared? She had been stared at before this man came along, but then, no one had ever posed such a threat to her independence.

"There was the fever again in London early this

49

spring—and Landaker's young wife was taken."

"D-dead?" Daniella could only stare at the jewel-like sheen of her father's drinking glass.

"Dead." It was Lord Landaker himself who spoke.

Daniella sat down so suddenly that the big hound asleep by the heavy oak chair jumped to its feet. She had no sooner sat than she got to her feet again and stood with her hands pressed against the front of her rose-colored gown as if she was trying to flatten it to her thighs.

"Oh . . ." she cried softly, moving toward the man of whom she'd thought so unkindly. "Lord Landaker, I am sorry. How you must still be grieving."

"Indeed." Lord Landaker sadly gave a nod. "That I am."

With a look of thorough pain, Lord Landaker took hold of Daniella's slender white hands. She could not understand why the man's touch made her experience strangely tight sensations inside, as if all her nerves had gathered into one place—and now into Lord Landaker's large, strong hands. His fingers were very long—narrow, hard. He had removed his gloves, she noted. His touch was—she cringed—almost intimate.

Then Daniella chided herself for being so mean. And, oh, how sorry she felt for the poor soul!

Still holding Daniella's lovely white hands, Lord Landaker said, "Sweeting, we shall grow closer because of this." He took in her misty-eyed frown, then went on. "You will see, my dear. We shall like each other, in fact, immensely." He stared and Daniella was instantly mesmerized. "There are things we need talk about—"

"Not now though." Edward, seeing his daughter's distress, all of a sudden stepped between Daniella and Lord Landaker. His hand went to the dandified

50

gentleman's arm and that one stared at it and then lifted his eyes. "I insist," Edward went on, "that you rest before dinner. You will like Vivien's repast. She is the best cook in all the Carolinas—I promise you."

Daniella's stormy gray eyes were sharply trained upon Lord Landaker, and then they shifted to her father. Why this strange tension?

Once again Daniella felt that odd thrill when Lord Landaker spoke, and, oddly, rivers of pleasure traversed her spine and thighs.

"I—oh . . ." Lord Landaker felt his head. "Aye, Edward, perhaps a rest is just the ticket." As he spoke, his lazy, hooded eyes rested on the inquisitive Daniella. "Indeed, my sleep was poor just the week before . . . at sea. I fear I am not altogether . . . uhhmm . . . steady."

"Oh." Daniella shot forward. "Let me help—" but her father caught her hand, whispering in her ear, "Not this time, Dany, perhaps another. I fear . . . ah . . . Lord Landaker is rather shy."

"Shy?" Daniella stared at her father's slim face. The fop was no shy provincial lad but a sophisticated Londoner!

"Uhm . . ." Edward cleared his throat, repeating, "Shy and—confused at this time."

Steven Landaker's next motion did not confirm her father's statement as he swept a flourish before her, then bent over to take her hand in his to kiss it. As if burned by his touch this time, Daniella pulled her hand away and her lashes fluttered as she colored with embarrassment. Lord Landaker paused at the edge of the carpet, turned to sweep Daniella another gallant bow, almost scraping his nose on the floor as he executed the polite gesture, then gave his yellow-and black silk vest a yank over an immaculate, if somewhat effeminate, white, blousy shirt with lace-embroidered cuffs.

Daniella clamped a fingernail between her pearly teeth as she watched the genial dandy in the flamboyant attire cross the hall to the staircase.

"He is a bit of a peacock, Papa," Daniella said with soft laughter as she stood shivering beside her father. If he noticed how emotional she was, Edward said nothing of it. "But interesting," she added.

Daniella could sense her father's mood; she didn't even have to turn her head to look at him. He seemed slightly withdrawn . . . slightly bemused, too. He was as puzzled as she herself was.

"Poor man." Edward sighed and shook his head.

Daniella thought she hadn't heard correctly. "What did you say, Papa?"

"I feel sorry for the man."

Her voice emerged soft and low. "I am not sure I share that same sympathetic view . . ." She faced her father. "How did you meet him, Papa?"

"Steven lost his ship in the Florida Channel during a storm and came here, having lost all—his wife, his ship . . . everything."

Daniella's smooth brow formed a frown. "Surely he has holdings in England somewhere, perhaps a townhouse in London?"

Edward went on as if he hadn't heard his daughter voice her concerns. "He'll need all the help he can get."

"Of course, with his wife dying so sudden and all."

"And companionship."

"Oh . . . yes."

"Love."

"Ah . . . naturally, Father."

52

Around midnight, Daniella moved restlessly upon her huge brass bed, caught in the throes of a deeply impassioned dream. In it, her childhood playmate and sweetheart chased her over the arched bridge and down into the deep oak forest where it was dark and mossy. She laughed happily as Robert caught her about the waist, drew her close, and as his mouth closed over hers, she sighed deeply. Then the kiss changed. He was gentle no longer, but brutal and demanding as he pulled her against him and ground his lips and thighs into hers. When Daniella began to struggle and push away, his body became even bolder and more intimate, and Daniella cried out and bolted upright in bed.

Dear Lord, someone was in her room! Daniella sat up in bed, and shut her eyes tight against the invading spectre. The man walked swiftly into her dark room and stood at the moon-dappled bedside, reaching out a hand and giving her shoulder a shake.

"Daniella . . . Miss Wingate!"

Her large, luminous eyes were startled open, and Daniella stared up at the dark figure at her bedside. She was still frightened until he moved and she heard the soothing murmur of his mesmerizing voice. At once she relaxed.

"Lord Landaker . . . Steven."

"One and the same, fair damsel."

With big silver-gray eyes, Daniella watched as the dark shape of Lord Landaker's arm and hand came away from her shoulder and went to hang limply at his side. She knew he was staring at her, but she didn't realize how clearly he could see her with the whiteness of her thin nightgown and creamy skin haloing her form in the pale moonlight streaming in. Daniella could hardly see Steven Landaker at all, for his long black hair shadowed his features, making him blend with the night.

"Are you still frightened?" His voice was soft in the night-enveloped room and his cloak moved like bat wings.

"The nightmare is gone," she whispered, wondering if he had been out walking by the moon-dappled river.

"It must have been a bad one, for you were shaking all over."

Daniella could feel him bump against the bed and knew it was not done intentionally, but he surprised her by sitting down on the edge and resting his dark hand on the whiteness of the sheet. A shiver raced through Daniella as she stared down at the ungloved hand with its long, graceful fingers and trimmed nails. "In truth," she suddenly added, "the dream was one I hope will not return."

He laughed soft and deep. "I hope it was not of me, for I know I'm not that easy to look at."

"Oh, no." Dany took hold of his large wrist. "It was not your presence at Braidwood that troubled me in my sleep." Her hand was soothing on his arm. "You are not . . . not all that hard to look at, my lord." *In fact, you are quite the handsome peacock,* she almost blurted. Instead she stated the altered fact: "You are very easy to look at, sir."

"And you also, my dear. In fact, you are most comely."

"I . . ." Daniella could feel herself blushing. "Please, sir, do not speak so. We are in my bedchamber, you must realize."

"So we are." Lord Landaker took hold of Daniella's hand, startling her for a moment before he patted it and let her go. Then he stood slowly to his feet, saying, "I shall leave you now. If you should need me again, just call out. My room is just across the hall, my dear."

His tall, shadowy form moved to the door. There was the silence of a pause, and then the door closing softly sounded in the room. Daniella brushed the askew hem of her nightgown back down over her pristine, slender legs; then with a deep blush staining her creamy white face pink, she lay back on her pillow, knowing that the bad dreams had fled and would befoul her sleep no more this night.

Chapter Four

At the western chamber the peaceful moon
  was rising
And a breeze glided in, leaving the door
  ajar.
Stirrings of flower-shadows kept me
  surmising.
Has my love come, with the brightness of
  a star?

           —Anonymous, Chinese

Daniella's bedroom was large enough to hold a chest at the foot of her four-poster brass bed, a sturdy table for her various books, a huge wardrobe, and a white, French work desk. A bow window right above the grounds looked out over the Cooper River, partially hidden from view by a tangle of myrtle scrub and palmetto. There was a faint blue haze in the distance, and Daniella loved to stare out there, imagining it was the sea's misty horizon. She could feel the deck of the ship roll beneath her feet . . . when in actuality it was nothing more than the solid wood floor in her room. Though her father owned several ships, Daniella had never yet traveled the seas in one of them.

Outside it was a sparkling morning, with the sound of birds pleasantly singing at her window. Daniella was emerged in lavender-scented water, washing herself with a rough, soapy washcloth. Warmth, wonderful liquid warmth engulfed her for a few more minutes. At last she gave a deep, satisfied sigh and sat up straight in the copper-and-wood tub.

She frowned then, but for only a moment. After all, much could happen to improve the situation before the sun went down. She hoped that Robert was still in town and in a more reasonable frame of mind than the day before. She needed a friend to talk to.

Why—she told herself—he could even be on his way to the house right this minute! Much cheered by the thought, Daniella worked even faster to get done with her bath.

When she had rubbed rosewater lotion onto her cheeks and brushed her tresses to gleaming, she decided to do honor to her father's guest from London. Now a smile came to her lips and there was laughter in her translucent gray eyes. Lord Landaker intrigued her, to say the least.

She would take her new yellow gown from the chest. Fashioned by the most talented dressmaker in the Carolinas, the gown had been her father's birthday gift to her.

"Yes, I shall do just that. Papa will be so proud of me."

The hard wood of the floor glowed with the rich, warm shine of Mary's loving care, and Daniella's bare feet softly padded across it. She hummed the melody of a love song as Bettina came in to help her dress. When she had the gown on, yards of rich sunny yellow brocade billowed about her. Bettina stared with eyes agog.

The gown's daringly low cut bodice was edged with a foam of fine cream lace. Panniers caught up with small pale-pink rosebuds billowed over her slim hips and the rose color matched her delicate French fan. Over her shoulders she wore a fragile shawl of cream lace that had belonged to Elizabeth. It was attached with a large pin of gold and pearls with a glass locket in the center. Daniella loved pins of any kind, especially unusual ones.

"Oh my," Bettina said in a soft voice, her eyes wide with awe, "You are a sight, Mistress Dany."

Daniella's lilting laughter sounded. Bettina joined in, and their happy sounds mingled. Bettina stepped over to pull the bellcord which would signal the arrival of Daniella downstairs. "Here you go now, love."

The sparkling pale-yellow gown gave Daniella a feeling of feminine grace and poise. "If only . . ." she said to her reflection, then let the words trail away. This was no time to be dreaming of Robert and what could have been. "Bettina," she said on a sigh, "I am ready."

Edward was waiting in the hall below, and pride and love shone in his blue-gray eyes as he watched his beautiful Daniella descend the wide stairs. Dear Lord, that he should have to leave this life and never gaze upon his splendid grandchildren—and splendid they would indeed be . . . But how was he to tell her that the doctor had given him only a few months more to live? He could not.

Daniella looked past Edward and Mary, across the hall where Lord Landaker sat gazing into the low fire which cast his features into an even more dandified mold. He had not seemed to detect her presence as yet. Daniella's lips parted in a tiny secret smile.

Edward came forward to offer his arm, whispering, "We have only the one guest to entertain so far, Dany. Relax, my dear."

Daniella's eyes searched the long hall, but just then the door of her father's office opened and just as suddenly Daniella's lovely face brightened with intense pleasure.

Across the hall, Lord Landaker watched her and then saw the object of her joy — a young man coming through a door on the left. Leaning a little forward, the black coils of hair lying against his cheekbones, Landaker's deeply shadowed eyes narrowed, scrutinizing the young woman's every gesture and movement.

Captain Alain Carstairs paused by the table to greet Mary Tilford and then caught sight of Daniella. His own smile greeted her sweet lifting of rose-tinted lips. Daniella had missed her friend Alain; he had returned only yesterday, having brought the *Seafire* safely home from a long voyage.

Quietly, intently, Lord Landaker put his mind and his eyes on the lovely vision in the room, conscious of every turn of her head and ankle and blink of her long, sweeping lashes.

The captain of Edward's newest fleet ship was a big man from England's Cornwall. Alain was very young-looking but was actually middle-aged, with brown hair and tanned, leathery skin the color of sandstone; he seemed to have been carelessly carved from that same stone.

In the doublet and hose of plain brown cloth — which Alain usually wore without brooches or chains — he could have stepped only this day from his shire, instead of some fifteen years ago, to join the Wingate family.

"Good evening to you, Lady Daniella."

Daniella blushed prettily. Alain was always calling her "Lady," and she reveled in the name. Some called her Wild Dany, and she supposed that could be true of her also at times. She had been accused of being not only a bluestocking but an adventuress at heart, and so far it had only been that, for her father had held tight reins.

The only person for whom Alain was ever tempted to purchase sparkling trinkets in foreign ports was Daniella. And this one was a special gift, gotten from a Portuguese seaman. Mysterious he'd been, one who sailed with the vessel *Spanish Wind*. Alain held the bauble in his hand now as he stood before Daniella and bent to gallantly kiss her soft, lovely hand. Straightening again, Alain looked at Daniella with a twinkle in his sea-blue eyes.

"Lord Almighty, Lady Daniella, but you have grown into a fine young miss. I can say it all in truth now!"

"Oh, Alain," Daniella said with a dimple peeping on either side of her naturally pinkened cheeks, "what have you got there in your fist? Is it for me?"

Drawing his hand forward, Alain opened it to reveal a small pin in the shape of a tiger, with crystal-and-black enameled spots, tiny, beautifully fashioned emerald eyes, and a ruby heart.

Daniella became very quiet, saying almost inaudibly, "Oh, you know how I so love pins! This one is so very lovely." Tears stood in her eyes and shimmered, sapphire over the gray shade.

"Very lovely indeed, Alain." Her father came forward to fasten the graceful tiger pin on Daniella's sleeve, as if linking it together with one of the pale-pink rosebuds. He then glanced up and across the room, turned, and took a sidelong look at Lord Landaker as he was making his way to the table, his long black hair swaying as he swaggered.

Just then the butler Crookshank entered with a large steaming platter of succulent meats and stood by the sideboard. There was also succulent crab, red rice, and cherrycake ready to be served to the guests.

Daniella took her place between her father and their guest, with Alain and Mary Tilford on Edward's other side. Edward stood to say the blessing, and as they had their eyes lowered, Lord Landaker brought his gaze to rest upon the alluring Daniella. One corner of his mouth was pulled into a slight smile of mockery. He noted a proud, contained beauty in her face, but there was also a look of wildness there, of an impatient spirit that needed only to be set free.

With the blessing over, Daniella lifted her eyes to catch Lord Landaker gazing at her raptly just as she'd known he would be, for she had felt the touch of his disturbing eyes upon her. Her own deep-gray eyes were wistful and misty with a glimmer of indefinable emotion in them.

While the dining proceeded, Daniella became wrapped in another world. A thought she cared not to acknowledge surfaced. When Lord Landaker had been standing close in the Blue Room, she had known he had wanted her. Wanted her as a man wants a woman. And now Daniella felt that same strange tug of emotion she had felt before and puzzled at the immensity of feeling.

Emotions written clearly upon Daniella's face played in her luminous eyes, and when suddenly she raised her head, she caught Lord Landaker again studying her. Mixed feelings buffeted her and she lowered her eyes in confusion and felt momentary panic race through her heart.

Edward and Alain Carstairs did most of the talking; Lord Landaker was still the moody peacock, and Daniella's own thoughts wandered so restlessly that it was an ordeal to sit still through the long courses of delicious rich food without squirming.

Finally, with a wide smile, Daniella found an

opening and plunged in when the talk was of Charleston. "The social structure of Charleston has not crystallized as yet. People in trade are accepted as they would never be in England. The only standard here seems to be money. If a man has land enough and slaves enough and can build a fine house from the profits of rice or hides or timber . . ." She paused. "Where do you make your home at the time, Lord Landaker?"

Indifferent to that question, Lord Landaker, with a weary expression, flicked a pea across his shiny plate. "At the time, m'lady, I have a room in Charleston, but my home is in England."

"Hmm. Some of our neighbors were telling us about foreigners being kept captive on a pirate ship. Would you know anything about that, Lord Landaker? I heard tell of a Spanish ship that was chased off the islands."

Landaker flicked the sleeve of his lace-embroidered shirt. "Have you heard about a ship that was full of onions?"

"Onions?" Daniella lifted a tawny eyebrow. "Tell us about it, sir, I have not heard about that one. It sounds most humorous."

"Right." Landaker cleared his throat. "This pirate by the name of . . . ah . . . let us just say 'Lucian' had counted on gold bullion. As it turned out, he was so furious upon finding he had taken only onions aboard as his loot that he had all the onions thrown overboard—and now all the islands down in the Caribbean will be grown up to onions sooner or later."

Daniella looked away, but not before Lord Landaker had seen the astonished look on her face. "That is a most strange story, Lord Landaker."

Just then, Alain took a brownish twist of tobacco

62

from his pocket, cut off a portion with his knife, and held it toward Lord Landaker. "Chew?" he proffered it to the dandy.

"Thanks, but I've never learned to use the stuff."

"Calms the nerves," Alain said with a chuckle.

"So . . ." Lord Landaker said. "Tell me about the government of this colony."

Alain warmed to the subject. "As you probably know, this province was chartered to eight lords in England by Charles the Second."

"Yes." Lord Landaker pulled his gaze from watching Daniella. "Go on."

"Their grant gave them all the land between the St. Mathias River on the south and the thirty-sixth parallel on the north, westward to the South Seas. The lords are supposed to pay to the Crown one-fourth of all the gold and silver ore found on the land, and a yearly rent of twenty marks. For that pittance these lords own and rule South Carolina, sell the land outright or lease it on quitrents, and control all the rivers, mountains, forests, and human souls with it—"

"Proving that if one wishes to own a province he should be a lord in favor with the Stuarts," Daniella cut in.

"But how," Lord Landaker asked, "does the House of Hanover stand toward these lordly proprietors?" He did not expect Daniella to be the one to answer his question, unaware that her statement led into his question.

She was swift. "The charter gives them the right of inheritance. So now young men are in a position of authority over this colony—through their regents and deputies, of course. Every proprietor has his deputy. Carteret was appointed palatine, and his deputy is the governor. This Council makes the laws,

63

repeals them if they choose, all with the sanction of the Crown."

"The Assembly concurs, of course," he went on, testing her intelligence. "Who belongs to the Assembly?"

She smiled. "Landgraves, cassiques, important men in Charleston, usually elected with the approval of the governor and the Council. That is one of the great grievances at present, that the Assembly does not represent the whole people. *One* of the grievances, for there are many, Lord Landaker."

Daniella's eyes grew openly amused as she watched the fop for his reaction. "Men of ideas, men who must pay taxes to support the military and the churches and defend the country in time of need, are more or less disregarded," she explained. "Some merchant will buy the ship's cargo because it can be had free of duty. Our only recourse is to sue . . ." She laughed lightly. "Or to let the people know that the goods have come into the country without payment or duty. Increasingly, people are refusing to buy duty-free goods because of their resentment that the act was repealed."

"I see," Landaker said with a strange glint in his shadowy eyes as Daniella sipped her tea and dropped her tawny lashes; then her gaze went rushing toward the wall with the tall French doors set into it.

Moonlight through the crystal-embroidered windows showed how little was left of the enchanted evening, and her restlessness increased, for it would soon be time to go to bed. How lovely it would be to walk outside before the house turned down for the night and Daniella would be checked on to see if she was safely abed. After all, as Mary Tilford often stated, "there are all sorts of riffraff roaming the streets at night, Dany." But she would be safe in the garden, Daniella's thoughts informed her, and she never intended her walk to go any farther than the garden paths . . .

Daniella sighed deeply. Surely they had been sitting here at the table for hours and she couldn't stuff in another morsel or sip another drop.

The day was rushing to a close. Everything was changing. Her friend Robert would soon go back to Cornwall—or the high seas . . . She could sit still no longer, not with Steven Landaker's gaze capturing and brushing intimately every blushing inch of her, setting her aglow and tingling.

Without a care that it would be anywhere near rude to leave the table and her father's guests, Daniella shot to her feet, then hurried down the steps of the dais and across the hall toward the tall front doors.

Jumping to his feet, Edward called out. "Dany!"

Surprisingly, Mary spoke up in defense of the young woman. "She seems furiously restless, Edward. She wasn't really hungry, either, I could tell by the way she was pushing her food around on her plate." Mary's eyes became secretive as they drifted over to take a look at the foppish Steven Landaker.

Edward sighed and sat back down. "I suppose you are right, Mary. You always know what's best for Dany." He looked at Lord Landaker. "I only wish I had Mary's talent for discerning Dany's wishes and needs."

"Trust Mary. I would." With that, leaving dessert behind, Steven Landaker rose gracefully from the table, stepped swaggeringly across the hall, and mounted the wide staircase. Carrying on like a happy child with a treat, Edward looked down at the rich pastry oozing with berries, then forked a large slice into his smiling mouth, speaking through the side of it, "I do believe our guest has a little twinkle in his eye for our Dany, and she likewise."

Mary smiled happily and announced with all her ladylike graciousness, "More than just a little, m'lord."

Edward leaned to Mary to whisper. "He is not really such a peacock after all, you know."

"I know, Edward." Sadness was in Mary's eyes. "I know . . . because you told me everything yesterday."

He just didn't remember.

The impulse which had driven Daniella outside furnished her no direction; she was like a ship without a star path. And still she was unwilling to return to the manor. She did not even go to the garden.

As Daniella walked, humming a tune, the moon broke through the restless clouds to bathe the twisting paths before her. She could smell the mossy earth, the marsh grass, and the silver-highlighted river. She paused, pulled herself into the moonless shadows, wondering if she had heard a sound behind her; then she told herself it was only her nighttime imagination playing tricks. Letting her breath go, Daniella stepped back onto the moonlit path.

Just then a tall, caped figure turned quickly into one of the paths which led to the river. It was as if he guarded her every step, meant no harm, and stayed just one ahead of her. Daniella shivered but kept right on moving until she was on the main road. She knew the wagon up ahead was her neighbor's, and she moved faster now in order to climb on the back to hitch a ride into town. It was not much farther now. Excitement tingled within as she realized the caped figure was now astride a horse and following. Robert? Or maybe Steven Landaker? She hated to think beyond these two.

The wagon lumbered down to a street which ended close by the Driftwood Tavern, and Daniella knew this was not a safe district to be in, even in daylight. Beyond the tavern, ragged buildings straggled toward the river. She had come this way often enough, true. Here was where the wretchedly poor lived, and she had grown accustomed to its squalid appearance; every town and city in the world had an area such as this one, Alain had informed her. Daniella slid from the back of the wagon.

Now in the dim moonlight, however, Daniella was more aware of what she took for granted during the daylight hours when groups of ragged children grubbed with half-starved dogs in the gutters and bewhiskered tramps rooted around in garbage heaps.

Slowing her steps, Daniella glanced over her shoulder. For some reason, the image of Robert Drake walking these streets in his rugged sea boots, as he used to, rose before her. And just now she caught the movement of that dark cloak in the archway of a building. Why did Robert Drake keep coming to mind when she spotted the cloaked figure? *If only I could wish Robert well before he departs.* Their friendship had always been special and she didn't want an angry parting to stand between them. She loved Robert too much for that . . . loved him as a sister would love a brother.

Daniella shivered but still experienced a youthfully confident freedom of the streets she'd traversed for so many years. But she'd never before been out alone after dark, and as she hurried along in the purple-and-gray night, shadows seemed swifter than her own movements. A low mist crawling from the river eerily joined forces with the moon to form a silvery suspended light behind the trees that were like heavy, dark shadows.

Daniella saw the looming shape of the horse first, standing motionless by a thick clump of cypress trees, then the tall, masked figure which moved to block her way. Astride the horse, he was dark and shapeless and seemed to wear a long, hooded cloak.

Daniella felt herself shiver. Was this the same man she'd seen not long ago, darting in and out of trees along the road? Who could he be? Dear Lord, not a murderer, she hoped!

Daniella started off in panic, her heavy skirts hampering her legs. The apparition of horse and rider were gaining on her and she would have screamed, but her voice seemed to be frozen in her throat. Why hadn't she taken the time to saddle and bring her own mount to ride? She could have gotten away from her pursuer then. Now, suddenly, he closed in as she tried to swerve in the direction of the river.

Panting for breath, Daniella risked a glance over her shoulder. She could see another figure, this one coming in at an angle. He seemed slightly taller, and she was glad for his swiftness. But was he indeed coming to save her. . . ?

As he came crashing recklessly through the bushes, the misty moonlight that scudded forth from the clouds fell on his darkly cloaked figure. Her gaze skittered madly to the other. Daniella's thoughts raced and her adrenaline pumped furiously. *Two of them!* Who could tell friend from foe?

Now Daniella put all her strength into running. Frantically, for a moment, she thought they both pursued the same prey — *her!*

Breathing in shallow gulps, Daniella kept on twisting and evading as best she could. When the heavy hand clamped upon her and seized her by the shoulder, she stumbled and fell, hearing the curse follow her down.

The second figure was upon them, and Daniella's assailant jumped back to protect himself. She heard yet another growl and curse from his deep cowl.

Two! Daniella could not tell which one to look to for help, if either.

When she finally scrambled up from the ground, her rescuer — if he could be called that — had got himself between her and the masked man.

Now there was the sickening scrape of metal in scabbards. Dear God, they were going to fight over her!

In the feeble light beneath the trees, Daniella saw the only brightness become the flash of a pair of wicked blades. Neither swordsman had given the other time to throw off his hooded cape. Their dusky formlessness and the silence of swift and efficient movement lent yet more strangeness to the scene.

There was the flash of something familiar from the unmasked figure — the way he moved or the turn of his head. Robert! Oh how she prayed she was right and it was really he.

All of a sudden Daniella stiffened and moved back a step. There was something strangely out of place about this swordfight. One of the figures teased and evaded and thrust the point forward, quick and snakelike. The narrower blade had only lightning quickness in it, as if branded within the metal, and a dancing alertness behind the hand.

Could this be Robert who moved like a graceful dancer?

Surely, Daniella thought, the "dancer" would tire first. Yet it was the masked man who overreached in one stroke. He faltered an instant and that was all it took. The swift point met the unguarded shoulder and the sword, half raised in desperation, flew from the slim hand and almost struck Daniella. With an involuntary cry, she stepped aside, and her champion turned his head.

"Robert!"

But the wounded man had not seized the opportunity to unsheathe his dagger and instead had used the moment to reach his horse. She whirled to face her dancing hero. "Are you al—?"

She looked behind her for the one she thought might be Robert but could not see him in the purple darkness under the trees. He did not come forward. This was strange in itself, she thought, for Robert would never have deserted her at a time like this. Unless he didn't want her to know he had been her hero. But that could not be the case, either, since Robert would surely leap at the chance for such a lofty position in her eyes.

Casting one more look into the darkness behind her, Daniella then quickly followed the streetlamps up the hill. There was a lighthearted step to her gait. Maybe Robert *had* been the one to save her . . .

She found the wagon returning up the plantation road, hitched a ride back home, and reached the manor, slightly out of breath from all the excitement.

Before her hand found the latch, she saw her father's head at the window, the comforting firelight haloing it. He came into the hall, stood waiting for his daughter to approach.

Tremulously, Daniella smiled, unaware that her face was a little dirty. She was lucky her father was not a violent man. But she had much explaining to do this night—that was a certainty.

Chapter Five

Like a windstorm
Punishing the oak trees,
Love shakes my heart.
— Sappho

The morning sun drenched the eyelet-covered brass bed in golden warmth when Mary pulled the snowy lace curtains back. Mentioning nothing of the night before, Mary set Daniella's breakfast of sausage and biscuits on the bedside table and explained that Vivien couldn't go to market. "Would you be so kind to take Bettina with you and go in her place, Dany?" Mary asked.

Lord Landaker and Edward had each gone to their separate assignations that morning, and Daniella had the books done. She needed something to occupy her time. "As long as *you* asked me, Mary . . ." Daniella said, popping a sausage into her mouth, then spreading a biscuit with creamy butter.

Mary busied herself folding some feminine garments and placing them in the bureau drawers. "Lord Landaker spent quite some time in Vivien's kitchen while that one gossiped in his ear for one solid hour straight!"

While Mary was telling this, Daniella blanched, wondering just how much Lord Landaker had learned of her little escapades with Robert Drake.

No doubt Vivien had made Steven Landaker's ears burn with her scandalous lies! Daniella would dismiss the woman herself if Edward did not praise the woman's cooking as the best in all the Carolinas.

As Bettina and Daniella set out, baskets slung over their arms, Daniella thought perhaps she might meet up with Robert Drake in the street—if he had not yet set sail. Had Robert actually been her hero the night before? She liked to think so.

When they reached the market itself, Bettina's steps slowed, along with Daniella's. With rapt expression, the comely pair drew deep breaths of sun-warmed straw, the bittersweet smell of farm animals, the earthy savor of fresh-pulled roots and herbs. Bettina's shining cheeks grew even pinker, and she moved happily along the dusty avenue with her beautiful companion.

The maid and the young mistress shared a quiet companionship. Any other morning, Daniella would have been livelier company. She would have pulled Bettina into the social side of marketing, the joyful part of shopping for the household, but today Daniella did not wish to be hemmed in by any of the leisurely groups refreshing themselves with cider and crusty pastries and neighborhood gossip. Her mind was on Robert.

Daniella greeted friends and acquaintances alike as briefly as good manners permitted and passed on with Bettina in tow until her eyes, scanning the crowd, lit upon a friend of Robert's.

"Guy . . . oh, Guy Tilberry!" Daniella called.

Guy's face lit up, showing wideset eyes which were bold and curious. He turned and strode toward the women and smiled into Daniella's eyes.

"Good morning, Dany." He tipped his blue cap to the maid, too. They talked of simple matters for a few minutes, then Guy took the pressing question right out of Daniella's mouth, "By the way, Dany, have you seen Robert today? He was in Charleston this morning, but I haven't seen him since." Guy chuckled. "I saw him with Charles, and that one was wearing a bandage under his shirt—a big one. Boy, Charles must have had *some* rough night."

Daniella caught her breath, and Guy's bright eyes, which missed nothing, fastened upon her as Daniella's voice emerged somewhat shakily. "Wh-who was wearing a bandage?"

"*Charles,* honey, *Charles.*" Guy cleared his throat and, looking sheepish, he corrected, "Oh, but I don't think Robert joined him in the . . . uh . . . rough night."

Just then Morgan Fields stepped up to them. He had heard the last part of their conversation. "Did I hear someone mention Robert?" Morgan laughed with a snort. "Was it *you* who sent him off looking like thunder?" He was looking at Daniella, and her eyes suddenly widened. "I am sorry to say this, Dany, but I think your beloved friend is bad company. If it was a Drake ship out of Cornwall, as I suspect, they are no better than pirates and had the devil's own boldness to sail the *Raven* straight into the harbor."

"You are sure the ship sailed"—Daniella almost whispered—"with Robert?"

"Aye, lovely lady," Morgan drawled, wishing she were not so concerned about Robert Drake. "All sails spread, making good time out of Charleston Harbor. Good seamen, those scoundrels, I'll have to give them that," he ended on a bitter note.

After Morgan and Guy had moved along, Daniella stood detached from the crowd. Robert was gone. It had been inevitable, she supposed. All yesterday she'd known he'd go. Daniella chewed her lower lip and frowned. Charles . . . wounded? Or was it only mere coincidence that Charles had been hurt in the same place, just like the masked man? Why would Charles Blackman wish to kidnap her off the streets? For what reason? Who *was* her hero, the dancing swordsman, if not Robert? She shook her head. Robert would never fight with Charles anyway.

"Daniella?" Bettina plucked at her mistress's arm. Still the young woman did not respond. They should make their way back to Braidwood now, for it was getting late.

"Yes, Bettina, I know. We are finished now."

Returning to Braidwood later that afternoon, Daniella spoke from the driver's seat of the wagon. "Take the market baskets in, Bettina." She snatched a shiny red apple from the basket as the maid alighted. "Tell Mary I've one more errand to see to." She clicked her tongue, turning the wagon back in the direction they'd arrived from. "Get up there!" she called to the team, feeling the trailing Spanish moss tickle her cheek as she set off down the lane again while Bettina watched for several moments in curiosity.

Daniella gave the wagon and horses over into the care of a hostler and set off on foot, staying away from the busier section of Charleston. She needed some time alone with her restless thoughts and at once turned them to worrying about Robert.

If, as she'd thought last night, Robert had not been far from her when she'd taken that walk and had waited for a suitable time to mend their quarrel, why then had he gone away without word or message after saving her life? Had mere chance brought him to her? Had Robert come to her aid only as he would have done for any stranger and left with his anger unchanged? Then . . . what about Charles Blackman and his wound?

In deep thought, Daniella clutched the shiny red apple, slowed her steps, then came to a complete standstill. What had she seen in the dark of the moon? Perhaps, she admitted, unreasoning instinct had made her hero be Robert, and she had clung to that with no more evidence of face or voice than she had of the identity of that other cloaked and hooded figure. One thing she was sure of, the rider who had been wounded had been masked, and he'd been the slower swordsman of the two. Charles Blackman was not, as rumor went, very good at swordplay . . . Oh that was utterly ridiculous. Charles would no more kidnap her than the boy next door would. He wouldn't even do it if a friend begged or paid him. Robert and Charles would not have played such a cruel joke on her, either!

Without noticing, she had wandered down to the wharves where warehouses were clustered tightly together. The harbor was as teeming and clamorous as the market itself, its stir sweeping Daniella along in the stream of sound and movement that flowed beside the magnificent ships . . .

Scents of spice and silk and leather; a blast of bawdy song and shrill laughter from a riverside tavern; water lapping the hulls. Foreign face and dress . . .

Suddenly a boy flew into the air and landed, light as a cat, at Daniella's feet. Startled for a moment, she looked down at him, wondering where he had come from. He had a round, freckled face beneath a blue sailor's cap, and Daniella decided he must be a ship's boy. Some sprig of a bawdy house run off to

75

sea, as Edward or Alain might say. Surely, she thought, looking at him again, this must be the boy's first voyage. He was small and skinny.

"Hello," Daniella softly greeted him. He reminded her of a spider monkey.

The boy said nothing. Executing a bow that Robert could not have bettered, he straightened and mutely stared at her. All of a sudden a sense that someone was watching her drew Daniella's eyes to a ship—three-masted and fresh with emerald-green paint above the black hull. What really drew Daniella's attention was the ship's figurehead of a beautiful tiger ready to spring, its muscular limbs reaching along the bowsprit as if to pull free and dive toward the water. A varnished wooden face was open in a dangerous snarl, straining forward.

It was unlike any figurehead Daniella had ever seen. She could see no sign of life aboard the ship save for the figure of a man disappearing into the aftercastle. The movements of his body told her he was powerful, and no doubt agile and alert. Who was he? she wondered.

An odd shiver of pleasure ran along Daniella's nerve ends. Her cheeks pinkened, her heart picked up its beat. Had the tall, broad-shouldered man on the ship been staring solely at her as she had greeted the boy?

Moving on to where the *Rampant Rose* lay waiting at anchor, Daniella again felt as if she were being watched . . . watched very closely. She told herself she would not turn around to look. *I will keep my eyes from running to mischief. After all, I am about to become Lord Steven Landaker's wife.*

Daniella came to a halt beside her father's ship. The *Rampant Rose's* deck was unencumbered by crewmen, who were no doubt kicking up their heels

76

in town. The *Rose* waited proudly to discharge the cargo with which she'd outsailed rivals and storms and pirates. She had been given Daniella's own second name and had been launched on her fifth birthday.

The *Rampant Rose* was a beauty, Daniella thought lovingly. A brig, more than three beams long, with the lower, slimmer lines and taller masts which gave speed. After admiring the ship for a few more minutes, she turned back the way she'd come. Daniella was not quite certain of what she would meet, or whom, but something was in the wind. She could feel it. And she thrilled to the expectation.

Sebastián Landaker, captain of the proud *Emerald Tiger*, which had docked in Charleston Harbor three days before, stood with his feet planted wide and his dark sea boots gleaming dully under the afternoon sun. He had lashes and brows of darkest gold, and the small scar on his cheek twitched impatiently as he gazed from the deck over the waterfront.

He was dreaming of making swift and profitable trips, of taking out cloth and corn and bringing back spices, oil, and Madeira sugar, Spanish fruit, saffron, ivory, and silk traded with Portuguese ships from the East.

Sebastián knew how to wait something out. And wait he would, always aware that fate would continue to school him, hone him, try him. Daniella came to mind just then. Though young and unpolished, she had a great influence on what her father did in business. Because he loved his daughter and thought only of her security, Edward Wingate was very careful what he ventured into. He had not joined the Company, and the position of the Windstar Fleet was becoming more difficult without Wingate's help and influence.

Sebastián looked up at the fluffy clouds scudding eastward in the azure sky. There was a crystal quality to the bright, sunny afternoon. But the peace was broken by the raucous peals of revelry which spilled from the waterfront taverns and bawdyhouses nearby.

He breathed deeply, filling his lungs, further expanding his wide chest. It was a good feeling to have his feet planted on the deck of his own ship once again. Marcos, a fine seaman, one of Sebastián's own best men, had been following the *El Draque* which had held him prisoner for so many months, and the *Emerald Tiger* had not been sunk in the Florida Channel, as he'd been afraid she might have.

At the moment, Marcos Marela was polishing the compass and greeted his captain with a beaming grin.

"Where's Rascon?" Sebastián called, with a wide smile of his own and standing there with hands on hips, tall, handsome, and square-shouldered.

"Just saw him hopping off the deck," the man said in a thick accent, but with a precise use of English words. "Captain, he comes and he goes, he swings here and he swings there. Like a monkey he is. His name should be 'Rascal'."

Sebastián's jade-green eyes glittered with delight. "Rascon is close enough, Marcos."

"He's an imp, Captain!" Marcos laughed aloud, easy in Landaker's presence, as were all the men of the *Emerald Tiger*'s crew.

"And you, Marela, are a superior imp from Hades, because how the hell did you ever find me?!" Sebastián shook his tawny head. "Never mind." He would receive a long, drawn-out explanation and he

78

was not in the mood for one now. He only recalled how confoundedly happy he had been to see the man emerge from a clump of rosebushes in the Wingate garden three days before, *pssst*ing, then whispering that his ship was awaiting him in the harbor. Sebastián could not recall rightly, but he believed he had kissed the man right upon his high forehead!

There was a joke that ran between the crew members, because of some trouble amorous Marcos had gotten himself into while in Florida. The story went that after tumbling the wife of a wealthy Spanish aristocrat, Marcos had been forced to run for his life. Sebastián had saved Marcos's skin that time; now they were even.

"I know, Captain, you do not ship men who are branded on their rumps." Marcos pointed to his own.

"Hah! As you well know, Marcos, I do not examine the sterns or the bows of my sailors, scoundrels or not!"

Just then a flash of feminine color caught Sebastián's eye and he swung about. His heart picked up a crazy beat as wildfire surged through his blood. Captivated and thoroughly delighted, he laughed richly. The older man was left alone to his work as the captain returned to the forecastle deck aft of the bow, watching from there as Rascon leaped into the air and landed, light as a cat, at Daniella Wingate's feet. She appeared startled for a moment, then she stared down at the small, skinny boy.

Sebastián continued to watch. Daniella was saying something to the lad, but of course he didn't respond. Rascon just stared at the young woman's stunning loveliness. Rascon could not speak. He had not uttered a word since the day Sebastián had swept him from the deck of a burning Spanish vessel just sinking into the sea. It had been another act of bravery from which Sebastián had thought never to survive—much less bring aboard his ship the little drowned rat his crew had christened Rascon!

Sebastián continued to watch the lovely Daniella with a slow sweet fire burning in his loins. Rascon could, if he chose, make sign language. The crew often joked that some huge cat must have gotten the boy's tongue, but Captain Landaker thought otherwise. He believed he had been greatly abused under the careless hand of some heartless knave. The child bore the scars of many whippings on his bony back, no doubt from his wretched captivity.

Now Daniella was studying his ship, unmindful that Sebastián watched. Before this, he knew, she had not been down to see the *Emerald Tiger*. The ladies, and the *putas* alike, were always taken a little breathless with his ship's figurehead of a magnificent *tigre* ready to spring.

Sebastián knew a dark moment as he stood there, feeling the venomous snake of emotion coil up through him. Vengeance. He could already taste it and soon it would be his. Soon, ah yes, very soon Daniella would lead his prey to him. It might take months, perhaps even a year . . . time that would be spent very pleasantly indeed.

As Sebastián stood watching Daniella, catching her unawares so far, desire mushroomed in him until he had to turn away in case she glanced up and observed the proof of his desire.

After a sufficient lapse of time, when Sebastián thought she'd be gone from the harbor, he returned to the deck only to see her walking away from the *Rampant Rose,* the Wingate's brig. Rolling down the sleeves of his green shirt and fetching his buff jacket, Sebastián started out after her, leaving a frowning

Rascon and puzzled Marcos staring after him as he stuffed a black wig into the inside pocket of his jacket.

While Daniella walked, the wind picked up and blew fine strands of hair around her temples and lifted the hem of her skirts. Before she entered the crowd of leering sailors just coming off a newly arrived ship in search of some amusement for the coming night, hard fingers locked around one arm, lifting her aside. Daniella spun about, her dainty body prepared to do battle if one of the sailors had it in mind to molest her.

"Oh . . . Lord Landaker, you gave me a fr—" She blinked, noting the color of his hair that was not black but rather tawny gold. "I . . ." she stammered in confusion.

Sebastián stared at the soft full lips that were parted. He was studying her up close, so mesmerized again by her beauty that he failed to hear her indrawn breath or see her unclench her fists. All he could do was stare, transfixed, held by a pair of stormy gray eyes.

"You are not Steven Landaker," she said, almost to herself.

He laughed, a warm, rich sound, then his voice dropped to a husky tone as he said, "So I am not."

"You are not the gentleman I mistook you for, sir." She did not much care for this insolent stranger.

Sebastián stiffened, but not from her words. He grew very still, thinking, Soon, soon, any day now, and he would show her how *ungentle* he could become. He would make her suffer for the sins of her lover and his evil brother, Lucian.

As Daniella walked, she could sense the stranger

close at her heels. She was alone. She had come to the waterfront often enough, but this day there was no one about, not even a member of any of her father's crews to come to her aid.

Daniella's skirts twitched and the captain ogled her boldly, not caring that they were being watched while sailors jeered and whistled. "The view is delightful from back here," he taunted, bending over to breathe down her neck before straightening again.

"You, *sir,* or whatever address you go by, are a vile rake!"

Sebastián smiled oddly at that remark, deciding to let it pass for the moment. "Captain . . . you may call me *Captain,* m'lady."

Daniella whirled to face the obnoxious stranger, and found to her disgust that his eyes were just lifting from below her hips. "Just who are you, sir?!"

She studied his devastatingly handsome face, feeling both excitement and terror wash over her. Her face was flushed with anger and fear, and she couldn't know how beautiful she appeared to the man who stood before her, aching with lust and desire.

Ignoring her retort, he reached out and took her slim white hand, speaking eloquently. "You are as fair as a lily, with hair as fine as a bolt of most precious silk and lips as dewy pink as a rose!" He mocked her with a half bow from the waist.

"Please!" She jerked her hand away. "You take too many liberties, Captain! I shall have my father call you out if you do not cease this nonsense!"

Once again he executed a mock half bow. "Have him call me out then, fair rose! But I will not cease—even were I 'pon my deathbed. You are too tempting a morsel to let alone, Miss Wingate."

"Just who are you?! I demand that you tell me!"

Daniella stomped her sharp heel into the ground, dangerously near his foot.

It was a long, tension-filled moment in which they regarded each other. Sebastián was frustrated and angry. He should not be feeling anything but the desire for revenge. His eyes focused on Daniella's.

"Ah, my dear sweet flower . . . so you can send your henchmen after me?" He smiled, but it was shortlived.

"Yes!" she cried angrily.

He was actually enjoying the situation! She took a deep breath and counted to ten. No help there. Before she realized what she was doing, her hand had reached out and struck him boldly across his handsome face with her open palm, all her force behind the blow, leaving a bright red imprint.

While she stood transfixed, her big eyes apprehensive and widening in shock over her dangerous blunder, he was feeling along his jaw testing the spot that was already sore.

"My, oh my, you do pack a wollop, little lady!"

Without thinking twice, Daniella whirled about and ran into the copse of oak at the edge of town. She should have noticed how far she had gone past her wagon!

She soon realized her drastic mistake upon hearing the quick step come up behind her and the lock of hard fingers once again closing over her arm. Daniella fought for breath as she looked down at the tanned arm, so close she could see the deep auburn freckles sprinkled upon his flesh and the tawny, glinting hairs that ran up and down his muscle-knotted arm. She looked up, up into hooded eyes, then almost fainted when, after what seemed an eternity, his gaze at last fell to her lips.

An expression of bewilderment and fear crossed

her face. Daniella knew what the bold stranger was going to do even before he commenced with the action, and she hardly welcomed it. She wasn't prepared for the shocking, thrilling touch of those firm and at the same time soft lips against her own moist flesh. At first he kissed her ever so softly, then with a little firmer pressure; he kissed her thoroughly. Daniella began to feel little fires igniting in strange, secret places throughout her untaught body. She knew a sudden urge to stand on her toes and wind her slim arms about his deeply tanned neck.

Breathing huskily, Sebastián rested his lips at the corner of Daniella's sweet mouth. "You are a tease, m'lady!" He pulled her closer, moving his face into the baby-fine strands above her ears. To get even closer, he adjusted his sword belt and the pistols he had tucked into his waistband, having realized they had been grinding into her soft flesh. His tongue flicked out and she jumped a little. *It will be good when we at last join — and I will have you soon,* he was thinking.

Wonderingly he stared down into her moody gray eyes, tinted with passionate blue flecks at the moment.

As she broke away at last, he was quick to snatch her back. Dipping into her bodice, with one long dark finger he brushed over her flesh and seared the tip of her breast that rose against his touch like a taut bud opening up. She gasped and shivered with the first full awakening as sweet coils of desire hungrily ground into her.

"Your flesh is like a hot velvet rose." He looked her full in the face as he said these words, and then he vowed inwardly, Dios, *someday soon you and I will be one!*

"Who . . . are . . . you?" Daniella pushed away,

and her eyes flashed stormy gray again.

He bent his back, executing a courtly bow that surprised Daniella, a gesture that she found vaguely disturbing for some reason.

"Your captain, m'lady, at your service—and so I shall be!"

The cryptic remark flew right over her head, and his eyes twinkled merrily with unhidden lust. Eyebrows raising, he peered at her closely, his slanted eyes holding a hint of wry amusement.

"I should inform you that I am soon to become a bride." She lifted her chin a little. "Lord Steven Landaker's bride."

"Well, well, well . . ." He lifted her hand to kiss the back of it. "Congratulations are very much in order, my dear. And I am so happy to hear that you will be part of the family."

Daniella blanched. "Part of—?"

"Indeed. I am a *very* close friend to the Landaker family."

"Will you . . ." Daniella paused to catch her breath. "Will *you* be attending the wedding?"

Sebastián stared at her for a long moment before answering. "I'm afraid that's impossible."

"Why is that, Captain?"

"For one thing . . ." He ran his fingers along her arm and felt her shiver to his touch. "I will be . . . ah . . . otherwise occupied."

"With a female," she guessed.

"Naturally, and a very beautiful one, I might add."

"And the other?"

A roguish grin worked at the corners of his expressive mouth. "I think, m'lady, you'd rather not see my scoundrel's face there!"

"You are correct, Captain. Only gentlemen shall attend *our* wedding!" she snapped, feeling the erratic thumping of her heart.

She whirled and over her shoulder called a crisp "Good day!"

Damning the telltale hardening at his loins, Sebastián bowed low after her graceful exit from the wooded copse.

Straightening, his eyes glittered a dark, ominous green as he murmured softly, "Good day to you, too, my dark rose." He lifted a lavender-scented handkerchief to his nose, one initialed with a leaning "D" beneath an embroidered purple flower. The lace square was feminine and unforgettably exquisite. Ah yes, just like its owner.

Sebastián donned the black wig, then made his way to a nearby inn where he could freshen up and apply the dark kohl to his eyes and brows, the loose powder to his face . . .

When he was done, he stepped back from the cheval glass, hardly recognizing his own face within the paler features and darkened eyes and brows as he donned the foppish clothes and quit the inn.

Chapter Six

Daniella jumped up from the mauve padded bench, her sweet face flushed pinkly across her cheekbones. "I cannot shake these jitters, Mary!" She toyed with her diamond-and-pearl necklace.

"Upon my word . . ." Mary began. "It's only your wedding day, Daniella Rose—not your execution!"

Daniella looked at Mary Tilford and the woman stood back with her hands folded within her crisp white apron. Had she detected an expression of pity in the woman's kindly face? Pity because she was marrying such a peacock?

Daniella smiled weakly and mused aloud. "It's just that I know so little about Lord Landaker."

"Steven is his name." Mary fussed with the folds of white satin and adjusted the length of white tulle veil. "You *must* learn to call him that, dear."

"Steven," Daniella repeated. Yes, the name fit him very well. Steven was very kind to others, she'd learned, kind and soft-spoken in her presence, too. He wasn't always at Braidwood, for he'd taken lodging in a townhouse at the edge of the road going out of the city . . . for the sake of propriety. Daniella was indebted to him for that.

"You will get to know Steven Landaker once you're wed," Mary said, fluffing the veil about Daniella's elaborate high-piled hairdo. "Make no mistake about that."

"I . . ." Daniella began and chewed her lower lip as she faltered. She smiled at the woman she'd known all her life, but for some reason she could not bring herself to speak about that which troubled her the most: her wedding night.

Mary looked very fetching in her best lavender silk, and Daniella had already seen her bridesmaids, old friends from schooldays. The bubbling girls wore gowns of stiff turquoise brocade which rustled elegantly as they entered her room to fuss over her like clucking mother hens. Each of them would carry a nosegay of rosemary, bergamot, and southernwood and lilacs for scent. Daniella wore white hyacinths in her headdress.

She reflected back to two weeks before . . . the day she'd met that scoundrel captain and been mauled by him. She wanted never to see him again, she thought as a knot rose in her throat. Never! Never! Not even in her dreams.

Daniella went on to recall something of a more pleasant nature. Her father had drawn her close beside him on the sofa two weeks ago. His eyes searched her face as he asked, "This is of your own free will, dear?"

"Of course, Father. There is no other choice I wish to make. Truly." She'd noted the relief Edward could not conceal and she also knew he'd been so counting on this marriage between her and Steven Landaker. She was now accustomed to the idea, because she did not feel threatened by Steven's debonair manner.

Edward wanted the wedding to take place at the small Protestant church, a vine-and-moss-covered structure in the woods. The church was already hronged with people in the churchyard by the time Daniella and her attendants arrived.

Daniella made a poignant picture as she paused, her beautiful satin dress belled out around her as she listened to the flutes and tabors of the bride's minstrels which could be heard across the field from Braidwood.

Daniella had wakened that morning smiling and peculiarly lighthearted, with some sixth sense that her mother was near and shared with her in every step she took this day. If only Elizabeth could be here in the flesh, she wistfully thought.

Now the tiny church bells began to peal and there was a thrusting forward in the crowd as the wedding procession moved inside the beam-ceilinged foyer. It was unusual for church bells to sound before a wedding, but it was as Edward ordered it, for he wanted every luxurious touch for his only daughter's wedding. Daniella saw her father at the front of the church, handsome in his finery, and she smiled happily.

Then her face clouded.

Of late Daniella had noticed Edward's tense, overly-anxious look. But she was grateful to notice that now that the wedding day had arrived, he looked much better.

The day she'd come home from her nervewracking encounter with that scoundrel captain, her father had said, "Lord Landaker and I have talked this morning early. He told me he would like to make you his wife and—" Edward had cleared his throat following a loud cough—"the sooner the better. My dearest Dany, there is no one I trust more than Steven Landaker to take good care of you. He can, very well, you know. He is the owner of several merchant ships—" Edward was about to add that Steven was head of the Established Merchant Fleet, but a sharp cough ended his sentence.

For a moment Daniella had stared at him in fear. Could her father be ill?

But Edward had assured her all was well with him just then, and she'd thought on it no more. She had been terribly surprised to bump into none other than Lord Landaker out in the hall. With gallant gestures and movements, he had bowed low over her hand and kissed her palm while peering oddly up into her very wide eyes. He had straightened, gazed deeply into her waiting expression, and said, "I can see you are taken by surprise with m . . . and so he has spoken of the marriage?"

"Yes," Daniella had answered on a swift, breathless note, her heart in her eyes. "I-I am r-ready."

"Ready?" He had chuckled, and the heavily applied powder on his too-handsome face had made him appear almost effeminate. He'd looked very dapper in his fine clothes, his navy-blue silk vest, tall highly polished boots. "Do you need more time, my dear?" His long black curls swaying between their shoulders, he had gazed down at her lily hands clenched in front of her, then back up into her face. "I had so hoped to make you like me better, my dearest Daniella."

Landaker's look had been so wistful it almost broke Daniella's heart. So crestfallen was he—the almost pretty face had turned down so much at the darkly lashed eyes, the nose, and mouth—that Daniella had been moved to compassion for the gentlemanly soul.

"Oh—I do not need more time." Daniella knew her voice had sounded overly eager. The arrogantly handsome captain of that rakish ship had come to mind and she had earnestly cried, "No more time, sir. I would like to wed as soon as possible. I mean it, a-absolutely."

"Ah, Daniella." Landaker had taken a quick step forward, and then seemed to check himself from whatever he'd been about to say or do. "My dear, I shall not have you pushed into this. Are you positively certain?"

"I've already said as much, Steven."

"You do not wish more time to think it over, demoiselle?" he asked, calling her an unmarried woman . . . *But was she a virgin?*

"I—" Just then the golden sun slanted through the tall casement windows and Daniella gasped softly, because Steven Landaker had reminded her of someone else—just for a moment.

Daniella again fumbled for words, staring at the blue silk of his vest, but then went on firmly. "Most marriages are arranged and turn out well enough—I do not see why ours would not, Steven."

"I mean something else . . ." He'd glanced aside, looking almost embarrassed, then, "You . . . you do not have to take me like a bitter posset, sweet Daniella. There is no force involved."

"Oh, Steven." Daniella stepped closer, unaware how deeply she blushed. She was able to smell the clean, masculine sent of him, and, curiously, she delighted in being so near the man, though his manner was indeed foppish. Raising her face for a kiss to seal the bargain, she found him turned away suddenly. "I'm not taking you like . . . like . . ." She laid a hand on his superfine sleeve. "I have learned how very kind you are, Steven, and it's easy to see why Father and Mary think so highly of you."

He breathed deeply. "But . . . do *you*, m
sweet?"

She had become very fond of him, true, bu
there was something still that made her leery o
Steven Landaker. What was she to do, she pondered
miserably. She must trust her own heart, for she'd
witnessed nothing but goodness and thoughtfulnes
in the man whom the kitchen gossips called a pea
cock.

As he gazed into her eyes, she felt compassion
take hold once again, and she nodded slowly. H
followed suit, and, tucking her lily-white hand i
his elbow, he kissed her cold fingers and they wen
in together, to receive Edward's blessing . . .

Now Daniella, the bride in resplendent virgin
white, stood beside Steven Landaker, having no idea
how she got there. She must have moved like a
sleepwalker all the way down the aisle. She let her
gaze slide and drift over Steven. He was wearing an
oyster-colored suit and cream silk shirt with match
ing vest; even his cravat was a pale shade of shim
mery material that begged to be stroked. He
smelled clean, good . . . even manly.

After what seemed mere seconds, her hand was
resting over the white glove Steven wore while he
slipped the ring on, and then he was kissing her. I
was short, sweet, and not at all as repulsive as she'd
anticipated. In fact, she couldn't believe the plea
surable thrill which shot through her like wildfire a
the brief contact of their lips.

"My wife," Landaker said close to Daniella's
burning ear, making her shiver inside while her
knees began a crazy dance all their own. He took
her hand again. Had she detected a triumphant vi

oration? Hadn't he been squeezing rather forcefully? Though Steven was gentlemanly in the social circle, Daniella wondered just how far his kindness would extend later on when they would be alone as man and wife. Would the preening peacock turn . . . *strange* on her?

All of a sudden everyone began kissing her. The wreath of tiny French roses with its delicate lace veil almost tumbled from Daniella's fair head, but Steven was quick to catch the quaint headdress before it fell to the floor.

Daniella looked into his face, and, sweetly smiling, she placed a gentle hand on his forearm. He stood looking down at the delicate white hand with its exquisite covering of fingerless lace gloves that reached to her elbows.

"Thank you, Steven."

"Think nothing of it, my love."

She flushed a charming creamy pink. While most of the men pumped Lord Landaker's hand, the women, on the other hand, chose to stand back and wish the dandy well from afar. Daniella wanted to shout at them, to tell of his kindness to her family and friends, of all in the household who already adored Steven and catered to his every whim and temper. If they only knew the man as she did, Daniella thought, giving his back a gentle, loving smile.

Bettina, the only one to step up and peck at the groom's cheek, now scattered leaves of rosemary over the couple, and Alain Carstairs was bringing the "joining cup" to drink from.

First Daniella.

Then Steven.

After they'd taken the first sip, they carried the

golden cup to Edward, and he, keeping an arm around Daniella—when she bent to kiss his cheek—gave Steven his hand.

"I wish you all the joys marriage can bring," Edward said, coughing aside, then telling them both, "I am very happy in my daughter . . . and in *my son.*"

"We could not have saluted a more beautiful bride!" Alain announced, and looked sheepish when Daniella stared somewhat perplexedly at her elegant husband. Alain saved the day, saying, a little more softly, "Ah, aye, and handsome groom." He grinned while the bridesmaids giggled from embarrassment. But Daniella thought Steven did not look embarrassed in the least by the laughing jest. In fact, she thought he appeared rather pleased with himself.

Throughout the merriment, Daniella couldn't help but think of Robert. She had reminded herself it was over between them, but she had not ceased to miss him, her friend—and never before missed him with the desolation which seized her now.

Suddenly a shadow fell over Daniella. Steven had come to stand there while she adjusted her pale rose silk slipper. She sat very still while he continued to stare, and she lifted her eyes finally to see the eager affection in his face. That sudden, unbidden image of Robert withered and at last faded under Steven's warming gaze. She told herself that the memory of that arrogant captain would no serve again to haunt her. She was a married woman now. She had no choice but to put Robert and the stranger far from her mind—and her heart.

*   *   *

94

Edward Wingate had insisted on a wedding feast with dancing afterward. The din of voices and the lilting songs of the musicians in the gallery lost itself among the high-ceilinged plantation house. There was a long succession of courses: deep sea fish, juicy meats, stuffed capons among other delicious foul, topping it all with rich colorful desserts of berries, fruits, and delicious cakes. With plates in hand, many wandered out to the rose-planted garden to watch the youngsters romping there. It was growing a little chilly outside by the time dusk settled in, and one group after another began to drift into the hall where a huge spring log was aflame and crackling merrily in the great stone fireplace. The room had been cleared for games and dances.

While the firelight flickered and the hall grew long with shadows, the groom found a seat against the wall to watch as the musicians tuned up for yet more dancing. Landaker smiled pleasantly around the room, but for the most part he watched his radiantly glowing bride, whose feet could not remain still for very long. She stood up with everyone who asked her to dance and was swung in turns by the handsome bucks until the room was whirling about.

The groom stood all of a sudden and cut a swaggering path to his wife. His unwavering gaze remained glued on her. She stumbled on the dancing feet of a couple and would have fallen, but Steven was there at once for his bride. He held her easily and swept on through the dancers, spinning her about in their second waltz, graceful and light, airy, romantic, dancing her over to a place by the hearth.

"Oh Steven!" For a moment Daniella felt lightheaded and placed the back of her hand against her forehead.

"You must sit before you collapse on your feet, Daniella. You've been dancing much too hard." There was great concern in his voice as Daniella did as he ordered. "Sit still, my love, while I fetch you a drink."

"No!" She grabbed hold of his warm hand when he would have moved away. "I am fine, really, I am fine now, Steven."

An inexplicable tenderness for her new husband settled over Daniella.

Daniella felt a jolt run through her just then as Steven bent to adjust the long veil about her shoulders, his dark hand brushing the bare part of her shoulder, and her skin became sensitive as she anticipated what was soon to come. Even the tips of her breasts felt like raw silk inside the taut bodice of satin as she experienced a sense of growing sensual awareness.

She knew her rakish husband was studying her closely, and his presence warmed her whole body even before she looked up at him. Wondering about him as he must be wondering about her, Daniella loosed another hot-and-cold shiver. His face was blank and he displayed no emotion at all as he bent his head over hers, long black curls tickling her flushed cheek.

The dancing was over. Most of the guests would spend the night. Pallets would be made in the hall for the overflow, but first a merry procession would escort Landaker and his blushing bride to bed.

"My love?"

Steven stood first, and breathlessly Daniella al-

96

lowed him to help her to her feet as he held out his hand. She watched as the riotous group came toward them, breaking bride'scake over them as they turned to the stairs.

As the hard fingers tightened over hers, Daniella's heart gave an odd leap while the music from the hall seemed to linger poignantly. A breeze flirted with the lace curtains as they at last stepped into the bridal chamber. She stared at the bed. What did she really know about Steven Landaker? she asked herself. He was from London, was a titled gentleman, owned merchant ships . . . Daniella swallowed hard, wondering what the night would bring as the door closed behind them.

Chapter Seven

They say dreams are only fleeting fancies.
But, I wish I could dream him oftener.
Where else could I see him, if not in a
dream?

— Myung Ok

At last the newlyweds were alone, the final cere-
mony over . . .

Daniella had known all along what would happen: The custom was that the bride and groom
must crawl into the bridal bed together, with the
candles burning low but not extinguished. And the
couple may not look upon each other as they dis-
robe and it was only after that was completed that
the attendants, following custom, were permitted
to leave the room.

With Daniella on one side, Landaker on the
other, they had stripped down to their smallclothes. His seminakedness apparently did not repulse the women, for in fact they wore expressions
of amazement, and the young bucks, seeing the
big man in only his underdrawers, wavered as if
they'd been hit with a ton of bricks.

Smiling nervously and trying to make light of
the moment, Daniella crawled into one side of the
huge bed — a new one all the way from France,

white with gold scrimshaw—and drew the comforter up to her chin. Holding her breath, she hadn't even looked up to see the astonished faces of those watching her husband slip in beside her.

Now across the bed, they faced away from each other.

"They have gone."

"Yes," Daniella murmured softly, "I know."

"I'll blow out the candles," he said, moving to slip out of bed. Her hand came upon his arm before his left foot touched the floor. "Yes. What is it?" His gaze skimmed over his shoulder.

"I . . ." Looking away, she asked, "Why are you going to blow them out?"

He cleared his throat roughly. "I thought you'd prefer it that way," he said softly, now gazing deeply into her wide eyes.

"I do not mind." She pressed her lips together. "Really."

"Well . . ." He got out of bed. "I do."

She kept her eyes averted. "I'm sorry, Steven."

Slipping back under the cover, he asked, "Sorry? Why?"

Daniella shivered, not unpleasantly, when his breath tickled the loose strands at her temple. "Why, Daniella," he echoed when she hadn't answered. "Why be sorry? They are only candles, and I blew them out so you wouldn't have to see and be afraid the first time I make love to you."

Daniella gasped softly but mistook his meaning totally as she whispered, "Oh, Steven, you do not repulse me in the least."

Moving closer, he reached out to stroke the long strands of shining blond hair. He growled deep in his throat. "I might be horribly malformed or have

99

scales like a fire-breathing dragon for all you know."

"I think not." Daniella's heart picked up its beat as his finger circled her ear and his breath came hotter still against her flushed cheeks; it was all she could do to breathe!

"You think not." He chuckled low in her ear. "Well then, let's rid you of this last bit of flimsy garment you wear, so we can stop beating around the bush."

Daniella looked curious. "What does that mean? I've never heard that expression before."

"It's quite new. You see, the king was chasing one of his mistresses and . . ." He cleared his throat, continuing. "I don't think you'd like to hear the rest. It's rather close to indecency."

"Risqué, you mean?"

"Yes, that's the word."

Daniella's eyes slanted downward. "Tell me then, my dear husband, what does it mean . . . ah . . . in our situation?"

"I . . ." He laughed and cupped her cheeks. "I'm sorry, I entirely forgot what I said," he explained. "Daniella . . . you are so tempting." He hauled her to his chest, making her feel his fast-beating heart. "I can't wait much longer to have you!"

Daniella stirred uneasily in the bed. "Oh, Steven . . ."

"What?" He very expertly slipped the straps of her chemise off her shoulder and, pausing in his delightful labor, he waited.

"I . . ." Tucking her face beneath his chin, she finished in a murmuring voice, "It's just that I did not think you would go this fast with me. You're . . . you're not the same of a sudden."

He groaned. "It has been hell having to be around you these past weeks and not able to touch you . . . where I want to really touch you: your coral lips, your glorious hair, your fair white skin. All I've been allowed is the sight of your loveliness and I have drunk in all that a sane man can stand before going crazy. I am at my wit's end, Daniella!"

He dragged the chemise over her head, and Daniella's flesh heated over every inch his hard fingers traveled. When at last the thing had been flung to the floor, Daniella lay stiff as a board, waiting for what was to happen next. He did nothing more alarming than cup her face in his big hands and bring it to within a hairsbreadth of his own.

"Daniella . . ." He felt around and grew puzzled. "What in tarnation is all this garb?"

"I . . . with the wedding dress, it was only proper to don as many undergarments as possible . . . to give as much fullness to the belled style as was called for. That is why the extra shift."

"I understand." He chuckled. "I think."

She felt herself blush. "Believe me, the bulk is *quite* uncomfortable."

"And hot."

She said, "That, too."

"I did not think you could get anything else under that flimsy chemise." He brought his face closer to hers, tickling her with his long black hair, which she now knew was not a wig . . . otherwise he would have removed it, she told herself.

She could feel the flaring breath from his nostrils and was suddenly reminded of last spring and the stud that had mounted her father's favorite brood mare. The actual mating had brought a feverish blush to her face and a ringing to her ears; so emotional had she become that she'd had to turn away before the stallion had finished what he'd set out to accomplish. The stud had been a powerful and magnificent male beast . . . and she'd never forgotten that day.

"You may possibly think of me as a peacock, strange to gaze upon," the amorous groom went on. "But let me assure you, my beloved bride, I am no simple, half-witted fool, nor am I lacking in vitality in this act. Do not fool yourself in thinking the performance will be a short one. I am quite, quite able"—he kissed her lips once, softly, quickly—"to do you justice, m'lady. And if I seem different, not the same man who pecked you in the church, it is only because I want to make love to you so badly at this moment." A total ravishment, he kept to himself.

His bold words brought to the surface her own conception of what it would be like to be made love to by him. It was, or had been, incomprehensible that he could turn the warm feelings on inside her and make her experience almost the same thrilling desire she'd felt while the insolent captain had stolen a kiss. Because of Steven's kindness and caring heart, she felt much more affection for him at this moment than she would have believed possible.

Wordlessly he stroked Daniella's bare arm, and it wasn't long before he was creating a longing in the pit of her stomach, and the sensation traveled lower, and lower yet. Daniella knew her affection for her husband was intensifying. She looked up at him and her heart began to pound madly when the moon stole into the bedchamber and bathed the huge bed and its hangings in a silvery light.

The powder and rouge that Steven had applied with a heavy hand had begun to mingle with the sweat from his brow. One day when the time was right she would speak to him about the makeup, for there was no need for him to wear it while they were together.

Shifting his weight, Steven rested his elbow on the other side of his wife while his hard-muscled leg crossed over hers and now lay between her own. Daniella gave a quivering response as the throbbing length of his desire came to poke stiffly at her tender thighs.

She was about to protest, but Steven rushed on. "Kiss me, dearest Dany." With his lips merely brushing hers, he smiled and implored, "Open them," while his tongue begged entrance as he circled the rosy bow of her mouth.

Shy and self-conscious, Daniella tentatively opened her mouth and tasted his tongue with her own. Her reaction was violent and stunned, when, at the same time he plunged into her mouth, his hips rocked forward to grind his hard desire against her feminine softness.

"Steven. . . ?"

His answer sounded harsh in her burning ears, "Yes, my beloved, what is it? Did I hurt you? I certainly did not mean to."

"It's just that I need more time."

"More time," he groaned. Sighing deeply, as if pained, he pushed away from her and moved onto his back, staring at the high ceiling. Without looking at her, he asked, "How much time would you like, Daniella? A night? Two nights? A week? A month?" He wanted to be inside her *now.*

"A few more minutes please?"

He came to his elbow as she left the bed, padded across the room, and as he heard the door opening to the necessary room, he decided he would avert his eyes when she returned.

His voice was deep and soft when she returned to bed. "Was that the reason for your violent reaction when I thrust my body against you?" he asked bluntly, raising the sheet for her to slip beneath . . . next to him.

Daniella blanched that he should speak so boldly and openly and he could see her whiteness, almost matching the powder he wore on his face. "Steven . . . *please.*"

"Was it?" Snatching her up against his chest, he demanded, *"Was it?"*

"Yes, my lord, it . . . it was only that."

"Daniella, you needn't call me 'my lord'."

"Thank you, my lord." She almost chuckled as she heard his exasperation.

"Now," he growled as he snatched her harder to him, "let's get on with this marriage."

"Yes . . . Steven." When he let her go, she lay on her back staring up at him. "But please—get it over with."

He stroked the side of one aching breast. "This is not a thing quickly over and done with. That is only the way of a man with a whore. You are more precious to me than that. You are my wife now, and I will treat you as such."

With a jolt, Daniella came to her elbows and stared at him while her heart did a wild dance in her breast.

"What are you staring at?"

104

"You . . . your body. It is . . ." Her eyes swept over him. "You are so virile, Steven, not the fancy Dan I imagined you would be in . . . this situation."

"So you thought me the cock-of-the-walk, hmm?" Taking her head against his chest, he cupped her chin, his long fingers caressing her fine cheekbones. "Are you certain the moon is not playing tricks, sweet?"

"No, Steven—the moon is definitely not playing tricks!"

"I will have to argue that point. I think the moon is affecting you, love." Rising from the bed, he went to the windows, first one and then the other, drawing the heavy drapes closed against the invading moon. "There."

Daniella had been watching Steven all the while he crisscrossed the room, and now as he returned, she bit her lip and lowered her head. She was positively shimmering inside, could feel the palpitation of her heart. While he had slowly risen from the bed, his buttocks lean and tautly muscled, she had unknowingly licked her lips at the sight of his dark and manly form. He was coming back to her now, and she could sense every movement he made even if she couldn't see him. Peacock? Bah!

He chuckled as his knee sank into the bed. "What were you staring at, my silken beauty, with your big eyes?"

"Oh . . ." She felt as if she'd just opened a treasure box containing a very lovely surprise. "Nothing."

Daniella snuggled closer this time and pressed her cool fingertips along his strongly muscled arms in a titillating dance. There was not the slightest hint of quavering in her voice, only a soft purring anticipation as he removed the balance of his clothes in a flash. Now his virile beauty sprang up between them, and Daniella felt its rigid life. As it was, their bodies were now only darkly outlined blurs that moved like sensuous creatures of the moon-and-starlit night.

With the force of steel bands, Landaker encircled her narrow waist to draw her nearer, and Daniella only relaxed and purred in his arms while he whispered in her ear, "Better . . . oh, so much better."

There was not an inch of clothing separating their bodies, and where they touched, they were both moist and hot. She was prepared to submit to the inevitable. He tapped her chin with two fingers.

"Open your mouth to me, Dany love, and kiss me like this."

Before she could obey, he pressed his mouth to hers and forced her lips apart. Between the tiny movements, he breathed against her cheek, "I am a very impatient man where you are concerned, my love." Now he moved down over her body, his kisses soul-blistering as he planted them here and there, going lower and lower until at last he found the treasured valley he'd been seeking.

His voice dipped lower. "Ah, at last you are my wife, in every sense of the word."

With the thrilling certitude ringing in her ears, he slowly eased her lissome thighs apart, feeling them quiver in his hands. When he plunged his tongue inside the warm recess, seeking with it the sweet taste of her, Daniella groaned and tried to slide upward. Taking the small buns of her buttocks in his big hands, holding her still, he proceeded to kiss her most thoroughly. When she couldn't control the delightful shiver that passed between her legs, he pulled back, thinking she found the act revolting.

"Is my touch so distasteful?" he asked.

The power arising in her voice revealed, in truth, not one speck of uncertainty as she firmly replied, "No."

Reaching out a hand, he stroked the blond tuft, making her writhe under his caress, then he bent to bestow another liberal kiss upon her thighs.

"Oh . . . *yes,* Steven. You can believe that I find your t-touch"—she breathed laboriously—"quite stimulating." Choking back a small sob, Daniella reached out slim white arms to him, mutely begging him to come to her.

"Ah, Dany, I fell for you heart and soul when first I laid eyes on you. My sweet, you don't know how it pleases me that you truly want me!"

"I do want you, Steven . . . I do!"

"Despite my foppish countenance?"

Daniella closed her eyes, counting to ten in her frustration. "I only shivered a moment ago because—"

His hand rested on the concave hollow of her stomach. "Because?"

She wanted to shout but softly answered, "Because, my darling, I wanted you to continue!"

"Ah, I desired for you to surrender willingly, Daniella. You know that now, don't you?"

She was beginning to think her husband was teasing her. But would he do such a thing? I think I am about to melt, Daniella thought to herself as he leaned over to bury his lips in the curve of her golden mound. She gave a small, broken cry deep in her throat. He moved up over her and brushed his fingertips over her engorged nipples.

Amid her deep sighs of pleasure as he put his lips first to one rose crest and then the other, Sebastián carefully parted her legs and pressed his bold fingers between her thighs. To his intense pleasure, he found Daniella thoroughly moist, but when she reached down, her small hand going around the thickness of him, Sebastián became undone.

For a tense moment, he only gazed down at her slim form, but when she arched against his manhood, he lost the last measure of control and prepared her for his mounting.

The first deep thrust was hard and quick, penetrating her with one smooth motion, leaving Daniella only a moment of stunning pain; and then the burning pressure eased as he began to slowly fill her and move backward and forward, each thrust touching the rigid folds of woman flesh. He was rewarded by the lifting of slender hips and buttocks. Slowly . . . blissfully, the plunges went deeper and her tenderness folded around him, touching with fire, fullness, hunger.

Sebastián's lips moved to the smooth white curve of throat she arched so that he could better get to it. Small, eager hands traveled over the whipcord arms and broad expanse of back and over the rigid muscles. With his hard member inside her, giving her so much pleasure she thought she'd swoon, Daniella's lips trembled and she wept and made desperate little utterances. His strength was unexpected, forcing her to take more of him.

"My fiery little tigress. You are so tight and good." He flexed within her and she answered by clenching around his hugeness. "We fit together perfectly, sweet."

"Oh, Steven . . . yes . . . oh, yes!" she cried as their fiery rhythm shook her to the foundations of her womanhood.

His thrusts went deeper, deeper inside her, and Sebastián groaned as she rose to meet him, and her slender arms wound about his neck as he sought the ultimate depths of intimacy within her. Daniella surrendered all and gloried in the tumultuous sensations beginning to build apace until they were both red-hot with passion's fervor. A new desperation mushroomed in her and she bit almost through her lip, tasting blood on her tongue.

"Ah," Sebastián cried, "ah, my *tigre roseta!*"

"Oh, God, Steven . . ." she whispered hoarsely as sensation followed sensation and throbbed through every vein.

Sebastián's mouth crushed Daniella's as they soared to unbelievable heights and flamed with a frenzied heat and then were wrapped inseparably inside a burning mantle of ecstasy.

Sweat-slick bodies moved together in a rhythm as old as time, and all thoughts fled their minds save their turbulent passion. When, after they had at last soared and shuddered and exploded like colliding stars, first her, then him joining, Sebastián whispered the sweetest of endearments a wife should ever care to hear, "Lady Landaker . . ." he began hoarsely. *"You* are the . . . the most exciting woman I have ever known. And this night, my moonlit rose, this night, bears repeating because I can't wait to let you drive me wildly insane again."

Agreement merely came upon a low moan as Daniella continued to float upon a downy cloud, of bliss.

The most exciting woman he had ever known! Those words were repeated over and over in Daniella's mind in the early-morning hours after her husband slipped from the bed and dressed while the moon was low in the sky.

She went through the gloom of the dawning day to the window, and pushed open the green shutters. The moon was a sliver of white-gold. The sky was still black, holding the glitter of distant stars fading one by one. The smell of wild jasmine in the dewy morning reminded her of the hours not long ago spent in her husband's arms. In truth, she was shaken to think they had made love so wildly and passionately just a short time ago.

Daniella's face took on a dreamy, almost rapturous look as she recalled when a knight in shining armor awaited her in her dreams. Now she had to come face-to-face with reality. Her husband certainly knew how to tease and pleasure a woman, for he'd deliberately prolonged the intensity of her wait until he had her shivering with sweet torment. Before last night, she'd never dreamed he would be that gentle, so giving, their bodies moving in perfect harmony.

After a leisurely bath, Daniella smoothed the folds of a pink-plum gown and put it on without Bettina's help, then paced her room. She was still troubled by Steven's passionately whispered words. *You are the most exciting woman . . .* Was she really so? She wondered how many times her husband had experienced such pleasure before she came along?

Daniella continued to pace the floor, feeling a frustrating tug on her nerves. His other women must have been very skilled in the boudoir. Perhaps they had been whores, for how else would a man have learned all he knew about making love? Come to think of it, Steven might have been in love with another woman, which brought her to the question: *Does Steven love me?* Why else would he have married her if he did not love her. *He must . . . surely.* She had to be content with that thought for now.

The men in her father's library were well known to Daniella. Among them were a few shipmasters of superior dignity and substance like young Garrick Warpinton, and the rest prosperous merchants . . . like Steven Landaker.

What were they all doing here so early in the day, Daniella wondered as she stepped quietly into the room. But they had not spotted her yet, so she decided to hesitate before barging in. Maybe she could learn a thing or two.

From the discussion in progress it appeared that the group of the more adventurous overseas traders were disturbed by the lack of success of their last voyage to Europe. What could the problem be? She overheard them speaking of the Windstar Fleet. Daniella hoped the problem didn't include her father's ships, or Lord Landaker's. She didn't even know the name of his fleet, or if he sailed them on his own as captain, in fact.

Then Daniella froze, hearing the ominous word "searobbers." For some inexplicable reason, Robert Drake came to mind. But she did not have time to dwell on it further, for just then Garrick Warpinton breezed past her and stormed out of the room, slamming the big oaken door and leaving a deep resounding echo all around.

Daniella paled. There *was* some trouble!

Lord Landaker, standing a little apart by the tall windows with the light striking his broad shoulders, moved his hands impatiently as he spoke. Daniella looked around for her father, but she could not see him in the room.

"Warpinton crows awfully loud for a young cock," Landaker said in his deep voice. "Dammit, he should have had more patience and listened more carefully. Some damage has been done to our Windstar Fleet and there will be other losses if they are not stopped. Is that young pup a fool?" He snorted. "If we sit upon our backsides, what have we gained? I would risk everything just to be able to dispose of those thieving bastards!"

Landaker spun to face the room, taking hold of the back of a chair, giving those present — and one who was well hidden — a start from seeing the savage countenance he displayed. His long black hair was flung back, his large hands balled into tight fists.

One man swallowed hard and shouted, "I am willing to put up a quarter of what we will need in guns, ammunition, and other supplies!"

Daniella stood glued, listening to the young man boom out his pledge to the Company, unable to move forward to save her life. She had never seen Steven in this kind of mood. Her expression, if one could see her, was raptly attentive. Following her wedding night, her beauty had taken on a shimmering quality, and if Landaker's eyes would have found her where she stood with the sun striking her recently washed blond hair and her body in the lovely plum gown, she would immediately have snatched his breath away.

They began to discuss costs, and as Daniella listened to her husband's resonant voice deep in explanation, she experienced a sting of pride in him, knowing she was falling ever more deeply in love.

Her father had chosen well for her, she thought, *for Lord Landaker is someone Edward trusts to carry on what he has worked so hard to build for me.*

Daniella started as her father appeared suddenly at her side and directed his words to the Company men. "I should like to contribute the *Challenger!*" was all he said.

All eyes riveted upon Edward Wingate, and Daniella gasped, bringing attention to herself. Nothing in the lower ports could outsail the *Challenger,* and no ship they might send to search the piratical coasts could cover more water or pick her way more nimbly in strange waters. But no man had cared yet to send the pride of his fleet to be battered on that dangerous hide-and-seek venture that was like a giant chess game on the high seas.

Daniella glanced across the hall toward Alain Carstairs, who stood rigid with anger for a few seconds then broke into a tirade. "Meaning no disrespect, Edward—but are you totally mad?"

"You've no wish to join us, Alain?" It was Steven Landaker's question; he studied Carstairs closely.

Alain's face was red, but not from thinking anyone might dare to question his seamanship or courage. "I have no wish to see someone else mishandle the *Challenger*. Luke and I are the only ones who have sailed her and no one else has the right!"

Stepping closer to her father, which placed her now in full view of the men, Daniella softly asked him a question only he could hear. A pretty blush rose in her cheeks as Steven swung his regard her way and nodded in her direction. She gracefully lowered her head in a respectful acknowledgement of his greeting.

Traveling leisurely over his wife, Landaker's eyes were crystal-jade slits veiled by impossibly long lashes. His lean face had been carelessly powdered almost to whiteness, and he was watching Daniella, who was putting on a nearly perfect show of not being aware of his bold study. There was something fiercely sensual about his look. It gave her a tingling sensation, for it was as if she could read his most revealing expression under all the thick, foppish makeup he wore to conceal what must be some minor flaws. Someday she would see him without the makeup.

Reluctantly dragging his eyes from Daniella, Landaker plunged right back into the heated discussion, almost as if she wasn't present. But he flicked a look over to her every few minutes to assure himself she was still there.

"That's only fair, Alain." Edward was saying. "You do have a right to speak your mind."

After a time, Daniella found herself frowning. There seemed to be a hint here that the merchant venturers wanted the Wingates to join their company. She looked at her husband, whose thoughts seemed preoccupied. *Yes,* she thought, *this must be the Company's idea.* They were all looking hopefully in Edward's direction. They had never pushed her father this hard, but Edward was not an easy man to win over to anything. Now that she'd become Lord Landaker's wife, what would this do to their position? Had they automatically been ushered into the Company after Daniella had become a Landaker?

Here it comes, Daniella thought, tensing up with a strong feeling of intuition.

"Count us in the Company," Edward said, nodding as if that settled that.

Staring hard at Daniella, then away, Landaker said, "I don't think Edward ever meant to hold out to the point of damaging himself. He just preferred to go on as he always has. Most of the Company has known him for years and did not press the matter."

Daniella spread her hands wide, pointedly asking, "What about *now,* my lord?" She had realized he was their leader.

There was a twinkle in his jade-green eyes as Landaker swiftly crossed the space that separated himself and Daniella and stood protectively closer, yet still within hearing of the room's occupants.

"There has been a movement to tighten up our defenses, my sweet. You have heard about the attacking of our ships, have you not?"

"Well, I have heard it just now." Moistening her lips, she gazed up at Steven as she spoke. "But they have yet to attack one of ours, you know."

"Yes . . . *ours* all the same, my love," Lord Landaker agreed, giving her a possessive look.

115

Daniella chose to ignore that statement for now. He could not be saying in this taunting tone that the Wingate ships were now in the Company's hands, to do with as they wished, to sail any one of them with a captain of their choice? *Could he?* He would not have played that trick on them, for Lord Landaker was too kindly a person. Once, though, while they had been making love for the third time, she had detected a possessive desperation in him. Yet, aside from that, the flames of passion had burned brightly in them both and she had thought that no deeper passion could have existed.

Daniella looked up at her tall husband, gave him a tender smile, and he went on. It wasn't long before her suspicions grew apace with the deep thuds of her heart.

Steven was looking right at her. "Whether you knew this or not, love, you have always had to obey most of our regulations, but your father is well liked and has many friends in the Company, so if it seems we are pushing you now, perhaps it is because we know it is time you got in. It would be a step in the right direction."

Steven Landaker nodded as Edward coughed softly into his hand, his face flushed, his eyes watering. But Daniella wasn't looking at her father just that minute. She remained frozen solid with her eyes riveted on Steven until Edward stepped forward, took her hand in his sweaty palm, and smiled down into her worried face. Daniella hid her alarm as she looked at her father. He had never before been nervous over business matters. Was he really ill then, as she'd suspected several days ago?

116

She spoke gently to Edward so as not to excite him. "The pirates are not attacking *our* ships, Father." But the look Landaker sent Daniella made her hackles rise. "You have not captained your own ships in a dozen years and have forgotten what it was like to sail as far as England. You used to tell tales of the winds failing, storms blowing you off course, days of crowded quarters for the men, food going bad, stench and grumblings. Not to mention the sickness and perhaps even mutiny . . ." She glowered at the Company men. "Even pirates."

Edward patted Daniella's hand. "My love, what are you trying to say?"

She looked across the room to find Alain Carstairs nodding in her favor. "Our men are not fit for such a . . . a dangerous venture on the high seas. We have only three ships, Father, and we need them all. Take the *Rampant Rose,* she is our favorite and . . . and we would be losing so many good men." As she continued, Landaker looked at his wife with new respect. "They cannot fight pirates, Father, they are but simple sailors, and our ships are only merchant ships."

Landaker stepped closer to his wife, gazing down into her clear gray-blue eyes. "Dany, the Company has several hundred men, and you needn't worry that we will sacrifice one of the Wingate ships as warships. The Merchant Fleet will supply those."

"Well then . . ." She spread slim white hands toward him. "Why do you need them at all?"

"Decoys, Daniella, my dear wife."

Leaving her gaping at him, he plucked her hand from her side and planted a kiss in the smooth pink palm. She tingled beneath his fingertips, hypnotized by his very touch. She recalled his kisses which had sent her senses into a wild swirl of passion.

Several of the men seemed bored with the conversation and were leaving. Lord Landaker bowed to his wife, nodded at Edward, and then went to the door with his Company friends.

Her father's voice sounded close to her ear. "It is time we joined the Company, Daniella. You know that, don't you?"

Daniella seemed deep in thought as she answered. "I suppose you are right, Father, I have seen it coming for a long time." But she didn't like it one bit.

Edward turned her hand over in his, looking down. "I think we know when we are overcome, Dany. The Merchant Adventurers are just too big to fight."

Daniella turned to say something to her father, but when she noticed how very pale he'd become, the words died on her tongue. Her ire rose. She was wed to one of the most powerful and influential men in the business of merchant fleets. There was really nothing either she or her father could do. She saw that now, and wished she had been more wary of Lord Steven Landaker and his motives.

Staring across the hall at the tall, lean form of her husband, she began to wonder if this wasn't exactly what Steven had been striving for all along. If it was, then their marriage was already turning into a farce. Steven Landaker had gotten precisely what he desired; how much more could he want from her?

"Dany?" Edward addressed his daughter. "Steven has informed me he will be sailing in just a week's time."

"Sailing? So soon?"

"You will be going to your new home—the Landaker estate in Cornwall . . . England."

The sudden lump in Daniella's throat was hard to swallow as she said, "But Braidwood *is* my home, Father. I don't need another place to go to."

"You have to go with your husband, Dany love, and it is my wish that you accompany him to the Landaker place in Cornwall."

"This is Steven's wish also?"

"Of course."

Daniella looked aside. What more could Steven Landaker want? she asked herself again. At this point, he only asked the *world* of her, that's all.

Chapter Eight

The time had arrived and by no stretch of the imagination could this moment be called thrilling, as she'd once thought it would be. "Home," she murmured.

Daniella stood at the rail and dared not turn her head to look back at the town, for she knew the tears would come fast. Besides, South Carolina was probably visible no longer. The shores were moving farther, farther away, and with them the small group waving good-bye . . . her father . . . they were all lost, torn from Daniella in blurred outlines.

Bettina stood beside Daniella. The maid had watched as the great sails unfurled and the ship was released from the hold of her anchors, then as she began moving majestically from her moorings.

With the tide carrying the ship along the meandering course, it wasn't long before they were on the Atlantic Ocean and America was well behind them.

The navigation of the windy sea was a long affair in a sailing ship. There were the cross currents, the boom of the wind in the spread canvas as the ship plunged and plowed the waves. For the most part, however, the going was easy enough and sent no one prostrate to their bunks.

For the entire first day out Daniella hardly saw her husband, but she was aware that he'd slept in the same cabin with her. Yet, if he had crawled into the same bunk with her, she never knew, for she'd been dead to the world that first night. Up and down, up and down . . . She had felt like a babe being gently rocked to and fro in a huge cradle.

Daniella drew very little comfort from the fact that Bettina had revealed the voyage would take only two weeks. Their first stop would be the Landaker house in Cornwall, and from there they would go . . . *Where would they go?* Daniella wondered. Already she missed her father and her home.

Steven Landaker had taken over her entire life, it seemed, making most of her decisions, even down to the color gown she would wear for the day. For an instant she had been tempted to jump ship and run home. Oh, she had given in meekly, but she was growing sick and tired of being told what to do. She wasn't a child any longer but a grown, married woman with a mind of her own!

Yet, after all was said and done, she still adored Steven. And so she should, Bettina told her when Daniella confided in the wise maid, who said it would be better for her not to grumble and complain so much.

"Come away from the rail, my lady," Bettina said. "You didn't wear all your petticoats and stays." She giggled softly. "The men are staring, and they are getting an eyeful, too, no doubt."

Daniella's cheeks pinkened when she realized Bettina was right, for the strong breeze that had come up molded her skirts to her long legs and thighs, not to mention the shapely curve of her buttocks.

Blushing, Daniella asked, "How long have they been staring?"

"Long enough."

Bettina drew Daniella's attention when she tugged on her arm. "Look who's coming."

Just then Steven walked up to them, his hooded gaze riveted to that section of Daniella's body that was being ogled by the men on deck. "Go to our cabin, Daniella."

"What?" She couldn't believe he was ordering her around as if she were a maid.

Before Daniella could protest, he again told her what she must do. She stiffened and tossed up her chin in mute defiance when his eyes narrowed and he spoke again.

"I've some things to see to. I'll join you in our cabin later." He gave Bettina a swift perusal, then added to Daniella, *"Alone.* Without your maid."

"As you wish," Daniella crisply answered, then turned in the direction of the bulkhead.

Bettina smiled saucily for the men—one in particular—as she walked to the bulkhead and the small cabin assigned to her on the *Emerald Tiger.*

Misery such as she had never experienced in all her healthy years stared at Daniella from the swaying walls of their tiny cabin.

"Oh, Lord," Daniella groaned, holding one hand to her head the other to her stomach.

"There now," Bettina crooned, "you'll soon be feeling better."

Tossing the blanket over her head, Daniella made a muffled groan. "Oh . . . I doubt that very much, Bettina."

The decks had been awash for days, and even when Daniella shut her eyes, it helped little in her terrible battle against seasickness. Bettina, who had never been in the least upset by the motions of a ship no matter how the thing rolled and pitched, did what she could for her lady, amusing her with racy accounts of the crew members she'd come to know and who seemed a pleasant lot — when they weren't ogling her backsides and making raffish comments!

One thing Daniella sorely missed and could not understand: Her husband had not come to her, not even the second day when he had ordered her to her cabin alone. When Bettina had been allowed to come to her, Daniella had felt much better, for loneliness had begun to settle in, but Daniella still missed Steven and his touch. Oh, how she missed *that!*

Now this terrifying storm had kept him from her even longer.

"Can you eat a biscuit?" Bettina asked with compassion in her dark-chocolate eyes as she walked at a slant across the cabin.

Daniella held her head and groaned again. Two days had gone by since she had even thought of food, and no persuasion could make her try even a morsel. Bettina went to a huge trunk in the corner of the cabin which had been sent aboard as a present from her lady's neighbors. She dug around the straw, took out a bottle, then uncorked and smelled it.

"What are you doing?" Daniella asked from her swaying bunk.

"God's teeth! Madeira!" Bounding across the cabin, she knelt on the floor beside Daniella's bunk. "My lady! This will put color into those whitewashed cheeks of yours."

"Away!" Daniella looked even more sick. *"Please,*

123

take it away, Bettina," she groaned. "I can't even look at it in fear I will have to use the bucket again."

Bettina could not help laughing, and then she sipped it herself and licked her lips. Then she began to cough. "Zounds! Strong brew, this!"

In a strangled voice, Daniella sank back on the pillow, grateful that Mary had seen to it that down pillows and the best blankets had been sent aboard to compensate for the hardness of the bunks.

"That's enough." Bettina jammed the cork back into the bottle, set it aside, hiccupped loudly, and then tucked poor Daniella into bed warm and snug. "You rest now, my lady."

"My . . . lady," Daniella murmured. She slept, and awoke feeling much better and even took some bouillon Bettina fed to her by spoon.

To be sure, the sea was calming somewhat. By the next morning, a wan sun struggled through the cobalt clouds. By noon they had run before the wind into a beautiful blue-green sea dancing with white-capped waves.

Wrapping Daniella in a thick cloak and blanket, Steven Landaker carried his protesting wife to the cushioned spool-chair he had produced for her in a sheltered corner of the deck. Wearing rakish clothes and a concealing cap low over his forehead, he gazed down at her. "You look no worse than a dozen other wrecks of humanity," he chuckled softly in her ear, making her shiver.

"What?" She looked up at him as if she hadn't heard exactly right. "How dare you, Steven . . ." Then she caught the crooked smile and heard the hint of laughter deep in his throat. "I believe you are making fun of me."

With his black hair waving about his softly powdered face, Steven looked almost handsome standing there, gazing raptly down at her. Drawing her chin up in his gloved hand, he kissed her eyes shut first and then brushed her lips, her white cheeks, while holding her quivering hand in a tight grasp against his thigh. "Love, I am so happy to see you are feeling better. Aided by sun and wind, you will soon revive."

Daniella laughed softly. "By slow degrees!"

"You have youth and you are strong, my dear. A courageous spirit such as yourself will soon be leaping and dancing like a sprite along the deck. I'm confident that nothing in the way of a storm could ever disable you for long."

"Storm?" Jaecko, the helmsman, stooped from his seven foot height to say good morning. His eyes were red-rimmed from the night's wind. "Did I hear someone mention *storm?* Imp of Satan!" His deep chuckle rolled across the deckboards. "That was hardly enough to make us furl t'gallants." He winked at Lord Landaker's lady.

All in all, Jaecko, with his straight black hair close over his ears and almost falling to his shoulders, was quite handsome for his massive proportions. Daniella realized just then that Bettina seemed quite impressed by the colossal sailor.

Laughing delightfully, Daniella looked up at Jaecko. "You do not frighten me, sir."

He winked again. "Wait until we really hit the big one with all hands lashed to the bulwarks!"

"You're just—" Daniella did not finish, for when she glanced up, she saw that her husband had vanished. "Where did he go?" she asked Giant Jaecko.

"Disappears like that sometimes." Jaecko emitted

a snort that fell short of a laugh. "Guess he don'
want us all to see how *pretty* he really is in the
brilliance of sunshine."

Another snort of laughter sounded behind
Jaecko, and Daniella looked over to see several of
the crew members gathered there around a petty
task. Daniella smiled with happiness, thrilling to
the bracing open air now that her seasickness was
passing. This could be a very exciting life, she
thought, for how could this crossing become mo-
notonous with the constant sense of gliding on toward the unknown?

Jaecko interrupted her musings as he leaned toward her. "How do you do it?" he cryptically
asked.

"How do I do what?" Daniella wondered aloud
yet beginning to feel a sense of embarrassment
creep upon her. If he was asking her what she
thought he was asking her . . .

"You know." Jaecko shrugged enormous shoulders. Just then the mute boy Rascon came to stand
by them, his deep amethyst eyes boring into Daniella's so intensely that it made her shiver.

"He sure makes a person wonder sometimes
eh?"

"Wonder?" Daniella thought he meant the boy
and she prepared herself to defend the poor raga-
muffin.

"Lord Landaker," Jaecko supplied, grinning ro-
guishly with large white teeth and twinkling seaman's eyes.

"We get along just fine," Daniella offered with a
beautiful smile. Then her cobalt-gray eyes turned
mischievous as she looked up at the giant again. "It
is usually dark in the room, you see."

"Dark?"

"Yes, of course. Dark." *When we make love.*

Jaecko made a sound like a grunt as he sauntered along the deck until he joined the other crew members. Rascon hadn't moved, and he gave her quick, glowering glances from his great sad eyes. He was so frail, but not timid by a long shot. What had happened to him to make him appear so angry and unhappy? Just like the first time the elfin lad had jumped down to suddenly appear in front of her, he stared and stared, as if he couldn't quite believe what he was seeing.

He had eyes. He could see. So Daniella refused to let him avoid her *that* way. She pointed to her lips, saying, "My name is *Daniella . . . Rose.*" She plucked at the material of her bodice, holding out an embroidered flower for him to see. "It means *flower,* my middle name."

Rascon blinked wide, then made a sound like a grunt and gave her a fierce look as he gesticulated with slim, graceful hands.

"I'm sorry. I—"

Astounded, Daniella gasped as the boy reached out and slapped at her hand, making her drop the delicate bit of flowered lace back to her breast. She had been totally unprepared for Rascon's unwarranted attack. Her eyelashes fluttered as she peered up at him. "Why did you do that?" she asked, pointing first at herself, and then at his chest. "Don't you like me?" Feeling desolate, she held her hand out to him. "I like you."

The angry boy stomped his foot three times upon the deck as if shouting, "No, no, no!"

A huge shadow fell over them just as Rascon whirled to run from her and he crashed right into

127

the hard male form standing there. When he looked up and saw who it was, he snatched up the long-fingered brown hand and kissed it furiously, as if telling the man he was sorry for bumping into him.

"Hey, it's all right," a deep male voice said comfortingly.

Mesmerized, Daniella watched the muscled hand reach out to lift the lad's cap and tousle his thick dark hair. Then, putting the cap back on, he spun the lad and sent him on his way with a pat on his skinny behind.

Daniella's stomach clenched tight as she stared at the sun glinting on hair that was like a living golden flame. Eyes dazzled her like costly jewels encased in a band of deeper jade. Thick golden lashes, long and lushly feminine, sparkled with moisture, as if he'd just bathed his face. Daniella's cautious eyes dropped like hot coals, aflame by what she looked upon: Black boots, tight breeches proclaiming his manhood, green silk shirt slashed open to a narrow waist, flat stomach, up again to broad shoulders, deeply tanned throat, teeth stunningly white in a dark, compelling face, strong profile exposed as the dashing man turned for only a moment to smile lopsidedly at something Jaecko had joked about.

Though her heart was surrounded by sudden warmth, Daniella gasped. She stared in shocked remembrance.

Now he turned back to her.

Daniella felt as if lightning had bolted from the blue sky across the decks, seared a path through his flesh and then hers. She stared up at him, her heart pounding madly as his husky male voice came down to wash over her. Waves of warm honey

128

poured rampantly through her veins.

Ragged emotions battled within Daniella.

With impassive coldness, she stared up at him.

The voice was deep and flagrantly sensual. "Good day, m'lady. Enjoying the voyage so far?"

Daniella's hands automatically clenched into tight fists. That scoundrel of a captain! She remembered her promise to herself to slap his lecherous face next time she encountered the devil.

Daniella began to rise, fury burning in her stormy eyes.

Sebastián saw her intent and reached down swiftly, catching both fragile wrists to hold her imprisoned. His tall frame hovered above Daniella, giving her time to cool her anger.

"How *dare* you!" Daniella's anger did not cool. She began to struggle, unintentionally bumping against his bent legs and solid thighs.

With a wolfish expression, he grinned down at her flushed face. "My goodness, but you are strong for such a little sprite."

"An impossibility!" Daniella whispered as he settled her back into the chair, staring wide as his arms bulged with huge muscles.

He smiled almost gently. "Not really, when you realize who is captain of this ship."

"You?!"

"Indeed, m'lady." He was still holding on to one wrist and had no intention of letting go, it seemed.

"Where . . . is . . . my . . . husband?"

Sebastián waved his hand in the air, then continued. "He has taken ill, I'm afraid."

"But that cannot be possible! He was here on deck only a short time ago." She cast her eyes about frantically, looking for a friend, but there was no one present, not even Bettina. Oh, where was she now in this time of need? *Anybody!*

Gently Sebastián eased Daniella's hand down onto her lap. "Seasickness comes on suddenly sometimes, little lady."

Daniella stared out to sea. "But . . . but the storm is gone."

"I'm sorry. Weren't you informed that your husband was ill while you yourself were indisposed?"

Daniella's eyes lifted over his towering frame. "You mean he has been bedridden, too?"

"That's right. So you see, m'lady, it can come back on one suddenly. And I'm sorry you were misinformed as to the true captain of this ship."

She boldly met his eyes. "Wh-what ship is this?"

"Don't you know?" He shot her a twisted grin.

"I . . . I didn't happen to look at the name when we boarded. The sky was rather overcast at that time."

"Then you failed to notice the figurehead, too."

"Which is . . ." Daniella blanched. "The ship with the figurehead of a leaping tiger." Now she went on as if speaking to herself. "The day I saw the ship in the harbor . . . the very same day I met you. *You . . .*" She looked up at him again. *"You* were the one watching me from the deck of your ship. *You* were the one who followed me from the waterfront and into the woods. This ship is *yours,* not *Steven's!"*

Eyes darkening with emotion, he bowed crisply. "The *Emerald Tiger* at your service, m'lady, as I myself am."

She blinked at the sun behind him. "You work for my husband . . ."

He executed a short bow, a dashing grin splitting

his strong chin. "You could say that, love."

"Why are we sailing on *your* ship?" she asked. "Why are we not sailing on one of my husband's?"

"It is not only *my* ship." He laughed softly, adding, "As relatives, and consolidated owners of the Windstar Fleet, we are in this together. We . . . ah . . . share."

Seeing the possessive look in his eyes, Daniella paled even whiter than her seasickness had bleached her. S-share?

He smiled as he placed a hand on her shoulder. "This is going to be a long voyage, Daniella."

"Not so far as you're concerned, Captain!"

Sebastián clicked his tongue. "You could start out making your voyage more pleasant by calling me Sebastián."

"My *husband* would not like that, Captain."

Tipping her chin up with a forefinger, Sebastián grinned into her blinking eyes. "Believe me, Steven won't mind."

"What do you mean?" Daniella pressed, half in dread.

He stroked her chin for a jolting moment, then waved those long fingers in the air, while she stared, mesmerized.

His look was bold. "We *share,* that is all I can say."

The stunning color of his eyes was so pleasing to look at that Daniella lost herself, unable to look away. Stimulating sensations Daniella had felt only once before overpowered her senses, leaving her dizzy. Having lost her tongue, she could only stare up at him.

When at last he pulled her to her feet, she didn't even notice, and when he tangled his fingers in the blond cloud of hair, the slight tug on her scalp didn't even bother her. All she sensed was his lean form, his manly odor, and his eyes, his beautifully vibrant eyes that were holding her spellbound and captivated as if she was caught in another world from which there was no escape.

Her husband had never looked at her like this man was doing at the moment!

His fingers banded her wrist and, pulling her closer, he gazed slowly into her lustrous eyes until she trembled against his body. As if holding a raw emotion in control, Sebastián's cheek twitched and his jaw was held taut.

Daniella's expression could only be called bewilderment. *What is she thinking?* he wondered. *Is she afraid of me?* Sweet, disturbing emotions roiled through him and he felt a strong urge to be kind to her. She had been ill. He would let her have this time to recuperate and then . . . ah yes, she held a breathtaking promise for him. She was so incredibly beautiful . . . Oh God, he'd also like to strangle her. Eileena had been beautiful at one time, too, but now she was nothing more than a helpless shadow. Someone had to pay for the crimes inflicted upon the innocent. He had to begin somewhere . . .

"Dark rose," he murmured, caressing her slim hips while his pulsating desire strained to reach her.

Daniella felt as if she were leaning on a door that was sealing her fate. The words had been said quietly, yet they now seeped into her mind as she stepped from the desperate cloud of sensuality which had imprisoned her and back into the bright sunlit day. She had been rooted in dangerous desire, unable to move or to think. What was he going to do to her now? He was captain of this ship, and couldn't captains do what they wanted to—to anyone? With Steven indisposed, would the captain exert pressure on her vulnerability? She hated to think what he would do once he had her alone belowdecks in his amorous clutches.

How sweet she is, Sebastián found himself thinking. He longed to step forward the few inches separating them and hold this beauty forever in his aching arms. *Idiot fool! You can have her anytime,* he told himself, *even though she belongs to another.* Her heart might be with Robert Drake, but he, Sebastián Landaker, had her on his ship and in his control now. The problem was, he knew Daniella, and she would only yield to her husband, Lord Landaker!

Then again, the situation *could* change . . . Indeed that might give away the whole show, he warned himself.

"Oh, here you are." Bettina came cheerfully to the deck. "Don't you think it's time you had some rest, otherwise . . ." Her words froze as she shielded her eyes from the sun and stared at the man gazing raptly into Daniella's face . . . and Daniella was doing the same thing. Weren't they aware they were being stared at? Mercy sakes, the way these two ate each other up they could go hungry the rest of their lives and still be sated!

Just who is this man? Bettina wondered.

"Ain't she a dolly!" Jaecko the giant hooted from a lower deck as he ogled Bettina from crinkly eyes. "Like to meet me later for a moonlit stroll, love?"

Bettina colored, and not knowing how to behave around the handsome giant, she cocked a shoulder haughtily, shouting down, "I've no time for the likes of you, big lad!"

No one had ever dared speak thusly to the giant! Then, surprisingly, when "ooohs" and "ahhhs" flitted among the sailors, Jaecko colored just as brightly as Bettina herself. Green eyes highlighted with light hazel shards turned on Bettina just then and she drew her breath in sharply, wondering where she'd seen those eyes before.

Catching Bettina's wise discernment, Sebastián moved away from Daniella to stand before the wide-eyed Bettina. "Do you see a family resemblance?" he asked softly when Daniella was out of earshot.

"Yes . . ." Bettina gulped. Lord but this man was beautiful. Even with a thin scar slashing his jaw, he was gorgeous. Rugged. A real man.

Whispering almost, he asked, "Who?"

"I . . . I'm not sure, sir."

"*Captain,*" Sebastián instructed with a large smile.

"Of this ship?" Bettina's mouth dropped several inches.

"Aye," he whispered. "Captain Landaker. Sebastián Landaker, at your service."

"*M-my* service?" Bettina blinked vacantly, all but swooning beneath the ash-rimmed green eyes.

Sebastián shook his head and cleared his throat, beginning again as he asked, "There was something familiar in my eyes?"

"You must be related to Lord Landaker then?" she asked tentatively.

His comeback was softly spoken. "For sure, you've seen something no other has — yet, little maid."

Bettina gasped low. "Oh, yes, that's where I saw

the eyes, even though they are more hidden in the dandy's face. That husband of m'lady's narrows his eyes almost to slits of nothing. You wonder what he's thinking at times, he's so mysterious. Oh, I'm sorry, you and Lord Landaker must be related."

"Yes." Taking her arm and leading her back to where her lady waited, Sebastián whispered to Bettina, "Let's keep it a secret then, Bettina."

"But I—"

"*Shhh.*"

Bettina gulped loudly. "Not a word, Captain."

Smiling, he patted her cool hand. "That's a good girl," he said, then when he turned to face Daniella, he found himself staring into the impishly grinning face of his mate Jaecko. Daniella had gone belowdecks, Jaecko's jerk of a huge-knuckled hand told his captain.

Soon there will be nowhere the lovely blonde can hide, Jaecko thought to himself as he watched his captain stride to the helm.

Sleep, Daniella soon found, was an utter impossibility in the afternoon heat. A puzzled frown hovered above her bright, crystal-clear eyes as she lay there in her bunk. Daniella's hand rested diagonally across her chest so that it lay between the firm, upthrust breasts which pushed their way half out of her shift.

Lips, as softly coral as a young robin's breast, were pouting a little as she sighed in boredom and twirled a long strand of flaxen hair around her finger.

For two days now she had seen neither hide nor hair of Lord Landaker or the captain. The rakish

135

man of mystery . . . What had he said was his name? It began with an "S" like her Steven. *Where did they hide themselves? Were they together? If so, what were they planning?*

Daniella rolled over in her bunk to stare at the watery designs on the ceiling, then at the circle of light on the bulkhead. It was a huge ship, true, but not all that huge that in all these hours not once had she caught sight of either one. She might as well get used to the loneliness. Her absent husband did not seem to care—so why should she?

But she *did* care. Steven had stolen her from her serene world, made her his wife, and introduced her to indescribable pleasures. And now when she craved those same pleasures, where was he? Could he still be ill? She moved restlessly in the bunk, her mind unwilling to turn to the scoundrel captain. But there was no help for her wayward thoughts.

Captain S. Who was he really? Robert Drake had told her they called him the Tiger, but in actuality, that was the title of his ship. The ship they were on. Was it a pirate ship then? Was he related to her husband somehow? Why, for God's sake, all the mystery?

As Daniella drifted in and out of sleep, lulled by the motion of a gentle sea, a shaft of dying sun slanted into the circle of galleon glass to fall across her face just as a tall figure stepped into the cabin to stand there quietly watching her.

Mother of God, she is beautiful! Sebastián's eyes burned with passion and hunger while his mind whirled dizzily with the sweetly tantalizing sight of Daniella. The Rose, Rascon had called her as he "signed" to the captain with a jealous frown.

Sebastián's warming gaze fell to the delicate bows

of her mouth, shaded in deep afternoon like tender-soft mandarin copper, and then he drank in her sleek limbs and fragile curves. His palms ached to cup her breasts, his fingers to stroke up and down her inner thighs.

In an agony of indecision, Sebastián stood, surrounded by the heady smoke of desire.

"Dany Rose." Just saying the name was enough to ignite the flames of desire in his blood. His mind was baffled. He had beheld unbelievable richness, rarest jewels whose glitter paled the noonday sun, not to mention women by the dozens, of rare beauty and courtly charm. But this one whose eyes and ethereal young face framed in a soft cloud of hair had filled him with a haunting sweetness that had surrounded him in longing all the days since he'd known her, was by far the most glorious gem, a diamond among other insignificant stones.

It was a pity he must use her in his plan for revenge and for the discovery of those responsible for the attacks on the Windstar Fleet. He would soon learn if she knew of Robert or Lucian Drake's whereabouts, but if she said she'd no idea where they were, he could not believe her. Not for one minute.

Sebastián had been informed by the gossipy cook at Braidwood that Daniella was aware of every move the Drakes made . . . and that she still loved Robert passionately. But he would never forget the nasty glitter in Cook Vivien's eyes. Why, he could almost believe the woman had been jealous of her employer's daughter!

Staring down at Daniella for a moment longer before he walked out the door, Sebastián told himself he would return later.

Before he could swing the door all the way, however, Daniella's voice reached him and halted him there. He stayed where he was while she spoke in a sleepy, dulcet tone.

"Steven. Where are you going?" Daniella sleepily lifted herself to one elbow. "Are you feeling better? Won't you *please* stay and visit with me a while?" Her voice lowered as she added, "I'm lonely."

Closing the door, Sebastián moved slowly to face the room once again, his eyes heavy-lidded as he softly answered, "Oh, I'll stay, m'lady. Make no mistake."

Daniella's eyes flew to the golden hair, the insolent smile. "You again!" she cried angrily.

One swift glance to her chest told Daniella she was indecent and needed to cover up, but in the bat of an eye Sebastián was beside her. "Please, m'lady, allow me." He reached out to help her secure the full, embroidered collar to her bodice, but before he touched the piece, her hand was slapping his away.

"Keep your hands from me, clod!"

Stepping back a foot, he bowed, "I am *so* sorry to have touched you, *Princess.*"

Securing the bodice with the glittering tiger pin Alain had given her, Daniella tossed her legs over the bunk's edge, unaware she was giving him a wonderful view of long, well-turned ankles and shapely calves. When she saw where his ardently glowing eyes rested, however, she yanked her skirts down and stood to her feet.

"Don't you have duties on deck, *Captain,* at the wheel or something?"

The captain was silent for so many minutes that Daniella thought he might have left the cabin.

"You didn't answer my question, Captain," she said, unaware how devious his thoughts were.

"Do I have duties elsewhere? Not unless there are several pirate corvettes or sloops of war trailing us. My man is at the helm. I won't be missed for a while yet. Does that answer your question, m'lady?"

Daniella only gave him the pleasure of a brief shrug of indifference.

Sebastián looked about the cabin, then riveted his gaze on to her once again. "Do you mind if I take a turn and ask you a question?"

Again the cool shrug. "Go ahead, ask away."

His eyes took on a strange light. "I think you are afraid of me," he said.

"That is not a question, Captain . . . you only surmise."

"Let me rephrase: Are you afraid of me?"

Indignantly she cried, "Certainly not!"

Sebastián watched her cross the floor and halt at the wavy mirror, where she drew the loose strands of blond hair up into a heavy bun and lifted her arms higher in order to secure the mass there with big ivory pins. No doubt the pins had been a gift from Robert Drake and his travels into pilferage.

"You needn't have worried about my urge to fondle you, m'lady. There isn't more than a thimbleful there."

Daniella gasped and turned to glare at him. His smiling eyes ran over her breasts once more, and he revised. "Perhaps . . . hm . . . a mouthful."

Much to Daniella's distress, the objects of their conversation began to tingle and grow taut. She whirled, showing him her back once again. "Indeed, Captain, you have become a thorn in my side. I do not wish to have your company any longer. There are other more important things to do than bandy words with you."

"Ah, m'lady, I am sorry to have caused you such aggravation." Moving slowly and silently across the space, he asked, "Shall I pull out the thorn to ease your distress?"

In the wavy mirror Daniella saw her features jolt as if she'd received a staggering blow. "Y-you don't have to do anything, Captain, just go away please. If you would be so kind as to send my husband to—"

When those strong fingers closed around her shoulder caps, Daniella's nerves twitched and a shuddering moved through her body, catching her off guard. He turned her then, slowly, and she faced the lynx-eyed scoundrel with a wide expression that he met with a confounding grin. Tipping her chin upward so that her coral-pink lips were not far below his, he spoke, ever so softly.

His eyes roved her features. "In time, m'lady."

Daniella's thick lashes brushed down, then slowly up again. "What are you going to do?" she asked in a surprisingly calm tone.

"First?" His warm and vibrant eyes shone passionately.

Nodding, Daniella could only stare into the mesmerizing jade-dark eyes as her pulses jumped alarmingly

"Kiss you." His eyes smoldered excitingly.

Daniella bristled. "This is not for you to do, Captain, but for my husband."

"Aye," he said, searching her face for signs of fear or loathing. But there was neither.

Then, catching him off guard, she shoved at him

and ducked from the circle of his arms. But he was quick to enclose her once again, pulling her closer this time. "That you must not do," he said, his breath fanning her cheeks. "Don't push away from me ever again."

"You are going to make me despise you more than I already do, Captain." Her hands clenched into hard fists at her sides and he imprisoned her even tighter.

"Why don't you call me Sebastián." He said his own name like a caress.

Her heart fluttered wildly as she quipped, "I'd rather not."

"Why?" he demanded with a lazy grin. "Why will you not call me Sebastián."

"Because I don't know you that well," she flipped back with a sigh of frustration.

Sebastián's mouth expanded in a tigerish grin. "Do you know your husband any better?"

"I . . ." Confusedly Daniella thought about that for a moment, then responded in a short breath. "I know him little better. Except . . ." She blushed, then forged on. "Really, it is none of your business."

"You are right." Sebastián stared at the floor. Desire for Daniella was aching in every bone and muscle of his body. He gave a resigned sigh. Later would be soon enough, he warned himself, watching the changing shadows of the crimson sunset drift through the tall windows.

"Captain?" Daniella softly said.

"Yes?" His handsome face was taut with control.

She had turned away and now kept her back to him as she requested, "Would a bath be asking too much?"

141

"No." He stared at the lovely, slim contours of her back. "You shall have it, m'lady."

"Thank you," she almost whispered.

A sly smile crossed Sebastián's mobile mouth. He walked quickly to the door and gave his mind free access to thrilling memories . . . and ones soon to be made.

Chapter Nine

All the world's a stage.
— William Shakespeare

Perhaps a mouthful.

The captain's distasteful comment repeated itself over in Daniella's brain as she soaped herself vigorously and then relaxed in the bubbles. The long blond ends of her hair floated in the water partially concealing her breasts beneath the shimmering surface.

It was so peaceful and pleasant that Daniella soon grew sleepy. Her head resting against the high rim of the tub, her eyes drifted shut. Her soft lips were parted, as if in anticipation of a lover's tender kiss.

The door opened and closed softly. Pale lamplight created a hazy aura about the tall figure just stepping to the side of the tub and fell on the gorgeous water nymph reposing so languidly, one slim white arm draped over the rim.

"Daniella."

"Oh," she exclaimed softly, snatching the towel from the low table and bringing it to her naked, moisture-dewed chest. Then her face relaxed into soft, sweet lines, her eyes limpid pools of gray. "Steven. I did not hear you come in. You are as silent as a cat."

His features were pale and drawn beneath the dusting of face powder, but she loved him just the same. She had been so lonely, but now that Steven was here she would be happy just to sit and talk with him.

"Stay as you were, love. You look very beautiful."

He took the towel from her and cast his gaze anywhere but on her nakedness, but his eyes returned to her when she sank back down into the water, only partly concealed by the floating shroud of hair. His keen eyes probed, and if she studied his eyes she would notice that they were gleaming with fervent ardor and possessiveness.

"You are such a gentleman, Steven," Daniella said, feeling a tingle of anticipation along her nerve ends. "Unlike . . ." She bit her lip, hoping he wouldn't ask her to finish her sentence. But she wasn't to be so lucky.

"Unlike?"

Daniella felt the question hang between them like an ominous black cloud. How much could she tell him? Would he understand if she tried to explain that his relative had stolen kisses? Had it been twice . . . or had she only dreamed this? She couldn't recall just now. She had no idea how close Steven and Sebastián were, knew not if her husband would defend her honor and fight the captain in a duel. She decided to say nothing.

He stepped closer. "Can I dry you, my love?"

She was so relieved that he'd not pressed her to elaborate that without a second thought she rose from the tub, dripping wet and splendidly beautiful, while he held the larger towel out for her.

Out of the tub now, Daniella stood still as his

144

hand rubbed the towel across her back, down her spine, and patted her buttocks dry. His lips parted. How he'd love to bend down and lap up the moisture from her softly quivering body.

"You have been ill," she reminded him.

His shoulders moved in a light shrug. "I have been worse."

With him behind her, Daniella could not see his expression as it roved the narrow waist, gently flaring hipbones, and soft white buttocks. As his hand lingered on her hip, Daniella tried to control her breathing that was becoming more rapid as the moments passed. The manly fragrance of him swirling about her was having a thoroughly devastating effect on her. Her eyes were as deep as tropic seas as she recalled the night Steven had awakened her to womanhood. Now that she knew what to expect, she couldn't wait to welcome him into her receptive body.

"How have you been feeling?" he asked.

Daniella smiled tenderly. "Fine, Steven. In fact I've never felt better."

It was natural and inevitable that they should mate this night. She didn't know about Steven, but she was ready to swoon in ecstasy at this very moment and he hadn't even kissed her yet!

When he moved to extinguish the lamp's light, Daniella barely gave it a second thought. Then she thought of the water. What if they should begin their lovemaking only to be interrupted by the lads coming to empty the tub? But Steven instantly relieved her worry, and it was as if he'd read her thoughts.

"The tub will be emptied later." He cleared his throat. "Much later."

145

"F-fine," she stammered, feeling a hot blush creep upward.

"Have you taken the evening meal?"

"No." She was breathless and she rushed on to cover up. "I am not very hungry, Steven." *Not for food!*

"Dany." His deep male voice beckoned yearningly in almost a whisper. "Come here." Deeper yet.

Daniella moved on rapture's wings and the sensual eyes watched her approach with tenderness in their depths.

"Come, love, transform this dragon into a charming prince with one kiss from your mandarin-rose lips."

Already pale moonlight touched the window, giving Daniella some illumination with which to make her way to the bunk. Trembling, wobbly limbs carried her there, and when she went into Steven's waiting arms, he whispered sweet endearments into her tumbling hair.

Burying her face against his throat, Daniella's fingertips bit into his shoulders and then rushed over his arms as his lips at last found hers in a fire-hot kiss. He wrapped his arms about her waist as he kissed her hungrily, demandingly, and scorched the interior of her parted mouth with whiplashing tongue.

"Ah, Dany Rose," he groaned. "You do transform me into a bold lover and make me feel almost handsome . . . almost manly."

Her eyes widened in surprise. "Oh, you are, my lord, you are most handsome while you are in my arms. You"—she sighed—"are my prince charming."

Hot shivers raced throughout their bodies as they

146

strained to get closer to the other, both reeling beneath the onslaught of furiously demanding desire. He pulled her tightly into his embrace and time stood still as they kissed and kissed some more. When Daniella caught at his long black curls, the wig slid from Sebastián's head, falling to the floor. Neither seemed to notice the loss, they were so caught up in the firestorm of mutual pleasure that besieged them as their passions took wing and soared ever and ever higher.

Their kisses went so deep that Daniella could taste the heavily applied powder and makeup, and even that elicited an erotic appeal. There was suddenly a great need for her to get closer to her husband, to feel every inch of his hard, manly body. He was a peacock to be sure, but even that did not take away from his masculinity one bit!

"Your clothes . . ." Daniella panted. "Steven, please take them off!"

"Yes. Yes . . . yes of course!"

Daniella almost giggled when she heard the sound of cloth being rent in the almost silent room, hushed but for the excited panting of their breaths. The room grew steamy both from the bathwater and their compelling enthusiasm to snuggle closer to each other.

Unable to control herself, Daniella pushed her husband back to the bunk and quickly straddled him. The rush of surprise that fell from Sebastián's lips—a deep groan of delight—fueled Daniella's inspiration even further.

His voice was deep and husky as he said, "I might hurt you this way. You are so small, Dany, my love. Oh, God . . . what are you doing?"

He couldn't bear the pleasure . . . he was about

147

to lose control! Daniella had been rocking her body so that her delicate little folds which surrounded his manhood rode up and down, playfully stirring his senses to total madness. He had never known such an innocent could be quite this wonderfully wanton . . . and she was his beloved wife!

"Stop—I shall be in you if you don't cease!"

Ceasing her erotic movements, Daniella stared down at him, feeling utter disappointment. "But Steven—that *is exactly* what I wished," she explained slowly.

Sebastián couldn't believe his good fortune. "Oh God . . . Dany." *Dios!*

All of a sudden needing to know, she blurted out, "Steven—I . . . Have there . . . been others before me?" Her blush could not be seen in the darkened cabin. "I mean . . . many *many* others?"

Daniella thought her husband was going to choke before he said, "I cannot lie to you, my love. You recall that I . . . hm . . . had been happily wed."

"I mean others besides her."

"Yes."

She tossed her bright curls. "But now it is only me! I am happy, Steven . . . so happy you could never believe how much."

"I am happy, too, Dany. Oh come here, you bewitching beauty!"

"Love me, Steven. Just love me now until I cry for you to cease before I die."

Pulling her down for a moist, thrilling kiss, Sebastián took hold of her buttocks and gently slipped two wriggling fingers into her furry mound. Moaning and writhing, she bucked forward and found herself impaled on a larger, longer, stiffer member.

148

Sebastián pulled her mouth down to meet his own and the kiss was heavenly sensual with her moving astride him while he tutored her in the movements, igniting a wildfire that set her pulses to racing. He helped her move faster, deeper, demanding the pressure of her pelvis to grind into him, and she drew him into her snug sheath as far as she could.

The outcry of ecstasy slipped through Daniella's lips as her body began to vibrate with release, and Sebastián arched up, rolled over with her, and drove himself into her quivering casing, hard, one last time. Daniella absorbed the strength and energy from Steven's fiery release and she heard his loud cry of triumph.

The heights of ecstasy reached, they began to drift slowly back down to earth and Daniella could feel the throbbing beat of her heart match the deep thunder of her husband's own.

Afterward there was no need for words as they rested within an embrace, limbs entwined, his face buried in her soft hair, their pulses gradually slowing along with their breathing. Without another word, they soon fell asleep while the moon's pale rays bathed them in a blissful slumber.

Deep in the night when he took her again, there was a oneness that made them cry out at the same time, and afterward they lay locked together for a long time. When he finally retrieved his wig and slipped from the cabin, thinking she was asleep, Daniella lay awake, softly frowning into the dark.

The word "love" had never been spoken and she wondered if it ever would be. Steven was a strange man. Cordial. Genial. Kind. Mysterious. A silk-stockinged dandy. A fop! She almost giggled, wondering how many wigs he owned!

Oddly, though, Steven was a master in love's passion, although she had no other lover to compare with him. She loved him, true, even thought she might love him more than her own life. She must. She had to! Her old friend Robert was lost to her. Steven Landaker was her husband and friend now and, knowing their love could soar to ecstatic heights, he was her only lover for all time.

Daniella frowned again, this time more strongly in her moment of guilt. Why had the devastating image of the captain intruded on their most rapturous moments? It was almost as if it had been *he* making love to her the last time. He who was kissing her. Why? Why? *Why?*

As the silver moon slipped past her window, Daniella found sleep, restless and tormented as, even in her dreams, the tall, dashing figure came to her, mocking laughter in his voice. At one frightening point, Steven was wearing a hideous mask, and when he whipped it from his face, he became Lord Landaker. But Steven was not the dandy at all, and, in fact, he was handsome and virile. He wore a shiny vest of gold incongruously over his Spanish pantaloons. His flesh was a deep bronze, his hair gold, like a great lion's mane about his wide shoulders. His eyes blazed pale green, but a light of pure mockery danced in their golden depths, making him look almost diabolical.

"Dark rose, hah-hah-hah!" he laughed, right before his form vanished like thin mist rising from a meadow's edge.

Daniella woke and sat straight up in bed, her arm reaching for her husband. "Steven!" she cried.

But Steven wasn't there. Her fingers brushed

something in the bed. Retrieving the item and carrying it to the table, she lit the lamp and stood staring at the lace handkerchief.

Her eyes widened incredibly. *This handkerchief . . . my own!* The thing had been missing since . . . she couldn't remember . . . Yes, it had been the time she first encountered that golden-haired scoundrel captain!

The captain hadn't bothered to return it. She had lost it while in his presence and remembered only after she had already been home for several hours.

How then, had it come to be in Steven's possession?

Extinguishing the light, Daniella crawled back into the bunk, plagued by new and disturbing puzzles concerning her mysterious husband. Just then a soft knock sounded at her door, then all was still again. She rose to answer it, hoping Steven had returned and she could talk to him about those mysteries which plagued her mind.

She opened the door to a vacant companionway. As she was about to return to the bunk, her eyes fell upon the covered platter of food. Her stomach rumbled to remind her how little she had eaten that day. She picked up the delicious-smelling tray and carried it to her bunk, delighted to find as she lifted the cover a cold breast of chicken, an orange, and a skin of fresh water.

As she ate, finding just how hungry she'd become, Daniella wondered who had been so kind to leave her the food. Steven came to mind and she smiled, wondering where he had gone, wondering if he was with the captain, wondering . . . Suddenly she was sleepy and wanted no more of the succulent chicken. She left the breast half eaten and the orange she would save for tomorrow. She took several sips of ice-cold water and replaced the tin cap of the skin.

While the ship rose and fell softly in the moon-silvered waters, Daniella continued to try to fit pieces together. The disturbing dream was already scattering to the far corners of her overworked mind, but there was so much she needed to know.

The mystery of the handkerchief. If she asked Steven, that would raise questions in regard to what was going on between her and the captain. If she asked the captain, he would . . . no doubt he would want another piece of her clothing!

How in the world was she going to find out anything? Daniella smiled in the sea-swept dark, counting the stars in her window. How? By keeping silent, that's how.

The men who sailed the *Tiger* were a tough and seasoned lot. They knew all the tricks of seamanship. But the captain was lord over all, the master setting the course and the sails, giving instructions to the pilot who kept his watch on the quarterdeck. Close by his compass, Sebastián called the course down to the helmsman and constantly checked his own compass against the pilot. He steered by the feel of the ship and the lodestone in his own spine. All were constantly on the lookout for hostile fleets or single ships, and the voices of the seamen were hearty and resonant as they sang: "Good is that which passeth, Better is that which cometh; An hour is past and another floweth, More shall flow if God willith; Count and pass makes voyage fast."

The *Emerald Tiger* was singing also, and scudling along at a good rate.

Ahhh.

Legs braced on deck, Captain Sebastián stretched. His deep golden hair which lay long on his brown neck reflected the fiery hues of the Atlantic sunrise, while the catlike tones of his eyes sparkled between fringes of dark lashes. His belly was hard and flat, the muscles knotted at his shoulders and flowing strong into long sinews.

Sebastián lowered his arms and winced. The scar on his shoulder ached still at times; it was a memento from an unreasonable, brutish husband in the Bahamas, the one whose ribs Sebastián had parted with a single thrust of his trusty blade. Naturally, the husband never beat his slender wife ever again after that, nor did he seduce any more little girls.

Captain Sebastián shouted down to Jaecko to bring the *Emerald Tiger* about. The great tiller creaked along with the rudder, and the ship skittered the aqua sea and bowed her majestic nose for the watery course. There was a chant from the deck and a song in the rigging as the past came up to meet Sebastián where he stared into the coppery-hued sea, feeling the rising sun warm his face. His jaw tautened. He remembered all too clearly . . . *Dios!*

Lucian and Robert Drake came to mind, like a horrible disease he'd desperately fought. He knew a deep flare of anger. Then he calmed enough to allow himself to think clearly. His mouth twisted upward at one side and his cheek itched where his scar troubled him now. He would dispatch Lucian and his brother yet, but he could not be in two places at once. It was not only the Landakers' score

153

to settle. It was his, too.

Of course he was driven by the desperate need to discover how many preyed upon the Company's ships and the Landakers' ships. The Landakers had been accused of preying upon English ships as well as foreign ones — unjustly accused while the real villains skipped free! Damnation. His *Swallow* had already been sunk by the rascals and he had a good idea Robert and his new friends had been guilty of the misdeed. Robert was new at the pirate game. He was young. And he was good.

Lucian Drake had killed two of the younger Landaker lads and burned their ships at sea. Sebastián himself was not a pirate, but he longed to meet his enemy on equal ground. For this reason, he might be forced to don the disguise of pirate captain.

Sebastián's eyes glowed with a savage inner fire. Now this flawless rose with the face of an angel and the body of a wanton beneath the fine brush of satin or silk would lead him to his enemies. Face-to-face. Sword-to-sword. With the man he had sworn to destroy.

If he had to crush a single fragrant flower to lure Robert and the other satanic fiends of that piratical band, he would, by God. For Eileena; for the dead Landaker boys; for Rebecca, his sister Rachel . . .

That was all in the past, Sebastián thought now as he brought his reflections back to the present and the monumental task at hand, while all the time he daydreamed of that one who was so fair, like a white pearl that has sipped the dew of heaven, that one who was so near all he need do was reach out and touch her.

Lifting her heavy blond hair aside, Daniella brushed the mass until it crackled and shone with the luster of golden silk. She listened to the bustle of activity on deck, wistfully smiling at the songs the sailors were singing. Sunlight streamed through the galleon windows like thousands of flickering candles and the diamond cut of the surrounding glass made delicate patterns on her velvet skirt, which she had put on when she'd discovered early that morning that it was much cooler today.

Setting her brush aside, she quickly turned and rose from the bunk and at once resumed her search for clues, believing there must be *some*thing in the captain's cabin that would help her solve the puzzle.

Watching over her shoulder, daintily lifting her skirts in one hand, she left her cabin and swiftly went to the one she had discovered the captain occupied. Closing the door quietly, she searched the drawers of the high cabinet of cypress-and-tulip wood and came up with nothing. She chewed her fingernail for a moment and then went to the crowded desk to rummage through the drawers and discovered a log book. She was ready to toss it back into the lower drawer where she'd found it if footsteps in the companionway sounded, but for now she read a few lines here and there, words she couldn't understand, for they had been set down in another language, one she was not familiar with . . . It could be Spanish! she suddenly realized. Yes, she'd sung some Spanish melodies, and the writings here resembled the lyrics Madam Gilberto had tried to explain in the sheet music.

As Daniella was putting the ledger back in its place, her fingers brushed a dark maroon book, leather-bound with golden scrollings upon its cover.

"Journal," read the cover.

Interested now, Daniella slowly sat with the book in her soft white hands. As she read the handsomely scrolled words — the handwriting the same as in the log but the words in English now — her heart began to palpitate with cascading excitement.

No date. "I am the bastard of one Captain William Kidd, a gentleman pirate this luckless son has never had the pleasure to meet."

She flicked a few pages and read on: "My soul yearns for my lost youth, but only for Rebecca, only if we had shared some happiness together. I hardly knew her. Still I love her and forever and ever shall."

Gently Daniella fingered the page she was reading and looked up to gaze into a hazy corner of her mind, not really seeing anything in the room.

The captain, a bastard? In love with a girl named Rebecca?

Hurriedly, Daniella flipped through the pages, wishing to find more about the mysterious young woman the captain wrote about . . . for this must certainly be his own journal.

For a space of time Daniella glanced up and around. This room was smaller than the one she occupied and was used as an office mostly, and she could see that at one time it had been partitioned off from the larger section. There was not much space to move about, for large pieces of furniture and a single hammock took up most of the room. Her eyes dropped back to the parchmentlike pages, eager to discover more information about the woman named Rebecca. She would ask herself why she was doing this later, but for now the riveting journal distracted her from the main reason she'd been motivated to come here in search of clues concerning the mysterious actions of both her husband and the elusive captain.

She read on.

"Staring toward the Strait, with the mist rising and Spain behind it . . . but first to Portugal. It is the next morning. All has changed since my last visit. Hammers of shipwrights resound in the yards, for craftsmen are busily equipping new and greater fleets, and the port is thronged with masts flying the flags of every nation in Europe. And I return as I have left, expected by no one, greeted by no one . . . no one important . . . no one to lavish love upon anymore . . . for Rebecca is not here."

With tears pooling along her eyelids, Daniella looked up from the now-blurred page and closed the book yet held her finger between its pages and kept her place if she should wish to return to reading the sad man's account.

She was prying into another's personal life, which was entirely improper, but she couldn't seem to refrain from further quest into the readings. Too, she was gaining a clearer picture of the captain and an understanding of his possessive and domineering nature, but still there were so many spaces in between that needed filling in. Steven was another mystery. The two of them were much alike in certain ways, though she had never observed them standing side by side.

For some reason it troubled her that the virile captain had loved this Rebecca with such fierce passion. How she, Daniella, would love to be desired so passionately! Just the thought of loving so thoroughly inspired a wanton beating within her blood and caused her eyes to shimmer with longing. To learn the deepest secrets of passion while holding one's beloved close, to discover the tender passion of love that could truly make her desire's slave. Ah, Rebecca must have been very beautiful to hold the admiration of a handsome and virile man such as the captain . . . and hold his heart in her hands as well.

Daniella wondered what had happened to Rebecca, for surely something must have as the captain wrote of her in the past tense.

Overly curious, Daniella flipped the book open once again.

She read.

She gasped.

She dropped the journal as if the thing had set her fingers afire.

Just then her heart leapt into her throat as she heard the now-familiar step in the companionway. She tossed the book into the drawer, then she went scurrying for a hiding place behind one of the larger pieces of furniture.

As she waited, swallowing her heart over and over, the words from the journal came to her again—words that had been recorded only two weeks before.

"Now the hour of my Vengeance is tolling. Let the Drake Devils beware!"

Daniella scooted back farther into her cubbyhole. That scoundrel captain was after the Drakes. Did this mean *Robert* also? But why? What could they have done to the captain to make his heart so bitter?

The footsteps fell before the door, and then it was opening, quickly, and then slowly, slowly, as if the person there had discovered something. Or someone . . . Her.

Praying that she wouldn't be discovered, Daniella hung her head between her knees, hugging her velvet-clad elbows. She waited while the words pounded ominously from her fast-spinning mind. "Let the Drakes beware."

Chapter Ten

For a moment Captain Sebastián paused inside the room; then the cabin door slammed behind him as he kicked his booted heel against the wood.

Once again Sebastián stood in thoughtful silence before he began to move slowly about the room, his nose twitching from the curious scent hovering in the air like a perfumed aura.

There was nothing Daniella could do but sink down farther, holding her breath in the darkened corner. Her ruffled skirts were pressed hard against her quivering limbs and her tender buttocks jammed into the buckles and straps of a leather portmanteau. Her position was so uncomfortable that she almost stood and gave herself up to that knavish captain who would no doubt exercise his carnal appetite if he discovered her in his cabin.

One thing she had not counted on was his hot-blooded display of bad temper as in one flash he sank a steely grip into the delicate curve of her shoulder to haul her unceremoniously to her feet.

"Ouch!" Daniella cried out, then repeated the exclamation of pain.

Pushing his face close to hers, he ground out deceptively softly, "What the devil is this all about?" When she remained still but for the shivering of her legs, he continued to interrogate. "Did you find what you are looking for? Or did you get lost on your way to the necessary?" Again he shook her until the teeth rattled in her jaw. "Answer me, girl, or I'll shake you until your brains spill out!"

"Girl!" Daniella shrieked, stomping so hard she ground her heel into his toe-tip. "I am not 'girl' to you, Captain, I am Lady Landaker!"

"I *am* sorry," he taunted with a sneer. "I thought perhaps you were the chambermaid come to clean my desk." His eyes rested on the mentioned object with suspicion. "Daniella . . ." His grip was hard on her shoulders. "Answer me. What are you doing in my cabin?"

The lump in her throat was hard to swallow, but she finally got it down enough to answer stutteringly. "I . . . I was looking for my husband . . ." she trailed off.

"In a dark corner of my cabin?" He stared at her dubiously. "Hardly."

Daniella appeared confused before she answered. "Th-there were some noises in here. I thought I heard Steven's voice from outside the door. I . . . I was taking a walk."

"Taking a *walk?"*

With her free hand she pressed two fingers to her temple. "I . . . I am not sure. I . . . I do not feel too well. Perhaps it is a trace of seasickness once again?" She peered up into the shadowy features that were still taut with anger.

"Well then . . ." He swept her off the floor before she could think. "I shall return you to your quarters before you fall ill in my cabin."

Daniella pushed at his hard chest. "Put me down this instant, Captain, for I am quite capable of taking myself back —"

His dashingly bold face was too close for comfort as he sneered. "Really? Why, m'lady, did I not hear you mention you were ready to swoon?"

Sebastián studied her, his breath coming harder now. Soft ringlets of hair, fresh as a bouquet moistened with morning dew, cascaded about her shoulders, while at her temples finer strands framed features as delicately exquisite as Spanish lace. She was staring at him with eyes large and vaguely slanted. They were such a deep gray, almost charcoal in her state of anger.

"Put me down in front of the door. I can make it the rest of the way, Captain."

"No doubt you can." Captain Sebastián disregarded her request, adroitly maneuvering the door with one hand while holding her quite easily in his other arm. When he had gotten her inside, he bent his leg backward and kicked the door shut with a deep resounding shudder.

"Put me down!" Daniella cried when he still held her dangerously close to his iron-thewed chest.

When he did exactly as she'd demanded, Daniella landed in a sudden hard plop in the middle of the floor and she stared up his long hard body from her most unladylike position.

"How dare you!" she hissed, regarding him with loathing. "You arrogant scoundrel —"

"Bite your tongue, woman!" he ordered. If his look could have been a weapon, Daniella would have been mortally wounded by now.

To the angry man who towered above her, Daniella was unconsciously and innocently posed like a lovely flower floating in a pond of azure as the velvet skirt puddled about her and dainty white petticoats foamed where the ripples ended the circle. Her rose-bow lips, half opened in surprise, revealed

162

her perfect teeth. Though she was startled out of her wits from her hard landing, her breeding lent her dignity.

Daniella was a picture of sweet innocence and purity . . . but Sebastián knew better. She was the Dark Rose. Beautiful spy for the pirates Drake. She would be used well before this game was concluded, for he had already set forth plans to employ her as his tantalizing decoy.

For a moment Sebastián stroked his chin as he continued to stare down upon her. At last he spoke.

"Did you find what you were rummaging around for in my cabin?" He was referring to the map of strategies he'd planned for Drake and the *Raven's* crew.

With as much dignity as she could muster in this humiliating situation, Daniella came slowly, like a lazy feline, to her feet — with no help from the snickering captain! She stood looking up at him like a diminutive queen, one of the rope pearls she'd woven into her locks having freed itself from her crown and swinging loose close to her rosily flushed cheek.

Her voice was huffy when she asked, "What do you demand of me *now*, bold captain?"

"Why, m'lady, I demand nothing save that you return what you . . . ah . . . filched from my cabin."

"What?" Her arm went flinging back with such momentum that a tiny button of her bodice popped, fell with a "tink," and went rolling across the floor. The creamy rise of her breast was laid open to the heat of his leering gaze, and Daniella's eyes became even wider as she hurried to flatten her palm against the recalcitrant flap. She looked up and almost gasped at the piercing jade eyes stripping her.

Suddenly she felt naked before his heated gaze and shrank back until her backsides touched the wall. "I took nothing, Captain." Her voice was almost a whisper.

She stared as his hands rose between them, strong and well kept, the fingers long and supple as a swordsman's. He was going to touch her, perhaps kiss her, Daniella thought with fear as a kindling of desire began to heat her innermost being. *No! No! No!* her mind screamed. This cannot be happening! *Dear God—I am a married woman!*

"Daniella," he murmured, moving closer and closer until his knees brushed her thighs. "By all the saints, m'lady, you grow more beautiful with every day that passes!"

Sebastián moved like lightning, seizing her at once to prevent a struggle. He captured her lips with his full, sensuous mouth, the ache in his loins sharpening as her exquisite body trembled and quaked against him, but she didn't struggle as he had anticipated.

Sebastián reached down and caught one of her hands, entwining her fingers with his to stop their trembling. Kissing her just behind the ear, he murmured there, "I swear I find you more desirable by the minute, Lady Landaker—a tantalizing bit of fluff."

A flash of intense anger swept her quivering frame, washing away the last vestiges of her shameless desire. Bringing her tiny, balled fists against his chest, she pummeled and shoved until he stepped back, gallantly letting her have her way.

"How dare you address me in such a lecherous

fashion!"

His dark face sobered, leaving no humor. "Watch your tongue, *Lady* Landaker." His eyes narrowed. "Do you deny feeling any desire in that kiss we just shared?" With a flick of his dark wrist to arrange the sleeve of his blouse, he said, "I think not."

"Captain, I shall answer for myself if you don't mind."

"Ah well then . . ." He swept the room with his arm. "Answer away."

She paced the room to pause, finally, and leaned on the back of a rough-hewn chair. "What is it you want?" Spreading her hands, she went on. "I have not taken any of your precious belongings, Captain. You may search . . ." Daniella shot back and clamped a hand over her mouth. "Oh, I mean I . . . you can take my word, sir, I have nothing that belongs to you."

You have my heart, my lovely dark rose, he almost bit out. His arrogant smile had vanished and a deep flush spread over his handsome features. Daniella was astounded, for she had never believed this man could be tormented over any situation.

"Aye, m'lady," he drawled. "You indeed have inflicted suffering upon my person. Would that I could have acquired you in body and possession, truly as my own love, forever and ever."

But you love Rebecca, Daniella wanted to remind him. Yet if she were to speak the words, the captain would have instant knowledge of her stealthy investigation into his private belongings. Besides, what did she care that he spoke these false words; she was a married woman and he was but a knave.

"I must confess, m'lady, you sorely tempt me to take you to that bed." He took a folded handker-

165

chief from his cream-colored breeches and mopped his forehead free of dots of moisture.

"Captain, I must remind you I am a married woman, and with all due respect to the Landaker name—"

An angry sound blurted from his lips. She knew he had cursed—but in what language?

"What did you say? Was that Spanish you just spoke?"

The captain shrugged wide shoulders. "You wouldn't like to hear it in your proper English, m'lady," he explained. " 'Twould make your proper English ears burn."

Daniella's mouth dropped open. "You *cursed* me."

He tilted his golden head. "Have not other men? Those who have not been able to touch a single curl on that flaxen head? Tell me, did you have to force yourself into a passionate pretense with Lord Landaker?"

Daniella clenched her fingers into tight fists which cut into her palms. "How dare you . . . you ill-bred knave!"

"How dare you," he mimicked in a tiny voice. Swaggering across the room, he once again stood before her, lifting a springy blond coil of hair from her shoulder. "My my, you've a very limited vocabulary, m'lady. And how would you have knowledge that I am 'ill bred'? You know very little past history dealing with myself or my family."

Bastard. Daniella instantly thought. She said aloud, "Many have called you adventurer—and lover," she blundered. Her cheeks flamed and her heart thudded.

"Lover?" He chuckled harshly. "Who has told

you this?" Eyes of deepest jade narrowed suspiciously.

She spread her hands. "I only refer to your infamous reputation, Captain."

He blinked innocently. *"What* infamous reputation?"

A smoothly rounded shoulder moved in a light shrug as she said, "You are the man they call Tiger." She recalled her conversation with Robert which had made her believe Sebastián was a pirate. "Are you a pirate . . . or only a privateer?"

"There have always been 'privateers', Daniella," Sebastián explained, "During wartime every country uses them. Then again, pirates go at their own risk . . . and others'."

"That does not answer my question sufficiently, Captain."

Sebastián rested his chin between thumb and forefinger as he studied her thoughtfully. "Do *you* think I am a pirate, Daniella?"

She seemed startled. "Oh, no, I never said that, Captain. I only—"

His hand left his chin to settle on the side of her cheek, manly fingers stroking the velvet of her skin. "Who really is the expert when it comes to these matters, Daniella? Is it . . ." He cleared his throat softly. "Could it be Robert Drake?"

Her eyes flew wide, her tawny lashes nearly brushing her eyebrows. "R-Robert Drake?"

His fingers pinched her chin. "I believe you know the man quite well, Daniella. At least, that is what I have learned about you and Robert. You and he were more than friends I take it?"

The beat of Daniella's heart quickened as she recalled her conversation with Robert: "You may lose something in this dangerous game you're playing," and she had promised him she'd lose nothing. She was still safe, wasn't she? Marriage to Steven had given her lasting security, hadn't it?

"Daniella . . ." Sebastián's voice broke her reflections. "You haven't answered my question. Were you and Robert more than friends."

"He . . ." she could not lie. "Yes, Robert and I were friends, but nothing more than that. I mean . . . at one time there had been the thought that he and I might someday be together forever. It was only wistful thinking."

"Not *wish*ful?"

She shook her head. "No. Wistful has to do with feeling unsatisfied, Captain. I do not believe I should be having this conversation with you, sir, for it does not concern us in the least. After all, I hardly know you."

Sebastián's wide shoulders lifted with the deep sigh from his throat. "Now that we have opened the subject of your 'friend'—what more can you tell me about him?"

Daniella stared up at him while thinking her words out carefully. "I believe we have nothing more to discuss, sir."

She dared not tell him she knew of his terrible plans for revenge; then he would know she'd snooped in his journal. She continued to look into those sensual, mysterious eyes.

Daniella was feeling deliciously warmed by his presence. She told herself she would have to come to grips with this dizzying desire she felt when he was around. Otherwise she would be lost. Their relationship while on this long voyage—for it certainly was turning out to be one—was becoming storm and tempest, and she was drifting into uncertainty as to the best way to handle the captain and his virile charms.

Each day, Daniella's desire to have him around her increased. She was afraid that one day she would yield to the stimulation he provided when he stepped near — as he was doing now — and touched her as if they shared a precious passion.

Daniella looked away from his deep perusal, her limbs shaking. *What am I thinking?* she asked herself. *It is love I feel for Steven and not for this knave!*

The captain chuckled deep. "Come here, my sweet rose."

She slapped the hand aside that was reaching for her waist and stepped around him, but it wasn't long before she whirled back to face his puzzled frown.

"Leave Robert and my husband and me out of this, Captain Sebastián. Steven knows nothing, and *I* know nothing of your dealings with whomever or whatever. Neither have I taken any of your precious belongings from your cabin. Now . . ." She pumped her hands onto her softly flared hips. "I wish to see Steven, if you would be so kind as to send him to me. I have questions to ask, and would rather he give me the answers, and not you, sir. For instance why is this trip to the Landakers in Cornwall taking so long?"

The dark expression departed from Sebastián's face, leaving one of amusement in its stead. "You have questions to put to your husband, m'lady, and yet you just asked me one of them. And I shall give you your answer. The reason this crossing is taking so long is because we are meeting someone in the

Azores. At this time, all you need know, m'lady, is that we are riding the North Atlantic Ocean."

At the door to her cabin, he paused long enough to leave her with, "Later I will send your husband to you. Good day."

Daniella's face was pale as she sat on the edge of the bunk. She was so white that she glowed like an alabaster sculpture in the light coming from the galleon glass.

Azores. Islands in the North Atlantic? *Of course.* She had read that the humidity in the atmosphere there was so great that paper-hangings would not adhere to the walls and the veneering of furniture strips off. Delicious fruits abounded in the islands — oranges, apricots, bananas, lemons and more.

Shocked at the captain's admission that the voyage to Cornwall was being delayed for a time caused her mind to be even more plagued by fresh doubts and fears.

Clenching the covers at the edge of the bunk, she thought how cruel the captain could be. Taking a deep breath, she tried to relax, but the effort was useless and caused her greater discomfort.

Her eyes grew large and liquid. She was more frightened than she had ever been in her life.

Daniella came to her feet, determined to see her husband now!

She could tell that the wind had picked up, so she snatched up her flimsy shawl and crossed the cabin to the door. Steven would answer her questions; he was always kind and considerate of her feelings. Yes, she would find her husband and demand that he order the captain to turn the ship around. She was also determined to stand at

170

Steven's side when he confronted the captain with her request. No, *her order.* She would not be bested by that boorish captain!

Daniella was desperate now. Taking hold of the knob, she tried opening the door. But it would not budge!

He has taken it upon himself to lord it over me and imprison me here! Daniella raged inwardly. *I'll have none of it!* She pounded the door and shook the knob, but to no avail. "Let me out!" she shouted. "I demand to see my husband at once!"

After several minutes of battering the door, Daniella spun about and placed her back to the wood, her eyes blazing and sparking. With an overwhelming sense of desolation, she took a deep breath and went back to the bunk to sit there—staring at nothing.

Take courage, she told herself. *This, too, shall pass.* Bettina would soon come to her with dinner, and then Steven would be there to soothe away all her fears. There was nothing in the world to worry about, really.

Daniella hugged her shawl about her body and curled up into a ball to sleep.

Chapter Eleven

Nothing of him that doth fade
But doth suffer a sea-change
Into something rich and strange.
     —William Shakespeare

The waters of the Atlantic were blue and brilliant, the breezes brisk but warm. The lookouts were doubled, and the talk among the crew—invariably of Juan Tomaz and the Drakes—doubled, too. One or the other should show on the horizon at any time now and the waiting was beginning to wear on the crew that was restless for action of any kind.

It was with relief one morning that the long-awaited cry of the lookout sounded across the sunswept decks: *"Sa-ai-l ho-o!"*

Knowing full well what the call portended, and anxious as he was to hurry topside, Captain Sebastián remained in his cabin to dress carefully for the coming crisis. Or perhaps it would not be that, after all, depending on how well his plans succeeded. He could not wait to see Juan, but for the Drakes, Lucian or Robert, he could not say the same. Juan was his friend; the Drakes were his enemies.

From a trunk he had unlocked he carefully selected a heavy vest of gold, a red sash, and a loose

white cambric shirt, all worn over a pair of handsome Spanish pantaloons made of leather. At last,
a golden ring dangled from one ear. He now looked
every inch the pirate. What, he wondered, would
Daniella think once she saw him?

By the time Captain Sebastián stepped out on
deck, the crew members were in a lather of excitement and some apprehension. They, too, had
changed their clothes and resembled pirates, and
the flag that flew above the *Tiger's* decks portrayed
a white tiger rampant on red and black with a sinister spiral coiling at its tail.

Marcos Marela had just climbed down from the
mizzen shrouds. He telescoped his glass with an air
of finality and gave Sebastián a significant look
that was more eloquent than his simple statement
of fact.

"A corvette, sir. She's closing on us fast!"

Sebastián leaned over the rail and glanced down
at the helmsman who watched him with anxious
eyes. The huge man's body was tensed as if expecting the command to put the helm down.

"Keep her full and by!" Sebastián ordered, then
turning back to the lieutenant, he lowered his voice.
"What do you make of her?"

Marcos tendered his glass. "I suspect she's the
Raven, Captain."

Sebastián stroked the rough bristles on his chin.
"I was hoping to meet up with Juan Tomaz first."

"No sign of the *Desdemona,* Captain."

Marcos threw a nervous glance at the oncoming
sail. "Satan's backside! Why don't you run? She
carries more guns than we do. You are not aiming
to fight her?"

173

With his long leather-clad legs planted firmly apart, Sebastián gave him an icy stare that chilled Marcos's exuberance. "Mister Marela, be good enough to rouse up all hands!"

Marcos exhaled heavily. "Aye, sir." He gulped and hurried away to bawl the captain's order.

The *Tiger* was standing on the wind, but from the way the foresail flapped against the mast, Sebastián knew the breeze was lulling. He took the telescope from Rascon, who had tumbled down from above with the captain's glass and now climbed atop the hammock nettings, linking his spidery arm through the shrouds to brace himself. Sebastián followed suit and the lad grinned with excitement alive in his deep amethyst eyes.

Through the glass, Sebastián could spot the corvette clearly. Her three lateen-rigged masts were one, which meant that she was headed dead for the *Tiger,* and she appeared to be bringing her own devil wind, for she bore down on them at a spanking clip. The *Raven* had spread every black stitch of canvas until she soared like the bird of darkness itself.

Sebastián swore softly. *Death she might be, yet beautiful and sleek in spite of all.* Perhaps he just might own the *Raven* one day. When he saw the skull and crossbones at her peak, he collapsed the glass and climbed down.

"Get back on your course!" the captain barked at the steersman when he'd let the *Tiger* come up into the wind. "Where the hell is Jaecko?" he shouted. He had been there only minutes before.

Rascon was gesturing wildly with his hands, and then the captain knew, for Jaecko had taken to protecting the little maid Bettina, indeed had been courting her as if the decks of the ship were a rose garden in which they strolled arm in arm. Jaecko must have gone to warn her to stay hidden in case there was trouble—and there was going to be plenty when Sebastián took Jaecko to task.

The crew members muttered ominously as Sebastián stepped to the quarterdeck rail above them. He stood tall, princelike in his gold vest over a white, ruffled shirt, Spanish pantaloons hugging lean legs and hips. His full mouth twisted slightly, his eyes half laughing, half mocking as one dark hand idled on his gleaming sword hilt. And the red sash fluttered low on his lean hip.

Just then Jaecko appeared, looking sheepish as he stepped to the captain while a grinning Rascon waited for the tongue-lashing to descend, but all Sebastián snapped in a low tone was, "Unlock Lady Landaker's door." Then he couldn't help smiling himself, for his mate Jaecko appeared so smitten by his newest ladylove. "You are getting soft, big man. Now hurry, we will soon be under attack."

In a low, grumbling voice, Jaecko asked, "Won't she wonder where *Lord* Landaker has taken himself, Cap'n?"

"She will be too busy to notice his absence!"

"Aye, Cap'n!"

Unable to tolerate the suspense, an old sailor blurted the question rising in every crew member's mind! "Ain't we going to do somethin', Cap'n?"

"Indeed," barked Sebastián. "But in my own good time!"

The balance was delicate. Everything counted on his timing. He glanced at Marcos; the lieutenant was staring off to starboard where the sleek corvette had altered its course to bear athwart their bow. Sebastián knew a moment of disquiet which had nothing to do with fear . . . And then it came!

A white puff mushroomed from the corvette's bow-chaser, and a moment later the report reached them as the ball splashed into the sea a half-cable's length ahead.

The men gaped where they stood. In the ensuing silence, Captain Sebastián called calmly to the helmsman, "Bring her up into the wind, lad! We'll heave to." He turned back to the men. "Courage, lads. You've heard the *Raven* shriek, now listen to the *Tiger* purr. And don't forget, my neck is as priceless to me as yours to you, and I don't mean to strain it."

"You ain't going to fire back?" they chimed in unison.

"No need, actually. If we move circumspectly, we can show a pretty piece of meat and have them where we want them."

"Ah. The cap'n means the little lady, lads. He means to use her to lead them in a merry chase to the islands where we'll have the *Raven* trapped."

Moving like a restless cat in a cage, Sebastián strode the deck, his feet light as tiger paws. At the head of the companionway, he met Daniella just emerging into the sunlight. Her lovely face was flushed. The crew members stopped all conversation to stare at the little lady, a gorgeous vision for sore eyes to encounter.

A gown of dove-gray wild silk encased her slender form like a summer breeze, and she looked very prim and proper, her bodice with its tiny pearls buttoned all the way to the slim column of her ivory throat. Her step was light . . . and then she paused as if receiving the shock of her life.

"I . . . I heard a shot," she stammered. "Then I saw the ship. What is happening? Are we in danger?"

It was then that Daniella's step faltered as she noticed Sebastián's attire. In the loose cambric shirt with flowing white sleeves, open to the waist to reveal a muscled bronze chest, two huge pistols stuck into a red sash, she thought he looked every inch the buccaneer. A golden earring winked and made him look sinister and appealingly dangerous.

The blue waters of the Atlantic swirled in a blur as she got out, *"You!* Y-you are a . . . a p-pirate! I should have known!"

Captain Sebastián bowed deeply, as if to give confirmation to her stuttered words. He watched her color deepen as her eyes traveled his lean frame, and she lifted her eyes then while drawing herself stiffly erect.

"Wh-where is my husband?"

Sebastián's tanned throat worked and he heard the deep chuckling of Marcos and Jaecko. Thinking they meant to make her the object of their humor, Daniella then made to go below, but he blocked her passage.

"Stay," he ordered coldly. "If necessary, I shall have you bound and gagged to that mast over there."

By now the *Raven's* crew had spotted his lovely decoy, and he smiled his pleasure watching the sleek pirate ship, her sharp bows tossing the seas aside as if in contempt as she awaited the *Tiger's* next move.

Daniella glanced over her shoulder and up, noting the flag that blossomed defiantly from the *Tiger's* masthead.

Molten anger suffused Daniella and she reaffirmed her assumption out loud. "You *are* a pirate!"

She had never witnessed a more devastatingly handsome sight as the captain boldly displayed his stunning male physique. But he was so . . . *different*. Her eyes lowered and she held her breath. Flushing brightly, she tore her regard from the tight pantaloons.

"I mean what I said, *Lady* Landaker."

The sunlight shimmered on her bright hair, and his, making them look almost as brother and sister, so alike in coloring but for her peachbloom cheeks. She said, "You would not dare tie me up!"

"Dare, m'lady? When the lives of my men hang by a hair? I'd sooner put a pistol ball through your lovely head by my own hand before I'd let you escape me now." He grinned, adding, "Dark Rose."

Daniella pondered the title as the breeze tugged at her long tawny hair. He had called her this before. But why? What did it mean?

Daniella looked him in the eye and squared her shoulders. "I will stay." Her words were like a whispered breeze.

"What? I didn't hear what you said."

Tossing up her chin, she repeated, "I will not try to run."

"You have made a wise decision."

Sunlight shone fully on Captain Sebastián's face as he looked in the direction of the *Raven*. Now they would not fire but follow close at the *Tiger's* heels—right into the lair where the *Desdemona* would be waiting!

Daniella was beside herself with apprehension. What was happening? She swayed against the bulkhead, her eyes, now limpid pools of dull gray, searching the captain's stern features. She couldn't believe this man could be so ruthless and cruel when only days before he had held her in his arms letting his mouth linger on hers for a radiant kiss.

With a certainty that made her stomach churn, she wondered when he would claim her? It was obvious her husband was nowhere in sight, and no doubt the captain would take liberties as he saw fit. But just where was Steven? Why had he deserted her in her time of need? Was he ill again? Had he been tossed overboard by the evil captain?

The thick sweep of Daniella's lashes fell on her cheeks, then lifted in shock when Captain Sebastián pushed her out into full view of the ship which preyed upon the *Tiger*.

Not knowing if he could trust her to obey, Sebastián was sorely tempted to bind her to the mast, but after a moment's hesitation, he decided against the sterner measure. That would get him nowhere with the Drakes. His expression reflected remorse and he looked away before he was trapped in the sad grayness of her eyes.

Sebastián had earlier discovered that Daniella's eyes not only changed color with her moods, but met with the moods of the sky. Gray for gloominess as now, he thought grimly, and that brighter shade of blue when she was aroused to the passionate hungers of the flesh.

Almost against his will, Sebastián turned from

giving orders to his helmsman and returned his attention upon Daniella. He reached out for her.

"You are a monster, Captain," she hissed when he drew her close to his side.

"Cease your struggles, Lady Landaker. It will only make your situation worse."

Daniella could almost foretell what would happen later. Though he spoke softly, she knew he was angry with her. She shivered, wondering how she would be able to stand his ruthless lovemaking after the tender sweetness of her husband's embrace.

Hoping that Drake was getting an eyeful, Captain Sebastián reached around Daniella's shoulder and cupped her fine chin in his large hand. As he tried turning her face to meet his for the kiss, Daniella struggled for all she was worth. She stared in amazement as his lean, muscled arm came up from her waist, his long fingers to cup a tautly rounded breast in full view of all—including the ones aboard the other ship.

Sebastián's thick shoulder-length hair flowed around a stern face that made Daniella tremble like a frail blossom in the wind. She put her shoulder against him and squared her chin in determination not to let him best her.

"Turn to me, Daniella. Give me your lips for a kiss."

"I refuse to have you make a fool out of me, Captain Sebastián."

"Then you leave me no alternative."

Although Daniella made fluttering motions with her hands against his chest, she was entirely helpless when she was turned to be molded along the hardness of his long body, wrapped in a warm embrace from which there was no escaping. At first he kissed her lightly. She knew she was at his mercy and he could kill her if he wanted, and, in fact, he'd said he would do just that if she fought his demands.

Swept along by the kiss, she ceased her struggles. Suddenly she was on a cloud, flung into paradise, as his lips and tongue trespassed where no man had gone before—not even Steven with his wildest kisses.

With renewed mastery he delved deeper. The interior of her mouth was thoroughly explored, her tongue was toyed with vigorously, and she began to experience a buoyancy that lifted her ever higher into desire's realm.

The captain was an enigma to her, a powerful force to be reckoned with. The intensification of his thrilling kisses never failed to arouse her. But this kiss was consuming her in liquid fire, making her heart beat like fierce waves pounding the hull of a ship. She was well aware that he had started something that would have to be finished sooner or later!

Sebastián was thoroughly aroused, to the point of almost throwing her down and satisfying himself with no care or thought to anything or anyone else. He had been snatched into an enchanting snare, one which his own selfish kiss had begun. He was captive of his own evil machinations.

Sebastián's arrogant head lifted and he smiled into her wild blue eyes. "You are a beautiful witch, Daniella, one I mean to exorcise from my blood."

Her already taut bodice straining to the utmost, she panted her words into his dark face. "Was that

181

not suitable to your lustful ideals, Captain?"

"Oh quite, m'lady," he drawled, even angrier with her than when she had first defied him. "Now you may return to your cabin."

Daniella stiffened her spine resolutely as she walked away, flung a glance in the direction of the lagging pirate ship, and then she almost looked back at the captain. But no, she would not give him the satisfaction of knowing she had discovered his ruthless game.

Decoy! She had been used as decoy . . . oh dear God, just as Steven had intended using the *Rampant Rose*. They were all in this together, and no doubt Steven had abandoned her to the evil captain's clutches, a pirate no less.

They had gotten what they were after — *her* . . . and her father's business which she would inherit when he passed away.

Everything was lost to her. The center of her chest felt hollow. She would never see her father again, nor would she dwell in the halls of Braidwood. One thing was certain: She would fight this devil captain tooth and nail when he came to satisfy his lust. And somehow, some way, she was going to find her way to Robert Drake, the man who truly loved her, the one who would lavish love and protection upon her. Robert would see to it that the captain and his friends never used her again!

"You used me! Damn you for the black pirate you are. You used me!"

Her hands were clenched into fists she would love to dispatch speedily into the captain's grinning face! But she could only return to her cabin as he so arrogantly had ordered.

Giving her retreating form a mock half-bow, Sebastián concluded with, "And *well* used, m'lady!"

With her back presented to him as she entered the bulkhead, Daniella missed the gleam of irony in his hard and passionless catlike eyes.

Throwing back his tawny head, Sebastián laughed full and heartily while the stealthy *Raven* watched and preyed and watched some more, unaware she was being led close to Dove Island in the Azores.

Chapter Twelve

They were underway once again. The hostile ship which had continued to prey on their heels for hours was nowhere in sight now. The sea witnessed the harmless play in her rippling, night-dark surface; and a visit from a long overdue guest arrived by longboat.

The *Emerald Tiger* plowed through fitful, moonswept waters with the enchanting music of her rigging and sails playing a song of the wantonly capricious sea. Another song was being sung by a woman, a song beginning with soprano notes, sweet, virginal, thrilling the soul of everyone on board as her voice carried from her cabin. Men ceased their labors to listen as Daniella put the lyrical words to music:

"Oh . . . say not Woman's love is bought
  With vain and empty treasure!
Oh . . . say not Woman's heart is caught
  By ev'ry idle pleasure!
When first her gentle bosom knows
  Love's flame, it wanders never,
Deep in her heart the passion glows;
  She loves, and loves forever!

Daniella's voice recalled to the weary men half-forgotten memories of golden dawns when the world had been young for them, and some faded sailor's eyes were dim with tears for a childhood that had been sweet and true. Hearing her, jaded men remembered the faces of the women they had first loved. Then her songs were done and the men returned to their work.

Daniella moved restlessly about the cabin after having sung her heart out, not caring if anyone heard. She had carried out her frustration to the limit and by the release, felt better for it. But she could not believe she was actually preparing to dine at the captain's table after what had transpired just that afternoon.

Now her frustration had returned, but she was all sung out. The situation was unfair, *maddening*. While Bettina was allowed to come and go as she pleased, waiting on her lady's needs, seeing Jaecko whenever she wished, Daniella was locked in her cabin like some common thief. Bettina was not her jailer—that was left to the big oaf Jaecko who stood just behind Bettina while she bustled in and out, her face remorseful over what she must do.

Daniella could not blame Bettina, for the simple maid only followed orders from that black-hearted captain who surely roared with laughter every time the clanking key was put to the lock.

Now she was being allowed to dine as the captain saw fit. How blessedly fortunate was she!

"Oh thank you most kindly, Sir Pirate." Daniella gave a mock curtsy, a graceful movement befitting a duchess presented at court. She continued her one-sided conversation with the wavy reflection in the tall oaken-dresser mirror. *"I shall eternally be grateful and shall never forget your gentlemanly*

actions of this afternoon. How you boldly displayed your amorous attentions for all the world to see." She gritted her teeth. *"How you set me up to be employed as your coveted decoy. Now, Sir Pirate, you have the utter gall to graciously invite me to your abundantly laid table!"*

Daniella paced the confines and then let herself down with a flourishing plop.

"The rollicking knave!"

She was fairly seething by the time she rose from the sagging bunk after the alarming click of the door sounded.

The towering figure of the captain darkened the doorway, and his dark-green eyes lit dazzlingly when they fell on the graceful lines of her mulberry dress fashioned of velvet with its creamy, embroidered trim. His eyes rested on her delicate slippers before drifting upward again.

His voice was a seductive murmur. "Good evening."

Daniella stared with slack jaw. The feeling in the pit of her stomach tightened as she slanted her eyes to give his handsome form a sweeping regard. The captain himself had arrayed his lithe frame in a smoke-colored frockcoat, tight breeches, and knee-high leather boots polished to a sheen. The evil look of the pirate had vanished, and he now resembled the gracious and gallant prince.

"Dinner, m'lady," he announced, giving her his mighty arm.

Daniella reacted with reckless impudence, thrusting out her chest. "No thank you, *sir!*"

As he eyed the pointed delicacies, he said softly, "You've the countenance of an ill-tempered badger,

186

m'lady." His smile was wistful and mocking at the same time as he added, "With the voice of an angel."

"You might tell me what all this is about," she said with a feeling of growing apprehension.

Bettina and Jaecko appeared just then, and the big man winked at Lady Landaker as he awkwardly remarked that it was a pleasant evening.

"I wouldn't know," Daniella Landaker replied with imperious haughtiness. "I have not taken my air this evening." She gave Sebastián a scorching look.

"Why, m'lady. The evening will be most enjoyable, I promise. Why spoil it." He stated without question, snatching her arm back.

"My day has been otherwise," she quipped. "But I don't suppose that will weigh heavily upon *your* conscience." Daniella pulled her arm back to her side.

Captain Sebastián seized Daniella's arm this time with firm pressure, smiling amicably. "You have only graced the captain's table once before. Come. You will enjoy the repast this evening."

Her lips moved in a doubtful smirk as she tried to move away from him, but her efforts were lost as he pulled her along like a ship with slacking sails and gently but firmly propelled her into the spacious cabin. Bettina and a grinning Jaecko trailed behind.

As soon as they entered, a tall, dark, handsome man rose from the long table. There was a pleasantly congenial look about him as his fierce dark eyes took in the beauty of his friend's companion. He had fine taste in clothes, and he admirably observed the soft mulberry velvet gown which opened upon an underbody of pale primrose spread to the floor with the sweep of the young woman's slender height, and which enriched her flaxen hair and ivory coloring.

"Ah, so this is Lady Landaker," Juan Tomaz murmured as Daniella seated herself, far from where the captain stood. He leaned close to Sebastián to whisper, "The lady's eyes are the stormiest gray I've ever seen."

"Don't let yourself gaze too deeply into them," Sebastián advised. "You might find it easy to lose yourself in eyes like hers."

"But have *you, amigo?*" Juan asked.

When Sebastián said nothing in answer, Juan remarked, "She's quite young . . . much too young and lovely for all you are putting her through. I heard her sing — *Madre de Dios,* with such sweetness and passion!"

Sebastián at once steered the conversation to other topics, watching while a cocksure Rascon poured a glass of glimmering wine for Daniella. Juan smiled across the table observing the comely maid fussing to make her lady comfortable while the big man stood behind her chair as if guarding the lovely lady from all the smiling officers looking her way. For now, Daniella smiled sweetly and answered the questions put to her, but her eyes roved continuously to the door as if she awaited another's coming. Her husband, perhaps?

Juan grimaced to Sebastián and the two handsome heads across the table came close. Juan spoke low, and Daniella took her gaze elsewhere to concentrate on the comings and goings at the squeaking door.

"Upon leaving Dove Island, I was desperately afraid that we would be too late," Juan said. "We could only make out the black sails of the *Raven* and thought she'd got to you already, my friend. I tried to put this thought out of my mind, but it persisted. I could well imagine the *Tiger* raked by their broadside, her hull battered, her rigging cut to shreds, fighting valiantly on to the inevitable end . . . sinking into the sea."

"You paint a grim picture indeed," Sebastián remarked and took a sip of his wine. "Yes. I could feel trouble in the air when I awoke from a few hours' sleep this morning." He peered over his glass to Daniella, pondering the enormity of the situation at hand. "I am almost inclined to let Drake have what he wants . . . when the *Raven* catches up with us at Dove Island."

Clearing his throat, Juan said, "And that means the lovely Lady Landaker."

There came a nod from Sebastián's tawny head. "It would save us much trouble. In the hold I carry an array of costly spices, which I don't intend to lose." He frowned and ran an impatient hand through his tawny hair which swayed silkily when he moved.

"You mean to give the lovely lady to the *bastardo* Robert Drake?"

Looking out at the dusky-blue starlit darkness, he said, "With her seductive walk and angelically wanton eyes, she is more trouble than she's worth."

"I don't doubt it, my friend. Most beautiful women are."

189

"I've given her the name Dark Rose."

"But she is blonde . . ." Juan remarked in puzzlement. Then, "There are *two* Drakes. Robert and Lucian."

"As far as I'm concerned, you cannot tell one from the other—they both spit hell's fire and leave destruction in their wake."

"The older brother, Sir Lucian, stays at home most times now, I hear tell, *amigo,* but as luck would have it, Lucian is prowling again."

Sebastián wore a wintry smile as he snarled, "I had the *Raven* right in my clutches!"

"Why didn't you fight then, man!"

Sebastián's sensuous mouth thinned in a grim line and a tawny brow cocked. "I thought you were so worried about us."

Juan gave him a bland smile. "Don't change the subject, my friend. You know as well as I, *you* were the worried one. Worried over that fine piece of womanflesh you have aboard the *Tiger. Madre de Dios,* I'd not want to risk losing her, either."

"Ah, it is not that. I have already told you Daniella is more trouble than she's worth."

Hmm, I wonder, Juan thought as he watched his friend closely. With such an intoxicating beauty on his hands, Sebastián could not be as unhappy as he appeared at the moment. There was something more. Between the frowns, he thought he had noticed a lovesick expression flit across Sebastián's features. It was true, a beautiful woman could put a man through hell, but it certainly was worth it, especially if love was being kindled; and for sure a fierce love was developing between these two.

190

Juan studied them both. Indeed, it was as if a thick mist obscured the horizon of their attraction. *What,* he wondered, *would become of this poignant affliction?*

Once again Juan cleared his throat. "It is rather rude to ignore her. We have been talking for several minutes now." He wanted to ask Sebastián more, but this was neither the time nor the place; they had to make plans as to how they were going to capture the searobbers without too much damage to their own ships.

With little interest as to its contents, Daniella stared into her glass of Spanish wine, a warm amber hue sparkling as though the sunlight which had ripened the grapes had been captured and distilled into the golden liquid. She had never taken much wine, for at home she had preferred the fruited drinks like lemon-lime and cider. She took yet another sip, then another. Her spirits were improving in consequence and she had a strong urge to giggle.

Enough is enough! Daniella set aside the half-empty glass and reached into the fruit bowl for a persimmon. She searched around the table for a knife to slice the fruit in half so she could pick out the tiny delicious buds of sweetness, but she could not find a utensil sharp enough for the cutting.

"Need help, m'lady?" the deep male voice suddenly beside her inquired.

When she looked up, Sebastián found himself gazing into her flawlessly beautiful face. His eyes roved downward. Indeed, nature had perfectly fashioned Daniella Rose from head to foot, for he could find no fault or imperfection. Her beauty fascinated; her charm conquered and radiated from within; her grace was singularly exquisite.

"I could cut that for you," Sebastián offered as he pulled a chair beside hers, brushing his muscled leg against hers as he sat.

Her reply was a chilly "Never mind." She set the stubborn fruit beside her water glass, which Bettina was just refilling.

When Daniella glanced up at her maid, she noticed Bettina was regarding the captain most strangely, almost with awe.

After Bettina had laid another platter of meats to the table, she walked over to Jaecko and linked her arm in his while each gazed into the other's eyes worshipfully. Watching them, Daniella felt a flush come into her cheeks as she realized Jaecko and Bettina were in love.

Leaning back in his captain's chair, Sebastián watched Daniella as she stared at the lovers, as if fascinated by the whispering, the preoccupation for each other evident in their eyes and touches.

She has beautiful hair, Sebastián mused as he stared at the silken strands of Daniella's tresses, and suddenly he was consumed by a great need. His soft breeches pinched where they fit Sebastián more snugly than ever and his lean body was tossed into a state of torment which could not be alleviated—not by merely looking at Daniella. But there was a cure. *Only one.*

Just then Juan came around the table, taking a seat on the other side of Daniella. Before long she realized that he was an excellent talker as he began to speak of the topics which interested her most.

Sebastián sat silently, listening to the intelligent young woman converse with his longtime friend.

Daniella took a breath to go on, warming to the conversation, while Juan looked at her with astonishment at her knowledge of the world of transactions. "There is more wealth now in London than in Venice, but incomparably more in Antwerp. It might even seem that the sea itself, at the moment when it opened to Europe's dazzling new opportunities, has chosen to do Antwerp special favor."

Juan Tomaz changed topics lightning fast, leaving Daniella a little dizzy, and too, she had begun to sip her wine again, unaware that Rascon kept filling it before she could ever get to the bottom.

Juan described the excitement of the Spanish ports—the riot of new wealth and color and gossip. He himself was using all the influence he had to get a mapmaker in his service aboard a Spanish galleon. Juan looked at Sebastián as he spoke of the *Spanish Wind,* and Daniella missed the winking of the Spaniard's eye.

As Daniella listened, she was back in a world that had grown more alive, its colors rich and brilliant. It was no longer Robert's words which made her see the wonder of each treasure ship's unloading, the fabulous stream of gold and gems, strange fruit and spices. Just when she was reflecting on all this, Juan added to her imagination the picture of strange men, captive men.

"Spain is setting up another slave market to sell their labor," Sebastián was saying, mostly to Juan, for Daniella had slipped into the cobwebs of the past.

Daniella's imagination made a vivid picture.

Even though these were free men who made the bargain themselves, it had disturbed her vaguely to see men and women stand there to be appraised and chosen. She pictured red men there, too, making no bargain of their own. All sorts of ships brought back slaves—black men from Africa.

"Yet to sell men must be against the laws of God," Daniella stated. "I do not believe in it."

"Nor I," Sebastián said, relieving her somewhat.

Once again Juan switched topics and asked her if she knew the *Tiger* was carrying spices. Daniella's eyes slid to Sebastián and she shivered inwardly as the glittering orbs at once caught and held her in their dark-jade embrace.

"I know not much of spices" was all she said, shrugging to hide her sudden confusion. If Sebastián was a pirate, was then Juan also a searobber?

Sebastián cleared his throat, warming to the subject, for spices were his specialty market. "Pepper, ginger and cinnamon and camphor are weighed upon apothecaries' scales, the windows being carefully shut during the operation lest a draft should blow away the tiniest fragment of the costly dust."

Daniella found herself giggling after another sip of wine. "How costly?"

"You didn't know?" Juan asked in surprise.

"I'm afraid I lived in a very small world in the Carolinas."

"Consider the risks of import . . ." Juan began. "The East lies at an immeasurable distance from the West. The trade routes by land are perpetually threatened by robbers, while pirates abound at sea. Great are the difficulties of travel, immense the risks to which ships are exposed. Consider this:

194

The first hand of the series is the most poorly recompensed—that of the Malayan slave who plucked the fresh blossoms, carried them to market upon his brown-skinned back, and received little more than his own sweat for his reward. It is his master who reaps the profit, the master from whom a Mohammedan merchant bought the load, paddling it in his *prahu* beneath the broiling tropical sun from the Spice Islands to Malacca, not far from Singapore. Here sits the first of the bloodsucking spiders, the lord of the harbor, the sultan, who demands tribute from every dealer who wants to tranship his goods."

Sebastián leaned forward, taking up where Juan left off. "Not until the dues have been paid, however, can the aromatic freight be transferred to another and larger-bottomed ship in which, by sail or oar, it would be removed a farther stage in its journey—to one of the seaports of Hindustan, for instance. Months have to be spent in such successive transhipments, for, in these latitudes, the merchant ships are often becalmed week after week beneath cloudless skies or must run before fierce hurricanes and escape from searobbers by headlong flight.

"Not only toilsome but fearfully dangerous is the voyage across two or three tropical seas, where, as a rule, at least one out of five ships is sunk by storm or plundered by pirates." He heard Daniella gasp softly here and continued. "With good luck, however," he smiled as he said this, "the Gulf of Cambay can at length be crossed; the southern coast of Arabia rounded; and Aden reached—if the destination should be the Red Sea and Egypt—or, if an earlier landfall is sought, Ormuz at the entrance to the Persian Gulf. If one petty ship out of five reaches home, after three years, well freighted with spices—as we are—it will bring in a handsome profit indeed."

Whether she could believe him or not, Daniella could not decide just now. His detailed account and Juan's seemed plausible enough. Was he only trying to convince her that he was not in league with the searobbers? Daniella frowned. She cared not what he really accomplished, for she still worried greatly as to her husband's whereabouts.

When Daniella glanced up from her plate, she noticed that Juan had gone around to the other side to drain the contents of his fiery drink.

Across the table, Juan caught Sebastián's attention finally. Nodding and motioning with his hands as he rose from the table, Juan indicated that he was going to the quarterdeck to check on his ship which softly treaded the *Tiger*'s moonlit wake.

The captain's officers were deep in conversation, noisily commenting upon the luscious attributes of a comely maid or two they had met in this port or that. Rascon kept the wineglasses filled, while Bettina established a path from galley to captain's table, luring the attentive downward slant of Jaecko's gaze to faithfully return to her swishing skirts.

With heavy-lidded eyes, Sebastián's gaze lingered upon Daniella's finely boned fingers as she picked at her food. He spoke softly and all of a sudden. "Your thoughts are elsewhere this evening, m'lady?"

Daniella did not look up at him as she answered, "You are right, Captain, and you would not like the path they travel."

"I feel an argument in the making," he said, staring at her profile.

"Then do not speak, Captain," she said energetically, looking down at his manicured hands resting on the table near her elbow.

"You are angry." He sipped his drink.

Her voice, soft and breathy, she said, "That is an understatement, Captain."

"My name is Sebastián." He tossed his head, setting the silken strands of his hair into a liquid, gliding motion.

"Your name is not unfamiliar to me."

"Then why continually refer to me as 'Captain'?"

"Because, sir, that is what you are. In fact, you are a pirate captain." She speared a piece of broiled Spanish mackerel.

"What makes you think so?" He stared down at her fish.

With a breathless anger, she said, "You test my intelligence, Captain *Sebastián*."

"No. I merely asked you a question."

"And I answered. You looked every inch the pirate earlier today." Daniella pushed aside the lime wedges surrounding the fish.

Sebastián laughed. "Do clothes make the man, Dany?"

She looked up into his face, realizing he was a shrewd interrogator and that he was trying to convince her he was not what he had seemed today.

"You are no longer a wolf in sheep's clothing,

Captain. I have your colors now." Taking a lime wedge up, she paused coolly.

"Brilliant, *bellissima!*"

He made emphasis on that which caused a fleeting blush to skip across Daniella's flaming cheeks — an *endearment*.

When Sebastián realized what she had unwittingly stated, he threw back his tawny head and began to laugh. A strong arm came around and banded her tiny waist, making Daniella feel small and vulnerable. It was a husky voice that murmured into her ear, stirring the gold strands there and tickling Daniella's flesh.

"We fit well together, m'lady."

"We fit together not at *all*, Captain," she fumed, driving a fist into his chest as she tried to escape his threatening presence.

Drawing back to look her full in her beautiful face, he said, "You think not?" His chuckle was deep. "I know better."

For a moment Daniella sat feeling stunned. His powerfully lean body was so near her own that she ached with shameless desire. This should be her husband seated here at her side not this despicable pirate captain . . . her husband who should be realizing the extent of her desire.

"Captain!" Daniella shot to her feet, leaving him to stare up at her with heart-reaching eyes. "I demand to see my husband now! Did you lock him up? Is that it?" Her eyes flashed around the room, ignoring the curious looks she was receiving. "Or perhaps you have already seen to his demise." She caught a flicker of emotion in his mocking eyes. "So. You have done away with Steven Landaker!"

For some reason this brought a gale of hearty chuckles from around the room. Daniella began to back to the bulkhead. "You are all searobbers—all bloody pirates! I shall see that you rot in prison . . . for the murder of my husband!"

With that, Sebastián's sardonic laugh turned with the others into uncontrollable, boisterous laughter. Daniella whirled to catch even Bettina hiding a giggle behind her hand, and when she saw her lady, the maid stared around the room as if she wondered what all the hilarity was about, for truly she did wonder.

When Daniella whirled back to the reckless faces in the room, she caught sight of Sebastián just rising from his chair. He pushed it back, straightened his back, as if in preparation of an important announcement.

When the words came, Daniella's gray eyes grew larger and darker, her cheeks paler.

"You are so right, m'lady." He executed a sweeping bow. "I have done away with Steven Landaker. I *am* sorry. But it was time. His usefulness had run its course."

"Usefulness!" Daniella shrieked. "You . . . you cold-blooded murderer. I hate you!" She turned and flew to the portal, her mulberry skirts atwirl behind her as she raced from the cabin.

Before Captain Sebastián Landaker followed in her distressed wake, he turned one last time to the now-hushed room, ordering them all to resume their seats and finish their dinner and drink. Bettina's eyes were round and frightened as she turned to stare at Jaecko. And Jaecko stood stroking his bearded chin, his expression a keenly worried one.

But Bettina looked almost pathetic, ignorant of the captain's clever deception.

"Jaecko," she said, "You know something I don't. Yes?"

"Yes," Jaecko drawled.

"And . . ." She swept an arm about the room, indicating the others who had followed the captain's orders. "Do *they* know what's going on, too?"

"Aye." He looked almost sheepish. "They do now."

"What do you mean?"

"Haven't you wondered what happened to Lord Landaker?" He lifted Bettina's hand to tenderly caress it, rubbing large fingers over the freckles dotting her soft flesh.

"I suppose I have." She blushed. "But I haven't thought much of it lately." Deep went her gaze into the large man's eyes, but seriousness returned as she feared for her lady's plight. "He won't hurt her?"

"I'm afraid I don't know all the captain's plans, but I think he won't hurt her too much. He just needs her to do something for him."

"What?" Bettina's heart pounded as she stared at Jaecko, waiting for him to be earnest with her.

"He hasn't told me, Bettina."

"Why did he kill Lord Landaker?"

Something flickered in Jaecko's eyes as he leaned forward as if about to reveal a much-guarded secret.

"That one was killed a long time ago, in a duel with Lucian Drake."

Bettina shrugged her shoulders. "I don't understand, Jaecko. You mean *there is no Lord Landaker?*"

"That's right."

As Rascon came by with a tray of drinks, Bettina swiped one and tipped it to drain the contents in one fiery gulp. She coughed and choked, and then sputtered and stammered as she faced Jaecko's grinning face.

"Let me get this straight, Jaecko. Lord Steven Landaker is a ghost that the captain's just done away with."

"Now you understand, Betts."

The lad Rascon stood by and frowned. Jaecko knew that Rascon would never be able to utter the words, and yet neither would the lad betray his captain even if he were capable of speech.

Her voice lowered as she took in the new solemnity in Jaecko's expression.

"Just *who* married my lady then?"

Bettina drew a deep breath, waiting.

Jaecko rolled his eyes to the ceiling. He only said: "Guess."

Chapter Thirteen

Damnable, both sides rogue.
—William Shakespeare

Outside the ship, the black night sky was radiantly sprinkled with stars and aglow with moonlight, but the passageway along the cabins was dim; only two small, smoky lanterns were fastened one to either side of the bulkhead walls.

The way was eerie, shadowy, and Daniella shook with uncontrollable anger as she made her way quickly to her cabin. Womanly intuition told her that Steven was not dead—not really—but had abandoned her. No doubt he was situated comfortably upon Juan Tomaz's ship, leaving her to fend for herself in the evil clutches of Captain Sebastián!

Oh, he indeed was a devil, and she wished she'd never heard the name Landaker! Hah! *Lord* Steven Landaker—no doubt he was no dandy gent at all, and perhaps he expertly concealed a rogue's face with his theatrical makeup, a deception that would be very easy to get away with. Of course it was the makeup! Dear Mary knew of many a demure and coy lady who used a substance called white fucus which was less dangerous than ceruse, but the latter gave the best immediate effect in whitening the skin and concealing flaws . . . or creating any desirable mark to deliberately hide one's identity!

Daniella's teeth flashed as she gritted them. "Oh, no, dear Lord, say it is not so!" she said out loud, her eyes flown wide and stormy blue-gray.

All of a sudden Daniella swayed dizzily and put out her hand to steady herself against the bulkhead. One hand flew to her stomach and she felt as if she might become ill. Then logical reasoning told her that of course—Lord Landaker and the captain never occupied the same space in the same room, at the same time. Never at the same time. Never had she seen them together . . . It must be!

Daniella shook with the excitement of her discovery and its subsequent import! No wonder the captain had appeared familiar to her and she'd mistaken him for Steven Landaker that day he'd followed her from the waterfront. He'd been without his black wig!

Wig! That made it certain. The roguish captain had disguised himself with wig and makeup!

"Oh!" Daniella smacked her forehead. *The wig . . . I'd always thought his hair was fake-looking . . . Why couldn't I have put two and two together sooner!*

Oh yes, she saw now, blind and stupid that she was!

Daniella started. There was the sound of someone coming along the passageway. She could hear footsteps. A door had closed, and Daniella realized shakily that the captain must be following her to make certain she was going straightaway to her cabin!

Opening her door in a rush, Daniella squeezed inside and splayed herself against the portal, waiting for the footsteps to come closer and finally stop outside the door. What would the roguish captain do now? He could lock her in again, or worse . . .

"Daniella."

Her breath came out in a rush, "Yes . . . what do you want?" She only wished he would go away and forget to lock the door, but that was not to be!

She stood back, waiting for him to come barging inside, yet his voice was unbelievably soft, almost a caress soothing her frayed nerves.

"I wish to speak with you. May I come in?"

He was *asking?* This was something new, unless . . .

Daniella's frightened gaze skipped across the room to the flickering lamp, realizing someone had come in to light it not long ago. More than likely Rascon, for that was the lad's daily job aboard the *Emerald Tiger.* Daniella turned slightly and she took in the young woman reflected in the wavy mirror. Was that herself? Looking so frightened and miserably vulnerable?

Now her eyes darkened to cobalt as she thought about the evil that had been done to her. She had been fooled by a well-dressed dandy! Tricked by a gentle, loving touch. She shook terribly to think just whose touch that truly had been!

Clenching her hands into fists, Daniella stared and stared at her reflection, not listening anymore for sounds outside her door. And she began to smile a sly, secretive smile.

"Captain . . . are you still there?" Daniella said succinctly, taking a deep breath.

There was a deep, waiting sigh, "I am here, m'lady. Will you give me entry now or must I lock you in, seeing as you wish to hide yourself in your room? I have with me a delicious dessert—bread pudding with whiskey sauce."

"That sounds most unpalatable, Captain," Daniella said with a grimace. "I do not care for anything with strong inebriants in it. You can set it down outside the door and let Rascon fetch it later."

"I shall do just that. Daniella . . . I do not believe you to be a coward, not at all!"

"Come in, Captain . . . oh, I mean *Captain Sebastián,*" Daniella said in a voice dripping with honey.

She swept the door wide, and could almost have swooned when the captain flashed his most charming smile, bowed gallantly, and gave her his arm. She stared at it as if he had offered a basket of bees that would sting painfully if she reached out, and she wavered, trying to decide what to do. Her sea-gray eyes flickered and fell on his lips. His smile was bland but not unpleasant.

What is he up to now? she cautiously wondered.

"M'lady. You spoke earlier of taking your air this evening. Perhaps now you would care for a walk on deck in the moonlight?"

Wildly, impulsively, Daniella said to him in a pleasant tone, "Of course." *Why not?* There was a pronounced improvement in his attitude, and she

did so much wish to take some air after her prolonged imprisonment!

She walked beside the tall captain, her skirts a
rustling moonlit wake brushing the deck and Sebastián's pantaloons, her dainty-heeled shoes click-
ing with a soft sound. It was with a suddenness
that he turned to her, slowing their walk to a
standstill beneath a spray of huge silver stars and
vivid yellow moonlight. The evening was romantic,
tropically warm, full of stardust. Whatever else the
captain had been about to say was halted as he
stared at her, his breath stolen away.

Tawny lashes, sparkling with stardust, raised,
and large gray-blue eyes watched and waited. She
remembered this man's lovemaking well . . . but
she remembered his skill in treachery even more!
Seething inwardly, Daniella lifted her lips for his
ardent kiss.

Brushing his mouth against hers, he murmured,
"You are as changeable as the savage sea, and just
as beautiful." His arms cupped her back. "Ah . . .
you are no longer so concerned over the disappearance of Lord Landaker?"

Daniella laughed with a throaty seductive sound.
"How can I be worried about one who is no
more? You have done away with him,
Sebastián . . ." She shrugged laconically. "What
can I say? What can I do?"

Wary now, Sebastián leaned back, stroking his
chin. "You did not love your *husband* then?" He
was watching her closely, his eyes moody and passionate.

"Of course I loved him." She slithered a white

206

arm about his neck and he groaned deeply as she pulled him closer. His eyes narrowed as she drifted her fingers over the nape of his neck, then slid beneath the collar, to the front, to his chest, to delve into the V of the smoke-colored velvet. "I have loved Steven since the first time he took my purity." She almost purred the word and she heard Sebastián swallow hard. "He was *so* gentle, *so* kind, *so* loving. I shall miss him sorely and mourn his passing. He *was* my husband, you realize."

He still is, dammit! Sebastián thought wickedly.

With another deep groan, Sebastián yanked her to his chest and lowered his starved mouth to take her sweet-nectared lips in a fierce, scorching kiss that seemed to last forever. His large hands took the small of her back and cupped her gently to his muscular frame, and her pulse drummed as, in a husky voice, he murmured against her cheek.

"I need you, *bellissima* . . . can you not feel how badly it is I want you. *Madre de Dios,* every lovely inch of you, Daniella Rose—every sweet turn of you." He stared into the hyacinth-gray of her eyes, thrilled to see the passionate shade in them telling of her rapidly growing desire coming from deep within her body.

"Daniella . . . let us go back to the cabin now."

"Surely you do not believe I will fall into bed with you so easily, Sir Pirate." Her voice was breathless and hardly recognizable as her own.

He reached out a hand to stroke the velvet texture of her heavenly angel face. "I am many things, my dear lady, but no pirate."

"Then what you and your good friend Juan Tomaz told me today was all truth? You and Juan and others associate with the Established Merchant Fleet?"

Sebastián laughed lightly, seductively, then softly answered, "We *are* the Merchant Fleet, *querida*. The United Windstar Fleet, to be precise."

Daniella's eyes narrowed as she walked around him, watching his warm gaze follow as she made a full circle. She came to a sudden halt before him, staring up into his catlike jade eyes. Oh, yes . . . the *eyes*—why had she not recognized the similarity between the two deceivers long ago!

"You must know Edward Wingate, my father, then?" she said slyly.

Now Captain Sebastián knew the contest, and he was willing to play it to the fullest to win this night with her before the lovely rose bared her thorns and pricked him until he bled. And bleed he would, for he had never known another like this intoxicating beauty! The fierce tiger would be bound by the velvet rose . . . but he would have his revenge, be its price a broken heart! *Ay di mi!* Never that, for first he would see *hers* broken in payment for what the devil Drake had made of the once-lovely Eileena.

"I know *of* him, *sí* . . ." Sebastián began, then deciding to tell the truth, he changed that to, "I have . . . met him."

"Briefly?" Tawny lashes flicked upward, baring her beauteous eyes for him to gaze fully into. "Or . . . uhm . . . *well?*"

"Let us not speak of anyone for now, Daniella." He breathed her name again, and again, like the softest of caresses.

Common sense dictated that Daniella beware the velvet touch of his hands and his lips, but as he drew her closer and fitted his lips to hers, she was lost in a heady kiss and oblivious to everything else save the sensual pleasure Sebastián brought to her.

Wild, reckless moments passed as she arched to him, aching to be closer, eager for whatever he would do to her. Sebastián crushed her to his taut body, clenching his buttocks while straining between her thighs, savoring the feel of her softness responding to his rhythm.

Daniella felt the manly shape press into her, and she closed her eyes as his thrusting tongue invaded and probed and made an act of love inside her mouth. With hungry impatience, Daniella met his tiny thrusts, sliding and playing along his tongue, lightly nibbling the corner of his mouth as he did the same to her. Pressing her bodice aside, his lips cherished her aching breasts next, adoration of their graceful femininity evident in every gentle pull and tug. He teased with a slowness that drove Daniella wild with thrilling excitement.

All determination to resist was washed away when Sebastián lifted her skirts and found the silken skin on her belly, and then he was winding his fingers in her soft, downy curls. Daniella gasped. This was Sebastián—the man she despised. This was Steven—the man she loved. Her beloved husband. Her lover. She began to move against him, her rhythm graceful and luring him on to the moistness of her pearlized flesh. He discovered the sweet mysteries of her vibrant body, ever deeper into the warm wetness did he delve. She gazed dreamily into his eyes, looking up into his handsome face, which seemed fascinated by what he had captured beneath his hard, plunging fingers. Daniella almost swooned.

Sebastián moved quickly then, and emotions wracked her senses as he strained closer, his hands lightning fast at the front of his pantaloons and then he was lifting her whimpering and wanting against the bulkhead, his hands cupping the soft flesh beneath her buttocks.

He was going to make love to her right here!

"Sebastián, no, no . . . not h-here!"

"*Sí*—here, my dark rose!" he hissed into her ear. "Here—*now!*"

"You will have to take me by force!"

"*Sí!*" The tip of him gently touched the sensually swelling part of her. Then he gathered himself for the forceful plunge.

Hot, fast, hard, he entered her. Daniella's sharp fingernails clawed at the smoke-colored material and then grasped to give her a hold as he began to move inside her.

Shyly then, her hips began to move with his and she scraped her breasts along his strong chest.

"That's right, my love—move!" He nuzzled the hot, velvety cheek. "I shall help you."

"Sebastián . . . oh Sebastián," Daniella cried wantonly. "I . . . love . . . you!"

Only for a moment did Sebastián freeze. Then the dark rose bewitched him anew and, with rapture burning bright, he thrust his swollen manhood deeply, impaling her graceful curves against the bulkhead.

Daniella felt the white-hot heat engulf her as he forged his body to hers, and breathlessly, glowingly, she burst into pulsating ecstasy. Not long after, Sebastián followed. The heaven-breathed moment claimed them both and they became one being, inseparable, the tiger and the rose, one creature, one entity. Wonderfully husband and wife.

When Sebastián moved away from her, Daniella straightened her skirts with quivering fingers; she was certain that from head to toe she was scarlet with shame. An agony of embarrassment washed over her, then she was suddenly furious and tore her hot gaze from his smiling, mocking face.

"Leave me be," she said with a groan. "You've gotten what you brought me up here for. Don't look at me like that! Y-you raped me!" she accused hotly.

"Rape? Hah! I gave m'lady only that which she yearned after." As he said this, he cockily smoothed the front of his pantaloons, which still bore evidence of desire which had become everlasting while in her bewitching presence. He himself knew he could never have enough of her. She was in his blood, like thick, sweet honey.

"Conceited knave!" Daniella tossed her disheveled hair and looked away to the moon-whitened sea. "You are a Spaniard—I could tell by your wicked speech!"

He chuckled, musically taunting her with, "Daniella loves Sebastián."

211

"Oh, please . . . just go away!" She kicked at her skirts and clutched a handful of the mulberry material to shoo him with a flick of her wrist. "I . . . I hate you!"

"Oh?" A tawny brow lifted. "Then who was that you professed your undying love to moments ago? Or does the blushing moonlit rose only cry out in the heat of midnight passion and refrain from foolish endearments in the light of day, hmm?"

"Steven Landaker is gone from my life. I wish never to speak of him again. He is a ghost." She hung her head.

"Oh, but *querida,* there is still the question of a marriage."

"Dare you speak to me of marriage?" She whirled on him, baring her teeth as she hissed the words. Softly she said, "There is no marriage, 'twas only a marriage of deception."

"You are bound securely to those marriage vows, Daniella—whether it is to your liking or not."

"You speak false, sir!"

"I say the truth. And you will not escape . . . Dark Rose."

"I asked you before . . ." Daniella began with panting breaths. "I asked if you knew my father briefly?" she paused. "Or well?"

Sebastián only performed a mocking bow.

"The question?" she persisted.

"Ah . . . briefly." Sebastián smiled, and smoothed the cuff of his elegant sleeve. "I knew Edward Wingate only briefly."

"Liar!" Daniella whirled around to face him,

lifting a hand to strike off the smirk.

Easily he caught her hand and held it above them, as if a weapon hovered there. "Why do you call me that?"

Deep stormy eyes and bright jade clashed and dueled while the moon showered its gleaming silver all around them, and they stood like make-believe lovers staging a theatrical piece.

Daniella pushed forward and then came away, free of him, and she began to back away, her eyes blazing her frustration and hatred.

"You deceived me! You played me false!" She pointed a shaking finger accusingly at him. "You are no dandy fop! You are not a gentle soul. Blast you, you conniving bastard, you are Steven Landaker and — Sebastián!"

Sebastián was upon her in a flash, his fingers biting with cruel vengeance into the soft flesh of her upper arm. Snarling into her face, he said, "Steven Landaker is no more," and shook her until ringlets of rich, shining blond fell forward and bounced at her temples. "Steven is no more! You are wed, bedded well, and bound to Sebastián Landaker! Do you hear?"

"You slimy . . . bastard!" She writhed at the grinding of his knuckles into her arms. "Let me go! I wish to return home! My father awaits me. He will know what you have done. Word will reach him. Alain Carstairs will flay your hide for your cruel deception!"

"He is . . . gone." Sebastián's last word was spoken in a hush. "I would have told you at the table, but you would not have taken it well."

213

"What do you mean, he is gone?" Her face paled to an ashen hue. "Who is dead?"

"Juan Tomaz brought word. Your father passed away just last week."

"What?" Daniella shrieked, shoving her fists at his hard chest. "Do you mean . . ." she began to sob now. "Do you mean to say while I was with *you*, my dear father was dying? With you . . . making love with a deceitful, unscrupulous, evil bastard *pirate!*"

Taking both arms against his chest, he drew her nearer, saying, "I should not have broken bad tidings just yet. This is too much for you to take all in one night. *Dios,* please forgive me."

While he stared into her heartbroken face, Sebastián pulled himself up short. He had just asked her to forgive him? What in hell, was he daft? *Diablo,* this was exactly the turn he had wished for, to seek and gain revenge on the Drakes — to capture the dark rose and use her as that devil Lucian had used Eileena Landaker . . . and she had just called him bastard!

Angry and thoroughly disgusted, Sebastián pushed her away from him. "Jaecko! Anyone who can hear me . . . come and take this wench from my sight and lock her away!" His deep male voice thundered across the decks and Daniella shivered at his sudden, violent anger.

With that he began to stride away, but stopped as she stumbled to the rail and hung her head, tears falling like huge drops of rain onto the sleeve of her mulberry gown. She slumped there, feeling as if the end of time had come to her, gazing into

214

the swirling midnight waters as if her answer might be miraculously discovered.

"If you are thinking of ending your life, *querida*," he said coldly, "go ahead and jump. But if I save your lovely neck, you shall owe me, owe me until your dying day. This warning I leave you with: Never, but never, call me bastard again!" He hissed the venomous words with horrible intensity.

With her back to the hard wood railing, Daniella stared at the captain's lean, ramrod-straight back as he strode away from her, missing the look of enlightenment dawning in her eyes. It was Robert Drake he hated so very much . . . but why? *Why?* Sebastián was using her to get back at *Robert* . . . she was Captain Sebastián's bait. Sebastián was using her as an allurement in order to destroy Robert . . . But then why, when he had the chance to fire on the *Raven,* had he not taken it, but instead allowed Robert to escape? Was there more?

Yes, Sebastián had more punishment in mind. He was not yet finished!

She had to get away! Just then she saw her jailer coming for her, and she went docilely. Actually what could she do? Jump in the middle of the night to her watery grave? Slay the captain while he slept? She would not get far with that, for where was there to run to and hide on this blasted ship?

Daniella hung her head as Jaecko took her gently and showed her to the cabin. She said not a word, not to Bettina, not to anyone. She was not even at this moment mildly embarrassed, for her thoughts were only on her father. *Oh Papa, you are gone . . . never to look upon your beloved face again.* In her mind, her father had deceived her, too. It hurt her terribly to think he would do this to her. As for the other—"Steven"—she would remember the all-absorbing passion they had once shared, and every moment she was with *him* from this day forward would be one of agonizing remembrance.

Daniella walked quietly to her prison, closing her heart to all she had once felt for Steven—and whatever she might feel for Captain Sebastián in the future.

Chapter Fourteen

Through a blossom-scented breeze, the *Raven* prowled outside Wind Island, continuing along the low shoreline with tableland rising into peaks. Vines and oranges grew luxuriantly on the sides of the mountains, scarlet foliage and exotic snow-white flowers abounded, and Robert Drake had spotted a few quail and partridge in his spying glass, wishing he could take the time to hunt some fresh meat — but he'd had a few crew members swim inland for a supply of tangy oranges and pineapples.

Robert had trailed the ship he could have sworn was the *Emerald Tiger*. Now, as he thought of it, biting into a juicy orange wedge, he could not fathom the flag she'd been flying. The figurehead had been the same, and yet the captain and his crew were dressed as pirates, and the woman — she had reminded him painfully of Daniella. He'd been intrigued, so he had followed, but not too close. Confusion had reigned, since he could not make up his mind whether to attack or not. If that was Dany aboard, he would not have liked to fire upon them, thus taking the chance of hurting Dany.

Robert had covertly trailed the mystery ship. Indeed, she could be carrying spices, he'd told himself — yet if truly a pirate craft she was, then he could not fire on her and be damned by the brotherhood of searobbers. And if it was truly the *Emerald Tiger* that pirates had captured, with a beautiful young woman aboard and the pirate captain clearly enamoured with her charms — again he could not intrude on his brothers!

Now the *Raven* had company, for she had joined up with another pirate craft, the *El Draque,* a swift-running dragon lady of the sea. And aboard her was none other than his brother, Lucian Drake trailing the *Raven,* tracking in her smooth, curdled wake.

At the moment, Robert Drake was not pleased with the way things were going. He was displeased with the whole world — and himself. But his luck was holding, and the men, having survived the encounter with the *Wind Star,* now believed Robert invincible, though they'd only tossed back and forth a few volleys and sailed their separate ways with no one the winner.

Finishing his juicy orange, Robert carelessly tossed the peelings into the summer-sparkling sea. With the *El Draque* behind them, the crew of the *Raven* had momentarily dismissed their dream of capturing a ship full of spices, and they were as impatient as stabled stallions, for Sir Lucian always had a few painted ladies aboard, they heard tell.

Watching tropical birds wheeling past, Robert stood at the rail, his dark brown eyes somber. Dammit all, he refused to worry at this point! Danger, like a beautiful woman, was a heady wine, and Robert was drunk with confidence if not happiness. He made up his mind then: He was going to twist the tiger's tail and take the prize! First, he had to find out if the beautiful creature he'd seen with the tawny pirate was truly Daniella. Through his spyglass he could have sworn that the haughty beauty was indeed Daniella Wingate . . . or Landaker now. He'd heard she'd married into the family, but had yet to see for himself if this was true.

Lustful craving for this one woman was becoming as elemental as food, drink, and sleep. He had never before known torment and yearning. He lusted after his beautiful flower—his Dany Rose. He had to have her to warm his bed. She would be as good as that Landaker woman. What had her name been. . . ? Eileena. But she had become limp and useless, no longer able to heed his or his brother Sir Lucian's commands to perform the lustful acts they'd shared with her. Eileena had become a mere shadow, and they'd left the poor mute woman for dead; and then the Tiger had found where they had left her like a discarded heap of clothing.

Robert smirked evilly. Useless Eileena. A few of his lowlife friends at Land's End professed she could not even utter her name, though some of those more haughty in demeanor said she had revealed her spoilers to the Tiger and his friend Juan Tomaz.

But Robert comforted himself with the fact that Daniella would show more spirit and fight than Eileena, for she had been full of mischief, and merry as a girl. How much more spunk she'd have, he thought, now that she'd grown into delicious womanhood!

Robert's hate-clouded face twisted in bitterness.

Now his Dany had become Lord Landaker's bride rumor had it. But hell . . . which Landaker? Most of the arrogant lot had already been dispatched by his brother Lucian. Could it be that the crisp dandy all of London and Cornwall had been gossiping about was not dead after all? Or had one of the handsome bastards survived after Lucian had given him the supposed death thrust in that duel? Some even went so far as to say Steven Landaker had not perished from the fatal wound; others said, "Well, but of course he is gone from this earth!"

And now it seemed the man Steven had come back to life. To seek revenge on his brother's head?

An unconscious shiver rippled through Robert. Damn, but he was deathly afeared of any semblance of ghosts, as was his cunning brother . . . Robert threw off his worries to give his full attention to scanning the sea. It quickened his blood to realize that perhaps somewhere in all that savage sea was his woman with skin like the dewy petals of a wild rose and an ardor-awakening fragrance all her own.

"I'll find her—and have the devil to pay to see her as my own," he said to the dancing sea. "And be damned if she'd wed or not!"

Sunlight touched the *Spanish Wind* where she was anchored in a beautiful wooded inlet of recently rain-washed Dove Island. Beneath a jeweled rainbow with the sun peeking behind lolled the *Desdemona,* a broad-beamed heavy galleon with

220

several decks like the *Spanish Wind*. She was high in the bows and stern, with three masts, and the *Spanish Wind* had four. Each was amply manned by sun-wrinkled sailors. Always Juan, like Sebastián, kept the crew members busy at one task or another, for idle hands were the tools of *el diablo!*

All ships had been provided—as had the *Emerald Tiger*—with Portuguese license to ship spices. Just days before, the *Wind Star* had almost lost her precious cargo, but she had survived the encounter with the hated *Raven*.

From the waist of his ship, Juan Tomaz saw the longboat shoot under the square stern of the *Spanish Wind* and nose alongside. That would be Sebastián's men, making the transfer from the *Emerald Tiger* to the *Spanish Wind*. The crew of the boat rowed easily in the calm turquoise waters, their conical caps heaving forward and back with the strong pull of their golden-brown arms at the oars. Spray slopped over their short, baggy breeches and they grinned like merry pirates.

Three more ships had pulled up to the inlet during the last hour, among them the *Emerald Tiger*. For a moment, Juan wondered how his friend had been faring the week past with the spirited Daniella, who no doubt by now had learned that Sebastián had been playing a dual role! The only part that bothered Juan was that his handsome friend had plunged himself into a reckless marriage, without thought as to the consequences! Ah, *Dios*—what wedded bliss could grow from a union such as theirs, when the lovely lady had been grossly deceived? It was a pity to have used her to his advantage when she possessed such rare intelligence and fragile loveliness.

Juan shrugged. But who knows, matters could drastically change, for they were both young and attracted to each other, whether they realized the truth of the matter or not!

Most of the Windstar Merchant Fleet had gathered by now and they'd have to proceed with caution, for pirates with swift sailing vessels were lying in wait along the inlets of Dove and Wind Islands to prey upon merchant vessels. So far, luck had staying power, for the *Raven* had not been spotted since the episode with the *Wind Star,* but once they went their separate ways to unload their spices, they would have safety in numbers.

The *Emerald Tiger* carried a treasure the *Raven* would be lying in wait to snatch once she saw her chance, but the precious cargo, including the lovely Lady Landaker, would not be aboard the *Emerald Tiger!* It was sad to think that his friend would go to such extreme measures, for he meant to use the *Tiger* and had already sent the *Rampant Rose* back to the Carolinas. This must signify something of import; that Sebastián would sacrifice one of his own instead of Daniella's?

Over Juan's dark, curly head furled sails shook in the rope yarns that bound them to the yards, and the swifters bracing the pine masts quivered in the mounting wind; still the sun continued to shine upon the little armada.

Juan turned from watching the longboat and grimaced to think what that new longboat might be carrying. Maybe a woman by the name of Geraldina, who was Captain Gancho's loose-moraled, wily daughter.

His dark cinnamon eyes fell on the *Spanish Wind*. She was a fine galleon, massive and sturdy, with a length three times her beam that made her speedy and seaworthy. It was to this ship that Captain Sebastián would transfer his precious cargo; perhaps he had it in mind to lure the *Raven* at last to her end. . . ?

The small armada sat like sea birds on the water. Great ships. Galleons. Smaller, bouncing caravels. Merchantmen. Their masts and spars rocked against the cerulean sky; among them were the longboats, the coasters, the pirogues which would disappear into the island's secret coves once the greater ships had returned to the open sea.

The members of the Established Merchant Fleet could navigate and they could fight. Sebastián and Juan had chosen them for their many talents; even Rascon was not without creativity, for he had fashioned the flags that rose to fly jauntily at the masts of many a Windstar ship. Sebastián and he had encountered the seasoned lot of crew members in the town streets. Their speech had the ocean tang, the speech of traders to the Mediterranean and the Baltic and of Devon rovers and salty shipmen. Certainly, love of ships, skill of the "lady sea," ran through them like a tide of blood-brothers united.

Some of the men pronounced their *h* as though it were a *y;* such as Senhor being Senyor. Juan chuckled softly, for he was one of those Spanish-Portuguese-speaking himself, and he and Sebastián *Saba* used to speak the same melodious language, back when they were small boys in Spain and did not even know the other existed. Then there was the time Sebastián had saved his life — the day they'd met.

For such a worldly sailor, Juan still smiled wistfully. Ah, *ciertamente* . . . such a time they'd had those first weeks together as friends — brawling and imbibing and wenching. Worries had not plagued this man as they did now . . . for Juan Tomaz wenched no longer — he had fallen headlong and strong in love with the only one in his world of friends, lovers, and acquaintances who did not know he even existed. But one day, he promised himself, one day he would make Eileena come alive to him. For now, all he could do was pray that she would one day emerge from the ravages of mind and heart and body. One day, sweet *Jaysus*. One day . . .

That night, without the wind's persistant tossing, the misty sea was calm and quiet making the sleeping cove even more peaceful. Pacing the larger cabin given to her, Daniella fruitlessly searched her mind for means of escape, staring around her in the dimness that filtered through the eyelike windows.

Daniella plopped onto the bed, her yellow cambric frock with white violets strewn across bodice and hem spread about her like a meadow of wildflowers and liquid honey. She wore the tiger pin above her breast and fingered it lovingly, remembering that Alain Carstairs had gifted her with the dainty reminder of their longtime friendship. Where was Alain now, she wondered?

MORE PASSION AND ADVENTURE AWAIT... YOUR TRIP TO A BIG ADVENTUROUS WORLD BEGINS WHEN YOU ACCEPT YOUR FIRST 4 NOVELS ABSOLUTELY *FREE* (AN $18.00 VALUE)

Accept your Free gift and start to experience more of the passion and adventure you like in a historical romance novel. Each Zebra novel is filled with proud men, spirited women and tempetuous love that you'll remember long after you turn the last page

Zebra Historical Romances are the finest novels of their kind. They are written by authors who really know how to weave tales of romance and adventure in the historical settings you love. You'll feel like you've actually gone back in time with the thrilling stories that each Zebra novel offers.

GET YOUR FREE GIFT WITH THE START OF YOUR HOME SUBSCRIPTION

Our readers tell us that these books sell out very fast in book stores and often they miss the newest titles. So Zebra has made arrangements for you to receive the four newest novels published each month.

You'll be guaranteed that you'll never miss a title, and home delivery is so convenient. And to show you just how easy it is to get Zebra Historical Romances, we'll send you your first 4 books absolutely FREE! Our gift to you just for trying our home subscription service.

BIG SAVINGS AND FREE HOME DELIVERY

Each month, you'll receive the four newest titles as soon as they are published. You'll probably receive them even before the bookstores do. What's more, you may preview these exciting novels free for 10 days. If you like them as much as we think you will, just pay the low preferred subscriber's price of just $3.75 each. *You'll save $3.00 each month off the publisher's price.* AND, your savings are even greater because there are never any shipping, handling or other hidden charges—FREE Home Delivery. Of course you can return any shipment within 10 days for full credit, no questions asked. There is no minimum number of books you must buy.

With a wistfulness born of boredom, Daniella sweetly hummed a wistful tune as memories, beautiful ones and poignant, brought a flutter to her breast.

Adventure? True, she had wanted that, but now she was sick and tired of being at sea, living on a ship. It was more like being surrounded by prison walls. From one prison to another, she thought. Bettina, Jaecko, and Rascon the lad, and several other crew members—as much as she could tell— had been transferred to the *Spanish Wind,* the huge, beautiful galleon she had only gotten a glimpse of as she was rowed from one ship to the other. She took it for granted that the captain was coming along, even though she had not seen his arrogant person since the night he had ravished her on deck.

One thing was different here on the *Spanish Wind*—this luxurious cabin could have served royalty! Indeed, Sebastián was no doubt thought of as such.

It was spacious in the extreme. Under the leaded windows were green settees, and at the forward end was a massive double bed. The bulkheads were elm, less likely to splinter if struck by shot, and ornately carved. A large, fixed table marked the center of the cabin, with heavy chairs to match; these were upholstered in the same jade-green as the settees. She had continued her survey of the more practical aspects of the cabin. There was a wardrobe filled with clothes of all sorts— men's, women's, in all sizes. Her heart had filled her throat as she had spied the captain's foul-weather gear hanging from a peg on the forward bulkhead. She also noticed with some trepidation the goodly supply of small arms—swords, pistols, and muskets, cutlasses, all set in neat racks about the mizzen mast. Charts were all in place; a telescope in its bracket. And a good compass.

Indeed, this was Captain Sebastián's own personal cabin, she'd been informed—and he would no doubt come to claim his rest, and her body, later on! But he would not find a wanton tigress awaiting his pleasure. Instead he might just find a fierce battle on his horny-toad hands!

Bettina entered with the ever-grinning Jaecko, and bringing up the rear two seamen lugged in a tub of hot water. When all the men took their leave, Daniella simply forgot her sorry plight in the pleasure of her warm, soapy bath.

While Bettina sponged the soapy bubbles down her back, Daniella softly inquired, "What's to happen to us, Bettina?"

"I'm not sure, my lady." Bettina's chocolate-brown eyes shone, for just that morning Jaecko had asked her to become his bride. "But soon as we return to the Carolinas, Jaecko and I are getting hitched!"

All of a sudden Daniella started and sat up, her eyes wild. "The Carolinas! When did he say we were to return?"

Home was all Daniella could think of. Braidwood. She was much saddened to think her father would not be there to greet her with open arms; at the moment she did not wish to speak to Bettina of her beloved parent, for she needed her strength for other matters, and the conversation would prove to be wearisome, she knew.

Daniella clasped her hands together. "Oh, when, Bettina, when do we return?"

She excitedly reached for the towel and Bettina used another to dab the drops of moisture from Daniella's slender back as she stepped from the tub.

"After Captain Sebastián's mission is complete and he's unloaded his cargo." Bettina shrugged, scrambling after her lady as she hurried across the floor, already reaching for her ivory-handled brush. "We'll have to dry it some first, my lady."

"Oh, please, Bettina, call me Daniella and please don't keep me in suspense!"

"I already told you, D-Daniella, Captain Sebastián has some unfinished business to take care of."

Daniella made a face. "Like using me as his decoy for another week or two, until his revenge has run its course, or until he . . . he kills Robert Drake!" She stared through the mirror at her wide-eyed maid.

"Oh, my lady, I wouldn't know about that," Bettina said with a shake of her fiery red locks. "Jaecko only told me about Lord Landaker . . . Oops!" The young maid clamped a hand to her mouth, staring at Daniella as if she'd bludgeoned her with a sword.

Daniella stood stock-still. "Oh? *What about* Lord Landaker?" Nonchalantly then, Daniella ran the towel up and down the glistening ivory skin of her arms. Unbidden heat built up inside her as she thought of the captain. "You know much more than you are revealing, Bettina." She turned and looked the maid square in the eye. "Am I correct in my assumption?"

227

"Uh . . ." Bettina gulped. Her face was suffused with red. "God's teeth, my lady, what am I supposed to do?" She flung her arms wide. "Be loyal to you, my lady? Or to Jaecko, my lover?"

"Your lady, of course!" Daniella said quickly. Then, taking Bettina gently by the arm, she led her over to the jade-green settee, and when she had sat, her towel tucked in at her breasts, she patted the seat for Bettina to join her. "Come now, Bettina, we've been friends for some time now. You like me, do you not?"

Bettina hesitated, then said, "Oh . . . of course, my lady!" She loved Daniella as if she were her own flesh-and-blood sister.

Daniella smiled as her maid sat as if she might crush eggs, then twiddled her fingers nervously before she finally began.

"Of course you know who Lord Landaker . . . I mean, Sebastián is — *was* . . ." She cleared her throat noisily. "You do know what I am trying to say, don't you?" A hand waved in the air. "Of course you do, Jaecko said so. He overheard them two handsome captains discussing it."

"They were discussing *me?*" Daniella leaned forward, her damp hair an ivory-tinted veil about her beautiful face. Raking her fingers through the bothersome strands, she rolled her eyes heavenward while Bettina kept her head downward, her teeth worrying her bottom lip. Taking a deep, impatient breath, she asked, "What were they saying? Bettina, please tell me?"

"Well . . ." Bettina blushed, freckles and all. "The captain said he'd like to toss you overboard, and — "

Startled for a moment, Daniella leaned forward with a toss of her damp head, wearing a waiting expression. "And?"

"And Captain Juan Tomaz said he shouldn't do that!"

Painfully, Daniella tugged the brush through her hair with some show of irritation. "Oh, that's so-o-o nice of him," she said, looking bored now thinking Bettina had finished.

"Captain Sebastián stated you're his wife, and he can do anything he wants with you!"

Bettina bit her lower lip — waiting.

"Ooooh, he did, did he?" With a snap of the brush over the ends of her hair, Daniella continued in the same vein. "Just like that, hmm?" Her eyes sparkled a mischievous cobalt blue. "I would like to see him try." The ivory-handled brush slammed down onto the settee. "That deceitful, unscrupulous, foul-born captain has used me for the last time!" She stood, walking across the cabin, tossing her shining tresses over her shoulder, clear down to the small of her back. "It is high time this woman fought back!"

"Good for you, my lady!" Bettina cheered her on, trailing behind to help her dress for the party on board that evening. Excitedly, she went on. "There is some luscious seafood and saffron rice left over from lunch if you'd like a snack, my lady . . . uhmm . . . Daniella. You haven't taken a thing all day."

"No, no, Bettina, food is the last thing on my mind just now. I am not hungry in the least!"

"Let me see." Daniella tapped her bare foot on the floor in front of the huge chifforobe. "Ah, here it is, just the one!"

"Oh, my lady," Bettina said with a gasp. "That gown is black — and indecent!"

Daniella's eyes glittered luminously as she purred from deep within her throat, "Uhmm — *very.*"

Chapter Fifteen

Ships that pass in the night, and speak each
    other in passing,
Only a signal shows and a distant voice in the
    darkness.
                — Henry Wadsworth Longfellow

Gold-veined waves, caught up at the crown of
Daniella's head and fastened with two glittering di-
amond-studded combs, cascaded down her gently
curving back almost to her supple hips. She'd
donned the bewitching black gown, and as soon as
she entered the dining cabin, all the males turned
her way and lustily gawked, so potent was the
spell she wove about them. The lusty Geraldina,
seated close beside Juan, sumptuous breasts pressing against his arm, looked up at the unblemished
beauty and flashed a smirk across to the young
woman.

Daniella knew at once here was an enemy to
reckon with and managed as graciously as she
could, withering the auburn-haired Geraldina's
confidence with a radiant, self-possessed smile.
Geraldina's shaken confidence suffered an even
greater setback as Juan Tomaz shot to his feet and
went to greet the lovely blond creature who had
stepped into the cabin like a glorious goddess
draped in black velvet. The midnight gown clung

to Daniella's slim curves, drawing amorous attention from many an officer and captain; their noses twitched at the scent of exotic spice perfume wafting after her.

"*Buenas tardes,* Señora Landaker," Juan greeted, and like the handsome gallant he was, brown fingers lifted her lily-white hand to press his lips in a gently adoring kiss.

"I am so happy to see you again, Captain Tomaz," Daniella said in her pleasing voice. Her crystal-clear eyes were glittering mischievously and Juan smiled into them, wondering what she was up to.

While Juan showed her to the chair on the other side of his, Daniella glanced at the irritated young Geraldina whose face was turned at the moment, and Daniella took in the high cheekbones which had been rouged with a heavy hand. Her eyes were beadlike, silver-bright, her laughter quick and throaty as she conversed with a hook-nosed man on the other side of her. Her russet hair was covered with a see-through spangled net depicting green-and-gold mermaids. Her skirts were satin and sumptuous. Geraldina acted as if Daniella were not even present in the long hall decorated with large Atlantean pieces of furniture and heavy drapes curtaining off one end in red and gold.

Daniella was introduced around the table. She had a hard time to keep from giggling when the homely face of Captain Gancho greeted her. He stood to bow from the waist in a gentlemanly fashion, booming explosively to her in Spanish, "*El gusto es mio, señora!*" and reached over to caress her hand lightly, then sat back down smiling at her with adoration in deep-socketed eyes which never seemed to leave her face and figure.

"I am happy to meet you, too," Daniella said to the man, then leaned to Juan to ask what Captain Gancho had said.

With a smile, Juan whispered, "He said, 'The pleasure is mine, señora!' "

As she sipped from the goblet which had been set down in front of her, Daniella grimaced, setting the strong drink aside and reaching for her tall water glass instead.

"You do not like alcoholic drinks," Juan noted, making it sound like a statement.

"You are very observant, Captain, and correct. Strong drink is not to my liking. I much prefer fruit juices — orange, lemon, or lime."

"I am drinking catawba. There is no liquor in it. Here, I'll pour you some from the pitcher and I promise you you'll like it."

After testing it and licking her lips, she nodded. "You are right; it is very good and refreshing." Though she was not imbibing inebriants, her cheeks were nonetheless pink and flushed as her overbright eyes roamed the table in search of . . .

Observing Daniella closely, Juan leaned closer, delighting in the fragrance of her exotic perfume. "Captain Landaker will be joining us shortly." He grinned handsomely as he passed the gulls' eggs and dark bread to her, and Daniella placed a portion of each on her plate.

She looked up at Juan and caught his knowing smile. With a toss of her bright head, she smiled back saucily. "I could have been looking for someone else?"

"Unlikely, señora." He followed her gaze to the curtained area and inclined his head as if relaying a secret to her.

Keeping an eye to the heavy damask curtain Daniella did her share of flirting with the men and conversing in her winning manner. It wasn't long before Daniella had dragged all male attention her way, leaving Geraldina fuming as she picked viciously at her delicately cooked salmon and cast haughty smirks toward the youthful beauty who was capturing all the men's hearts.

Geraldina had plans of her own where the other young woman was concerned, and had it in mind to capture the dashing Captain Sebastián's attention as soon as his presence was made known. She had overheard Juan address *her* as Señora Landaker, and she also had overheard some gossip concerning the estrangement of the newly married couple. As there was already trouble in the wind why not make a little more between them, was Geraldina's way of thinking. She rose from her seat, deciding it was a good time as any to begin.

As Geraldina came around behind the other woman's chair her silver eyes roved, curiously hostile, over Daniella Landaker. Juan remained silent for now, thinking how Geraldina reminded him of a white slug, a crawling creature which made its way between dark curtains, over walls, finding out what should not be known.

A lock of sleek auburn hair fell over Geraldina's eyes. Her gown was deep copper and of the stuff called silk-sarcenet that, it was said, had come long ago from the East with the Crusaders. It swirled, lightweight, and made her movements graceful; but Juan thought she could never equal Daniella in the blonde's liquid golden movement.

As Geraldina made herself at home beside Juan

her glinting eyes studied Daniella's black gown with green envy. A ribbon of silver bound it under the breasts and the neck was cut daringly low, displaying the soft satin-white flesh. The sleeves puffed and slashed cunningly after the manner of Italy, and the overskirt looped to show an underskirt of white, ductile silver.

"We must content ourselves with the dull flavor of this wine, *sí?*" Geraldina raised her glass, her mouth curving as she flashed Juan a wicked smile, whisking her gaze from the blonde's glamorous gown which flattered her classical features and made Geraldina pale in comparison. She grit her teeth hard.

"Pare!" Juan warned, and when Geraldina wondered why he had told her to stop, he went on in a casual tone. "Be careful, *chica,* the wine may be drugged."

Geraldina tossed her head with all the haughtiness she could muster. "Surely you jest, Juan Tomaz!"

He shrugged nonchalantly. "Perhaps."

"Certainly you are making sport with Geraldina, *eh?*"

"Again . . . perhaps."

Juan sat reflecting on the night he had met Geraldina. He had been in Lisbon, she visiting a cousin there. As he'd entered the great Spanish-brick mansion and saw her standing there, a quick understanding had passed between them and he'd experienced the flaming leap in his blood and the old familiar tautness like an ache in his loins. He made no mistake about it. She desired him, and like a rutting stag he, in turn, wanted her. Geraldina had received his message to meet him later, and she was waiting for him upstairs in her broad-ceilinged bedchamber that overlooked the moonlit garden. Their savage meeting had been passionate beyond anything he had imagined . . . *Dios!* almost animallike, he recalled now with a shudder of revulsion!

Juan tried not to remember the rest, but the memory of the distasteful liaison returned like fleas in a mongrel's shaggy coat. For six months they had lain together in sin. He had thought himself to be deeply in love with the auburn-haired vixen and thought to marry her to make it right. And then he had caught her in that same canopied bed with one of his best friends. Geraldina had wailed and battered her fists against his chest, but they were finished, and to this day she sought him out still. But Geraldina did not compare to his new love, for it was like standing a soul-killing witch beside a fairytale maiden.

"Eh, Juan?" Geraldina snapped him out of his vision as she cut across his lusty reflections with her slightly slurred voice. "What are you doing, hmm? Dreaming of another woman? Oooh, I will be much jealous if you are!"

"If you want the truth, Geraldina, *sí,* I was doing just that."

"So, *querido mio,* what is her name?" Geraldina cast a suspicious eye in Daniella's direction, but that one seemed still distracted by the curtained area of the room.

"Her name?" The woman he had fallen deeply and everlastingly in love with? The precious one he ached to love and be inside her heart forever? To be with her as two souls eternal. To have little ones with her. "She is Eileena," he said like a ca-

236

ress. But it might never be, he might never make love to the one woman in his life he cried for, because the one he loved lived in her own dark, frightening world from which she might never surface!

"Oooh *Dios,* Juan, you make Geraldina wildly jealous when you speak like this!"

"I will not say I am sorry, Geraldina." When she tossed him a sulky pout, Juan turned an indifferent shoulder to her and pressed for more intelligent conversation with the beautiful creature at his other elbow. "Señora Landaker." Juan laughed lightly when she turned a startled face to him. "Would you give me the pleasure of your company for a time? I am put out that you lavish all your attention on the other men present here and save not a morsel of your charming self for Juan."

Daniella's gay laughter tinkled like an enchanted silver bell, capturing all male ears — and hearts, too.

"But, Captain Juan, please, there are so many handsome gentlemen present I cannot make up my mind who to converse with next. They are all so intelligent, too. Why just a minute past, Captain Gancho was telling me — "

Daniella's heart leapt in time with her fast-thumping pulse as the curtain was drawn aside with a brisk flick of a darkly tanned hand. He wore a green silk shirt tucked into *gris pantalones,* taut over lean hips and thighs, while a long dangerous-looking sword was suspended from a deep-umber sash. He stood tall and commanding, savage and untamed as the turquoise sea. His island-green eyes swept the room, not deigning to cast so much as a glance in her direction.

Juan scraped to his booted feet, leaving Geraldina with a drowned-cat expression as her eyes passed from one handsome captain to the other. Sebastián and Juan. Such men, *ah!* Her thick reddish lashes came to roost heavy-laden on Captain Sebastián, and she knew she was lost to his virile, heart-stopping charms.

Ah, *Dios!* Lost again. She had tried with him and failed. He had been too much of a man for her, making her look stupid and girlish, sending her packing with a look that withered, but she now told herself she would renew her seduction subtly and first agitate the already shaky ground between him and his sickeningly lovely bride.

Wingbeats of heavy desire pulsated through Daniella as she stared at the man who claimed to be her husband. She was angry at herself for desiring this man who had deceived her so cruelly and opened the flower of love in her heart, now only to crush it beneath his booted feet as he ignored her, as he had done the past week and would continue to do!

Bittersweet emotions coursed through Daniella with an intensity she had never known before in all her nineteen years. Anger, frustration, confusion tumbled about in her mind. Oh, yes, she desired Sebastián with a passion that would forever and ever prevail. But she must remember that she had closed her heart to him and whatever she might feel for him in the future. Yet. . . !

A profound feeling of excitement claimed Daniella as Sebastián raked his scrutiny over her, and, finally, her own defiant eyes met his tigerish ones. Daniella's heart fluttered with a foolish beat, and she was the first one to tear her gaze from his.

As her tawny lashes fluttered down, her heartbeat caught in her throat, and Daniella knew she was caught up in a dangerous sinking desire from which she prayed she would someday be able to escape!

Now he was coming her way! And he looked none too happy as he halted beside her chair, gazing down at the top of her head, her shoulders, her . . . *dear God,* she was spilling out of the black gown! The amorous glaze fled his eyes, his breath was sucked in for a moment, then was released as the question rang out in the suddenly hushed room.

The line of Sebastián's mouth hardened. *"Dios,* where did you get that gown?"

"I borrowed it, *sir*—from your own cabin aboard this ship."

"My name is Sebastián—address me as such."

"Captain *Sebastián,"* Geraldina took up and gushed, holding out her hand for him to take as she reached across in front of Daniella's frowning face.

Sebastián glared at the proffered hand as if she were offering him a disease he didn't want to contract. Geraldina was miffed for the moment but everyone present knew she would recover soon enough, for Geraldina was persistent as shooed flies returning to a dung heap.

"Ah, Lady Landaker is so charming, *sí?"* Geraldina asked around the table, receiving nods for her strenuous effort. Geraldina saw that she was getting the response that she so desired from the handsome captain, for his anger was darkening into a wrathful jealousy. She decided to stick the honed blade deeper. "She has been entertaining the

239

officers and captains—and look! They all are smitten with her!" She was not letting this fish get away this time! "Ooh, *querido*, you are so fortunate to have such an *entertaining* bride."

The red-haired bitch! Sebastián swung on Geraldina, asking in a low, sibilant tone, "How in hell did you know Daniella was my bride?"

"Madre mia! Captain, darling, she was introduced as *Lady* Landaker, do you not know?" Geraldina shrugged as if it could not be otherwise.

Sebastián ignored Geraldina to hiss into Daniella's ear. "Go to our cabin and remove that dress . . . at once! Do you hear?"

Daniella looked up to see Sebastián's pinched face so near her own. "I most certainly will not!" she said, tossing abundant honeyed waves across one bared shoulder.

Sebastián sighed as if angrily impatient with a naughty child, then sat down beside her, taking her arm with a threatening little squeeze to her elbow. "No? Then I shall tear it from your lovely body right here for all men to see! And, *cálida,* my loving bride, the men will really be in for a sweetmeat to feast their hungry eyes upon . . . I might even be pressed to toss them a morsel or two!"

"What do you mean?" she asked, her voice trembling.

"I mean, my lovely dark rose," he began, looking with deep earnestness into her suddenly apprehensive face. "Their *eyes* will feast on your naked loveliness, as I've said. But I lied a moment ago, for I will forever be the only man who will ever *taste* of your charms."

He is jealous! Daniella thought, feeling light-

240

hearted of a sudden. She had actually succeeded in making Sebastián jealous . . . *It must have been what I intended all the while,* tumbled about in her mind wickedly.

"Now go, *querida,*" he ordered thickly, staring at her bosom . . . breasts he'd thought beneath a mouthful — but not this night! "Before I fulfill my threat!" he gruffly added.

Daniella understood that Sebastián meant every word he said, but she didn't want to be humiliated, like a child, to return with another gown on her back to replace the bewitching black one!

"Please, let us compromise, Sebastián. If you will be so kind as to have someone fetch me a shawl from my cabin?" She begged prettily and touched him lightly upon his silk-sleeved arm. "Please, *querido,*" she tried, recalling a Spanish word of endearment — she hoped! — she'd heard Geraldina earlier employ.

As if mulling this over, Sebastián stared downward, a thrill running through him . . . and then he looked up into her soulful sea-gray eyes, a passionate hue now that he remembered well when she'd been hungry with aching desire for Steven. *Dios!* she made him ache hard in the groin just looking at her. Desire for her filled him to the brim. His eyes slipped lower, to the hollows of her ivory throat he knew would be warm and silken if he should wish to nibble and slide his tongue along the ivory column.

"Sebastián?" Daniella's soft voice finally reached into the smoldering corners of his besotted brain.

Sebastián nodded his head in a small bow. "You may have the shawl." His eyes delved deeply into hers and he saw the blue rapture in them. "You may have anything your heart desires, *cálida*." If only she knew that *cálida* meant loving and ardent little one!

As Rascon scurried off to fetch the shawl, Daniella turned her eyes upon Sebastián once again. "*Anything,* you say?"

"*Sí.* Within reason." He picked at the salmon and popped the delicious morsel into his mouth, eating slowly, sensuously, while she watched the movements of his shapely mouth.

Daniella shifted uncomfortably. "I wish to return to the Carolinas, Sebastián!"

He swallowed hard. "Now?"

"Yes. *Now.*"

Casually Sebastián forked another piece of pink-fleshed salmon. "That is impossible. I have unfinished business that needs clearing up." He washed the salmon down with a long swallow of cool water brought aboard ship from a bubbling spring near the cove. "Ah . . . here it is."

The shawl, a dawn-mist silver, was brought to Daniella. She could not believe her eyes when Rascon handed it to her and smiled in a friendly fashion. He had smiled, actually *smiled* at her! *That* meant something, she thought, if nothing else did. Then the lad sighed, as if in boredom, looking this way and that as he blushed, then took off in a quick-walking gait to fetch more ale for those who were calling for it.

For several moments Daniella sat with a happy smile as she stared after Rascon. She had longed to be his friend, and as time went by, she thought she'd never see the day Rascon would smile at her or show any sign of friendliness.

"What are you suddenly so happy about?" Sebastián asked her, loving to see her looking so radiant and lighthearted. "I have told you it will be a while before we return to the Carolinas."

Daniella's heart dropped, for she suddenly remembered another area in which Sebastián had deceived her. "Never mind *why* I smiled. I have a question for you, sir. Why have we never reached Land's End but instead are on our way to some foreign country?"

"My beautiful wife is disappointed again." Sebastián chucked her under the chin as if she were a mere child in need of coddling.

Taken by surprise, Daniella's lashes flew upward and she stared into his handsome, smiling face. He never had called her "wife" before . . . and the sound of it pleased her intensely.

"We *are* going to stop in Cornwall, love, on our way back to Charleston Harbor."

"Oh, but for now we are chasing searobbers." She had given up the belief that Sebastián and Juan Tomaz were pirates, for Juan's conversation had returned to her in the still of one night, and as she'd watched the moon flit by the eyelike window, she'd recalled clearly every word they had told her. If they had been telling the honest to God's truth—which she believed they had—then they were no more pirates than the man in the moon!

Sebastián looked at her meaningfully. "They will chase us, and *we* will catch *them*," he told her softly.

"Strategy, Captain?" she asked, remembering the map she had seen in his cabin aboard the *Emerald Tiger*.

"*Sí,* love, strategy."

She was worried suddenly. "Is the *Rampant Rose* going to be used as decoy as formerly planned?"

"You've the memory of an elephant, Daniella. No, we are not going to use the ship your father named you af—"

Madre de Dios! What was wrong with him? Why did he have to go and mention her father just now when they seemed to be getting along so well. He should have closed his mouth on that subject—and now he'd gone and stuck his foot in it!

Tawny lashes flashed down, then up again. "You can say it, Sebastián. I am over the worst of it now. He is a loving memory, and somehow I am brought closer to him in his death. Never had I realized what people meant—that after a beloved one parted from this earth, the departed would be closer—*seem* closer. But now I do, even though he is not with me in the flesh, dear Papa."

Sebastián had the grace to look embarrassed. "I am sorry."

"Do not be, Sebastián." Her voice gathered forceful momentum then. "But now I *am* having a hard time forgetting how cruelly you treated me that night, how you all but ravished me aboard your ship. Not to mention that you used me as your decoy to trap the *Raven!*"

"As I had at that time, I mean only to confuse those pirates aboard the *Raven,*" he stated simply. "To get the captain going in circles like a cat chasing its own tail is the first order in my plan of action."

"But to use me as your decoy! That is unforgivable . . ." She shook her head. "And the disguise . . ." Why, she wondered now, why the

244

disguise in the first place? In case Robert or Lucian had showed up before or after the wedding? Had Sebastián been trying to look like someone else, like the *real* Steven Landaker, and would Sebastián don the foppish guise at the end of this dangerous charade, she wondered with sunken heart?

"I cannot forget what you did, Steven . . ." Her eyes flew wide. "I mean—Sebastián."

His voice went deep and husky. "Then let me help you forget, Daniella. Sleep with me in my arms tonight, *cálida.*"

Daniella was shocked. That he could even ask such a thing after all that had happened! Did he not realize how much she despised him? Why was her body betraying her, telling her she needed his touch to come alive, to be lifted from the lethargic state she felt after being absent from his arms?

Hugging the shawl closer about her, Daniella gazed up into his passionate tiger-green eyes.

"Will you?" He shifted closer, hugging her arm folded gently but firmly into the crook of his arm, brushing her lovely breast with a feather-touch of his elbow. "I shall make you swoon in ecstasy's bliss, and you will never forget this night as long as you live. I make that a promise to you . . . my *tigressa roseta!*"

There was an awkward silence after Sebastián had closed the door behind them and gave a sharply definite click to the lock of the cabin. He stood there watching Daniella with his heart in his eyes as she stared at the huge bed she had yet to sleep in. But this night and only this night would

245

he share it with her, her first night aboard the *Spanish Wind*. After he loved her, and thoroughly, perhaps for the last time, he would leave her and board the *Emerald Tiger*.

"Come here, Daniella, and let me do that for you." His voice was husky and passionate as he held his hand out to her to come to her aid with the tiny buttons at the back of the ravishing black gown. "It would certainly be less trouble if the fastenings were in front," he said with a deep catch in his voice as she came to him and showed him her back. "Ah, but that delight will come soon enough," he said. There was a slight trembling in his fingers as he undid the buttons, then bent forward to plant a dizzying kiss upon the nape of her velvet neck as he held the mass of fragrant hair aside. "You, too, are trembling. Do you want me so much, *querida?*"

When he was finished with his task, she turned half circle in his arms and pressed her cheek tenderly against his warm, strong hand. Her voice was soft. "Oh, yes, I want you, my tawny tiger." The bewitching black thing slid along the slender column of her figure, slipping sensuously along between their aching, sensitive bodies, until at last reaching the floor to form a black pool that was almost invisible but for the shot of pale silver twinkling up at them. But they were unmindful of anything but each other as Sebastián gazed down at the delicate lace of the undergarments she wore, then removed them slowly, maddeningly.

Lips, thighs, bellies, hips touched and ground together in a tender erotic play of shameless ecstasy, and then Daniella wanted to be even closer and stepped back to undress her husband—her

246

muscled, determined tiger who did not pounce but brought his body slinking against her gloriously undraped loveliness and cherished every ivory-fleshed inch of her.

Ever so slowly his hands moved downward, gliding along either side of her body and on down to her thighs, awakening again for Daniella total awareness of the delightful mysteries existing between man and woman.

His face was shining with love and lust as her mouth trembled against his own. "Daniella . . ." Their lips fused together while their tongues performed a lusty dance in and along each other's mouth. Sebastián stepped back then, breaking the lusty embrace, his glittering eyes luring her onward as he encircled her waist and led her to the comfortable love nest awaiting them.

The tall candles threw a welcoming, caressing glow over the deep, canopied bed, and Sebastián turned with her in his arms and fell back onto the downy softness, taking her with him, naked limbs entwining while Daniella placed her hands upon his shoulders and pulled his bronzed face to hers for a kiss that was like a dance of fire against his lips. Glorious long hair became tangled between their bodies and she softly cried out, and he shifted, releasing the long strand that slid along his belly, making him groan from the provocative sensation created against his already scorched flesh.

Daniella drew her slim arms in front of her with an instinctive, playful gesture, and then, seeing the naked silvery demand in his eyes, flung up her head, laughing with throaty delight as she wound her arms about his neck. She realized the power woman had over man, and her hips rose up against his seeking fingers. Now she clung to him in absolute surrender, his strength hard against her silken frame.

Sebastián's fingers raked amid silver-blond strands, stroked at her temples, and up and down her ivory throat. The strong, tormenting fingers dropped lower again and she tingled with bold responsiveness. Then he was kissing her all over, lifting her straight before him as he bent on his knees, burying his face in the cleft between her breasts, pressing her breasts to his cheeks. He moved slowly, maddeningly, to kiss her hips and belly and the two soft, sloping angles where her shapely body slanted lusciously inside her thighs. There he suckled the pink pearl of womanhood, sipped honeyed wine, and delved with thrusting, slashing tongue.

The sensation was wild, like being left wide open to a sensuous storm with savage waves slapping in and against her most secret hull. She was afraid to move, afraid to breathe for fear the powerful tugging and hot plunging would come to an end far too abruptly. Before reaching that final pinnacle, when she was tossing her head, and starting to shift her hips and arch, Sebastián moved up over her and ceased all moment. She gazed up at him, a wild look of torment shining in her eyes.

"Please, don't stop. Let me feel you inside me . . . Steven!"

He growled against her throat, "Sebastián." He commanded huskily, "My name is Sebastián. Say it and I will be inside you, *cálida!*"

"Sebastián!" she gasped and tugged his shoul-

248

ders. It took every effort she could summon not to scream and beg for him to take her!

As he moved between her legs, heating her whole body with scorching flames, Daniella's heart gave a wild leap. A musky male smell mingled with a sweet, feminine odor as he circled her entrance with the pulsing, red-hot tip of his desire, flesh to flesh, in a deeply passionate mating kiss. Stimulating the juices of love to flow, Sebastián readied her while Daniella bit almost through her lip as desperation mushroomed and a profound feeling of excitement flowed.

The invitation of her body flowered and opened like a rosebud in summer's first kiss of sunlight. Now, his teasing and taunting over, he gathered the tensed muscles of his thighs and hips in a fiery heat and plunged deeply within her. His silvered gaze burned into hers. He rode her and she bucked high, meeting him thrust for thrust. Frantic and wild, she sank her nails into his muscled shoulders, lifted and closed her legs about his thrusting hips, arching upward to meet him again.

Convulsive pleasure overtook her. He followed into the hot damp of rippling flesh and they rose together, almost flung across the room in their explosive coming. When the tempestuous tide receded, a shaft of moonlight pierced the window's eye and found them sheened with the silken sweat of love. She wanted desperately to question him of the Rebecca whose name she'd seen in the journal: "Rebecca . . . only if we had shared some happiness together. I hardly knew her . . . still I love her and forever and ever shall." The remembrance hurt like salt on a new wound as Daniella watched him rise from the bed, muscled, tigerish, masculine . . .

He stopped all movement to gaze down into eyes silvered from moonlight pouring into the high, leaded windows. "You were beautiful in that gown tonight, *cálida*. You bewitched every man there. I wonder how many pining hearts did you leave here tonight and behind in the Carolinas?"

A look of pain crossed her face, for she had been reminded of Robert Drake, the young man she had sworn in her heart to love and cherish forever, but that had been an immature yearning, not fully developed, not passionate or possessive— nor was it excitingly stormy as this relationship had proven to be! Daniella still ignored Sebastián's question, coming upright in a deliberate effort to avoid his knowing eyes reading the tormented look on her face. Oh, God—how she had come to need this man, as the flowers needed the sun and the rain and cool nights to fully bloom and survive!

Sebastián was silent, his face shadowed and impassive as he stared down at the bed, not realizing she'd risen until her soft voice came to him from out of the moon's fitful shadows. Then he felt her beside him and he listened to her answer his question.

"I left no broken hearts," she answered in truth, for Robert was there no longer, but out here, she believed, here on the moonlit sea searching for her. If he came for her, if he captured this ship, what would she do? Was Robert the real pirate? Would she willingly go with her childhood sweetheart, even if he proved to be a searobber? But Robert had been her playmate, her friend, nothing more, wasn't this true? Could she learn to love Robert and desire him as she desired Sebastián? She

250

thought not.

There was a slight edge to Sebastián's voice when at last he spoke again. "Why did my question cause you such distress, Daniella — so much, in fact, that you had to rise from the bed to be away from me?"

The brilliance of her gray eyes was visible now as the night deepened and the moon slanted across the heavens, showering moonbeams into the cabin. "I refuse to dignify your hasty words with a reply," she snapped, trying to pull away from the strong grip on her arm.

"You avoid what is plain for any man with eyes to see." With bent elbow he looked up at her, his other hand still holding her fast, seeing nothing but her glossy hair cascading down her sleek back. "Who is it that holds the golden key to your heart, *cálida?*" His hold tightened, biting into her soft flesh. "Is it Robert Drake?" His brow darkened furiously. "Is it, my cruel, tempting rose?"

Breaking free of his bruising grip, Daniella stood from the massive bed and crossed the room to gather her underthings. She dressed quickly, wondering all the while why he did not rush across the room to stop her. When she heard his deep chuckle, with an underlying element of anger, she stood still, her smooth, naked body cast like a golden Venus as the moonbeams reached her where she had halted.

"You professed to have fallen in love with Steven, if I rightly recall?" He reminded her of the breathless endearment she had cried out as they'd made love. "What of that? So fickle in your affections, Daniella, my love?" There was a mocking tone of laughter in his voice. "Am I the last besotted fool left brokenhearted by the prickly dark rose?"

"Why do you laugh?" she asked, ignoring that same curious endearment he always used when irritated with her.

"I asked you a question. Must you come back with one of your own?" When she said nothing, but stood there in all her sensual allure, he made her aware of her foolish gestures to fly from him. "Where are you going? Why are you dressing? You will only have to come back here to this bed you share with your *husband* this night."

With the black gown held loosely in her hand, her expression helpless, knowing she was his captive bride, she wisely questioned, "Why do you say *this* night? Will there not be other nights in which you will come to torment me, as you are doing now?"

Sebastián's eyes glittered as he pondered the situation. He came to his feet, lithe and catlike as the feline for which his ship was named.

"I'm afraid you have been deluding yourself, Daniella, if you think Lord Steven Landaker shared the same devotion you swore for him."

"Oh!" Daniella said with an enraged gasp, "you are contemptible! First you forced me into an unwanted marriage—"

"Unwanted?" He snorted, lifting a tawny brow. "Your adoration for Lord Landaker was well known. You could not wait to be wedded so that dandy could take you to his bed."

"Oh, it was not *his* bed but *mine.*"

He executed a mocking bow from the waist. "Indeed—*your* bed, *querida.*"

Realizing that she had been enticed and caught

252

by the bait, she seethed with injured pride and sought to remind him of his many sins, when hers had only been to love a simple foppish gentleman.

"You deceived me! You used me as a decoy! You disguised yourself to wed me! And for what? No one follows us even now! Oh!" She flung the bewitching black gown to the floor, little realizing the effect the sight of her clad in only her lacy underthings was having upon his recently cooled ardor. "How I wish that Robert would come!" She saw the blazing hurt in his eyes, and dug the thorn deeper. "He and I could have been lovers for all that we shared in our happy childhood — always together, promising that nothing would come between us. But you . . . *you* tore us apart. *Why?* Robert and I might have become husband and wife if you had not come along to spoil it all!" She took a deep breath. "You could never become the sweet, gentle man you pretended to be. I . . . I hate you! Do you hear? You are a wicked, conniving devil. I hate you!"

"Enough! You have already made your revulsion quite clear." He stepped closer. "But tell me this: Who will be your lover when you are lying in your bed of desire, when no one comes to ease the ache between your thighs? *Ciertamente* you shall pine long for your husband to hold you in his arms when the lonely nights are upon you. Who will have you then? Your beloved Robert? Hah! That one is hopelessly mad. I cannot believe you have not witnessed the crazed light in his eyes. All the Drakes are crazy as horned loons!" He bent to plant a warm kiss in the palm of her hand, then he began to back to the door, still bowing low. "I wish you *buen viaje!*"

With that, Sebastián walked out of the spacious cabin, leaving Daniella staring miserably at the floorboards. He had extracted from her exactly what he wanted. To see her miserable! To leave her suffering!

Cheat! Liar! Sebastián was the one who was mad!

But there was one thing he would never have again, a part of her she would hold henceforth from him—from any man. And that was her love.

Chapter Sixteen

From the enclosed inlet where, over the years, accumulated masses of fallen rock had gathered, the *Emerald Tiger* sailed out while the stars still stood out like a necklace of diamonds strung across an endless bodice of softest velvet gray.

Throughout the day, as the sun shot up to glare like a sea monster's yellow eye in the blue vastness, both the wind and the current were adverse, so that the *Tiger* made very poor speed.

Two days out, Captain Sebastián paced the deck forward and aft, his tiger-eyes alive and alert. His mouth was held tautly and his fingers clenched and unclenched. The gun crew held at the ready for any sign of the enemy, the faintest streak of color on the horizon. Any sudden burst of action, and they would rush to the black-snouted guns. There were only six guns in all—primed and on the ready!

Jaecko was not his usual self, no longer rending the crew to laughter and jeers with his tales of virgins won and abandoned, and of the boastful things that sailors forever talk about. Instead his mood was blue and gloomy without his brown-eyed Bettina. He looked over the side, watching the silvery-green tunny, mullet, bonito swimming in the turquoise sea. Still, all was not lost, for he was going to meet her in Cornwall—if that was where they ended up—and then they would be wed in the

Carolinas, as she wished.

Too, Captain Sebastián was not in one of his best moods. Everywhere he looked, Daniella's eyes seemed to lift from the blue-gray sea and mock his low spirits. From the pocket of his buff breeches, he pulled out the glittering tiger pin he had filched from among her belongings when she hadn't been looking. Turning it over in his hand, he stared down into the tiny, beautifully fashioned emerald eyes which seemed to mock him just as cruelly as her own eyes had. The creature's body was made of gold wire drawn almost to the fineness of human hair and soldered together in a pattern so intricate as to defy the skill of the makers of the finest Spanish jewelry.

Sebastián's long, tanned fingers ran over the ruby heart and he grimaced as the sharp pin in back pricked him and the tiny drops of blood mingled with the ruby red of the tiger's heart. He recalled now who had gifted her with the priceless object: Alain Carstairs. How many other precious baubles had the man given her? he wondered now as he replaced the tiger pin. Even more significant, Sebastián asked himself, why had he taken it with him? Would she even miss it? He had not seen her wearing it often . . . Sebastián also knew that Alain Carstairs had obtained the precious object from a crew member who served aboard the *Spanish Wind*, a man who no doubt sold the pretty bauble for a hefty price. When Sebastián had questioned Captain Gancho as to the man's whereabouts, he said Nino had left not long after selling the pin he'd stolen from a pretty señorita's bedside as she slept!

Sebastián's tawny brows beetled over the bridge of his nose. He had been compelled to don the

256

guise of Steven Landaker once again, this last time
when he had spotted the *Rampant Rose* on the horizon, and while Daniella napped aboard the *Tiger,*
he had hailed and caught up with the Wingate ship
and had his man take him by longboat. Daniella
had not known of his visit upon the sea to the
Rampant Rose. He had not talked to the captain
but to the lieutenant, who informed him that Alain
Carstairs was very ill. He wouldn't wish to contract
a fever, if that was what had been ailing the man.

The lieutenant was called Charles Blackman, and
for some reason, there had been something faintly
familiar about the man—his walk, his body movements . . . Sebastián couldn't put his finger on it
. . but one day it would come to him, and when
t did, he hoped for Blackman's sake that the man
hadn't crossed him or the Landakers in some way.
There were two, the Drakes, he was after now, and
he wouldn't like to make it three!

Sebastián's mouth curled with an unpleasant
twist. Actually it *had* been three, for he had already
taken care of the dark rose, and he only hoped that
he had left her with child. He had deceived her;
used her well and good; fraught her with confusion; caused her to fall in love with Steven Landaker . . . *Dios!* that was good for a laugh. The
beautiful Daniella Wingate in love with a swell
dandy, one who was dead to her, yet one he could
create within minutes if he so wished!

He caught himself up short. Wingate? The laugh
was on him this time. She was now Daniella Landaker. *His wife*. He was forever *married*. The name he
had signed to the document had been Sebastián
Landaker. Daniella's father had witnessed the name
his pen had put down. From their first meeting,

Edward had encouraged the marriage. Wha
Edward had *not* known was the subsequent ruse h
had invented while wearing the disguise in order t
catch the spy who had long been working agains
the Established Merchant Fleet. He was almost cer
tain the spy had been present that morning whe
they had held a meeting at Braidwood and Daniell
had appeared in the room like a bewitching angel i
the lovely plum gown.

Sebastián frowned. Another thing Edwar
Wingate had not been aware of was his true ap
pearance, minus the heavy makeup and black wi
he'd always worn while in residence at Braidwood
Sebastián doubted the spy had ever met with hir
before, nor did he have knowledge of who he reall
was.

For a moment, Sebastián wore a curious smile
Perhaps Edward himself had known all along, o
suspected something at the beginning. One thin
was certain: Edward had known he was dying an
wished to get Daniella far from him before his fina
suffering began. There was no need for Edward t
have told him because the older man's eyes had sai
it all: *Please take my daughter far from here s
that she might not watch me die!*

Sebastián sighed. Dear God, at least he had ac
complished one good deed, for a dying old ma
who had been so sad, with huge tears in his eyes a
he watched the carriage laden with baggage remov
his daughter to the ship. Sebastián had looked u
to see Edward's hand move, frail and white agains
the window as he waved. And then later he ha
appeared to see her off. Again, there was a worl
of sadness in his eyes as he watched his daughte
sail away, watched her wave from afar for the las

time ever. *Dios.*

Suddenly Sebastián's fist crashed against the bulkhead, and then he pressed the pained member into his palm to seek some comforting softness after the hard shock of the blow. Edward Wingate had loved his daughter dearly, and placed her in his care . . . *placed her in his care* . . . and what had he done? *Ay di mi!* He had done exactly the opposite, and tangled up her life so badly that she couldn't know who to trust any longer. He was no better than those whose blasted hides he sought revenge upon. Yet, clearly, Daniella was in love with Robert Drake, at least *thought* she was, the little fool!

Who is really the fool? he asked himself. He'd taken her with him in order to lure the *Raven* to him. Why hadn't he taken the *Raven* when the chance was presented to him like an apple-stuffed pig on a platter?

Sebastián began to pace the decks, ruffling his thick tawny hair with his fingers. He knew why indeed! The reason he had done nothing was Daniella—the *only* reason. His cruel treatment of her had been uncalled for, and he had seen the play of surprise in his crew's eyes as he had handled her roughly and threatened to bind her to the mast. He was the devil who should have been lashed to the post and given a sound beating!

Then he told himself he could let her go . . . give her her sought-after freedom. He needn't ever darken her door again, and she would live happily ever after without him tormenting her. But the tables were turned and the torment would be his—especially when the night descended and soul-raking desire to have her wrapped in his arms overtook his better sensibilities . . . No, he could not live in the same house without going to her, and even now he wanted her with a fiery desire that gave him no ease from his torment!

God help him, he had come to need Daniella, as he needed food and water to sustain life. How long, he wondered now, could he live without being near her, the vibrant and lovely rose who was like a glorious flame to him? He had left her with the same warning, that she would pine for him when he was gone . . . but would she? Did she miss him even now? Were there tears in her eyes because he had deserted her? Or had she recaptured happiness in the thought she would soon be going home to Braidwood?

Perhaps, he told himself as he walked to the wooden rail, when a year was played out, the tale would be told. *Sí,* he would leave her alone for a year if he could . . . if she did not grow heavy with child and send for him. But would she see him even then? He thought not.

Sebastián had departed three days before, confident that Captain Gancho and Juan—whom he'd left in charge of Daniella—would not allow any harm to come her way. If there should be any sort of trouble, they had been ordered to take her to Cornwall posthaste. All spices, excluding his own load, had been transferred to the *Sea Horse, Trade Wind, Wind Star,* and *Wind Spirit.*

Sebastián's lonesome reverie was interrupted by the lookout's shout. "Ship astern . . . four points to starboard!"

Exploding into action, Captain Sebastián ran aft again, his officers coming at right angles. Standing back, the captain began to shout orders at the top of his lungs, and instantly the billowing shrouds were full of figures that strained and tugged at their tasks.

"She's a corvette, Cap'n, with lines as clean and trim as—is it the *Raven,* Cap'n?" his mate asked.

"Gunners!" Sebastián shouted. "To station! And furl the mainyard up there, mateys!" He stripped to the waist and, tossing his shirt aside, pulled the sash from his waist and bound his head in the gold-and-red cloth, adjusting the knot and flowing ends off to one side. He whipped out his sword and held it just against his hard, lean hip. "Open the scuttles!" he yelled, pacing the quarter-deck, burning with impatience as he caught sight of the *Raven* drawing abeam.

Sebastián knew fear as a great noise burst from the *Raven's* line of guns and the corvette disappeared behind the cloud of smoke. He hit the deck as the balls whizzed over and missed him only by inches. Why this sudden fear? Why hadn't he given the order to fire when it was time? Could this be the fearless Sebastián, who everyone had named the Tiger at the young age of thirty, who had enjoyed all the experiences open to a warrior on land or as a sailor or captain at sea? Again and yet again he had risked his life with devil-may-care attitude, and he had seen an exhausting amount of the world. For eight years he had been tried and tested in the grueling techniques of war. He had learned how to handle both sword and arquebus, tiller and compass, sails and artillery, spade and lance. For long, he had studied navigation and had gained knowledge how to keep a ship's reckoning, was as good a leadsman as the most experienced of pilots, and was as precise a manipulator of the forerunners of quadrant and sextant as any master of astronomy. What others had learned timidly from books, he had learned boldly by repeated experience of calm and storm, battles by land and sea, rapine and siege, onslaught and shipwreck. In the duration of ten years, upon thousands of nights and days, he had learned to await the will of the boundless ocean, ever ready to seize the skirts of happy chance. Too, he had made acquaintance with men and women of all kinds and colors—

Sebastián, in that moment as the balls sang over his head, realized he had been at the mercy of sworn revenge, not sweet but stinging misery, and, as so often when a man seems to be at the mercy of the winds, he was in reality being blown back upon his own self!

Suddenly Sebastián did not wish to die! He did not even want to court danger. He had the wildest desire to live on forever . . . in Daniella's arms. There had not been enough laughter and love and sharing between them. There had been only the bitterness . . . and his selfish anger!

Dios, but neither was he a coward, Sebastián told himself as he snatched up his sword and shot to his feet. Brandishing his sword-arm, he called in a booming voice while the gunners crouched beside their black-snouted pieces, awaiting his signal, "Wait!"

"Wait?!" they echoed back to their puzzled captain.

The corvette was riding so close now that Sebastián could read the name on her bold prow: *El Draque,* he spelled out.

His fists clenched into balls of raging steel, Sebastián cursed the name of Lucian Drake for his

262

involvement in the many deaths of his friends. Twice the Dragon had interfered in and interrupted the lives of those he loved most, and his days of living at the expense of others were nearing an end!

"Gunners!" Sebastián shouted. "Give them hell!!"

Sebastián swiftly motioned another command, and his ship at once veered toward the *El Draque,* and he lifted his sword and then sliced downward, eagerly anticipating sweetest revenge. The *Emerald Tiger*'s stout little guns boomed. "Fire at point-blank, mateys!" Another belly-deep roar from the attacking ship and Sebastián ducked as the balls sizzled overhead and into the sea. "Give it back to them faster than they can serve it to us, mateys!"

The guns roared out one after another, and just when it seemed they were gaining ground, a broadside from the *El Draque* struck them full on. There was the sound of splintering wood and screams of wounded men, and acrid smoke filled Sebastián's throat so that he could not call out the next order.

Suddenly Jaecko appeared at his side, stupefied as he pointed aft, and Sebastián rose to his feet, unaware until that moment that he had fallen to the deck. He turned, his eyes growing enormous with amazement at the closeness with which the green-and-brown hull of the enemy had drifted . . . It filled his whole range of vision. Then the three ships came together with a grinding crash . . . *three ships* . . . for the ominous *Raven* had the *Tiger* pinned from the other side!

The ringing slide of metal as blades left scabbards reached Sebastián's ears as Jaecko announced, "They're boarding us, Cap'n!"

"Aye, and don't I bloody well know it," Sebastián arrogantly sang in his best Englishman's accent.

Reaching for his green silk shirt, he swiftly donned and buttoned it up and plastered his hair down slick with a heavy hand. Then he stepped out, with sword in one hand as he postured and made a dandy leg.

"Aye . . ." Jaecko drawled, "always knew you was the cunning master of disguise, Cap'n. They'll never know you as Sebastián Landaker. The captain will be thinking you're a real fruitcake . . . looking like a pirate one day and then dressing up like a cocky dandy the next!"

"Why, Jaecko, my friend." Sebastián made a leg as the ugly pirates started for them, chipped swords, eyepatches, ragged pantaloons, and all. " 'Tis the bloody pirates. Come ahead, me pretties," he crooned, testing his sword by slashing it wickedly through the air. His blade sang. It danced. It mesmerized.

"What the devil goes here!" a voice cut across the decks, alive now with fighting men.

Boldly, Lucian Drake barged through the swinging swords and plunging daggers amid screams and gurgles of death, stepping to the corner of the ship where several of his crew stood transfixed, unable to attack the dandy who looked no less than a crazy man with smoke-darkened face, white flashing teeth and eye-whites, slashing his sword and testing its tip in the air.

"I'll see if the bucko's got a piker or not!"

The Dragon nonchalantly undid his black cloak and dropped it into the hands of a mate who had stepped up to serve his evil captain. The new gibbous moon glinted on Sir Lucian's sword hilt, and on the cross-handled dagger at his belt. He sneered at the English dandy, and at Jaecko who stood at he man's elbow. The dregs of derisive laughter reverberated in his throat as he spoke . . .

"This strutting peacock would have his feathers pulled!" Sir Lucian spread his thin legs and struck a pose, with his chin held high, his black beard coming to a V pointing directly at the smoke-darkened dandy with the head of hair plastered down like a simpleton's while he coughed aside and sniffed loudly.

"What?" Lucian sneered. "An attack of the vapors?"

Now Sebastián danced and postured, and he had gathered quite a crowd as blades ceased to clash and ring and blood to flow, as men stood with dripping cutlasses and mouths agape, wondering if the dancing dandy himself was a mad simpleton.

Sebastián once again lost his reckoning of danger; he felt only the strong malice before him, the deadly hostility in the glare and the white line of teeth like the death's head flashing in the black beard of Lucian Drake.

Lucian's lips were set thin, and the moonlight ran along the steel blade like diamonds spilling to the deck. Red flecks danced in the Dragon's eyes, and he swung his sword in a half circle, then slicing down viciously with his blade. "Now, peacock," he snarled viciously.

Eager and ready for this fight, Sebastián flung his hair back, making it stand on end in some places. "Pull feathers if you can!" He beckoned with one hand. "Come on . . ."

"Ah," Lucian murmured with satisfaction. A cloud that darkened the moon blotted his inky doublet and hose, leaving only the two points of steel and his evil-grinning smile. The smile was set and

murderous, like a wicked scar it slashed his face. I
was a baleful triumph, a black evil that conjure
up images of Satan himself.

For a few minutes the play was halted as Lucia
ordered his men to take the cutlass from the pea
cock's hand, but when the younger man resisted
brandishing a dangerous arm, the Dragon's crew
leaped back. "Ah, peacock," he said, taking an
other sword from a man standing by, "I only wan
you to fight with a rapier . . . as long as you seem
to be such a dandy. You should feel right at home
with 'thrusting,' hmm?"

Sebastián took the rapier. He had never used on
before and tested it. He liked the way it felt in hi
hand; it was light. The shorter, narrower blade wa
new to him, for he was used to fighting with th
cutlass and longsword. But he would not let Lucia
know that he had never handled the shorter swor
before . . .

Lucian took time to gauge for the opening rush
but Sebastián was on him before he could move
The slightly older and thinner man parried with hi
shorter sword, and they locked hilt to hilt, thei
bodies staggering together and straining like wres
tlers. There was no hit either way.

"You're a murdering knave, a bastard villain,
Sebastián hissed, causing Lucian to start with som
surprise at the intense hatred on the younger man'
face.

They broke, and sprang back!

With that first parry, Sebastián had felt the Drag
on's power. He knew now he must employ all hi
own; he balanced in a quick recovery and, best a
he could, he braced for footing on the blood-slip
pery deck.

Now Lucian came at him with a mighty thrust. Sebastián met one, turned it, countered another with a quick swerve of his sword, and his men cheered him on! But the pressure of the second thrust forced Sebastián sidewise. He shifted stance and sank his boot heel for a firmer footing.

"Sebastián. . . !" Jaecko warned.

Sebastián recognized the danger. The Dragon was inching in, attacking on his sword arm to take him at an angle, desirous to drive him into the rail and finish him there. Swooping, Sebastián feinted toward his opponent under the guard. The Dragon took the feint on his blade, and at the same instant, Sebastián swung up with a spring of his lithe body, leaping by the other man and landing on one knee.

Sebastián was up when his opponent whirled.

They were on equal terms now. They held their blades at the level of their hips, points forward, swords extended, and circled each other warily. A kind of exultation tingled in Sebastián's blood at the chagrin on Lucian's face.

"Come, Dragon," Sebastián purred as if enticing a lover. "Show me your fiery blade!"

"Spare your breath, peacock," Lucian said with an evil sneer.

The Dragon plunged in without warning, and Sebastián warded off the plunge, taking the weaker thrust on his own and cutting from beneath. The cut slithered across the Dragon's sword quillings, and his weight spun them both around and tossed them wide of each other.

They became interchanging blurs that rushed together murkily and writhed and flung upward and broke away. Rips and scratches showed on their clothes. Sebastián's left sleeve hung tattered from the shoulder. Both were bleeding, Sebastián on the forehead and cheek and shoulder, Lucian in both legs below his doublet.

"You are very good, peacock!" Lucian sneered with an arrogant stance. "Perhaps you even fought the bloody Tiger and won this ship as your booty. With cutlass in hand, no doubt. But you never fought with the rapier, I notice. Tell me, strutting lad, where is the tawny-haired wench with the winsome face? My brother has told me of her. I would like to sample the slut before I let my men take her. Eh? How would you like to see your prize—?"

He never finished. As the blade reached out, pale as venom in the moonlight, the Dragon spun to the left and leaped. The action saved his tendons, but the blade sliced across the flat of his hip. At the same moment Sebastián's own point lunged inside the wide dagger guard and drove through Lucian's side. He dropped his rapier, and took Sebastián's blade with both his hands. He shoved himself backward, sliding off the steel. A third of its length came from his body, and the Dragon fell to his knees.

"The peacock"—his voice whistled—"*is* good."

Breathing heavily, Sebastián leaned on his rapier. Blood was gushing from his leg and soaking his buff breeches a crimson shade. Over the blood soaked decks, a surprised Jaecko came toward him with Robert Drake close behind, running over to his brother.

"Mother of God," Robert whispered, disbelief in his eyes.

Jaecko stared with eyes bugging from their sockets as Sebastián put his hand to his thigh and then

268

spread the same hand in front of him, blood dripping through and from his long brown fingers.

Grasping his brother's wrist, Lucian got out, "The peacock has sharp quills . . . like a porcupine."

Robert shot to his feet, snarling, "Or like a tiger!"

"What do you say, Brother?" Lucian looked up from his sprawled position. "The Tiger?" he chuckled. "Bah! He is only a peacock. I shall show him one day . . ." He coughed and wheezed. "If I live this one out."

"Fetch the ship's surgeon!" Robert shouted. Then he turned to Sebastián and what remained of his crew, for the crews of the *Raven* and the *El Draque* vastly outnumbered those still alive on the *Emerald Tiger*. "I have searched your ship, man. Where is the young blond with the comely face and figure? I demand that you tell me!"

Favoring his wounded leg, Sebastián narrowed his eyes and gave a casual answer. "She is with us no longer."

Robert Drake stepped closer, snarling into the other man's face. "You *are* a bloody peacock, aren't you?" He poked his finger at Sebastián's face and smeared the blood all around, even into the tawny hair. "The young wench looked very familiar to me. You see, when you were all raked out as pirates, I saw from my ship as you took the lady in question into your arms. She looked very much like *my* woman." His eyes narrowed and flared wide. "Like Daniella Wingate!"

Sebastián's eyes were hard, like green ice. "Sorry. The name is not familiar—at least the name is not one that rings true."

"What do you mean by that statement?" Robert gave a glance to his wounded brother as they carried him away to his own ship. Turning back to the wounded man, poking him in the chest, he said, "You speak in riddles, peacock."

Sebastián made a painful bow. "With my own blood smeared about my face and running down my leg, I must look very colorful indeed."

As the crew was being led away, Sebastián felt his spirits rise somewhat as they chuckled at his cheeky words. Truth be known, he was weary, losing blood, tired to the bone, and defeated.

With the back of his hand, Robert struck Sebastián three times across his bloodied face, the sharp ring stinging smartly.

"We shall see *just* how cheeky you are"—Robert thrust him into the hands of grinning pirates who shook out the chains that Sebastián would wear—"when my men toss you into the dungeons of the Tinto hellhole!"

The pain in Sebastián's hip became worse as he was put into the shackles and led away with his men into the dark hold of the *El Draque*. He knew it was the Dragon's ship, for when they had been taken from the *Emerald Tiger,* they walked to the right. The *Raven* flanked them on the left.

In the stinking hold, Sebastián felt the ship finally move after what had seemed hours of standing still. Leaning his head against the bulkhead, while Jaecko stanched the flow of blood from his thigh, Sebastián wondered at the fate of the *Emerald Tiger.*

"That's a handsome slash in the head you got, Cap'n," Jaecko was saying.

"*Gracias a Dios,* perhaps I'll not need makeup if

270

I should be forced to don the comely disguise of our friend Lord Steven and resort to foppery once again."

Tears glistened in the giant's eyes as he ministered to his captain's facial wounds with the utmost care. "You was never a frilly fop, Cap'n."

"You're a softhearted fool, Jaecko."

"Aye, Cap'n." Jaecko nodded. "Where do you suppose this high-pooped monster will be taking us?"

"Why, Jaecko . . ." Sebastián made an effort to laugh, but it hurt too much. "This is not a galleon like the *Spanish Wind,* but a tempest-winged corvette."

At his own mention of the *Spanish Wind,* Sebastián's soul took flight as he wondered where Daniella was at the moment. Would he live out his gloomy days and dark, lonesome nights in the dungeon dreaming of that winsome princess who had stolen his heart? *Dios,* he no longer sought revenge on that glorious lady's soul and she was no longer his dark rose. For now, he realized Daniella was his love. His tiger rose. And he prayed that she was safe . . . wherever on God's vast moonlit sea she might be.

The night sky sparkled with delicate, winking stars, while inside, Sebastián sat up from his slumped position on the cold cell floor as a rotund man entered the dank corridor. The jailer had two bowls of watery soup in his hand, one for himself and one for the grumbling wretch in the corner of the cell; these the jailer set down on a bench as he fumbled for the key. Another guard stood by, his meaty arms crossed over his chest as Sebastián feasted on the soup, which had bits of garbage floating in it.

While Sebastián ate hungrily—not because it was palatable but to rebuild his strength—he watched the two outside the cell stuff themselves like pigs with oranges, dates, and chunks of crusty bread soaked with honey. The thin man beside Sebastián eyed the richer fare with greedy eyes and wiped his mouth on his sleeve before he spoke.

"Wish I could have me some of that honey oozing sweet in me throat."

Sebastián stared at the strange man with toothless gums and wrinkled brow. "Perhaps the honey, old man, but the bread I think you'd choke on!"

The old man smacked his greasy lips. "Ah, you're a cocky one, ain't you?" For a moment he did not speak, only stared at the younger man. "Where'd you come from, lad?"

"The sea."

He chuckled. "Me name's Spider."

"That is an odd name for a Portuguese."

"I ain't a Port-guese. I only look like one. Truth be told, I don't know what I am. Been Spider for long as I seen the sun come up and go down."

"How long have you been here in the Tinto dungeons, Spider?"

"You go mad the first year in the Tinto cells and after the fifth they forget you are here," he simply said. "By the tenth, they forget to bury you."

"You are not dead yet so you must not have been here ten years."

"Nine."

Sebastián shivered. "Have you ever tried to escape?"

272

"Need money to do that, and I ain't got a *blanca*." He leaned closer to whisper, "There's a way you can escape, laddie. But now, hear me, your risk is your own." He wiped his sleeve on his tattered shirt, which was open in the front and smeared with filth. "You got any money? Jewels?"

A highly unlikely possibility, Sebastián thought but something clicked just then in his brain. *The tiger pin!* He shifted and felt around in his soiled breeches. *It was there!* "Ahh, but how can I part with it?"

"What's that, laddie?"

When Spider leaned close once again, Sebastián almost passed out from the fetid odor of the poor wretch.

"I said, let's get on with it then, man!"

Sebastián came fluidly to his feet, and the hollow-eyed skeleton followed suit, but not as swiftly.

Sebastián drew the squinty gaze of the other as he pointed. "What is that over in the corner?"

"Hah hah," Spider chuckled. "That was the day I thought I died and went to heaven." The old man crossed himself.

Taking a look over his shoulder to see that the ravenous lads were still occupied, and in fact were getting quite inebriated on the huge jug they shared, Sebastián walked over to take a closer look at what was lying on the floor. He picked it up, hefting it, and then realizing what it possibly could be, said, "It looks like a bone."

"Big, ain't it!" Jealously, Spider snatched it back. "Jawbone from a hog. Least that's what creature the jailer over there said it was. Beto over there got himself liquored up one night. Hah, he does almost every night, but this one special night he got him-

273

self half a hog from his relatives. I had me a feast
. . . hogs' brains and—"

With a shudder clear down to his toes, Sebastián
said, "Enough!"

"You don't want to know what I did with the
eyes?" There was a twinkle of mischief in his own
rheumy ones. "I just plucked 'em out and
popped—"

Sebastián grabbed Spider's arm, groaning, "I
have an imagination, Spider." He shoved the huge
bone away from under his nose where Spider had
been waving it. "Now then," Sebastián told the old
man, "Here's what I want you to do—"

Before Sebastián could voice his plans, Spider
grabbed hold of his arm. "They was cooked, you
know." Their eyes locked and held for a moment,
and Sebastián had a sick look on his face. "They
really was cooked *real* good."

"I realize that," Sebastián said, his stomach turning. "You needn't trouble yourself in telling me
more!"

A short time later everything was ready. Sebastián sauntering to the cell door, called out, "Beto!
Might I have a moment of your time?"

"Huh?" Beto, who had been slumped against the
wall, wine jug held loosely just above the dank
floor, came wide awake with a jolt. "What do you
want?" he asked, in Spanish. "You already had
your slop. If you have a need to use the conven-
iences . . ." He chuckled. "Use the corner wall." He
smacked his thick lips, trying once again to get
comfortable against the damp wall. "Spider'll show
you."

274

Sebastián answered in that same language. "I've something you might like to see, Beto. Do you like jewels, Beto?" Sebastián's deep, soothing voice beckoned and tantalized the other to sit up and take notice.

Leaving the other sound asleep and snoring, Beto swung his jug as he ambled over to the door. "Jewels? What are you crazy or something?" Giving the young prisoner an indifferent look, he said, "*Sí*, you must be crazy. I'm going back to sleep, and don't be bothering me again, you hear?"

"Beto . . ." Sebastián called in a softly crooning voice. "Come here and see for yourself."

The rotund jailer came to a halt halfway back to his chair.

Again, in a smoothly soothing voice, Sebastián said, "It's magic."

"Magic?" Beto swung the jug to the floor and fumbled with his keys. "What kinda magic?" he asked with childlike wonder in his half-inebriated voice.

"Wondrous magic, Beto. Come closer and see for yourself." Sebastián stepped back, holding the cold object in his hand with the ragged and smelly blanket draped over the whole.

Thoroughly engrossed with his cellmate's cleverness, Spider stood off to one side. Excitement, for the first time in nine years, flowed through his emaciated limbs giving him renewed vigor. His young friend had promised to get him out of here—*if* this far-trumpeted plan of his came off right.

Beto, prompted by extreme curiosity, walked right into the cell, leaving the door wide, cunningly trapped like a fly in a spider's crafty web. And snores from the one outside the cell were the only sound as Beto stepped up to the smiling young man.

"What magic have you got there?" Beto was in the process of hoisting the retrieved jug to his lips when his arm was halted halfway to his face. He stared dumbly as the lean, brown fingers pulled the jug away from him, and as he stared, mesmerized, into the yellow-green eyes, Sebastián set the jug on the floor in back of him. Moving slowly and with caution, Sebstián straightened while the heavy man kept watching, as if hypnotized by the younger man's movements.

Some sense returned to Beto's drink-fuzzed brain and he frowned darkly, growling, "Wait a minute, is this some kind of *gambado?* You wouldn't be fooling me, would you?"

Sebastián performed a courtly bow, as if he'd been tutored in the queen's throne room of the Spanish palace.

Once again Beto was mesmerized, and he looked down as the young man raised his hand ever so slowly. "What's under that blanket?" Beto's hand went to the dagger at his low-slung sheath. "Let's see your magic, but I don't want no fast movements or else you'll get a taste of my blade!"

"No se preocupe!" Sebastián said not to worry as he pulled the soiled blanket off the jawbone, and Beto blinked wondering where all the magic was coming from.

"Que demonio! What the devil?" Beto snorted and pulled out his dagger. "It is only a bone!"

"Wait!" Sebastián held it a little higher and the glow from the torches caught the glint and glimmer of the jewels from the tiger pin. "Magic! *Verdad?"*

276

"Sí. It is magic." With a greedy glint to his eyes, Beto reached out to the shining tiger pin. "Ah, I will see this thing for myself." The new prisoner moved the jawbone a little, and the fat man jumped back as it stuck him. *"Ay!* The *pequeño tigre* bites!"

"Sí, yes. You must learn the magic words and then you may touch it." Sebastián chuckled deeply. "You might even have it for your very own, Beto, eh?"

"You are not fooling Beto?"

Sebastián spread one hand, "Would I do that to you, *mi amigo?"*

As a thump reached Beto's ears, he whirled about to see what the commotion in the corridor was about—and that was when Sebastián struck!

Lifting the jug from the floor, he smashed the heavy pottery against the man's thick skull, but Beto did not go down as easily as Sebastián had hoped. He gave him another blow, and that did it! The jailer's eyes crossed and he went down like a sinking hippopotamus.

"I got this one!" Spider called, hefting the guard's jug to his lips and sucking deeply; then, smacking his lips in satisfaction, he gave the knocked-out guard several kicks to his shins. "This is for that time . . . and that other time . . ."

"Spider!" Sebastián was all action now, stripping Beto's pockets and emptying the contents. Something jingled with liberal promise. "Ah . . . the keys to the whole blasted prison! Come on, Spider. We have some men to release!"

Taking another hefty swig from the jug, Spider kicked his heels in the air and lit out after the young captain like a young colt just let out to pasture!

Alain Carstairs, captaining the *Rampant Rose,* made to sail into Pirate's Lair, the hidden cove where he had often met with the Drakes. He had spied for the Brethren of the Sea, namely those linked with Lucian and Robert Drake and Charles Blackman.

The Drakes had been fighting with the Landakers for years, and he, Alain, had often wished to see Robert and Daniella become man and wife, for they had been so very happy as children when they had had their innocent adventures along the river-banks.

Alain's face was as if carved from stone as he stood at the rail of the *Rampant Rose.* He had taken the ship with her legal cargo and been law-fully cleared for an open port. Then he had made for the second port where he traded in contraband as he'd done for years, without the Wingates know-ing where part of their profit had gone. He had done it for Robert—for his and Daniella's future. But he had made a mistake when he had given the tiger pin to Daniella, for it had somehow mystically linked Daniella with the Landakers.

The *Rampant Rose's* goods had been unloaded in a Spanish harbor and picked up by merchants who pretended no knowledge of the voyage. As he had told Charles Blackman the first time he had sailed with him, "It goes like this: The merchandise itself is not contraband, mind you; it is only forbidden to import it. But no one is the wiser . . ." He'd chuck-led. "Especially the officials."

Alain shared a small portion of his gain with the

various officials, and then, to discourage investigations, the functionaries pretended to seize the *Rampant Rose* and toss Alain Carstairs into prison. The crew was branded and whipped, but not too hard—and the incident was thus reported to the court that they had prospered and the captain and his crew had been submissive. Then, after all was done, the ship would revert back to the captain and Alain sailed away merrily with pockets considerably heavier than before!

And the sea raids had long been blamed on the Landaker ships—but it was becoming increasingly difficult to put the blame on them, with the Tiger and his men growing in number and strength of ship.

Now Alain came alert. Charles Blackman rushed to his side, for he had been at the lookout, now reporting that a ship was in sight. "It looks like the *Emerald Tiger,* but how could it be? Lucian said they had that English dandy of a captain thrown into the dungeon!"

Alain smirked into Charles Blackman's face. Robert Drake should never have sent Charles to do a man's job. He had not succeeded in abducting Daniella, had flubbed the job terribly. A mysterious swordsman had stepped out of the shadows at the Charleston riverfront and given Charley a wound to his shoulder. They all were, Robert Drake included, still in mystery as to the dancing swordsman's identity, but someday, and soon, he would learn his name!

With the wind in its favor, the *Rampant Rose* could overtake the *Emerald Tiger* easily, but what Alain did not count on as it turned and put up more sails was the ghostlike appearance of another

279

ship that loomed up as if out of nowhere . . . She was the *Trade Wind*.

They had neglected to cover their stern, and all eyes were upon the heavy galleon moving slowly toward them. A surprise was waiting for the *Rampant Rose* as she drew close, for the *Emerald Tiger* suddenly appeared and swung to port exposing its whole side as the gun ports opened to the *Rampant Rose*.

Within seconds a deafening roar came from the heavy galleon. The shot whistled over the *Rampant Rose*, in a warning for her to come around.

"This is a trap!" Alain shouted.

"Why don't you just give in and let them come aboard?" Charles asked.

"And be drawn and quartered? Lord Steven Landaker will discover our deception and he will know we have been anything but honest with the Wingate profits!"

"You mean Sebastián Landaker," Charley reminded. "He is the master of disguise. You see, there is no *Steven* Landaker. He died from wounds suffered in a duel after he fought with Lucian Drake."

"What are you telling me? That one is a ghost!?"

"No, he is quite real—believe me!"

"Then *he,* the Tiger, is the man you fought with as you were trying to abduct Daniella in Charleston Harbor and bring her to Robert!"

Charley groaned. "He is the Merchant Fleet's spy!"

"We are done for," Alain said. "We should have returned to Charleston as he ordered and we could have gone on spying for the Drakes. But now it's too late."

280

And so it was. Alain decided their only course was to run for their life. The galleon continued to lay down salvos as the *Rampant Rose* pulled away with the wind in its favor. And the shots fell short.

On the *Emerald Tiger,* Sebastián was shouting, "Gun ports open and full sails! We'll run him down now!"

When the galleon, the *Trade Wind,* made a tack, she set out to follow the caravel, with the *Emerald Tiger* not far off to her side. The captain of the *Trade Wind* looked to Captain Sebastián mutely asking for orders to fire upon the smaller ship. When Sebastián was about to give permission, he took a closer look at the ship they were tracking and held up his hand. *Madre de Dios!*

"Wait!" But only the men on the *Emerald Tiger* could hear him. "It is the *Rampant Rose!*" He stroked his chin, wondering why Alain Carstairs had not returned to Charleston as he had been ordered. Enlightenment came over him then and he said aloud to Jaecko, "Aha! We have our spy, Jaecko! I am positive it is Alain Carstairs who has been aiding the pirates!"

"We'll get him, Cap'n. Look, he's heading for that cove. The *Trade Wind* and our ship will trap him now. Hah! He's done for."

Sebastián's eyes darkened with intense emotion. *"Sí.* We have our man." Another of Daniella's infamous friends!

"Charles Blackman is on that ship, too, Cap'n." said Jaecko. "So now there's only the Drakes to finish off—"

"My pleasure." His voice was firm . . . final.

Chapter Seventeen

To die and part
Is a less evil; but to part and live,
There—there's the torment.
— George Granville Landsdowne

Like a huge-winged bird, the *Spanish Wind* rode
the white-capped waters of the Atlantic, and before
long, Cornwall's coast was in sight. From the rail of
the ship Daniella could see the grass-covered crest of
the rocky cliffs. Though the sky was misty and gray,
it was a beautiful morning, with white gulls circling
above massive granite towers of rock and landing on
the sandy beaches below.

When the *Spanish Wind* drew yet closer, Daniella
could see more of the harsh rocky landscape . . .
and there, seeming to cling like some dark-browed
predatory bird, stood a magnificent house surrounded by towering trees, ancient and gnarled, with
fingerlike branches that pointed away from the sea as
if beckoning the wayfarer. Daniella experienced a
feeling of warmth looking at the house. Warmth,
anxious expectation . . . and something else she
could not place her finger on just yet.

One thing was certain—she could not wait to be
off this ship after living at sea for nearly two
months! She had been feeling ill of late but had
insisted that Juan take her across the Atlantic, none-

theless, home to Braidwood. Gently, firmly, Juan had argued that she needed to rest, and the nearest point of refuge had been here in Cornwall. He had won his point.

Daniella had cried her eyes out many lonely nights after Sebastián had deserted her. Juan had promised her that he would someday appear again, but for now Sebastián had especially pressing business to tend to.

Many nights and even during the daytime hours, Daniella asked herself why she should care if Sebastián appeared again or not, for she had vowed no man would have her love again. Steven/Sebastián had played a cat-and-mouse game with her and she would have no more of his machinations and evil intentions. He could not love her and act the way he did, she told herself.

When the *Spanish Wind* was finally shut down, her sails furled, her many anchors lowered, Daniella could hear the dull pounding of the breakers that boomed and crashed, foaming gray, blue, and the cliffs angrily spewing back white spray. It was all very strange to her, and how lonely and afraid she was, coming to this new place where she did not know the people and uncertain if they would welcome her or not.

Bettina was feeling in high spirits, and she only wished her lady could feel some of the same, since the comely maid was certain that Jaecko would return to her with the same fond love he had felt when they had parted. Bettina was bound and determined to make Jaecko wait until they would say their vows as man and wife, and only then could he claim his husbandly rights.

Daniella had lost some weight and her cheeks had

become winsomely hollow. Her eyes had taken on a haunted look. The sea-colored depths had been transformed back into the lonely gray pools of her childhood. She wished somehow that she could be with Robert Drake once again but knew she had to make the most of her situation for the time being and endeavor to return to Braidwood as quickly as possible. She had felt so ill the last couple of weeks!

Standing at the rail, Daniella looked over to where Geraldina stood aloof, keeping her distance from her and Bettina. Geraldina herself had complained of seasickness. But Daniella had a suspicion it was more likely that Geraldina had a secret desire to look upon the young woman Juan had often mentioned with a lovesick expression riding his darkly handsome face. If Geraldina pleaded ill, then she would not have to stay aboard the ship with her father, as she had often done in the past. It was clear that Geraldina despised Eileena already, though she had not even met the woman with the pathetic illness. Juan had spoken so much of her, while he and Daniella had shared quiet moments in the dining hall, that Daniella felt she already knew Eileena Landaker. The only thing she could not yet believe was that Lucian Drake has used her in such a fiendish manner, but Juan insisted that it was the God's truth. Daniella knew she would have to see Eileena herself to know for herself what ill fate had befallen the woman!

Daniella sighed with relief as they finally stepped off the galleon, a few of Captain Gancho's men rowing toward the sandy beach through the rugged gray waves. Daniella had learned much about pirates and smuggling in the area of Tallrock, and Juan told her that Captain Gancho meant to take some of his men to St. Ives to speak with the excise man and village folk to see if there had been any smugglers in the area recently, since he did not want any trouble while they were here. The caves along the beach were often used for the unloading of smugglers' contraband and pirates roamed the area of Tallrock and Land's End freely at night, defiantly begging to be caught as they had for years, bringing their stash in from the turquoise waters leading into the English Channel.

The manor house of the Landakers came into view again at the top of the slope and Daniella was struck by the savage beauty of the landscape, the vast holdings and the lush green-misted forests beyond. She could not help but wonder about the lives of those within the thick stone walls. Bettina kept close to her side and Rascon—ever near Daniella of late—helped carry some of their belongings.

The manor house faced the sea, its stately wings spreading out from the main portion of the house, and Daniella could see the beautiful gardens that reminded her of her beloved Braidwood. She was happy that someday soon she would leave here and return to Braidwood as Juan had promised. One thing was certain: She had no wish to be here when that devilishly handsome captain decided to come and claim his husbandly rights. As far as she was concerned, he had none whatsoever, and there was no marriage to speak of.

Nearing the house, Daniella was struck by its magnificence. Built of massive red stone, with the huge wings and main block in the pattern laid out like an H, rows of mullioned windows had been set deep against the ravages of wind and weather. Twin chimneys pointed skyward like sentinels and the house looked as if it would stand forever and ever into time

285

itself!

While walking up the slope, Daniella's roving gaze had been so busy admiring the landscape that she had almost forgotten she was entering into a strange house and even stranger family.

It is beautiful, Daniella thought with a sigh. But nothing . . . absolutely nothing could ever take the place of the home where she had known only love and laughter . . . even though she had at times been lonely. Suddenly she couldn't wait to be back in the Carolinas where she truly belonged, and not out here chasing searobbers and sharing adventures with members of the Established Windstar Fleet! Though Juan had been very kind to her, and she was thankful for Bettina's pleasant company throughout the long days aboard the *Spanish Wind,* she missed the halls and grounds of Braidwood terribly.

The first person Daniella met was Dame Charlotte Somerville, Master Landaker's widowed sister who had kept the house since the children were small, and there was Ellen, the maidservant, who was a treasure, and Robert, the manservant who had been with them for years.

"This is it!" Juan had announced as they stood in the lofty ancestral hall and the imperious woman and the little gray-haired dumpling of a woman whose face broke into rosy smiles greeted them.

"Juan Tomaz!" Dame Charlotte said, pulling him to her bosom for a hug. "Welcome," she greeted more softly, standing back to look at the others he had with him.

The smaller woman stepped forward, this one the maidservant. "This is Ellen," Juan announced, and Daniella was surprised when the smiling woman walked over and gave her a hug and a hearty kiss on the cheek. "You are lovely . . . beyond description." And Daniella blushed, thanking her for her sweet compliment.

Then Juan was hugging Ellen and she scolded, "Don't you be setting my cap crooked, you handsome scoundrel!"

The unmistakable warmth of greetings touched Daniella's heartstrings and impulsively she thought she had made friends for life; Bettina curtsied and Ellen shook hands with Daniella's maid. Daniella decided there was no reason to fear these folks any longer—at least those she had met so far. There were only Eileena and Teague to meet—and of course Master Landaker himself.

"Come in, dearlings, come in and make yourselves at home!" Ellen said. "Come over to the fire in the hall; you'll be cold and tired after that climb. Master Landaker and Eileena are out, and indeed they will be sorry . . ." Her face fell, and she revised, "At least the master will be, for you see, Eileena has not been herself lately. The master has taken her for a ride about the country. She likes her air, though she don't . . ." Ellen shook her apron. Tears stood in her eyes. "I'll be seeing you to your rooms now!"

"Come in here," Juan invited, and Daniella and Bettina followed, while Geraldina stood peering at the elegant furnishings.

Dame Charlotte appeared again. She was a tall, large-boned woman with a fresh color, who looked, in spite of her severe dark clothes, neither elderly nor delicate; rather, Daniella deduced, she could be called *handsome*.

"We thought you had forgotten us, Captain Tomaz," she said to the dark Spaniard. "I am happy to finally meet you," she said as she turned to Daniella.

287

Dame Somerville took Daniella's cloak then and remarked, "You are very like your mother."

Daniella was astonished. "You knew her?"

"Yes. We met in London when she had a season there." Dame Somerville touched Daniella's arm gently, adding, "Lord Landaker knew her, too, but alas, he is with us no longer."

Daniella shook her head lightly, to clear it, as Dame Somerville turned away. *Lord Landaker knew her mother.* But not the same Lord *Steven* Landaker that Sebastián had pretended to be . . . surely not!

After a warming drink of cider by the fire, they all retuned to the hall where the Landaker servants bustled about preparing rooms while rushing up and down the stairs with clean towels and linens. Daniella had never seen so many servants — so many happy faces glowing with ruddy health.

When Daniella turned, she received a jolting shock, for there, hanging halfway up the long, curving staircase, was a huge painting of *him,* Lord Steven Landaker, and it was incredible how close to resembling the man Sebastián had made himself. Ah, indeed! A formidable master of disguise.

"Ho!" Dame Somerville exclaimed as the lad stepped up to the bottom stair to lower his bundles. "And who is this rascal?" She gave his hair a fluffing with her gentle hand.

His cinnamon eyes bright with excitement, Juan returned to the hall just then. "This is Rascon."

"Ah well, I was close, wasn't I?"

"Here we are!" Ellen announced, then turned with her cheerful smile as she saw the boy. "Hello there, and what is your name?"

Juan was puzzled. "Do you mean to say Sebastián has never brought the lad to meet you?" he asked the women. Both shook their heads in the negative. "Well then—it *has* been a while since Sebastián has visited!"

"You were with him last time you came," Ellen said with a curious look. "Don't you remember? You came to see . . . Eileena."

Rascon was tugging at Juan's arm and making motions with his hands; Juan finally read what the lad was struggling to tell him.

Juan nodded. "Ah, ladies, you must forgive his unintentional rudeness. You see, Rascon cannot speak, but he has just informed me with sign language that he chose to remain on the ship while Sebastián visited. He went on to St. Ives with several of the crew members that last time."

"Ah, that explains why we've not met the laddie then."

"Take the ladies upstairs, Ellen," Dame Somerville said. "I shall see what can be done about supper." Winding her arm about the lad's thin shoulders, she said, "And you can come with me. We'll find you something to eat."

At that news, Rascon's face lit up like a summer sky, and he went along with the friendly woman who kept up a string of chatter all the way to the kitchen.

Gratefully, Daniella was then shown to a room in the east wing, where she could look out over the greensward that was graced by lovely gardens, terraced and flanked by unusually shaped trees. Beyond this she could see the rolling waves and the salt spray that crashed upon the huge, rocky cliffs. The breathtaking sight was all sea and sky.

When the maidservant left her, Daniella turned to study the room, walking over to run her hands over the taupe-colored spread on the great carved bed.

The room had been tastefully furnished, and most of the pieces were massive and dark, Atlantean, not a woman's room by any standards. She wondered if this was the room Sebastián occupied when he was in residence, and, too, she wondered how much she could learn from the kindly folk at Tallrock. So far, she had not met a single Landaker!

Daniella tested the huge feather mattress while she peeled down to her smallclothes, removed her shoes, flung everything aside, and then lay down for a nap. Her wedding night came to her in a restless dream like a tide rolling in and out . . . and she was again in her husband's strong embrace, feeling his caressing weight, hearing his stirring words; *Let me assure you, my beloved bride, I am no simple, half-witted fool, nor am I lacking in vitality in this act. I am quite, quite able—to do you justice, m'lady. I want you so much, Daniella, my love!* The moon had stolen into the bedchamber and bathed the huge bed and its hangings in a silvery light. The powder that Steven . . . Sebastián had applied with a heavy hand had begun to mingle with the sweat from his brow. It was hot in the room . . . very hot indeed. *Your body . . . You are beautiful, Sebastián!*

Flinging a restless arm up over her head, Daniella stirred and rolled to her back, reliving the feel of his long fingers caressing her fine cheekbones. *The moon is not playing tricks, Sebastián!* He rose from the bed to draw the heavy drapes closed against the invading moon. She was positively shimmering inside . . . could feel the palpitation of her heart. He had slowly risen from the bed, his buttocks lean and tautly muscled. He was coming back to her now . . . coming . . . coming—

All at once Daniella sat up in bed, and she blinked

the dreamy blur from her eyes. A flash of recognition brought her instantly awake. Why had she not realized it before? The handkerchief, that was explained now, too, why it had come to be in Steven Landaker's possession after that scoundrel captain Sebastián had been the last one to have it!

Daniella swung long, slim legs over the bed, lifting her blond hair up from her perspiring neck. Though she realized it was actually cool in the room, her body seemed enfired with heat!

Flinging back her head, Daniella leaned back on her elbows, closing her eyes to summon the dream back but with an awareness of feeling that the dream had lacked. He had demanded that she open her mouth to him for a soul-blistering kiss that had moved lower and lower until at last he had discovered the treasured valley. He had eased her thighs apart and plunged his tongue into the warm recess, kissing her most thoroughly. Her smile had been glorious. Her lips were parted and moist . . .

"Take me now, Sebastián. *Please!*"

Of a sudden the door opened a crack, and Daniella jolted up in a brisk motion, her cheeks red as Bettina stood there asking if she would like some fresh water so that she could bathe before going down to supper.

"Everyone will be waiting, m'lady."

Bettina was looking at Daniella strangely. "Oh, yes, of course, Bettina!" Daniella came off the bed with a guilty flush staining her velvet-petal cheeks. "Bring the water in — and yourself."

"Are you all right, m'lady?" Bettina peered around the room after she had closed the door. "I thought I heard you talking to someone."

"Ah . . ." Daniella nervously fiddled with the ties

291

of her chemise. "No."

"You're sure you aren't ill again?" Bettina turned with fresh towels in her hand. "You were feeling poorly before we reached the coast of Cornwall."

Rushing to Bettina, Daniella laid a now-cool hand on her maidservant's arm. "I have not been feeling all that well, Bettina, but let that be our secret."

Bettina stared at Daniella for a long moment, then said, "You look different, m'lady, almost . . . well, radiant. I mean, you've always been lovely, but now it's almost as if you have a wonderful *secret*."

"Yes, Bettina, that is what I said. Please do not speak of this to Juan, or . . . or the others."

"Why?" Bettina continued to stare at Daniella with suspicion. "Ohhh, Dany . . . I mean, m'lady!" Bettina dropped all respectfulness. "You don't think you're going to have a *baby*, do you?"

"Well . . ." Daniella gave her head a little sideways jerk. "That possibility *has* crossed my mind." The blonde appeared uneasy as she looked up from fingers she'd been twisting together nervously. "I really don't want to think about it or discuss it, Bettina. If the others hear about this, they just might make us stay longer, and I do so want to go home to Braidwood! You *do* understand, Bettina?"

All of a sudden Bettina was not so happy with her mistress. "You just want to run away before that handsome captain of yours comes along and discovers what you've been hiding . . . Oh, I am sorry, m'lady!"

Daniella's voice was whisper-soft. "The matter has just come to my attention. How could I know that all along I was with child?"

Bettina spread her hands to give emphasis to her next words. "Captain Sebastián is your husband, m'lady, and you can't run away from him forever. He might have done you wrong at first, but now I believe he truly loves you. Can't you see that?"

If Bettina had not said that with affection, Daniella's feelings would have been solidly hurt. Then it struck her fully, what Bettina had just announced, but she was not in the mood for Bettina's romantic theatrics.

Busying herself, Daniella took the pitcher and poured its contents into the basin, stepping back and bending over to splash cool, refreshing water onto her face. Concerned, Bettina watched Daniella for a moment, waiting for her to finish so she could hand her the fluffy towel. When Daniella blindly reached for it, Bettina hung it on Daniella's blond head and, turning in a huff, the maid went to busy herself straightening her lady's room where things were scattered all over the place. This was just not like her lady at all, to be so messy!

"Bettina?" Daniella pulled the towel down and briskly dried her face. "What, pray tell, is the matter with you? Why are you so angry? It is not my fault that scoundrel tricked me into marriage and then left me with his seed in my belly! I am the one who should be angry!"

With one hand on a generous hip and the other filled with Daniella's carelessly discarded underpinnings, Bettina gave Daniella a wintry look. "Now I must speak my mind, even though Jaecko told me to seal my lips." As Daniella drew closer, her eyes lit curiously, Bettina wondered if she was doing the right thing. But frustration and love's cause won out, and she blurted the most dramatic revelation she could think of. "Sebastián is the bastard son of one Captain William Kidd—the deceased pirate of the

Bahamas."

Daniella blinked and said in a breathless voice. "I . . . I read something concerning that in his journal, but I never realized just how that would have affected his life . . . to make him so bitter about circumstances—"

"You read his journal?" Bettina shook her red curls slowly. "It must have been before you learned just what was going on."

"Just what *is* going on, Bettina? How can Sebastián be Captain Kidd's bastard child when his name is Landaker?"

"I believe the person who can tell you all about that is Teague Landaker. You'll meet Teague at supper"—Bettina bent to retrieve a slipper sticking out from under the bed, chuckling—"if you ever get there, m'lady!"

Daniella was now most curious to learn as much as she could about her intriguing husband and his mysterious past.

"Who have you been collecting all your astounding information from, Bettina? Surely not from Dame Charlotte or the sweet little maid Ellen?"

With a toss of her head, Bettina said, "No."

"Well, who then? And do not tell me Jaecko has been the only source to divulge such fascinating news to you. There has to be another, hmm?"

"All you have to know, my lady, is that your handsome gallant of a husband loves you most dearly."

Walking over to the bed, Daniella wrapped a slim white arm about the intricately carved bedpost and asked, "If you are so well informed on my husband's dazzling history, then tell me: Who is Rebecca, the one he claims his undying love to?"

Bettina gasped. "Where did you hear that? I never

heard about any such named Rebecca!"

"Well . . ." Daniella tossed her head, shaking out velvety blond waves to her still-tiny waist. "I did — in the journal."

Bettina shook her head, wearing a slight frown. "I hope you're not just making that up so that I'll plead your case, m'lady, and help you return home speedily. If you do that, you might just never see that wickedly handsome husband of yours again. He's coming here, and if you're already gone, I don't think he's going to go off chasing you all the way home!"

"Why not?" she asked her maid. "You say he is madly in love with me."

"Aye, but . . ."

"But what?" Daniella cocked her head when Bettina turned away and she could not read her expression. "Tell me, Bettina. Please don't make me suffer your silence and hold back on me."

"Well, Jaecko says the captain talks to himself sometimes when he's pacing the deck." When Daniella softly giggled, Bettina looked up from the chemise she'd been folding into the drawer. "He was muttering to himself something about you despising him thoroughly for all he done to you."

"And so I do!" Daniella whirled from the bedpost, wearing a petulant frown. "I want to be gone from this place by the time he arrives, love or no love, I do not care if he is the king of England or the bastard of Captain Kidd." Daniella ended with the crack of a beginning grin.

Unable to help themselves, they both broke out in gales of laughter. They'd never spoken so freely with each other nor had Daniella ever proven to be so feisty in attitude.

After sharing a fit of the giggles, Daniella grew serious once again, looking toward the window where the restless wind danced over the wild gray waters of the Atlantic. She felt nostalgic all of a sudden, wishing for home, yearning for something else she was afraid to name, and feeling as scattered about as the winds tossed the foaming whitecaps.

Steven. Sebastián. Lord Landaker. The Tiger. Bastard son of a pirate—but himself not a pirate.

Daniella swung the mass of her flaxen-gold hair forward over one shoulder and in the same motion reached for her hairbrush. She gave the long silken tassel the boar's hair bristles with sweeping strokes, then paused. *I fear seeing him again.* To gaze into those tigerish eyes. To feel his eyes roving her until she was engulfed in passion which burned her from head to foot and then settled like a writhing flame in her middle. To have him take her in his arms and know that her body betrayed her once again . . . She must be away from here before he came for her—but how?"

And did she really wish to escape?

That was the burning question. Soon, God willing, she would know all the answers.

Chapter Eighteen

The storm that had been brewing all afternoon broke that evening. Thunder reverberated and bright lashes of lightning played to illuminate the vaulted ceiling and thick white candles set in silver sconces were set to shivering.

They would dine at eight o'clock. The women in the house traversing the great halls pulled their heavy, colorful shawls close as they made their way to the dining room. All but Eileena, who was carried to her chair at the table and pampered like a child by everyone present.

It was this scene that Daniella came upon as she entered and saw them all clustered about one female. As she drew closer, draping a willow-green silk shawl over her arms, what Daniella took in was a dainty girl who might have been pretty if it had not been for a sullen, discontented look. The long strands of her hair were definite browns and golds, though lacking any luster, as if she never put a brush to the heavy mass of hair or let anyone else do so. Her eyebrows dipped downward, giving her an almost angry look. The lips were wistfully petulant and the hands that clutched a book of Shakespeare's poetry were slim and lovely, though her nails looked untidy. Even seated, Daniella could tell her figure was lithe, but her posture seemed to have become affected by her sullenness.

A thick-waisted, chipper man noticed Daniel
hesitating and his gaze drifted appreciatively over h
plum gown down to her purple velvet shoes wi
their rose-and-green ribbon, then lifted to her beaut
ful face.

"Ah, and this must be Daniella," he said wit
chivalrous grace as he went to her and introduce
himself. "I am Gregory Landaker, master o
Tallrock. And this is my son, Teague." He drew
suave-looking gentleman over with a gesture of h
beringed hand.

Teague bowed low over Daniella's hand and lifte
it to his lips for a gentlemanly kiss.

"Come over here, Sophie," Gregory said, drawir
the pretty brown-haired woman over with a flick o
his hand. "This is my daughter-in-law, Teague
wife." He gave a half-forlorn sigh, and very bold
announced, "She has yet to present me with a gran
child."

Daniella could not help staring at the woma
Sophie, like her gown, was lovely. Her gown had
full, long skirt, sweeping the floor at the back, an
was fitted sleekly on her womanly hips and confine
high under her breasts by a deep amber belt. Th
sleeves were long and fitted and the tight bodice ha
a low, U-shaped neckline. Almost off the shoulder
it was generously fur-edged and descended in fro
to waist level. The turquoise gown was a new styl
one that Daniella thought very feminine.

Daniella's own was somewhat more old-fashione
The neckline was fairly low but cut wide, almost t
the edge of the shoulders, the sleeves fitted and e
bow-length, ending in long tippets. The fitted slee
of the undergown extended to the first row of knuck
les on the hand, its outer edge decorated by a row o

pink pearl buttons. The belt, worn at hip-level, was articulated with jeweled metal placques. Daniella had saved the gown for a special evening such as this one.

Sophie wore a placid smile for her father-in-law, and said to Daniella, "My dear, it's so good to meet you. But you must excuse Gregory—he is very outspoken as you will soon learn." She gave the older man an affectionate smile. "And Father, we have just learned today that I am with child!"

"My lord!" Master Landaker exclaimed. "You waited long enough to tell me." He pulled the pretty brunette to him and gave her a tender hug. "I am very happy indeed," he said with tears standing in his sharp blue eyes, and then he drew his eldest living son into his embrace, hugging him while he patted him on the back. "You finally did it, lad! Well then . . ." He pulled back, summoning the servants with a wave of his hand. "This calls for a celebration! Bring on the best brandy in the house—and a light wine for the ladies!"

"I am sorry, Master Landaker, but the cook was so excited by the birth of his third daughter that he burned the dinner!" Ellen said, wringing her hands in her apron, rattling keys, scissors, thimbles, and the many other items which hung from a belt fastened loosely about her thick waist.

"Well then!" he shouted. "Even more occasion to get pleasantly inebriated. Bring on the drinks, Ellen!"

It was then that Juan Tomaz appeared, with mellow drink in hand, announcing that he had been in the kitchen seeing what could be done to salvage the burned dinner. "I've cooked up something—delectable oysters, shrimp, and green turtle soup. It should not be long before we will be dining."

"Ah, Juan!" Master Landaker blustered. "Yo have saved the day . . . but let us have our drink while we are waiting."

Daniella hid a smile, for here was a man wh would rather await dinner and become "pleasantl inebriated" in the meantime. He reminded her s much of her father that she felt more lonesome tha ever for home . . . But Edward would not be there t greet her when she arrived at Braidwood, sh thought with sadness.

The drinks arrived and Daniella, not wishing to b left out, sipped leisurely of the white wine while th others imbided more deeply.

Daniella felt as if she were already part of th family, for they were so very easygoing and accepte her into their circle as if she had always been a par of them. Sebastián must have felt entirely welcom here, she thought, and suddenly she was lonesom for him and could not fathom the intensity of he feelings.

The family was relaxed toward one another, an even the servants were drawn into the homey circle Robert, the friendly Landaker manservant, and Bet tina, mingled among those present.

Eileena stared around the room, sipping now an then at the herbed tea Sophie slowly fed her as if sh were a child in need of coddling. But Daniell thought otherwise; she noticed a light of awarenes shining in the girl's eyes that followed the handsom Spaniard Juan about the room. It would take som doing, but Daniella was of a mind that Eileena wa not lost forever and someday would return to th normal woman she once had been.

Suddenly Geraldina made a dramatic appearance

dressed in a silver-and-green gown that fluttered above her dove-gray kid slippers. The gown was cut so low as to bare the shoulders and a goodly amount of bosom . . . the French called it decolletáge. Even the black gown Daniella had worn that night on the ship had not displayed so much bosom. Daniella was slightly embarrassed at Geraldina's outrageous display, but the auburn-haired woman sashayed into the room with nary a trace of unease.

Geraldina was greeted with an appreciative smile by Master Gregory Landaker, and, missing the companionship of women, as his wife had been long deceased, he drew her aside and pressed a generous drink into her hand. She gladly accepted with radiant smiles for Gregory, but when the elder Landaker was not looking, Geraldina turned her eyes to the man of her lusty dreams, Juan Tomaz.

All this Juan took in, and under his keen stare that settled on Eileena, a slow and painful flush crept upward from the girl's neck and burned in her cheeks; it was almost becoming. When the man who loved her beyond all else stood before her chair, Eileena began to turn her head to one side until her face was hidden from Juan's inquisitive cinnamon-dark eyes.

Across the room Bettina watched, saying to the manservant, "Ah, he loves her. I can tell, that's the way Jaecko, my love, looks at me." She turned to the man beside her. "Have you ever been in love like that, Robert?"

"Can't say that I have, miss, but it looks good to me."

"It is," she said, wishing Jaecko were with her now as she sipped her drink and remembered the nights under the moon when he had strolled the deck with

301

her and their kisses and touches had started fires in their hearts.

Dinner was served, a delicious fish from the waters of the Atlantic. The other food was just as delectable and there were desserts of cakes and pastries making one's mouth water before they were even tasted.

Afterward Master Landaker called for more after-dinner drinks, but Daniella declined, sipping at her tea instead. She was caught up in the wondrous love Juan felt for Eileena and the mastery with which he sought to bring her out of her pitiful world.

"Who are you?" Juan was asking Eileena.

"What *is* he doing?" Geraldina asked Sophie. "This surely cannot be the one he is in love with. *Ay di mi,* she is nothing but a sickly *child!*"

"That was not the way people saw her before the disaster befell her," Sophie retorted. "She was very beautiful and charming, with every young buck in the country asking for her hand."

"*Sí,* that may be true, but I will wager that they do not ask for it now!" Geraldina tossed back, suddenly very jealous of the young woman who had once been very beautiful.

"Eileena, answer me," Juan pressed. "Who are you?"

Eileena shook her head and gulped much like the child Geraldina had called her, and with her hair twined about her fingers she looked away from the handsome sea captain as he addressed the room:

"She *does* understand—I know it!" Juan said with ravaged eyes.

From her quagmire of despair Eileena cast the man a swift look upward. Since the "accident" she never stared at anyone directly but always upward,

302

from bent head, or sidelong with one cheek hidden in her curtain of dull hair.

There is both lonesomeness and misery in her beautiful eyes, Juan was thinking. Suddenly he said, "You live in a beautiful house, Eileena. Do you know everyone here?" His arm swept the room while he kept his eyes on her beloved face.

Eileena stared around her surroundings blankly, as though she'd never seen them before. Her mouth hung open and the pretty flush returned to her face.

The glitter in Juan's eyes grew brittle with despair. "I see," he said. "You would rather not talk. The pretty bird in a gilded cage. Or are you *homely,* Eileena?"

It came as a surprise to everyone when Eileena shook her lackluster hair all around her slim shoulders, and a wild expression was in her eyes. How could she tell anyone how she felt? Stark terror in her nightmares. She saw herself so clearly in those dreams, but by day she was a prisoner within herself. No one understood. Her lips began to tremble. Nobody!

"Please . . ." Ellen said as she came forward. "She cannot hear you. She cannot speak. You know this yourself, Juan."

"Feeling sorry for yourself is not going to help," Juan pressed on despite what Ellen said, "Unless you enjoy it — and I rather suspect that you do, Eileena."

Eileena blinked, at a loss. No one had ever before challenged her right to feel sorry for herself . . . not since she had become "different." Everybody she knew felt sorry for her, and showed it, too. By all sorts of overindulgence, which she dreaded, and this always fed her self-pity.

Teague stepped forward and broke in, "Come,

Juan, let us speak of your voyage. Everyone sit down, please," he said, for they all had been standing around, tense, wondering what Juan would do or say next. After Ellen and Robert helped Eileena to a more comfortable chair, Teague struck up conversation once again. "So, we all know by now that Sebastián has made this lovely lady his wife. Where is he now? When will he be joining us?"

Daniella blushed. "I . . . I am not sure." She exchanged a look with Bettina who had been waiting for her answer. "He . . . I think he is unloading his spices . . ." She laughed lightly. "Or chasing searobbers."

"Of course," Teague Landaker said. "I hope he catches them, too! We have long been blamed for *their* crimes—namely the Drakes'!"

Daniella could not contain the gasp that came easily to her coral-pink lips. "The Drakes? Your enemies?"

"Always and forever it seems, m'lady," Teague said softly. Daniella was seated beside Juan on the settee, while the others chatted comfortably around them, seeming not to eavesdrop on their conversation, but Geraldina had her ear cocked their way while she kept an eagle eye upon Juan who still had eyes only for Eileena!

"Tell me about Sebastián," Daniella politely asked Teague Landaker. "When did you meet him? How did he come to be taken in by your family?"

Placing his drink on the table beside him, Teague began. "I first met him when he was twelve I believe I was about seventeen. I was one among many who were escorting him to the palace . . . in England. Ah, that bright curly hair, and tanned skin—what a combination! He set the girls' hearts to skittering immediately. From the age of twelve to twenty Sebastián was royal ward to the queen."

Wordlessly, Daniella stared at Teague as he went on. "The nobles and the courtiers came to greet us when we rode in; I couldn't believe the attention he was receiving. I even called him 'my lord'," Teague said with a laugh. "It was then, that long ago day, I realized he was someone important. Important, *indeed!* Sebastián became the court darling."

"Who was he?" Daniella suddenly wanted to know.

"Sebastián never gave acknowledgment that he was a . . . a bastard of Captain Kidd." There was an embarrassed silence in which Teague cleared his throat. "His father never legally claimed him as his son, and who could blame him? Captain Kidd was a married man with many children, we've heard."

Gruffly Master Landaker interrupted. "And this is the reason he took to us, his adopted family," he blustered, sloshing his drink. "One with Cornish foundations. We loved him like one of our own, and I am not ashamed to call him son!"

Daniella's mind was spinning with what she had learned.

"Suffice it to say, Sebastián is like my brother," Teague added with honest pride. "You see" — his eyes were darker now — "I lost my *real* brothers to the evil blade of Drake — the one we call the Dragon. And know that his younger brother is no better!"

Daniella gasped and Bettina stepped forward to press her lady's arm.

"And the bastards almost killed my sister!" Teague angrily ejaculated. "If it weren't for Sebastián and Juan Tomaz, she would be dead now!" He sent a loving look to Eileena, then reached an arm around her back to give her a loving hug. "We are a family that cares about one another, Daniella."

Master Landaker lifted his glass to Daniella, who appeared close to fainting, and saluted. "To *Lady* Daniella Landaker—may she live a long and happy life as such!"

Gregory Landaker was near to tears—and Daniella was profoundly touched.

Daniella's slender jaw dropped, and so did her silver-handled brush. With a shiver along her spine, she turned at the sound of the dearly familiar voice, and stood with her hand upon the lace bodice of her nightgown, for there in the shadows of the heavy drapes stood a hooded figure.

"Sebastián?"

"*Sí, querida.*" He stepped into the room, slowly removing the cowl of his long taupe cloak from his head.

"Wh-what has happened to you?" she gasped, unable to drag her eyes from his broad-shouldered form—but it was his face that she was truly frightened of! Was it only makeup again, she wondered? But something told her this was not so. Then she was aware of the narrowing of his tigerish eyes.

With a low bow from the waist, he said, "Do not worry, dearest, I am truly the foppish one you originally fell in love with."

Her sea-gray eyes met the green ones as she walked across the room to turn the light a bit higher. "Y-you are limping," she stuttered. "Have you been hurt?"

"*Sí*, yes, I have been hurt." The cloak swirled from his shoulders as his long-fingered hands swept it off and draped it over the foot of the bed.

306

So that Sebastián would not catch the telltale shimmer of tears in her eyes, Daniella bit her lip and averted her face. With her back to him, she asked, "How did . . . it happen?"

Hungering to press his body close to hers, Sebastián stared at the thin nightgown, imagining he could see more through it than he actually could. As it was, the feminine shape of her softer parts was softly revealed, and he longed to cup the delicately curving buttocks in the palms of his hands and feel the smooth thighs brushing against his legs, her belly against his manhood.

Basking in the sight of her, he said, "It was a duel, *cálida*."

Instantly wary, Daniella panicked when he stepped closer. Though he had moved silently, she could sense his nearness, his tenseness, and a bounding feeling of excitement filled her. She could smell the salt-tang of his clothes and his disturbing maleness, feel his breath, almost hear his thundering heartbeat.

Sebastián clenched his hands, wanting desperately to love her, but he had promised himself he would leave her alone for a year. *If she did not grow heavy with child and send for him.* But he was here now since he could no more stay away from her than the moon and sun could keep from spinning across the sky!

Daniella stepped out from under the spell he had woven about her as she'd stood there immobile, just anticipating his touch, and then she moved away, not knowing what to say or do next. She said the first thing that came to her mind, "Have you eaten supper? Are you tired?"

Sebastián chuckled. "I took a light supper with my men earlier, and, yes, I am very tired."

Fingering the silken bedcover, Daniella found her voice, "This is your room when you come here, is it not?"

"Yes, Daniella, this is my room." When she kept averting her face, he said, "Am I so homely with a few little scars that you must turn away? Are you afraid to look at me, Daniella?"

Her head jerked up and she looked him square in the eyes, trying not to see the angry red scars but failing miserably, for she could not remove them from her vision.

Desire stirred within Sebastián until he was taut with urgency and could not catch his breath. The night deepened outside and the moon spilled more pale light into the spacious bedchamber. Daniella was unaware of the admiring gaze that fell upon her as she turned to do some simple task, if only to keep her nervous fingers busy. She was smoothing the counterpane when his voice sliced across her already taut nerves. "Daniella, I don't know how to say this and my wish is not to be a bearer of bad tidings—"

"You told me of the sad news of my father's fate . . ." She waved an arm in the air. "Pray, what news could equal the pain of *that?*"

"Could we sit?" He indicated the rust-colored chairs positioned across from each other in front of the Italian marble fireplace. "Over there where you do not have to worry that I shall become intimate."

Daniella looked up and her heart tumbled at his soft-spoken words. She had felt an ever-increasing anticipation from the first moment she had become aware of his presence. That he should show such concern for her feelings and not press her into making love caused her to wonder. Or was it only that he had grown weary of their stormy relationship? She was afraid she would never understand the complex-ities of his nature and, thinking this depressing thought, she nodded and moved over to the chair he had indicated.

When they were seated across from each other, Sebastián on the edge of his chair, Daniella comfort-ably enveloped by the huge cushions with her feet tucked under her, there was a silence that could have been sliced with a blade it was so thick.

For a pressing moment Sebastián chewed his lower lip, then he cleared his throat and leaned his elbows on his knees while one hand molded its palm into the other.

"The *Rampant Rose* is no more."

Daniella blinked, then said, "She has . . . *sunk?*" The word finally got out.

"Yes. And perhaps the worst of it is . . ." He looked up at her with ravaged eyes. "Alain Carstairs went down with her."

The back of Daniella's hand flew to her mouth and she pressed it there, her face a study in profound sorrow, and her hair fell forward over her face as she wept softly, tearing out the heart of the man across from her.

"*Cálida . . .*" He leaned forward to catch her hand, but she yanked it back to clutch the nightgown at her side as if she knew a sudden pain there. "Please, love, let me explain. There is more in the telling."

Recovering, she said almost in a whisper. "Go on, Sebastián." She lifted a trembling hand to sweep the moistness from her cheeks. "Please . . . go on."

"I'm quite certain your precious Alain had been aiding the pirates." He heard the soft intake of breath. "When ordered to take the *Rampant Rose* back to the Carolinas, Alain instead defied my orders and went on to unload the spices, and I knew this for certain when he began to run—"

Daniella clenched her hands upon the arms of the chair. "You *killed* Alain!"

"He was a traitor, Daniella." He looked at her grimly. "You know the sequence: The captain takes the ship with her legal cargo, gets cleared for an open port, then makes for the second port where he trades in contraband. Alain must have done this for years, Daniella . . . don't you understand?" He watched her ravaged eyes as she shook her head. "You and your father had no idea where part of your profit had gone. No one had been the wiser, especially the officials. But the real crimes, my love, were the sea raids being blamed on the Windstar Fleet, some of those ships belonging to the Landakers. For years there has been hatred between the Landakers and the Drakes. In fact, the Drake Manor is not all that far from Tallrock."

Daniella thought of the Drakes. Alain. "Is . . . is this how you received your wounds?" she asked Sebastián, finally able to look at him but digging her fingernails into her palms to keep from crying in front of him again.

"No," he said harshly. "That is a different story. But all these unbelievable happenings are strangely linked together."

"Tell me, Sebastián, who gave you the wounds? If you do not tell me, I have no wish to further this conversation. Who were they?" she said in a whisper.

"We will have to go further back if you wish to hear the whole story."

Daniella smiled softly. "I have all the time in the world, Sebastián." She resumed her comfortable position, folding her slim hands in her lap.

Sebastián noticed the little shivers that moved her shoulders now and then, so he went to fetch her white velvet robe and draped it over her shoulders with such infinite tenderness that Daniella was moved by his kind gesture. She thanked him and he went back to his chair across from her. He held up a hand then, and told her to wait while he went to build a fire, and after it was lit he returned to his chair. His smile was gentle as he explained. "It felt a bit chilly in here . . . Do you mind?" He indicated the building flames.

Just as in the fireplace, soft flickering flames began to quiver through her. The warmth permeated the chill in the huge room, as did the unwavering stare of his wondrous green-gold eyes warm her flesh, her heart, her soul.

With a boyishly handsome grin, Sebastián looked at Daniella and felt the same things happening inside him. "Please don't be angry, *cálida,* for I will tell you now the reason for the disguise." A corner of his mouth lifted; his eyes grew serious. "Promise me?"

A light laugh was drawn from her. "How can I promise when I do not know the reason yet? You will have to tell me . . ." She tilted her light head. "Then we shall see how my temper holds."

"There was a spy amongst us." His eyes glittered with feverish impatience. "Can you not guess *who?*"

With sudden clarity it came to her, the reason for everything that had happened! But how . . . ?

With a wild shine in her eyes, she whispered as if someone might overhear. "Alain Carstairs." Then she frowned. "Surely . . . you cannot believe . . . Why would Alain wish to deceive us? For years he had been best friends with my father, but we did not

311

belong to the Established Merchants . . . we were not members." There was a flare to her nose as she looked at him. "What else is there I should try to understand?"

"Our last meeting was held at Braidwood." He leaned forward. "Do you understand now?"

Once again Daniella frowned. "I did not note everyone present."

"Daniella, you are avoiding the real issue. We are speaking of Alain Carstairs and his deceptions."

"Please, I do not wish to discuss Alain's double-dealing." Daniella stood and began walking back and forth, her tempting silhouette gliding across the orange-and-magenta hues of the hearth. "How do you discover so many things? How do you do it?"

He chuckled warmly. "In . . . ah . . . various disguises."

"Then it is true . . ." She held in her breath. "You *are* a master of disguise!"

"M'lady." He stood and executed a dashing bow, sweeping low with his arm and a phantom hat clutched in his fingers. "I am your servant."

Daniella could not help the giggles that erupted, even though she was furious with him. "You are a blundering *fool*," she said, not meaning it. He was every inch the dashing rogue. The gentleman pirate. Captain Sebastián. Queen's ward and court darling. Master of disguise. The Tiger. Handsome gallant. Love . . .

And suddenly she was more angry than she had ever been. "Sebastián, answer me this: Why did you take me away from my father? You could have left me there. I should have been with him as he took his last breath."

Sebastián worried his bottom lip. "He wished for

you not to see him on his deathbed, Daniella. But wait before I get ahead of myself and you misconstrue my real quest."

"Please . . ." she said with a little sniff. "Continue. I would truly like to know the reason you took me away from my father!"

"*Dios,* Dany. I told you it was his dying wish. But . . ." He had the grace to flush. "I had ulterior motives, and you already know what they were and—are."

"Of course. I was your 'dark rose', decoy for the horrible pirates Drake . . . and you used me to lure him to his watery grave. Tell me," she said with flashing eyes, "have you also done away with Robert Drake?"

"No." He grinned. "But we had a mild confrontation at sea."

A flaxen-gold eyebrow rose as she said, "I would hazard a guess—the reason for your scars and limp?" Daniella stared, mesmerized, as his nimble fingers loosened his dagger belt, then let it drop to the floor. "Tell me, Sebastián, did you and Robert fight? Is he dead . . . or alive?"

"To answer your first question: No, we did not fight. The second: The last time I saw your 'beloved *friend,*' he was very much alive." His eyes darkened as he recalled the arrogant manner of Robert Drake, how he had smeared the blood all around his face and then sent him on his way—to the dungeon. "You needn't worry yourself, your lover is quite safe."

Daniella gritted her teeth. "Lover?! Robert and I were not lovers, and well you know it! Is that what you want, Sebastián, to argue?"

Sebastián's head jerked up, his eyes leaving the

313

hearthstick he'd been using to move the logs tighter in the fireplace. "How could I not believe you were Robert's little love when that feisty cook Vivien burned my ears with tales of your woodland adventures along the river?"

"Vivien! I should have known!" Daniella gasped. "She always did have an unkind word for me and was always eager to stir up trouble between my father and myself and—Alain." She sniffed at the mocking smile Sebastián was sending her way, and she shrugged. "So what if Vivien was a little sweet on Alain. So what if she was a little . . . jealous?"

Sebastián walked around her now. "You and Alain Carstairs must have been very close." He removed something from of his vest pocket. "Here, this is yours." With nimble fingers he carefully attached the tiger pin to the sleeve of her robe. "From Alain—with love."

With questioning eyes, Daniella stared up at her handsome husband watching her closely. "I noticed it was missing the day after you left. Why did you take it with you?"

"To remind me of you, *cálida* . . ." He lifted a flaxen-gold lock of hair from her shoulder. "Your smile; your walk; your talk; your . . . touch." With a lock wrapped about his finger, he brought the fragrant strand to his nose and breathed in deeply. "Your scent. Like a moonlit rose."

All the tears of loneliness she'd experienced with his absence stood in her eyes. "Why did you leave me?"

"Suffice it to say if I had taken you with me, I would never have forgiven myself. You might not be alive, or you might be in the hands of . . . pirates. You wouldn't like the . . . ah . . . place where I spent three terrible nights. The food left much to be desired," he said as if that was the very worst deprivation he had suffered in the dungeon.

"But considering everything we've been through, we arrived here miraculously fast and all in one piece." He thought of Spider, one of his new mates who insisted he owed Sebastián his life, since he'd spared Spider from a cruel, lonely death in the dungeons of Tinto. "Now, angelic enchantress, I shall leave so that you can get your beauty sleep." His eyes thirstily drank of her loveliness. "Not that you will need it."

As he stepped back, she stared at his sensual mouth, and asked, "Where will you sleep? This is your room. Perhaps I should move to another sleeping quarters."

"What?" He stared at her incredulously. "That would not be the gentlemanly thing to do, *querida*."

She laughed brightly. "And when were you ever the complete gentleman?" she questioned on a whisper-soft thread. As he smiled and gave her a gentlemanly bow, she bit her lip knowing Sebastián was going to make his way to the door. "Won't you leave the same way you came in?" Her voice carried a desperate note as he swept up his cloak and draped it over his arm. She was used to the thin scars on his face by now and the added mystery the tiny flaws lent him.

"I bid you a good night, m'lady." His voice was strong yet oddly gentle.

When he was about to slip out onto the moonlit gallery, her voice, whisper-soft again, carried to him where he was just closing the drape, out of her sight. He became still, wondering if she had really said the words. They were repeated.

"Don't go . . . Please stay."

Her lids came down over her huge, liquid eyes and she swallowed hard, knowing he had already gone, but when she opened them again, he was standing just inside the room!

"Lovely lady," he said with ravaged features. "Will you repeat that please?"

Her teeth worried her lower lip, then she said, "I . . . I do not wish to be alone . . . Sebastián." She turned her back on him so he wouldn't catch the glimmer of tears pooling in her great sea-gray eyes. "I have lost so much."

Muttering huskily, his arms were around her in a flash, hugging her from behind as he pressed his chin to the side of her head. Daniella could not see the infinite tenderness on his sun-roughened face and she buried her own against his chest as he swooped her into his arms and carried her to the huge bed. Her slender arms went about his powerful neck and she pressed herself against him until he responded with a deep groan of satisfaction.

Daniella was still clinging to him as he gently removed her velvet robe and light muslin gown with the delicate lace bodice. He lay down, fully clothed, and wrapped his arms about her protectively as she wept, softly releasing all the pent-up tension she had been holding inside, and all the loneliness, all the fears, her losses over her loved ones, and much, much more. With the length of him pressed to her securely, Daniella's sobs ceased and, much like a small child, she heaved a deep sigh, loving the feel of the strong yet gentle hands that cradled her head against his chest. All was quiet then.

Hearing her contented sigh, Sebastián kissed the top of her head, his voice a whisper in the room that

316

was growing dimmer all the time as the candles sputtered out and the fire in the hearth lost its blaze, soon to become mere glowing embers. "I have dearly missed you, my love," he softly breathed into the long fair tresses that tickled his chin.

Daniella turned in his arms and suddenly clung to him, cuddling at his side. Sebastián sucked in his breath as her slender fingers loosened the ties of his green silk tunic, bringing a warmth of sensation flowing through his blood. One tanned hand lifted, and he murmured her name as he caressed the burnished locks, twirling the silken strands while with slow madness she undressed him. *Dios mio!* he thought, ravaged.

When he lay naked against her, he murmured, "Your hair is like radiant diamonds, *cálida*." He grasped the thick skein to wind it about his powerful neck, drawing them even closer than before. "There. Now you have me bound to you. *Forever*."

She only smiled. Sebastián touched her with reverence, then moved back to study her in the low lighting of the radiant embers, his eyes falling to the alabaster flesh of her thigh, and the tightness in his loins was felt even more. She was supple and soft and silken. He was lean and hard . . . And he wanted her with a fierce passion raging in his blood!

Daniella felt Sebastián's manhood stir and grow hard against that most intimate part of her and his mouth clung to hers as he pressed her back to the bed to make their contact that much more felt. The insistent pressure held her captive while his mouth and tongue created glorious shivers of desire throughout her body. When he moved lower, Daniella moaned and arched as his slippery tongue softly stroked her nipples, and then moved lower yet to the gold velvet patch between her thighs, and all of Daniella's dreams came true as his mouth tickled and stimulated and sweetly tortured. Then he moved suddenly, up and over her, and with a plunge, knowing she was ready and eager, he thrust his swollen shaft inside and plunged again and again, and she arched her back, taking him and glorying in the heavy thrusts.

They reached passion's pinnacle once; then the lovemaking began all over again. She clutched his arms as he entered again, his powerful body thrusting deeply, deeply, his hard body atop hers and her bare breasts tingling against his hair-rough chest. He bent like a bow and his lips gently brushed her taut, thrusting nipples and she gasped and panted and mewled as he rode her, her hair falling like stardusted rolling waves around them, a foaming cascade twining and holding them captive to each other.

Pulses quickened and their faces were suffused with the moist shade of lovers nearing the shattering peak. He crushed her to him passionately, and when she bucked up, he drove the last thrust that brought them to sweetest release. He folded his powerful arms about her waist and she whimpered in delicious rapture.

Flipping over to his back, bathed in a coppery glow of sweat, Sebastián rolled his head and stared at the figure beside him. After their passionate joining, her hair curled in swirls about her temples, pressed damply against her velvet-rose cheekbones. "That was wonderful. Would you not agree, m'lady?"

Breath caught between her words. "Most assuredly, m'lord."

Still panting, he scoffed, " 'M'lord' is it now, eh?"

318

He reached over and squeezed her thigh and she squealed as best she could with her depleted strength. "I believe my lady likes a few scars here and there to decorate her lover's body. *Dios mio!* You are a little tigress all over again . . . just as you were when Steven loved you."

Choking back a gasp, Daniella spoke. "Did *you* love me, too, Sebastián? Or only when you were in disguise?"

Hiding his regret over his hasty words, he rolled his head on the pillow. "Surely that is a silly question, my love. Steven and Sebastián are one and the same."

Wordlessly she stared at the high ceiling, barely making out the corners of the room. She would not press him to say the words outright, out loud, as she wished to hear. Things were not completely resolved between them. She had known too much hurt! She had to learn to forgive. But *could* she forgive, that was the question? One thing was certain, she would wait to tell him that she was carrying his child . . . if indeed she was.

The next day they walked about the grounds in the early-morning swirls of fog and delighted in the presence of each other. It was as if Sebastián were courting her, as if they were lovers just beginning. In the afternoons they rode horses, and rode so far one afternoon they could spot the tumbledown manor of the Drakes. Daniella was still having difficulty believing that Robert and Sir Lucian were the cause of all the heartache the Landakers of Tallrock still were experiencing. One day she'd learn the truth herself, she knew it!

319

All of a sudden Daniella blurted, "Where do you come from, Sebastián? I mean your true family history." She bit her lip, waiting.

For a moment Sebastián frowned down at her from his perch aboard the huge black stallion, "My past is not one I am proud of. I am the child of an illicit union between a pirate and a beautiful Spanish lady. My bastardy is terribly unpleasing to me."

Now it was Daniella's turn to scowl. "But it is not your fault you are illegitimate. It is your father's, and not just a little fault of your mother's, too!"

"Dios mio!, no one has ever blamed my mother, and this makes me angry, Daniella!" He brought his mount to an abrupt halt and Daniella had to struggle with her own surprised horse until Sebastián reached over to steady the nervous beast.

They stared, and neither blinked a lash.

"Did your mother go to the pirate willingly?" When he remained silent, she said, *"Did* she?"

"Sí." He sighed. "I believe she did."

"Well then," Daniella said with a shrug, using her logic. "Your mother was not entirely an angel. How could even a simple pirate acknowledge an illegitimate child, since that would only diminish what his legitimate heirs would one day possess?"

"Hear me, Daniella. I am not greedy, and do not lay claim to anything that is not rightly mine, even of a simple pirate's, and never even thought to borrow when I was badly in need of it. It was too late for a father-son relationship anyhow. He died before I could ever come to know him. True, my mother and the pirate had an illicit relationship"—he took a deep breath—"and I never thought to hear myself say this, but now that you brought it to light, Rebecca was somewhat weak-willed to have allowed Captain Kidd

ccess to her bed so readily, especially as she did not
ove him. When I was a boy, she told me she had
never once turned the pirate away."

"Rebecca?" Suddenly it hit her; *the name in the
ournal!* "*Rebecca* is your mother?"

Rubbing his chin, Sebastián stared hard at Dan-
ella. "How would you know about her?"

"I must confess that I looked into your journal,
but only because I was searching for answers to
many perplexing puzzles. All this time I thought another woman occupied your heart, Sebastián!"

"*Sí*, she occupied my heart, Daniella, only as a
beloved parent could. There has never been anyone
but you, Daniella, *querida mia.*"

A blond eyebrow slanted. "*No* one?"

"*Dios!* I said it and I meant it!"

Daniella's smile was radiance itself, and as she
gave the swift gray mare a careful jab in the ribs, he
reared and performed a curvet, then she took off like
a flash of beautiful unleashed lightning.

"Catch me if you can!!"

The words of heroic challenge rang in Sebastián's
ears several moments following the leap of her horse
over a low white fence. "*Eiyahh!* Come on, Valen-
ino!, what are we lingering on our backsides for!"
he yelled at the black horse and they took off, leav-
ng the space on the green misty earth unoccupied
. . . until a man with dark-brown eyes came and
stood in the same place they had recently vacated, a
hill that looked out over Drake land.

Chapter Nineteen

Fortune favors the bold.
(Audentis fortuna juvat.)
— Virgil

"Hellooo?"

It was an amazing room with colors rich and dark
Plum, crimson, cobalt, green, and royal purple. Da
niella let her gaze wander from the oxblood red vas
with the three white-painted magnolias to the Japa
nese fans on the draped mantel to the dark-green
embroidered throw on a deep-cushioned chair to th
creamy white curtains with their rich blue borders.

Daniella slowly walked about the room she ha
slipped into from the open patio doors. "Hello, i
anyone home?" she called again.

Silence.

Finally, after several long moments, Daniella lifte
a book from a table beside the deep-cushioned chair
sending puffs of dust scattering about to float lazil
in the air. Holding her hand over her mouth, Dan
iella coughed and then sneezed. She set the book
back in its place, where no doubt it had lain un
touched for weeks or longer.

She was inside the Drake Manor, and she was be
ginning to regret the curiosity that she'd felt as sh
studied the unkempt estate from the hill — curiosit
that had finally lured her here!

Daniella was about to return to Tallrock, knowing that should Sebastián discover her visit she'd have much explaining to do, when a familiar voice spoke to her from the doorway.

Daniella spun about.

"Robert!" she cried.

The dark-brown eyes probed Daniella's very soul. He was thinner and new lines of maturity were visible about his sensuous mouth, and his vivid darkness had grown swarthier . . . and somehow sinister.

Daniella found herself staring. Nothing could really change him, she thought, for across any crowd, in any unexpected place—such as here!—she would always know Robert Drake instantly. There would always remain in her heart a very special place for him, one she prayed he'd never do anything to damage.

"Dany Rose." Softly, disbelief written in his dancing dark eyes, he mouthed the words before rushing forward to lift her hand to kiss it.

"Oh, Robert!" Daniella said with a nervous laugh. "You are going to eat my hand if you do not stop."

"Ahh, Dany, do you realize how you steal my breath?" He squeezed her dainty hand so hard that Daniella grimaced, but Robert hardly seemed to notice her distress. "Are you not happy to see me, my sweet? Did you think I could be easily disposed of?"

Still clutching her hand, Robert leaned forward to kiss the soft spot near her lips. Still feeling a sting of pain Daniella slowly pulled her fingers from his hand. She had greeted him with the warmth of real affection, but not with the overly enthusiastic reception he had given her.

"Dany, you little fool, didn't you know it would always be just the two of us?"

Daniella was worried now. "What are you saying, Robert?"

Robert allowed Daniella to free herself and, leaning indolently against the mantelpiece, laughed at her confusion as if he had provoked her with one of his old schoolboy tricks.

There was a murderous feeling inside him, for now he was certain that she had been the ravishing beauty he had seen in his spy-glass! Just yesterday he had seen her so happily riding about the misty grounds of Tallrock. He had witnessed an affectionate kiss that had ripped his insides apart. One day he would kill the man who had not only deceived Dany but himself as well!

"Ah, dearest Dany, you've grown lovelier, if that's possible," he said, his eyes hooded like a hawk's.

Robert Drake's chuckle was deep, sinister, bold.

He has changed, Daniella thought. Or had Robert always been like this beneath his playful exterior? Under his appearance of ease was a wariness she had not noticed before. He was grinning wickedly now and Daniella gave a start.

"I can still read your mind, Dany." His laugh was deep and sinister. "I knew you'd come. You felt it, too, didn't you? You could not stay away. You knew, somehow, I was here, waiting for you to come to me, just like you used to come to meet me on our wooded path near the river."

Daniella was too intent to be diverted. "What do you want, Robert?" He was right, for she had indeed felt the tug which had led her to visit the Drake estate.

"Oh! Can't you read *my* mind anymore? Suppose we say I'd like to sail away, far away, and take you with me?" His voice hardened. *"Audentis fortuna*

324

juvat."

"What does that mean?" Daniella asked Robert.

"Fortune favors the bold!" He laughed at her surprise, teasing and careless again like the old Robert.

"That was Latin, Dany. It would be amusing to sail East—to fortune, wouldn't you say?"

Daniella's mind was in a spin. Long eyelashes brushed down, then slowly up again. "There is Sebastián now," Daniella said.

A jolt of intense hatred went through Robert, but he acted as if he hadn't heard her and stood smiling down at her. "Must you amuse yourself with playing *Lady* Landaker?" His voice was cool and nonchalant.

Daniella was suddenly angry. Neither she nor this new Robert with the mocking smile were the same as yesterday's children. Time, indeed, had wrought many changes.

"I am not amusing myself *playing* Lady Landaker," she said in a sudden declarative tone. "I *am* Lady Landaker—Sebastián's wife."

Robert's smile warped downward as he shrugged. "I am sorry to have insulted you . . . ah . . . Daniella." He chose not to call her by that other name for the moment because he could see it bothered her.

With a renewed smile, Daniella said, "I forgive you, Robert, for haven't I always?"

"That you have." Suddenly he seemed very excited. "Come aboard the *Raven* . . . I would love to show her to you!"

"The *Raven?*"

"Of course. My ship. I told you that I owned her. Don't you remember?"

Warily, Daniella nodded. She had no wish to hurt Robert, but she wondered if he actually knew she was the same woman he had seen from his ship . . . or perhaps he had not recognized her. If he had, he was not saying. What could it hurt if she went aboard the ship? This was Robert . . . and she had always trusted him. And she had truly missed him, so what could it hurt?

When they were finally aboard the *Raven,* and he had shown her around, however, Daniella looked around with a strange tingling up and down her spine. She didn't much care for the dangerous-looking men she had seen watching and ogling her with eagle eyes!

Robert's dark eyes were slitted. "What do you think?"

He stood against the ship's rigging and Daniella forced a smile to her lips because, in truth, she thought the ship could really stand a good cleaning—just like his brother Lucian's manor!

Daniella had no time to answer, for all of a sudden she felt the swaying motion of the *Raven!*

She whirled to face Robert. "The ship is moving!"

With gentle consideration, Robert put his arms around her. "I had to make something happen, Dany, when you had muddled things up for us." He gave her tiny waist a squeeze. "Now is our chance to be away!"

"You must be mad, Robert!"

"Tonight we shall be far out into the Atlantic. You're safe with me, Dany Rose."

"Oh, Robert," Daniella said with a groan, "you cannot mean this. You could not be so wicked!"

Fright and bewilderment overwhelmed Daniella, and she struggled to get away from Robert, but he only tightened his arm. His breath, reeking of strong drink, blew across her face and she wondered momentarily when he had imbibed, for she hadn't noticed the sour smell before coming aboard the *Raven*.

"Tell me it is wicked to say we have always belonged together, Dany Rose?"

As he talked, he walked slowly and Daniella did not wish to be left alone so she followed him, feeling more lost than she had ever in her entire years—approaching twenty.

He continued. "We grew up knowing that, and it was the best thing in us both. Whatever comes between us must be put to death, Dany! Hell, I tried making you see that, but you kept mixing it up with things that can't matter, until I realized I'd get nowhere trying to talk you out of them." He whirled to face her, and his eyes were dark and strange. "Can you fault me when there was no other path?"

Daniella gasped. "You are crazy!"

With a lightning-fast movement, he grabbed her arm. "Don't *ever* call me crazy again, Dany!"

"Robert . . ." She tried to make her voice sound loving. "I do not wish harm to come to any of us, especially not you when Sebastián finds—"

"Let me finish! Things went wrong in South Carolina, Dany. This time I had to make plans, and now the stars must be with us. We'll live the sort of adventures we used to play make-believe at—you sailing with me always. Tomorrow we'll sail toward Spain—"

"Spain!"

Daniella looked at Robert, aghast at his reckless audacity. "From the first time you returned to Charleston Harbor, this plot was in your mind! You wanted a ship to go to Spain—to join pirates! I will not be a pirate's wench, Robert!"

He shrugged with an indifferent air. "Freebooters

327

or venturers, what difference is there? I am one, your lover is the other. We go farther to seek our treasure, if that makes it more respectable. We'll help ourselves as do the merchants in their lawful quest. Dammit, we are free as the wind, Dany!"

Robert was restlessly pacing about the cabin they had entered, striding as if the *Raven* could not go fast enough for him now.

"Take me back, Robert," Daniella said. "Now."

"Turn back?" He laughed. "I've never known you to take fright, Dany."

"Please, I wish you would not call me that. I am Daniella Landaker now."

He ignored that and went on speaking as if she had not even interrupted. "We are safe now."

"Safe?" Daniella could only echo hollowly.

Ceasing to pace back and forth, Robert went to perch at the edge of the narrow table, one foot swinging, his eyes bright, dark, restless as he stared around, his eyes resting often on Daniella's breasts.

"My mates found an inlet days ago. It's a perfect hideout. Only a short run to sea after dark again, and time to get clear of the coast without the *Spanish Wind* spotting us."

"Oh, God. You are only fooling yourself, Robert."

Under his breath he hummed a song, and then began to recite the words in a singsong voice:

"High on that thorny rose-tree
  There is a fair white rose.
Down here no one can reach it;
  Above there no one goes.

"Come on, Dany, join me in that beautiful nightingale's voice of yours."

She looked sad. "No, Robert, I'd rather not sing st now."

The *Raven* lurched so suddenly that Daniella was rown back onto the weak-framed bunk, and then e corvette came gently to rest. "What happened?" he sat up to rub her bruised ankle, tossing her loos-ed blond hair back over her shoulder.

"We're in," he simply said. "Did you hurt your-lf?"

"It is nothing." She leaned forward along her an-le, not wishing him to see her grimace of pain, for e would rather not have any comfort or affection om him.

"I'm going to go have a look topside, Dany. Stay ut."

As if I could go anywhere! Daniella grimaced gain and, as soon as Robert had made his exit, she ot up from the bunk and discovered that although er ankle was badly swollen, she could walk a little. he studied the small cabin. If she watched for a hance during the day, she might be able to slip shore, perhaps to find a place to hide, or reach ome farmhouse. She knew they could not have gone ll that far from the English Channel . . . Yet she new she could not move quickly enough to cover ny distance. There were the pirates, searobbers of e *Raven*'s worst lot all watching her every move. "hey would take care that she did not escape to be-ray their hiding place and she had little hope of easoning with Robert in his present mood. He was ke a man crazed!

Daniella sighed forlornly. There was nothing she ould say to change Robert's mind, for he would put : down to her quick temper and annoyance at his rick. He would recall how often they had quarreled and made up . . .

Daniella finally decided it was best to avoid
scene; she would watch and wait for her chanc
When she had poured a drink from the water ca
and washed and tidied herself as best she could, sl
felt somewhat refreshed and strengthened.

The curtain had been drawn across the winde
and, pushing it aside, Daniella could see the sl
coloring behind the dark trees that closed round tl
ship like a deep emerald shroud. She then lit a la
tern. She was standing there quietly when Robe
returned, and, strangely, she felt his comforting pre
ence as she always had.

"A perfect mooring," he said with satisfactio
"We have been here before, I only forgot. This is
lonely spot. There is not much danger of a chan
person stumbling upon us. If someone *do*
come . . ." He only shrugged, his hand resting at l
sword hilt.

Daniella understood that Robert was taking h
partnership for granted now, reassuring her of the
safety.

"Ah . . . what does Sebastián look like up clos
I've only seen him from a distance." He was thinkii
back to the swordfight on the decks of that ship l
was sure had been the *Emerald Tiger,* for no one el
on the high seas owned a ship with a figurehead su
as that. He was reminded suddenly of the Engli
dandy who'd almost ended his brother's life, but L
cian was healing, though he'd lost an enormo
amount of blood—no thanks to that tawny-hair
devil!

"Sebastián is like no other," Daniella answere
and it was true, since she'd never known a man th
seemed to be so many persons wrapped up in on

And he is like many."

The cryptic description flew right over Robert's head, and he decided to change the distasteful subject since Daniella seemed to wear a dreamily romantic expression all of a sudden, one that sickened him!

"Sean is taking a post downcreek to keep watch. But we can expect a quiet afternoon here while Roger goes inland for two copemates who have kept in readiness to join us. We could have headed out sooner, but I've been wanting to take them with me."

Disinterestedly, Daniella asked, "Who are they?"

"Just friends. But someday I want you to meet my brother, Sir Lucian." He chuckled and joked, "He's the devil himself."

"Oh" was all Daniella uttered with a shiver.

Robert had carried with him a brimming measure of wine and a plate of white cheese and biscuits; these he set on the table and brought down two mugs from the locker.

"I would have fed you sooner, Dany. I'm sorry, but we have been too busy to eat — we just now had a look at the *Raven*'s stores and we shan't go hungry or thirsty at any rate. Sit down, over here, love."

Robert took in her grimace at his calling her that but shrugged it off as he did so many other things, doing as he pleased.

"Let us drink our first cup to the venture." He sloshed the wine and gaily hefted his mug. "To lady fortune — may she smile on us!"

Daniella snickered. "Ha! A pirate's fortune quite commonly ends swinging at the rope, Robert!"

She was making a desperate effort to sober him and make him see things her way rather than with the twisted reasoning of his mind.

His laugh was sinister, and he drained his wine

331

without a blink. "Drakes make the most un*commc* pirates."

Her eyes tilted up at him. "You are a pirate then

He sighed, pouring himself another. "You loc better already, Dany. More wine?"

She looked at the glass she hadn't touched. "Yc know I do not drink."

Robert was flushed not only with wine but wit triumph also. The bitter lines about his mouth whic had been the first change she'd noticed in him we gone. He looked the boy again, playing this out as it were a boy's game, as if the rules were no mo difficult, as if he had grown no wiser. Yet he ha managed the plan shrewdly, and his reckless humc was more dangerous now than a boy's willfulness.

Daniella watched Robert stuff himself with vor; ciousness, then loosed a loud belch.

"I had hardly noticed I'd missed my supper," H mumbled between mouthfuls of crusty dark brea "You're my luck, Dany Rose." He belched agai "We pulled it off."

Daniella heaved a deep, slow sigh. Poor Robe . . . so lost.

He was filling his mug again and raised it to he quoting the rest of the lines he had earlier recited

"My thistle burned till morning
    And yet it still shows blue.
Now that the sun is shining,
    I know my love is true.

"Sing, Dany, sing!"
Shaking her head, Daniella's heartbeat quickene as she listened. She had heard these last lines befor aboard the *Spanish Wind*.

332

"What does it mean?" she asked, hoping to keep Robert sober with conversation, for she did not know what he would do to her if he became thoroughly intoxicated. She hated to think what could take place aboard this filthy ship . . . and she shivered though Robert barely noticed.

But Robert sat back, only to swig more wine "There is a certain summer evening when all the girls in Lisbon set their candlesticks in their windows and burn thistles in them. If the edges of the flowers are still blue in the morning, then their lovers are true."

"That is . . ." Daniella thought for a moment. "Lovely. Romantic." Sebastián was on her mind. Was his love true? How long would it take before she was certain of his love? Her blood pounded hotly as she recalled the last night they had shared and he had enflamed her with his tender caresses . . . And then there had been the afternoon in the sheltered woods when they had made love beneath a shaft of warming sun. And just yesterday . . .

Silence reigned in the small cabin until the door was suddenly flung back with a resounding slam! Robert dropped his wine cup and was half to his feet when the deep voice filled the space, thrilling Daniella to the core!

Not quickly enough, Robert's hand moved.

The deep voice again. "Keep your hand from your sword, Robert Drake!"

Sebastián! Daniella gasped. *How could it be?*

A swift rush through the entrance was executed before Robert could clear the bench to draw; then a wicked blade was pointed to his throat.

Sebastián stood out of reach, his sword point keeping its advantage all the while, and chills crept along Daniella's spine. They were going to kill each

333

other!

Robert, hampered by bench and table, empty-handed, shouted furiously at Sebastián's head. "Let me up and fight fair—you damned simple merchant!"

"Keep your hands on the table!" Sebastián ordered coolly. "Get back, Daniella!"

"No!" she cried. "Not this way! Let him go, Sebastián. Let's forget this ever happened. In God's name let there be no blood shed here!"

His eyes not wavering, Sebastián kept his full attention on Robert. "We can't all be as open and honorable as pirates," he sneered. "If your man strays drunkenly into the woods, Drake, someone may be watching to sneak up on him. And if you light your cabin . . ." His glance took in the lantern—still burning, though scarcely needed now—and the window whose curtains Daniella had left apart. "Someone in a hurry might just forget to knock!"

Daniella looked to the window where she had left the lantern burning, where she had opened the curtain. The lines came back to her, *I know my love is true.* Sebastián had found her!

Now Robert snarled, "Stop talking, curse you, and fight!"

"Simple merchants like to know the score before they settle it." Sebastián postured before Robert, looking every inch the English dandy. "Know me now, Drake?"

Daniella looked from one to the other, wondering what Sebastián was referring to. Then her conversation with him returned and she thought she knew.

"The peacock!" Robert snarled, gritting his teeth. "I shall give you a few more scars to add to your collection, *Tielo* Tiger!" *The master of disguise!*

334

Robert was free of the table and saw his advantage when Sebastián looked Daniella over to see if she'd come to harm. Robert attacked furiously. They meant to kill each other and any cry that she made now, any movement to hinder, might free one sword for a murderous stroke!

This was too incredible . . . Sebastián was giving way! He seemed to just manage to cover a retreat, then he was through the passage, Robert pressing him hotly, and Daniella scrambled to her feet, sick with terror but following them out into the companionway.

They came to a standstill on the afterdeck, and now Sebastián was holding his ground — yet not so much holding it as defending swift movements. He would not fight close, and every effort Robert made to force it was evaded. There was none of the forthright cut and slash practiced in singlestick about this, and for a moment it seemed to Daniella less dangerous . . . but she was so wrong.

Since Daniella had stepped aboard the *Raven,* each successive shock had seemed untrue and unbelievable. For a startling moment now the present slipped from her, and she watched not this scene but one not long ago in the streets by the riverfront. For an instant this eerily seemed the very same duel, the same duelists . . .

It was there, near the riverfront, that she'd seen this odd, dancelike advance with the sword point. Robert kept trying to close and, always fended off, returned to this thrust and parry as something not yet natural, as if he had not learned as well as the other swordsman. Had Sebastián purposely retreated from the close quarters of the cabin?

Now she knew! Sebastián had come along to save

her when . . . when Charles Blackman — of course
. . . Charley had been trying to abduct her to bring
her aboard the *Raven!* For Robert!

Sebastián had been that dancing swordsman who
had saved her . . . the wounded arm had been
Charles Blackman's!

Now Sebastián's purpose was deadly and Daniella
was no longer dazzled by the light, swift play that
had seemed almost a game. Both were breathing
much faster now, and the pace was quickening!

Oh Lord, Daniella groaned inwardly — all these
dreadful things had begun because of her stupid
folly in going to visit Drake Manor. No, it had all
started much farther back in the past . . .

And there was nothing she could do. She dared
not move or distract them in any way that would
bring the deadly stroke to one or the other!

They were evenly matched for height, but Sebastián was by far the quicker and surer footed, though
Robert was several years younger.

Sebastián's thrust seemed headed straight for
Robert's heart in the next instant, and Daniella
couldn't stop the words that came automatically.
"Stop . . . please *stop!*"

Robert only snarled his venom, wiping the sweat
from his brow with a hunched shoulder. "Go away,
Dany!"

The nickname, spoken like a soft endearment,
went clear through to Sebastián's heart much as a
clean thrust would.

Robert barely parried Sebastián's next thrust, and
before he could recover, the darting steel was back
again and easily, contemptuously, as if it had chosen
that spot, pierced his sword arm.

Sebastián lowered his bloody point, but Robert

snatched with his left hand for his falling sword. "I am not finished yet, damn you!" he cried. "Come . . . I am ready for you again!"

Impetuous and every inch the brave woman, Daniella chose that moment to throw herself between them as an accumulation of anxiety, self-accusation, and fright was wiped out suddenly by a fierce anger . . .

Indeed she was angered with both of them, with Robert who had tricked her, with Sebastián who could use others as suited him . . . both of them settling her affairs without a by-your-leave, and brawling, killing each other under her nose!

But Sebastián, on the other hand, had witnessed something more and he'd already decided he could not bring himself to kill a man who was pathetically insane. He had seen the gleam of madness in Robert's eyes, but he knew Daniella mistook it for something else—such as jealousy. It was the Drake madness, no rumor as he'd thought many times. Now, looking at Robert Drake, Sebastián finally believed Robert was as mad as his brother Lucian!

"Get out of the way, Dany!" Robert shouted at her furiously, "Damn you, woman, you've always been defiant!"

Daniella acted swiftly. She kicked the sword Robert was reaching for across the deck and faced him like a spitting tigress.

"Stop, you fool! Are you mad?" She missed the look Sebastián sent her. "End this now!"

Robert had clutched his arm and a bright stain was spreading on his sleeve, but he looked down at it and his handsome face was dark with rage.

"It has to be bound at once," she said, already tearing a strip of cloth from her petticoat.

337

Sebastián neither moved nor spoke a word. Robert, watching the blood that freely dripped through his fingers, allowed Daniella to rip the sleeve open to roll it back and bind the gash firmly, carefully.

Suddenly Robert groaned. It was bleeding profusely, but she saw with great relief that it was not spurting and should do well enough without having to burn the flesh closed.

Robert, still enraged, saw this, too, and with renewed vigor his hand went for his dagger and he swung about suddenly to face Sebastián, shouting, "We'll finish this, you bastard!"

"No!"

Daniella clung with her full weight on Robert's injured arm, knowing quite well how sharply this must pain him, but she could think of nothing else. "You idiot, simpleton! Cease this play!"

Robert whitened and sucked in his breath. "Off my arm, wench!"

"I may choose to leave the pirate to the hangman," Sebastián said smoothly as he brushed his knuckles over his umber vest. "He was in on the conspiracy with Alain Carstairs and Charles Blackman—both dead now."

"Why you . . ." Robert pressed forward, but Daniella restrained him as best she could. "You think you have ruined everything, don't you!"

Sebastián gave a mock half bow. "Only half of it; there is yet work to be done. By the way, Drake, you'll have to work hard to retrieve your crew, they are scattered hither and yon, some wounded, some dead—but small in number now. That is, if I choose to let you go."

Daniella had to think—and fast. Sebastián was ac-

338

cusing Robert of being a pirate and that would also mean he would be accused of being instrumental in the sinking of the *Rampant Rose!*

"What piracy is there?" She spread her slim hands, speaking cold and clear. "I . . . I gave Robert the *Rampant Rose,* and whatever papers have to be signed I shall swear to."

Looking at Daniella, Sebastián shook his head. "My love, you know the *Rampant Rose* is no more. I realize what you are doing, Dany, and it won't work."

"But, Sebastián, you have always known the ships would go to me. They are mine to do with as I please. If I want the *Rampant Rose* sunk, then sunk she will be."

Sebastián only shook his tawny head. "Dany, Dany, did you mean for your father's ships to become a scourge to decent men? You know what this gallows bird would have used it for."

Daniella drew herself up straight and looked her husband in the eye. "You do not understand, Sebastián — I could not give the *Rampant Rose* for a wrong use . . . to anyone."

"Daniella . . ." Sebastián only sighed.

She had meant for her words to reach Robert, staking the best she had known of him on a desperate throw.

"You will lose every time," Sebastián said, as if he had read her mind correctly.

Steeling herself, Daniella turned back to Robert, who was now reclining upon a coil of rope, beads of perspiration standing out on his forehead. "Robert, our games used to be of new islands and seaways. You yourself talked of them only today. I . . . I shall think of you sailing the *Raven* in ventures I might have tried — if — *if* I had been Edward's son."

Robert snorted. "Are you offering me a parting gift, Lady *Landaker?*"

"*Sí,*" Sebastián drawled. "*Wholesome* advice."

"Why you boastful bastard!" Robert made to rise and Sebastián stepped forward to meet him, but Daniella again stepped in between.

"My God, stop this! Both of you!"

With Sebastián prepared to charge Robert with piracy, able to command this area as others, Daniella could see no course except the one she had impulsively chosen. It left her unable to draw terms now or seek a promise. She could only cling to the hope of reaching Robert through her trust in the lovely moments they had shared in the past. And despite the bitterness in his voice now, she persisted, but the need to talk to him around Sebastián's hostility was a damper.

"Robert . . ." she went on sweetly. "My dearest childhood friend, if you find passage in this venture, the rewards and honors for it will be so great that all my life I shall be proud of you."

"You are a fool, Dany!"

But Robert put his arms about her as he said this, and suddenly he kissed her. "A sweet, forgiving fool. I shall never again find anyone as precious as you!"

The man is devious, as well as mad, Sebastián told himself. Rolling his eyes heavenward, he leaned against the bulkhead, shaking his head while feeling mildly sick to his stomach. *Sí,* he could not stomach much more of this scene!

"Daniella." Sebastián straightened. He had had enough! "We'll be going now."

"Wait. Please."

Daniella realized she might never see Robert again.

He had deceived her shamefully and she had been shocked and angry and yes, frightened, too. If chance had not brought them to this end she would still have been desperately contriving one—yet for a moment in time Daniella clung to their past in desperation, and the anguish brought its own sharpened clarity. She knew now what Robert had always been to her. He was the brother she had never known, the special one with whom you share things and moments which all others you love cannot share. Robert would follow his reckless wind far from hers, true, and the women he would love would fit his new world.

Robert turned away from them, his countenance radiating evil, an evil that would see them all dead!

"I am afraid there is one more score to settle," Sebastián said, stepping forward to block Robert from Daniella's line of vision. "Eileena Landaker."

There was a snort from Robert.

"Yes, you gasp, you venomous snake. You have not forgotten that you have ruined her life, have you?" He clutched his sword. "I could easily kill you for that . . . if you were not so coddled by my beloved wife."

Beloved . . . *beloved!* Daniella's heart sang in her breast. Finally, he had said it to someone . . . but when would he face *her* to say it out loud?

Robert slumped, falling to his knees on the deck, holding onto Sebastián's legs. "I must go to her and ask her forgiveness!" *Really, what he wanted was to find that secret tunnel into the house. Then he could see the last of the Landakers and have all their wealth to boot!*

"I'm sorry," Sebastián said, looking down at him with contempt, "but if you do that, Juan Tomaz will have your head on a platter before you place one boot on her doorstep! I advise you to let me speak with him first—and after a while he might allow you to see her to ask Eileena forgiveness." Sebastián's fingers stroked his chin. "A very good idea, in fact, and I shall see that you carry it out—soon!"

Robert came slowly and painfully to his feet. "I must go and find Lucian. This was all his doing in the first place." Daniella missed the mad light in his eyes, but not so Sebastián.

"Oh?" Sebastián played dumb. "What are you going to do?"

"Why . . ." Robert drew himself up. "Wipe his evil stench from this earth, that's what! He taught me . . . that bastard taught me everything bad."

"No, Robert Drake, you *let* Sir Lucian teach you. Now, be gone from my sight before I decide the lady is a fool to allow me to let you go scot free!"

"Farewell, Robert." Daniella turned and, without looking back, she descended to the lower deck and stepped ashore where the ship's waist grazed the bank. "How will we get back to Tallrock?" she asked Sebastián over her shoulder as he followed close behind, checking her step to see she didn't stumble.

"I have horses." He threw his arm out. "In that copse where Spider and several of my men await. It is shorter than to travel by ship, as the crow flies."

"Ouch!" Daniella turned her bad ankle.

"You have been hurt. *Dios!* Why didn't I notice before!"

"Because you were busy, m'lord."

He swooped her up into his powerful arms. "Please cease with the titles, Daniella, I'm in no mood for playfulness."

"Why did you spare Robert?"

"I could not end the man's life; he has already done that for himself."

"What do you mean?"

"Robert is on his way to total madness, my dear wife. Neither would killing him, I've discovered, bring back Eileena's lost innocence or her sanity."

"I don't understand. Why do you say he is mad?"

"Madness is in his eyes. You have never noticed it before, this is why you cannot recognize it now."

"D-did I do that to him, by rejecting him when he wanted to take me away?"

"Madness runs in the Drake family, *querida*. Their ancestors used to keep a torture chamber for their slaves and captives."

"How horrible! I never realized."

Daniella shuddered to think this of her childhood playmate, the one Alain Carstairs had brought to her long ago. Strange, she thought now, that Alain, the traitor, had been the one to introduce Robert Drake into her family.

"Sebastián!"

Daniella had seen the horses up ahead and a funny-looking little man waiting, watching for them and wearing a brace of pistols that appeared lopsided on his small frame.

"It is only Spider, my love."

"I realize that. But something else came to mind when you were fighting with Robert. I realized you had been that swordsman who came to my rescue. You saved me from being kidnapped!"

"*Sí*, so I did. I was not about to let you be carried away when I had just found you and was about to become your beloved groom." He chuckled, drawing her close to his chest. Then he became serious once again. "Robert was a coward to have sent someone

343

else to do his dirty work—namely Charles Blackman."

"I know that now," she said; then she looked hurt as she said, "Why did you let me go on home alone that night, after the swordfight?"

"I was always near, Dany. I never let you out of my sight until you were safely at your door."

"Thank you for that, Sebastián." She sighed as he let her down near the edge of the woods. "What will happen to Robert now?"

"You have not seen the last of Robert Drake, my love."

"He was always strange," Daniella said of Robert now, "but I never thought there was a taint in his blood." Suddenly she turned her face to gaze into her husband's scarred face. "I have a favor to ask, for I would like to go somewhere before we return to Tallrock."

"Where is that, my love?"

"A church. I need to feel clean again."

"*Sí.* We'll go there." He chuckled. "We might even get married again!" But as he said this he was thinking of Braidwood.

Chapter Twenty

August gave way to September and the sea air brought with it a slightly cooler wind. The sky had been blue and swept free of clouds the day before, but this day the morning dawned dull and cloudy as Daniella and Sebastián set out for their ride across the windswept moorlands that would take them to their usual haunts, with the exception of Drake Manor, since Daniella had no care to go there nor even to pause atop the hill to look out over the wild, weedy place.

The night before, Daniella and Sebastián had gone for a ride when the sun had only just gone down, and it had been beautiful. They had ridden to Land's End, and Daniella had had the reverent sense of sitting in a great cathedral. There had still showed a little light in the west, and in the central dome of sky the stars had shone with such brilliance she felt she could almost reach out to pluck one. And then they had rushed for Tallrock, for along the western fringe of sky a cavalcade of rain clouds were marshaling their forces. They made love while the silver, sapphire, and magenta storm crashed and lit up the beautiful night world beyond their cozy bedroom!

Daniella had not yet let Sebastián in on her secret; in truth, she was afraid to tell him she was with child, not knowing how he would take it and if he would still remain faithfully at her side. She also did not reveal to him that she had wanted to be gone before he had arrived at Tallrock. Fear did strange things to her lately, and she wondered if it was only because of the coming babe . . . or if she was not as sure of Sebastián's love as she wished to be.

But Sebastián had told her many important things about Robert, things she didn't much care for. As for Alain Carstairs, after Sebastián had informed her of his deceit, she had recalled Alain himself complaining about pirates, saying that the "wild" Landakers preyed upon English ships as readily as they did foreign ones. Well, Alain was gone from this earth and Daniella could not find it in herself to think further ill of her former friend, one who had also been friend to her gentle father. She had asked Sebastián to tell her more, but he had curtailed her gentle interrogation and she dared press the matter no more.

Daniella found that the Landakers lived like the ancient families of England; all ships in the harbor below the city were theirs, and they owned several in London also. The villagers were in Master Landaker's service and some of the gentry had a share with him. But when Robert had said "there is much feasting and dancing, finer silks and jewels such as you have never seen, not even at court," he had been wrong. For Daniella had not seen any such treasures, there weren't any, not that she was aware of anyway.

On a walk to the overlook at the windswept cliffs, Daniella had paused to look out over the stormy gray waters of the Atlantic and she had reflected back as she did so often on these seren walks by herself while Sebastián was with his crew taking the *Emerald Tiger* out and then returning later to help repair the ship, damaged while they had been at sea. Sebastián did not speak much of how he obtained the scars and the limp, but that was growing less noticeable as his leg healed. And the scars were even becoming tighter, whiter.

One night Daniella had walked out to the cliffs when Sebastián had not yet returned. She had taken a spy glass with her in order to see, and through it, she had watched the beautiful *Emerald Tiger,* her canvas blossoming like a night-blooming flower, and she had slipped along as graceful as a swan. She had followed her course as she rounded majestically into the wind. The *Tiger* had seemed to curtsy to Daniella as her sails were furled and the lusty song came to her on the wind:

Mackerels' scales and mares' tails,
  Make lofty ships carry low sails!
  Pretty Jane airy skirts and legs,
  Carry to port with many a kegs!
  Oh ho! Oh ho! Oh . . . Jane!

In the soft starlight, with the wind caressing Daniella's flaxen-gold hair, she had looked breathtakingly beautiful when Sebastián had climbed the hill to find her standing there, waiting for him, and he had taken her slim hand and led her to their peaceful bedroom where they had made wild, glorious love. Later she had wondered if Sebastián had truly repeated over and over that he loved her in Spanish, but at the time she had been so engrossed in what was happening as they'd tumbled on the silken sheets, bringing each other to wonderful release.

The days passed uneventfully, and Daniella had never been happier. She already loved wild, wind swept Cornwall and knew she would return here often in the future, for she had made lifelong friends here on this wonderful peninsula.

On their long rides Daniella had learned much of Cornwall's history and it was interesting to hear her husband speak of this place he had come to love and had always returned to, and she understood why now: the Landakers and their home made one feel peace, joy, a loving care as she had never experienced before, except in her father's presence.

Desperately, Daniella wished to forget Robert . . . to let his memory rest in peace. Indeed he was a pleasant memory and she would rather not recall the day he had kidnapped her; only what she remembered of him as a boy and a young man would remain in her heart. Everything else was already forgotten, thanks to Sebastián, who hadn't pressed her for details of that miserable day. There was one thing she must face one day soon, however, and that was that Sebastián had vowed to himself, and to Eileena's wandering spirit, to make entirely certain Robert Drake kept his promise to come and beg Eileena her forgiveness. Soon . . . very soon . . . before they left for America.

The sea mists of autumn arrived, and Daniella wore her warmest cloak when Sebastián and she rode out across the moors. She had seen so much of Cornwall and Sebastián had laughed, telling her she was going to see even more before he was finished showing her about.

Cuddled in the window seat one gray afternoon she was remembering especially one day when

348

they'd ridden far because it had been much warmer. They rode to where the ground rose to its greatest height, where it was so completely exposed to the seawinds that swept across it from east and west that Daniella had been afraid horses and all would be blown into the sea! Ah, but the granite district west of Launceston was broken and picturesque, with rough *tors,* or hills, and boulders. It was, for the most part, a region of furze and heather; but after passing Bodmin moor, the true Cornish moorland asserted itself—bare, desolate, and untillable, broken and dug into hillocks. They'd ridden through the *meneage,* or rocky country, the Cornish name of the promontory which ended in the Lizard, or Lizard Head. Long coombes and valleys descended from this upper moorland toward the coast on both sides. The soil was rich and deep and warm here, and there were pasture farms. The sea winds, except in a few sheltered places, prevented timber trees from attaining any great size, but the air was mild and geraniums, fuchsias, myrtles, hydrangeas, and camellias grew to a considerable size, Sebastián had informed her, and flourished through the winter at Penzance and round Falmouth. In the spring, he said, all native plants displayed a perfection of beauty hardly to be seen elsewhere, and the furze and heather covered the moorland and the cliff summits with a blaze of the richest, most beautiful color! "Dany Rose . . ." He'd cupped her chin and gazed tenderly, lovingly, into her eyes. "Beautiful wildflower—just like my wife."

"And you, my beloved Tiger . . ." She had leaned against him, feeling his warmth and power. "The most handsome of all men in the world." She had thrown her arms wide and he had swept her from her horse and tumbled her gently in the wild heather . . . Much later they had arisen from the tall plants covered from head to foot with small bell-shaped, purplish-pink flowers. "Heather bells," he shouted into the moor-sweeping wind.

"What?" She'd giggled. "What do you mean, hell's bells?"

"No, *querida*." He held the plant he'd plucked up, explaining, "The bell-shaped flower of the heather!"

Their days on the Cornish coast were wonderful and sunny, for Daniella romantically lazy, even when the sun did not pour forth her lemony warmth. And the evenings were spent with the Landakers before a blazing hearth, the conversation warm and intimate. Everyone was in high spirits; even Eileena seemed to come out of her shell every now and then to glance up and smile at some amusing joke—usually it was Juan who caused the fleeting smile to cross Eileena's pouting lips. Daniella wondered what would become of them, since it was plain to see with every passing day that Juan grew more in love with Eileena.

Juan Tomaz watched and waited for his love to emerge from her fragile cocoon. She was regarded with anxiousness and some pity, but Geraldina covertly smirked across the room at the once lovely Eileena. The only one who realized the extent of her burning hatred for the hopeless invalid was Geraldina herself.

One night, when the moon was golden and high, Juan slipped quietly into Eileena's bedroom, thinking to find her fast asleep and was surprised to find her wide awake, staring off into the romantically moonlit gardens below her window.

"Eileena," he said carefully as he strode across the silver carpet.

She gasped softly when he came nearer, but he spoke to her gently and tenderly, as one would do with a child or a lonely, shivering puppy.

Again he murmured her name and took her hand to press it against his chest. "My love, do you feel the beat of my heart? Do you know even a little how very much I love you?" He spoke to her simply, with no flowery speech and no cajolery. "From the first moment I saw you, Eileena, I knew you were the woman for me. My only wish is to help you and make you well. My sole aim is to please you and bring you out of your hell so that you can truly see me for the person I am. Can't you say anything, Eileena? Why can I not get your response? I saw you smile at me the other night. Can I help you in any way to be free from this nightmare? Oh, Eileena, I am living in hell, too, for I cannot reach you. Will you not respond to me? Please, *querida*—I am begging you."

Fear kept Eileena inside herself, and she was so afraid that if she responded she would again be hurt, as those filthy men had hurt her, and she couldn't go through that hell again. It was a miracle she was alive! She had heard everyone softly discussing that, but for some terrible reason she could not dwell too long on what awful things those men had done to her.

Eileena pulled away and curtained her face with her hip-length tresses.

"*Jaysu,* is that all you can do is gasp or hide your face with your hair?"

He was angry with her again. She wished she could speak to him, but the words would not come.

351

He moved closer. "How would it look if I pulled it up and away from your face?" he taunted.

Eileena reacted violently when Juan did as he warned, and she yanked her long, light brown hair painfully from his hold and pulled her body away so that he could not look at or touch her.

Juan was persistent in his quest to reach her inner self and draw the real Eileena back out into the world where she belonged. Eileena was breaking all her relatives' hearts by living inside her tight, fragile shell.

Juan felt no desire to make love to her at this point — he wanted only to reach her.

"Ah, my love," Juan purred in his deep voice, "you are not all that far away. In fact, I believe you know everything that is going on, you just prefer to hide from the real world in which you found so much pain. But what about before that?" He took her hand again, and she did not resist. "You see, *querida,* we love you." She looked at him with her head cocked. *"Sí,* yes," he murmured. "I do love you, too, Eileena. My love, however, reaches far deeper. I can not survive without you, now that I have found my one true love, and I must make you awaken to me, little heart. No . . . do not pull away, Eileena, for I will not hurt you, I am here to help heal your wounds and set your world aright once again, and through the grace of God I *will* succeed."

Eileena's mind and heart rejected all he was saying, for she had learned that men were nothing but deceitful liars and took what they could from a woman before casting her aside. They, those evil dogs, had left her for dead!

"Good night, Eileena."

Juan exited the room as quietly as he had entered, and Eileena turned her head, very slowly, to see the door as it closed. A moment later she was staring out the window again, her heart closed to everything, her eyes staring with no emotion at the golden orb of melancholy moon.

Daniella struggled each and every day with her own problems, trying to keep the secret of her pregnancy, trying to decide for herself what ill fate had befallen Eileena. After a delicious breakfast of sausages and buttered muffins one morning, Daniella visited with Eileena — if it could be called a visit — but it was more like a one-sided conversation until another entered in and then Eileena looked from one to the other.

Sebastián joined them for a time, and Juan wandered in and did his usual thing — took Eileena by the hand and kissed her palm reverently, cupped her face in his tanned fingers, then went out for his morning ride. This time Sebastián followed Juan out the door, after giving Daniella a tender kiss and informing her that he had to pick up some items for the *Tiger* from St. Ives and that she should not expect him until later.

"See you then, *querida*."

"*Sí*," Daniella answered with a smile that lingered as she watched her husband disappear around the door. Their relationship had become more relaxed and it was easier to act like husband and wife now, due to the fact that the Landakers were so easygoing, such nice people to call *friends* and relax around the fire with in the evening. The happy atmosphere was contagious, and with Sophie's cheerful talk about the coming baby it was difficult to dwell on one's own problems. And everyone did their best to cheer Eileena—all except Geraldina who was leaving at the end of the week with her father, taking the *Spanish Wind* to the Spice Islands to trade more goods for their precious cargoes. Thank God Geraldina was leaving, Daniella thought to herself more than once during the week before the auburn-haired troublemaker and Captain Gancho set out.

One thing Daniella did know—and something she was very happy about—was that Captain Sebastián, her husband, her lover, would be taking her back to the Carolinas himself. He had confessed to her that he had thought to leave her alone for a year, but it seemed every time it touched his mind, she was in his arms all over again instead. They had laughed over that. He had made confessions; only she had yet to make hers . . . for some reason that caused her to become very frightened.

"Why so fidgety?" Sebastián asked her one day when she had gone out to the ship with him while he made repairs. He had looked up from his task. "What is it, *cálida*—what are you keeping from me?"

Daniella only laughed. "When I have a secret to keep, my dear husband, then I will keep it for a while and then let you know."

I have not kept my secret long enough, she thought, and allowed the anticipation to tell him to flourish in her breast. When she told him, it would be as exciting for her as it would for him! But would he truly be happy about the babe?

The day that Rascon finally approached Eileena was indeed a curious scene to behold. Daniella was

354

just entering the room with Sophie; she put her hand on Sophie's arm to keep her from interrupting the two who could do nothing but stare at each other. Sophie became very still, the shawl she had been carrying for Eileena trailing to the floor from her lowering arm.

Rascon had become so curious over Eileena that he could not stay away from the young, silent woman any longer. Curious, he stared at her now. *She is much like me,* Rascon thought, and wondered if she had suffered under cruel hands much as he had. He was so intrigued by her lifeless figure and haunting, staring eyes — deciding she was much worse off than he himself — but he could not bring himself to touch her. She looked as if she would break to bits if he did!

I wish I could talk to her, Rascon thought. *No one else has reached her, but maybe I can.* Rascon smiled. *Maybe if we just stare at each other for a while, then she might say something. But I can't talk, either, so if she did talk, I wouldn't be able to say anything back to her except with my hands.*

Eileena blinked. *Why doesn't he go away? What does this child want?*

Rascon blinked back. *She has pretty eyes. I bet she was really pretty a long time ago. If she fixed herself up, she could be just like a princess. Why won't you smile? See, I can smile.* Rascon's face lit up and he grinned like a mischievous monkey eyeing a banana.

Eileena's eyes slowly moved to the right and then lifted. Rascon spun about to find the two young lady Landakers in the entrance, and he flushed guiltily as they finally began to move into the room. He tossed about for an excuse, but he was

355

too nervous to sign anything just then.

"What are you doing in here, Rascon?" Daniella asked, setting a tray full of sweet cakes and a pot of tea on the table in front of Eileena. "My, that was heavy!" She looked at the boy again, smiling, trying to put him at ease. "Rascon? Go ahead, you can use sign language . . . I'll understand."

Rascon had employed the sign language with Daniella Landaker lately and she was beginning to learn all the motions and gestures he made with his quick hands and body.

Daniella read out loud what he was saying, "She . . . is . . . pretty. Why . . . can't . . . she . . . talk?"

Pouring the tea for Eileena as Sophie moved beside the invalid to prepare to feed it to her, Daniella turned to Rascon. "I am not sure. Why can *you* not speak, Rascon? Can you tell me? If it is too painful I will understand."

Slowly, painstakingly, Rascon moved out of his shell as he spoke to the lovely young women, wishing he could make the pretty Eileena respond, too.

"I am so sad to hear this," Daniella said as the lad told her of the pirate who had coldbloodedly murdered his parents, then took him captive and beat him every day, even if he looked at him the wrong way.

"The man must have been bad, Rascon. Does Sebastián know all this?" Daniella was sure he did, but she asked it now to keep Rascon talking since Eileena was staring at him most intently, as if she could somehow relate to the meaning of what he was signing.

Rascon nodded fiercely. Then, holding her eyes with his, he looked at her as if what he was about to relate was most important, then, with sign language, he said he had never known how to say the evil pirate's name—but now he thought he could do it for her—especially for her.

Daniella felt a lump in her throat, aching to know but afraid to find out. "Why would you wish to tell me now, Rascon?"

Because, he signed, *I want to help you with the pretty young lady. I'd like to see her get well.*

Daniella felt an eerie chill along her spine. "But, Rascon, what has your story to do with Eileena's?"

I think he is . . . the . . . same man who was bad to Eileena.

Sophie flicked Daniella a quick look, and, realizing that something bothered her, Sophie intervened.

"What has he been saying, Daniella?" Sophie wanted to know, for the lad intrigued her and she, too, thought he was trying to help in any way he could. Daniella quietly told her and Sophie said, "How unselfish . . . the dear little heart."

Yet, Daniella found herself having a difficult time trying to understand Rascon's next movements and gestures and the dark, gloomy faces he was making.

"Rascon . . ." Daniella picked up a spoon and traced a letter into the cake. Sophie looked at her as if she were crazy, but Daniella kept drawing the "letter." "Did you ever learn your letters?" she asked Rascon.

Regretfully, with much sadness in his amethyst eyes, Rascon shook his head, no, he had never had a tutor, for anything. He signed with his hands, for his parents had been too poor.

Now, feverishly, Rascon was pointing out the window and pretending he was drawing the curtain back—and again a dark look crossed his animated little face. Dark . . . dark . . . *dark* . . .

"Dark?" Daniella said, and Rascon nodded vigorously, but she could not make out the rest of what he was trying to say.

Eileena, still staring between the two, leaned forward and performed a most amazing feat. With a tremor in her slow-moving hands she removed the spoon from Daniella's fingers, and, like a child, she clutched the spoon in both hands, fighting for control, and finally gaining it, she hugged her knee with one hand while leaning over a fresh cake.

Straining forward, all three watched as, amazingly, Eileena began to make letters on a fresh cake, the largest one with icing on it: B . . . A . . . D . . . *D*. Daniella swallowed hard and said: "Badd. You misspelled it, Eileena." She sighed and nodded slowly. "Really, he was." And then she looked at Rascon, for he was jumping about madly, making his *dark* sign again, and Daniella frowned. "Dark. Why is the last 'D' on the cake leaning?" she asked Sophie.

Sophie only shrugged, her head tilted thoughtfully as she studied the cake. "Could it be the beginning of another word?" Sophie wondered then.

Rascon began acting like a bird, flapping his wings . . .

Duck. Male duck . . .

Swallowing a small cry, Daniella sprang to her feet from the cushioned window seat, her next words between a whisper and a croak. "Bad . . . *Drake!*"

Rascon clapped his hands wildly together and jumped up and down, making noises like a monkey but not realizing that he had given utterance for the first time in three years! And Eileena — as Daniella turned to her she saw the definite gleam of excitement in the pale-green eyes . . . and then down to her lap where Eileena's fingers still clutched the spoon as if she would never let go.

Not wishing to frighten Eileena, Daniella and Sophie carefully joined their arms about Eileena's waist and hugged her and hugged her until tears shone in the girl's eyes.

A deep male voice intruded just then. "What is going on here?"

Daniella and Sophie turned to see Juan and Sebastián standing there, with Master Landaker and Teague behind them, and Ellen and Dame Charlotte rushing up behind the pair. Rascon saw them and stopped jumping around. His face turned crimson and he nibbled at his lower lip, his eyes wider than ever as he made the motion to his captain that he was sorry for causing such a commotion.

Tall, windblown, wonderfully male, Sebastián moved into the room, and Daniella's heart sang. *He had been right!* He had been telling her the truth all along, and so had all the Landakers. They were not against her, as she had worried they might be, working for Sebastián and his cause. They were all in this together now . . . and Sebastián moved closer, his compelling eyes never leaving Daniella's.

Unable to contain her excitement, Daniella happily cried, "Eileena spoke. I . . . I mean she did not open her mouth, but she told us something. *She wrote it in the cake!*"

First Juan closed his eyes in thanks to God, then he opened them to see his love gazing across the room at him, and he went to her, bent on a knee as he lifted her hands and drew them thumb to thumb. With her palms in his, he kissed the back of each graceful hand almost reverently. "I am so happy," he murmured. She still looked at him as if clouds obscured her vision, but not as dazedly. He laughed in a deeply satisfied tone. "Step one."

Moved by the touching scene, Sebastián turned misted eyes upon Daniella. "What did Eileena write in the cake?"

"Bad-D."

"Is that all?" Teague asked as he followed Master Landaker into the room. "And what does Bad-D mean?"

"Well . . ." Daniella smiled at Rascon. "He said the first word."

"What?" Gregory Landaker said, looking at Rascon. "I thought he could not speak, either."

"He uses sign language," Sebastián explained, then he smiled at his wife. "Our Rascon is becoming m'lady's shadow."

"No," Daniella corrected. "I believe he will be Eileena's from now on. He is becoming very protective toward her, I think."

Sophie laughed. "Together they put together the word 'Bad Drake.' "

Juan and Sebastián exchanged looks. This only confirmed their belief that Sir Lucian had been the one to abduct Eileena and put her through his particular form of hell . . . one they wished not to speak of to *any* lady!

Then the import of what Sophie had just said struck Sebastián between the eyes. "They . . ." he said, and repeated the word. He spun to Rascon, lowering himself to hunker down to the lad's height. "Was it Lucian Drake who murdered your parents, lad?" Rascon nodded and Sebastián gath-

·red him close and held him for a long time while
he lad buried his face against the captain's buff
·est. *"Dios,* I am so sorry I did not have time to
isten when you tried to tell me that."

No. Rascon shook his head and then let his sav-
or captain know with quick efficient movements
. . *I did not know how to make the word.* He
pointed at the cake with the word Bad-D in it. "Of
course you did not, for there is none of that in
you" was all Sebastián said, clutching the lad's frail
shoulders.

When Sebastián let the child go, Rascon's eyes
searched for Ellen and he found her across the
·oom with tears standing in her eyes; she had found
a special place in her heart for the motherless child,
and now she beckoned for him to come to her.
Placing her arms about him, the housekeeper led
he boy into the kitchen where he loved to watch
her bustle about the fire while she fattened him up,
talked to him, and treated him as if he were her
own, the son Ellen never had.

Daniella's eyes met Sebastián's and he dipped his
tawny head. "Now, my love, do you believe?" His
words were soft and for her ears only.

Juan, with Eileena's cool, slim hand still in his
own, turned to hear what Daniella would have to
say.

"Now I believe."

His eyes moved over her face. "You always believed, Daniella—*in your heart.*"

Chapter Twenty-one

Sweet are the uses of adversity,
Which, like the toad, ugly and venomous,
Wears yet a precious jewel in his head.
                                    Shakespeare

The altered gowns arrived on the morning of
Eileena's birthday party, but Sophie whisked them
at once to her room saying that no one was going
to see them until she and Daniella and Eileena
were ready to appear in all their feminine glory.

They had begun their preparations early, and
when the last tiny button had been fastened, they
surveyed each other with great satisfaction.

It was too bad that Eileena could not under
stand how really beautiful she was, Daniella
thought, holding the polished metal hand mirror
at the best angles for Eileena to see herself. The
stiff turquoise-and-gold brocade which opened
upon an underbody of pale peach spread to the
floor with the sweep of Eileena's slender height
and enriched and brightened her own subdued col
oring. Eileena's face was pale and lovely in the
soft application of cosmetics—enhancing and re
vealing the beauty Eileena once had been—and her
hair had been curled into golden-brown ringlets
that dangled saucily over her ivory shoulders.

Wistfully, Daniella looked at Eileena. "You are

so lovely—and may this be the grandest birthday ever for you, to be remembered always."

Eileena looked at Daniella as if she understood.

The gown Daniella had chosen was simple, with an untrimmed bodice and full skirt of soft, sea-blue silk.

"Simply lovely," Sophie purred. "It needs no ornament, except perhaps . . ." She went to Daniella's jewelry box. "These."

Daniella smiled, and accepted the rings Sophie brought to her. On her right thumb she now wore her father's heavy gold signet ring with the Wingate seal of a rose blossom, and the ring Sebastián had given her the night before to serve as the betrothal ring since he had never given her one. It was set with a very fine bluish pearl and the carving of a leaf was delicately frosted with tinier pearls.

"Thank you, Sophie, I was meaning to wear them but forgot to put them on in the excitement of helping Eileena dress." She trusted Sophie completely, for the woman had become her true friend and she hoped they would stay in contact after Sebastián returned her to Charleston.

For a moment Daniella dwelled on whether or not her husband would stay on with her at Braidwood, or would he leave on the *Emerald Tiger* and never return? Their marriage had been somewhat like a fantastic dream. Would that dream be destroyed in the blink of an eye once she was back home, and would she awake in her bed one morning to realize it had all been a fantasy? One thing was certain: the unborn child in her belly would become a living reality. No one, especially not her-

363

self, could flee from that!

"My, don't we all look lovely," Sophie said with happy tears in her eyes. "Your eyes match your dress perfectly, Daniella. You have unusual eyes so pretty, they pick up the green or blue or gray of the dresses you wear."

"Where did you get these dresses? They are so beautiful," Daniella said, then grinned, and added "If a trifle ancient."

"That is the effect I want to create — something old and something new!"

"Oh?" Daniella asked with a laugh. "Who is getting married?"

"Well . . ." Sophie eyed Eileena, then shook her head. "No one yet. This is supposed to be a birthday party, but I wonder how much of it has sunk into Eileena's head." Sophie shrugged. "I hope she enjoys it. We haven't had a party around here in such a long while, ever since . . ." She sighed breaking off her thought but it was clear she had been remembering Eileena's "accident."

Daniella placed a rope of huge, heavy pearls about Eileena's neck. They hung to her waist where she fingered them as if she were blind and only stared straight ahead with a wistful expression.

"Oh, I have something for you to wear, Daniella!" Sophie announced, lifting a headdress out of a box. "All this stuff came from Lady Diana's — she was a duchess, you know. But I hardly ever see her anymore. She was a friend of a cousin of mine . . . and she left all this stuff at their house, but that was a long time ago, I don't even know if Lady Diana is alive anymore."

Sophie laughed then. "This looks almost new! What do you think of it?"

The headdress was elegantly fashioned of velvet in an outdated version of the "coif," and had a stiff crescent sewn with seed pearls in front and a pouchlike back into which they had to bundle Daniella's long curls.

Daniella looked into the mirror, blinked, and said, "It seems too heavy for my face and my neck looks long and thin—like a swan's throat!" She laughed, turning this way and that.

Sophie frowned. "You may be right—"

"*Por favor,* leave it, Daniella. It is lovely," Geraldina exclaimed, sweeping into Daniella's room uninvited, wearing a loud scarlet gown with black scrunchy lace, "*Sí,* leave it on!"

Sophie only shrugged, deciding it was best to let Daniella come to her own conclusion. Something *was* wrong, though—perhaps it made Daniella's dainty face look too small. Geraldina, for sure, would not tell the truth!

Daniella had counted upon adding a modish touch to her costume, true, but she just didn't know about this *thing.* "It makes my face look too small . . . like I have too much hair." She tugged, making the pouch even longer. "I just don't know. I wish that I could decide. If only Sebastián were here—he would tell me what *he* thinks."

"Sebastián *is* here," a voice from the doorway announced, "and I shall tell you what he thinks." Geraldina smirked at him and he tilted his head with acknowledgment of her presence and a smile that did not reach his eyes. He saw that his wife was not pleased with Geraldina's presence, either, and he was glad that Captain Gancho would soon be taking her from Tallrock.

With breath stolen away, Daniella stared at her husband who was resplendent in dove-gray velvet. The pourpoint—or doublet—was short, opening in front to show a white shirt, and the short skirt was held in place by a scarlet sash; the white shirt was slashed and puffed. His tawny hair had grown long, flowing to his nape in gentle waves. Now it was her husband who looked her over and his jade-green eyes flickered with amazement.

"Dios mio!" Sebastián ejaculated. "What is that thing on your head . . . that . . . *that bag!* You cannot mean you will actually wear it?"

Daniella laughed softly, her eyes exchanging glances with Sophie as she joked, "Well . . . it is what everyone wears."

"Everyone from other star-planets," Sebastián said, walking closer to her, around her. "Are you going to really wear it, *querida?"*

"Oh, 'tis the very latest fashion!" Making an effort to keep from bursting into fits of giggles, Daniella said with dignity, "You surely must have noticed that *everyone* wears a headdress?"

Sebastián looked at Sophie, who wore none, then at Eileena, who wore plain velvet ribbons; Geraldina, who did not dress normally in the first place, wore none, either.

"So?" Sebastián shrugged. "I see none other wearing a . . . uh . . . *bag* such as you are."

Daniella seemed to find this amusing. "I intend to look *respectable*—like Lady Diana."

"Ay de mi! Who the devil is that?" He stopped and gave the headdress a tweak which dislodged

suddenly and tumbled Daniella's long wavelets about her head. She faced him smilingly, her cheeks flushing.

"Dios," Sebastián said. "This becomes you much better, my love." He stepped back. "So does the lovely blue dress. But this thing!" He held the offending object out of reach. "Must definitely go!"

"Come on now," Daniella begged prettily. "You give it back to me, Sebastián."

"No *cálida!*"

With a fatal sound of ripping, the expensive headdress came apart. And Sophie, who had been hovering uneasily on the outskirts of battle, gave a gasp of shock, wondering what Lady Diana would think of this man spoiling her headdress without a second thought. Daniella came to her feet, pretending surprise, though little did she care what became of the absurd thing—and no doubt Lady Diana had thought the same as she had left it behind at Sophie's cousins. Daniella took a mock-menacing step forward.

Sebastián had bent the pearl-sewn crescent into a small cap and, with a deep bow, offered the altered headdress to his wife. "So, how does *this* look?" He gave her a boyish grin, hoping he had not gone *too* far. "Is this better?"

Daniella nodded, then burst into sudden laughter. Sebastián, with the now-diminutive cap in his large hands, intent upon his role as bonnet-maker, looked utterly absurd.

"It is Italian," Sebastián announced, looking serious as he handed it over to her, and Daniella breathed a long, drawn-out *"Oh. . . ?"*

"Geraldina, please come here," Sophie said, hap-

pily noticing that Eileena was understanding some
thing of all this, the ghost of a smile hovered on
her lovely pink mouth. *"You* must wear this . . . i
is simply *perfect* for you."

Sophie summoned Geraldina over with a whisl
of her beringed hand. "Come, come."

"Well . . . I . . . I do not know," Geraldina
stammered. With Geraldina anxiously holding the
mirror, Sophie fitted the tiny cap to Geraldina'
head. "My it looks rather well!" Sophie exclaimed
and suppressed a giggle.

Eileena's entire face brightened as she stared a
the funny little hat . . . and that mean auburn
haired woman's even sillier red-lipped expression.

"Hmm, *Italy* you say?" Geraldina inquired o
Sebastián who nodded swiftly back. She snatched
the mirror back from Sophie and stood admiring
herself with a little pout on her generous red
mouth. "Is this a respectable headdress for ladies
in It-ah-lee?"

"Oh *sí!*" Sebastián declared. "It is quite proper
too, for everything there is highly regarded by the
rest of the world. There . . ." he said as Geraldina
tipped it a little. "Leave it like that. Ah, *sí . . .*
He clapped his hands, again playing the foppish
dandy. "It is exactly right for you."

Great grief! Looking at the vain woman, Dan
iella swept up her cloak. "Dame Charlotte canno
say you have nothing at all in your head *now,"* she
quipped.

Geraldina spun about, "Daniella —? What did
you say? *In?"*

But Daniella prudently drew up the hood of her
white velvet cloak — which Geraldina eyed envi-

ously — and they went on downstairs.

Master Landaker was ready and waiting in the hall, and Dame Charlotte was there with him though she was not dressed for the birthday party, since she had refused to go. She hardly ever left the house, especially not to attend parties or balls. She felt too overdressed and out of place at the last one she had attended years ago. But she'd made a fuss over Eileena's birthday party just the same, sending cakes and candied fruits over to the Sherwoods' ahead of time.

Dame Charlotte gave Geraldina's headdress a queer look. "Have a gay time," she said, waving them all off at the door, and even Ellen was going, for she wanted to be there when Rascon attended his first birthday party. She planned to give him one soon and she was even going to ask Sebastián if Rascon could stay on at the Landakers when he went on to the Carolinas with Daniella and the others.

Bettina and Jaecko stood outside, holding hands and chatting happily while they waited for the others to emerge from the house to the three waiting carriages, one sent over from the Sherwood country cottage. The Sherwoods also had another larger house outside London.

They set out with Bettina and Jaecko carrying lanterns at the head of the carriage to light their way, while Spider and another man lit up the rear end of the third carriage as they walked beside it, wheeling spirals of light over the road.

The carriages rolled over the curving country roads and through the woods smelling of damp earth and moss, until at last, an hour later — as they left the deepest woods of all—a good-size dwelling came into view and the Landakers and company found that other guests had already assembled at the Sherwood cottage.

Its biggest room glowed with firelight and candlelight and was fragrant with the old-fashioned tang of spearmint and sweet boughs of hay. The gaily painted walls seemed to lead into a summer garden, for there were dried flowers and bergamot everywhere, and it was especially cheery within the circle of the hearth.

"How lovely you all look," complimented Lord Sherwood's little French wife, her silky blond hair wrapped in a coronet atop her head, her shining green eyes happy and gay. "And, ah!—my little love Eileena!" Gabrielle took the somewhat dazed girl into her arms for a big hug, and then the Frenchwoman stood back admiring the man beside her who had been holding tight to Eileena's hand. "*Oui,* and this must be Juan Tomaz," she purred in her delightful accent. "You will be a good husband for our Eileena," and with that she turned to greet her other guests with joyous hospitality while Juan looked at Gabrielle with a surprised look that she had seen so much and took so much for granted. Juan shook his head. Gabrielle Sherwood was exquisite and incredible!

Gabrielle's cousin, Lady Alysia Markham, was a little bit taller than Gabrielle herself. She wore amber velvet with a very stylish headdress almost like the old-fashioned one Sebastián had snatched from Daniella's head earlier. Now he stared, dumbstruck, and Daniella did the same, while Geraldina paraded about like a fashion plate in her "Italian"

370

creation.

Gabrielle introduced an elderly man in clerical habit who was, Gabrielle said gaily, "a very famous classical scholar!"

There was also a well-known physician attending the party, one who had been the Landaker's family physician for years and had taken care of Eileena ever since she had become "ill." Dr. Maxwell was surprised and happy to see Eileena looking so well. He held very advanced views on the practice of medicine and Daniella was soon to learn just *how* observant the old man was. His eyes were the brightest, most inquisitive ones Daniella had ever seen.

At the end of the meal, Sophie and Gabrielle and Dr. Maxwell's wife were clearing the table when Daniella asked if she could help and Gabrielle cheerfully replied that the cottage kitchen was quite small, and please would she simply relax and enjoy the conversation. Daniella took a seat beside Juan and Eileena, while on the other side, where sat an empty chair, Dr. Maxwell moved to sit down, asking if she minded.

"No," Daniella replied nervously. "Please do." She smiled as beside her on the other side Juan was slowly and painstakingly feeding Eileena the scrumptuously frosted birthday cake. Then she faced Dr. Maxwell again and was surprised to find him studying her most strangely.

"Will you tell me a little about the Carolinas?" Jonathan Maxwell asked. "I have never had the pleasure to have visited there."

Between the songs the commanding male voices were pouring out—Sebastián's deep baritone com-

ing as a great surprise and pleasure to her ears—
Daniella found she could converse quite easily with
the doctor, for, though he was so brilliant and
witty, his questions were put not to display his
cleverness but to show his profound interest in
what she could tell him of America.

As she spoke about America and Edward, she
thought of her father, and, looking wistful, she
could almost hear her beloved father's voice again,
telling of a surprise he had for her—the "surprise"
turning out to be Lord Steven Landaker! She
sighed forlornly.

Dr. Maxwell patted her hand, noticing the misty,
faraway look in her eyes. "I should have liked to
have met and known your father."

Daniella's lashes brushed down, then up.
"Edward would have liked you also, Dr. Maxwell."

"Please . . ." he said, still patting her hand as
Sebastián appeared at her side, sipping apple cider.
"Do call me Jonathan." His bright eyes twinkled
merrily up at the husband. "So, little lady, when
are you expecting?" he asked.

Sebastián coughed out loud and then, twisting
to the side, he spewed a mouthful of cider onto
the rush-covered floor.

"I . . . I . . ." Daniella stared at the doctor with
her eyes wild and blinking, and, for the life of her,
she could not force them to lift to Sebastián. "I
am not sure." She could not lie to such an all-
knowing doctor!

"What?" Sebastián growled low. He stared from
his wife to the doctor then back to her again.
"Daniella . . ."

Dr. Maxwell sat back with hands clasping his

knees, his turn to look from one to the other, as he said, "My wife warned me not to be too inquisitive of folks' health this night." He apologized profusely. "I am sorry if I have let the cat out of the bag!"

"Certainemente." Sebastián gave the good doctor a gentlemanly bow. "See no fault in your own kindly practice of your craft, Doctor, it is only natural." To Daniella, Sebastián purred, "Please, m'love, come with me. I wish to speak privately with you — *outside.*"

Chapter Twenty-two

How had the doctor known? Daniella asked herself several times on the way out to the silvered path which led to a quaint rose arbor in the center of the moonlit garden. She kept her back to Sebastián and dared not turn about to face him, for she knew he would look as dark and wrathful as thunder. She had asked for this — *it was her own fault!*

Sebastián's deep voice was soft when it finally emerged from tautly held emotions. "You are with child."

Daniella stared sidewise and said nothing for several seconds. When she finally answered, it was barely above a whisper.

"I . . . I cannot be sure."

With gentle caresses, Sebastián's hands moved over Daniella's shoulders and held them still. He gazed down at her moon-platinumed head, feeling love and tenderness move inside him until he thought he would burst with the affection he felt for this lovely woman.

"I've been truthful with you, Daniella. Why can you not be trusting and show me the same respect?"

Daniella spun about, breaking contact with his warmth and strength. "Truthful? Hah! You dare speak of truth to me, Sebastián? *You,* who once lied about having a wife . . . Oh, yes, I know, you

374

will tell me that was when you were posing as Lord Steven Landaker. But recall, you told my father your wife had passed on. *Who was she,* Sebastián? Was that, too, only made up or was there in truth a Lady Landaker who first claimed your husbandly passions? Did another lie at your side and—"

"Daniella!" Sebastián grasped her shoulders so hard that she winced. "Listen to yourself . . . you sound like a jealous shrew! What has come over you? We came out here to discuss the possibility of your being with child." He shrugged. *"Dios,* and what do I get? All of a sudden you bring up the past. *Why?"*

"Tell me about the other woman, Sebastián!" Struggling, she peeled his fingers from her arms. "Please, do not touch me until you give me the truth."

More softly this time, Sebastián tried to bring her to her senses. "Daniella, I have never seen you act this way . . . and if you remember," he said with a gentle smile, "I was out to make you my beautiful captive; why wouldn't I try a little deception to make sure nothing stood in the way of my success? In my deepest heart I knew not only did I want you for my . . . ah . . . *decoy* in nabbing the pirate Drakes, but I also wanted you for my willing bride. I wanted you so bad I would do anything to get you. Revenge on the Drakes has even dimmed, so much that hardly *I* can even believe the strength of my bitterness before you stepped into my life." He stepped closer again, his eyes delving deeply into hers, his fingers seeking the slim white ones. "You have brought purifying love into my life, Daniella. A love that shines and surpasses." He pressed her hands to his chest so that she could feel the powerful beat of his heart. "Do you know what that means, *cálida?*" he asked, his eyes drilling hers.

"I . . ." Daniella looked aside, feeling the blush painting her cheeks crimson. *Dear God, I hope he is going to say it.* Anticipation pounded in her heart. Say it, Sebastián. Say *I love you.*

Sebastián roughly cleared his throat. "Daniella, I — "

"Yooo — hooo!"

Sophie, not realizing the seriousness of the situation which had brought the couple to the moonlit garden, called from the back door. For a magical moment in time, Daniella stared into Sebastián's tiger eyes . . . and then the wondrous spell was broken by the voice calling out to them — and for the first time since Daniella had met dear Sophie she felt like strangling her.

Sebastián stood impatiently. "Daniella . . . I would like to know?"

Daniella's entire body reached toward her husband. "Yes, Sebastián?"

"Are you with child?"

"Yes, Sebastián." Swiftly, Daniella turned toward the cottage, her step a little heavier as she went. "I believe so."

Not long after the Landakers and company had left for the Sherwoods, Dame Charlotte picked up the leather-bound history books she had been reading. Among the books were some journals that her dearly beloved son — departed from this earth by the wicked blade of Lucian Drake—had written in daily . . . and now they were hers, all that was left of darling Percy.

Dame Charlotte dried her misty eyes and lifted one of the books stacked alongside her deep-cushioned chair where she loved to sit and read when she was alone in the house . . . which wasn't too often, but she snatched every chance she could to read in private; it was so very relaxing and enjoyable.

"I went to a wrestling match today," Percy wrote. And then Dame Charlotte's eyes skittered to the notes he had made on the opposite page . . . something to do with the Black Prince. History, she guessed. Dame Charlotte yawned, and growing sleepy, her eyes blinked and she read through blurry eyes. Her chin nodded and came to rest on her large bosom.

Dame Charlotte was asleep. A shadow lent by the candles fell over her sleeping form and the book was lifted most carefully from her fingers. A low voice spoke.

". . . in favor of his son, the Black Prince, and of his heirs . . . *Ah*." Robert Drake read slowly and cautiously. "An old relative of mine. The Black Prince. Too bad his bastards were not added to the eldest sons of the kings of England. That is all right, Blackie, I shall gain my fortune yet."

Robert stared down at Dame Charlotte who was slumped into the deep cushions, snoring softly, her stockinged feet turned one toward the other. "Fortunate for you, old girl," he whispered, "that you did not awaken moments ago. Not yet . . . but soon it will be your time to depart your comforts of home." Robert's fingers held a death grip on his sword as he looked hurriedly about the drawing room, then back to the dame. "Then I would have been so sad had I been forced to add you to the growing list of those 'deceased Landaker and friends.' But I shall leave you to your rest now, for I have much to do before the others return." His chuckle had a nasty ring to it — "like finding the secret passageways that lead to *the also* secret tunnel that leads to the outside." He pulled the hood over his head that likened him to a black priest on a dark mission. And so he was. There were many he and Sir Lucian would send to an early grave . . . and that would demolish the ancient lineage of haughty Landakers!

Chapter Twenty-three

The moon was a ghostly galleon
tossed upon cloudy seas.
— Alfred Noyes

Around the shrubbery and shining-leaved trees surrounding Tallrock, the scent of the sun-warmed woods lingered mistily. Two full days had passed since the night of Eileena's birthday party. This day had been pleasantly sunny and the air had seemed to sparkle with mystery even after the sun had gone down. Sebastián walked up to the stone bench that Daniella occupied in the garden—hedged in by drooping flowers and tall plants which still bore their tender foliage.

"*Cálida* . . ." Sebastián's voice surprised her, tempered by tenderness and kindness. "Let's call a truce, m'love. You have been avoiding me for two days . . . longer than that actually. Do you mind if I sit here beside you?"

With a casual air, Daniella glanced at Sebastián, then gave her consent with a single nod. Sebastián sat, leaning his elbows upon his knees, his tawny-green tiger eyes raised to look at the moon.

"Perhaps . . ." Sebastián began, "both of us want too impatiently to push things which cannot be pushed. Nothing presses on us in the Carolinas that won't wait while we get the ship ready. Of course, I could always send you back to Charleston by freight ship . . ." He looked over and down to her midsection. "But journey by transport junker would be a bit too jarring for you . . . ah . . . in your condition. Perhaps you should wait for the *Tiger.*"

Daniella was keenly aware of Sebastián's scrutiny. "That shouldn't be necessary."

He turned his head slightly. "What won't be? For you to wait for the *Tiger* or journey by a merchant ship that has gone to wrack and ruin?"

"Neither."

Sebastián sighed, then said, "Make some sense, Dany."

Daniella's shoulders moved as she explained, "I am too far gone to travel on *any* ship, Sebastián."

He looked hopeful. "Then you saw the doctor as I asked?"

"Yes, I saw the doctor."

"When . . ." Sebastián swallowed, "are you expecting?"

"December," she replied coolly.

"Dios! That is only three months away!"

"I am aware of that, Sebastián."

Daniella sat primly, so ladylike with her dainty hands resting in her lap like pure white doves.

Silence reigned for what seemed like forever while Sebastián pressed his lips together as he endured frustrating emotions. Under the elms, a few twigs pattered down through the branches like soft rain. *There is a time of speaking and a time of being still. Silence, in which great things could fashion themselves . . .*

Daniella gave Sebastián a sidewise glance. His

380

high boots were polished, his blousy shirt tied in front as carefully as if he were attending a ball instead of merely sitting beneath the moon . . . with her. She looked up at his moonlit face and noted the taut lines of his jaw and cheeks—he'd shaven the short beard he had sported—and looked so clean and handsome. He made her heart leap in a thrilling dance and the excitement he aroused in her became manifest again.

Suddenly he faced her and for several moments their eyes locked in a silent, golden conflict. There were no words. Daniella could hear him, breathing audibly.

Breaking free of his own brief uncertainty, Sebastián's arms closed about her like steel manacles and he pressed her lithe upper body closer and closer to his. "This is the way it should be, Daniella *querida*. Close; never far apart. No, do not pull away . . . you are my captive rose now."

She could not understand why Sebastián did not speak of love. He gave no verbal commitment though he used the word "love" often enough. He was gaining control and conquering her will again, arousing her desire with his mere presence. She was surprised to realize that she herself had seldom admitted any fondness for him. Now she felt his mouth move heatedly on the nape of her neck as he pushed aside the long strands of moon-blond hair and she felt a weakness that trickled into her thighs. His lips slid along her throat, from the elegant curve of her shoulder . . .

"No, Sebastián . . . leave me. Go back to your wife, or your mistress, or whoever she is."

"Rebecca?" He slid his tongue along her chin "She is my mother, Daniella—and she is on thi earth no longer. As for Geraldina . . . *Sí,* I saw yo as you watched me staring at her the other night. I that what you are angry about?" He did not wai for a reply. "I can see you are jealous. I love it," h said. "This only means you truly love and wan me."

"I do not love you, Sebastián." She straine against the barrier of his solid chest.

"I believe you lie, m'love." He shifted an brought up his hands to frame her beautiful, rebel lious face within his long, lean fingers. *"Sí querida* you love me."

"No! No! I do not," she denied hotly, an twisted to break free of his imprisoning arms. "Yo will not trap me and deceive me again, Sebastián.

"What is it?" He used all his strength to hold he still, for she was like a wildcat. "Just last week w were so in love and shared beautiful days, gloriou nights together. What happened?"

She became still. "What did you say? Last weel we were in love?"

"Hmm, yes, Daniella. In love." He snatched he back again and murmured into her ear, "I lov you."

The baldfaced lie made her angry and she begar to beat at his chest and kick at his shins. "Yo bloody rogue. You cheat . . . *liar!"*

Sebastián's jaw hardened like petrified rock "You, m'love, have become out of hand."

He snatched her up and carried her up the sid stairs, along the hall, and to their bedroom wher

382

e deposited her on the bed and knelt over her with
is powerful body as she tried to escape.

"You . . . you!" Daniella panted. "I want to be
ngry! I wish to *stay* angry! And you will not allow
hat, you blind fool!"

"You are so correct, Dany, I'll not allow you to
tay angry with me. I do not have another bride. I
lo not feel anything for Geraldina; she is a slut in
ny estimation." His mouth curled handsomely.
You do not have to be jealous of Geraldina, of
nyone." He grinned like a handsome imp. "And
ve are all blind until we truly see."

Because all she'd taken in was the word "jealous,"
Daniella's face burned hotly. "Jealous? Bah! I am
lot jealous of you and your women. I have more
espect for my emotions and feelings than that,
Captain Sebastián Landaker. Scoundrel! You are
he one who whisked me away; and you are the
iar!"

"We are going to talk!" Sebastián growled, his
yes blazing and shooting green and tiger-yellow
parks. "Now!!"

Moving onto the bed, Sebastián sat with his back
it the huge headboard, and a soft gasp escaped her
vhen his hard, muscled chest pressed into her back
ind his arms encircled her waist. Streaks of undeni-
ible desire shot through her. They sat, spoonlike,
ind several moments of rare contentment passed
ind soon there was a smile on Sebastián's mobile
nouth when she had snuggled farther into the
varmth of his body curved around hers. His
oreath, when he spoke, was like sparks of delicious
ire on her neck.

383

"After all has been said and done, Dany, I have only one thing to prove to you now." He gazed down at her face as she turned hers to stare up at him with a waiting expression. "And that is how much I love you."

Daniella felt him shifting into affectionate familiarity. "Sebastián . . . n-no!" she stammered.

But it was too late. A burning heat spread through her when he came out from under her and cupping her beloved face in his hands, he gazed down at her with worshipful adoration shining in his eyes. He shifted to get closer. Then, as his head lowered for his mouth to take hers, a thrill went clear through both of them while his fingers moved to the thick mass of angel-blond curls; he captured her lips and lifted her skirts higher and higher. His mouth and tongue moved in rhythm with his hand tasting, stroking . . . and then he moved lower, his tongue wetting the pinkness of her breasts as his fingers rolled back the bodice and exposed the firm tips. The other hand moved over her graceful thigh and the tender apex which joined the slender limb with womanhood's sweetest mystery.

After Daniella's clothes had been swiftly discarded by warm and eager hands, Sebastián removed what remained of his own attire and continued to make wonderfully magic love to her with a tenderness born of maturity. He made her feel as if her flesh were turned inside out, sensitive to every caress and brushing touch. Her mouth clung to his as he pressed her closer to his splendid male body, stealing her breath with his passionate and reverent kiss, then slowly trailing kisses that

384

burned along her arched throat. Suddenly he slid his whole body lower. He buried his face against the soft flesh there and caught the darker amber curls in his fingers while his other hand lifted her slightly, and he moved her masterfully and fervently, his schooled lips teasing and slowly to bring her to the edge of rapture.

"Oh, Sebastián—love, love, *love*," she cried in a soft panting voice. "Love me . . . now."

She watched him as he briskly moved over her, staring up into the face she had first seen in the Blue Room at Braidwood. The mysterious and virile man who had stolen the heart that had never belonged to Robert Drake in the first place.

"My exquisite beauty," he murmured. "You are the woman God has created for me. I will keep you forever . . . my beautiful and radiant Dany Rose."

With heart-stopping gentleness, he lowered his hips and thighs toward hers, his flesh moving slowly to enter the patch of thick dark curls, gently, gently, and Daniella arched to gracefully meet each long thrust, her nails biting into his upper arms. His loving caresses moved from the pink nipples to her waist and on to her shapely hips, then around in back to cup her buttocks and position her higher for his swift, hot thrusts. Her fingers tightened their grip on his powerful arms. Flesh like silk, hard and sleek, moved within and without, and Daniella arched her back to meet him, graceful as an inspired dancer while her hands rode upon rolling hips and her fingertips tenderly caressed solid flesh. He was a startling contrast to her own cameo softness.

385

As the jade-green eyes flickering with their yellow rays of sunlight met the turquoise-gray ones, there was now reflected the beautiful awareness of what lay beyond this moment ... And then it came flinging them higher and higher, wafting them through dazzling, soaring, endless clouds and then bursting forth into a sunlit clearing where the scarlet sun beat down on their naked selves, making them flames of fire, so complete in their embrace that hearts and souls seemed inseparable.

When at last they became as glowing embers on a rosy hearth, their bodies were, too, inseparable as they lay close in a loving embrace and he cradled her head against his chest with a tenderness nurtured of true love. He loved her, *sí*, his wife. When would she truly believe him? he wondered as he held her and kissed her delicately boned cheek and chin with gentle lips. *He must say it now. Again.*

"I love you, Daniella Rose Landaker," he whispered softly in her ear. Then, caressing the slight bulge of tummy, knowing well this night the mysteries of her woman's body, he added with a smile "Dany."

She smiled up at him through long lashes and radiant tears. "You do not know how desperately I wanted to hear you say that."

"Had I but known I would have said it long ago." He rolled his head on the pillow to look at her.

"You must know how much I love you, Sebastián."

He smiled and kissed her damp cheek. "With an all-consuming fire. After this night I would be a

386

fool not to believe that you and I will always cause the sparks to fly."

While the crystal light sea moved below the shadowed cliffs and dark creatures prowled the shrouded night, the two were engulfed in a much-needed sleep. Peaceful. Delicious. Rejuvenating, like a tonic. Uninterrupted . . . for now.

Chapter Twenty-four

Eileena was adrift in a thrillingly romantic dream
. . . She was all alone in an enchanted garden
viewing the summer moon, submitting to her
dreamy mood as she waited for someone special to
appear. Juan: he was suddenly at the far end of the
garden. He neared, and a delicious sensation
warmed her slumbering body.

A firefly paused between them for a brief flash
in time then blinked away into the silver-dappled
night.

He stood before her, his manner gentle and gallant as usual, his love-deep eyes roving her slim
shape. This was no whimsical manifestation of her
dream — Juan Tomaz was a flesh-and-blood man
. . . transported into her starlit and moon-dappled
garden.

And Juan had entered her dream, the only way
he knew how to reach her . . .

Four bedrooms down from Eileena's, Juan was
having the same dream.

He was alone at first and then Eileena was there.
Her ethereal loveliness and her lovely smile, meant
only for him, stole his breath as she moved with
supple and languid grace to welcome him; then she
reached out a hand to him. She was slim and
white. He grasped the marvelous fact that she was
naked. Her flawless and comely form seemed to

beckon and reach out to him. He went to her and her cool, slim hand was in his own. He pulled her gently into the circle of his arms. She was wonderfully soft, as he had known she would be. Though her mind and body spoke to him, conveying the message of her passionate and tender love, he knew he could not kiss her. He had never kissed her, so he could not know what her lips tasted like; he could not dream this if he had not experienced the feeling and sensation of her mouth in wakefulness. Many women had he known and tasted, many hot and grasping and greedy, but this one he needs go slow with, he told his desiring body and his dreaming mind. This one he loved above all else; this one he would die for. He would not allow ungratifying and shallow passion in his dream nor would he allow it in reality. Not until his love was ready. When Eileena said, "Yes now, my love," then and only then would he proceed to honor and make her his . . . And now her winsome and lovely form drifted from him and faded completely . . . Juan fell into a deep and dreamless sleep, knowing in his tormented soul that she would not be far from him when he awoke to the autumn morn.

Suddenly, Juan's eyes were wide open. *What was it?*

Roused from sleep, Sebastián slowly and alertly lifted his head, then jerked aside to check if Daniella was still beside him. He breathed a sigh of relief, for his wife was sleeping peacefully and he dared not disturb her sweet dreams. *Sí*, she was smiling softly in her sleep, traces of lingering bliss across her face. But he had to go check and see what noise had awakened him; if any had in truth.

After slipping into breeches and high-topped boots, he made his way with stealthful caution out to the hall, checked this way and that, then slowly and quietly crept downstairs. He would have forgotten the matter and gone back to his warm and inviting bed if some sixth sense had not urged him to fully check the rest of the house and investigate the downstairs for prowlers or thieves.

In the drawing room he found nothing but a few glowing embers in the hearth; then he moved on.

In the dining room all was still, the chairs in order and giving him the feel of an eerie graveyard with tombstones cast in high relief by the motes of moonlight beaming into the huge chamber. The moon-spill caught and mesmerized him momentarily and then his eyes moved away, as did his body which was invigorated with wariness and caution.

In the other rooms it was the same, eerie and spooky in the gloomy sleeping house, and he began to feel like a sneaking thief, prowling where he should not.

He was about to check one last room—the kitchen—when a furtive movement along the hall caught his roving eye. Of a sudden he wished he had taken a weapon from his room . . . and then he spied the suit of armor! It shone dully in the moonlight streaming into the ancestral hall . . .

As Sebastián had, Juan had come suddenly awake; some sixth sense instilled in warriors of sea and land had alerted him that all was not right in the big house. He stepped from the drawing room and began creeping along the wall—when something halted all movement and he froze. *There!* A dark figure had just crept from a room down the hall. Juan's powerfully muscled body came alert and he tensed for battle. He damned his stupidity for not bringing a weapon along; but then his eyes lit on the suit of armor at the foot of the wide, curving stairs!

Juan and Sebastián crept stealthily and unaware toward each other, each with only one thought in mind: to reach the twelfth-century suit of armor and lift down the heavy Passau steel sword to employ as a weapon if the need arose!

Neither thought of the commotion that would be created if that suit of armor should topple . . . and scare off the intruder.

They spied the dark and frightening forms of each other at the same moment peeping out from either side of the suit, and then both hands grappled for the sword. The struggle was on! There were grunts and groans and the shuffling of booted feet. The great cylindrical helm came crashing down, missing Sebastián's head by a mere inch. Next the triangular shield with its curved sides crashed and clattered to the hard floor. Then, while they jumped back just in time, the remainder of the disembodied medieval knight toppled over and made the most startling performance and loudest crash in the night either of these dauntless warriors had ever had the misfortune to give audience to. Both stared awestruck as the bodiless knight finally released his death grip on the sword and it went spinning along the hall, moonlight catching its shiny blade in the turnings.

This brought the house running!

The first to arrive was Dame Charlotte. She held a candle high above her disheveled head and blinked wide as she surveyed the situation at the foot of the stairs.

Then Teague arrived.

Next came Sophia and Daniella. They had almost collided in the corridor, almost spilled dripping wax on each other. Then, side by side, they had tiptoed down the stairs and saw that there were others standing below, staring with surprise and shock at the scene which greeted them, never realizing that it could have been a tragic one!

Master Landaker's voice preceded him as it boomed and thundered along the hall, and the now wide-awake master himself suddenly appeared in silly nightcap, gown, battered and tasseled slippers — and his face looked furious above the candle's little flame. "What the devil is going on? Who is that on the floor with his backsides in the air? Is that my suit of armor? E'gads, what happened to it? Have we been robbed?" He blinked as two men arose from the floor. "Sebastián? Juan? Are you both drunk?" He was about to ply the mute, blinking men with more questions when Rascon came running into the hall.

Sebastián watched carefully as Rascon came to a sudden halt, his face animated and his hands waving as he tried to sign, to explain. The man caught the boy's hands and held them still.

"Slow down, Rascon, I cannot understand a single thing you are trying to tell me when you act like a windmill in a whirlwind!"

Daniella stepped off the last stair and neared her husband and the lad, the skirt of her soft white robe opening and closing in her lithe movements. "He was trying to say something about food — but I cannot understand the rest." Then Daniella stared around at the tense and confused faces. She asked,

Where is Ellen?"

"For that matter," said Master Landaker, "where
s Geraldina?"

Sebastián dismissed the younger woman's absence
with a wave of his hand. "I believe she has already
joined her father aboard the *Spanish Wind*. We'll
not be hearing from that one for many months."

"Never, I hope," said Juan in a harsh and steely
tone.

"And where is Eileena?" Teague came out of the
shadows where he'd been examining the scattered
remains of the bodiless knight. "Did no one think
to check on her?" He looked around the room.

"How could we? We just arrived. It all happened
so fast," Sophie explained, and before anyone else
could speak, Juan was bounding up the wide stairs,
taking two steps at a time.

"Now," Sebastián said, and he turned back to
Rascon, "what were you trying to tell us?"

This time, more slowly, Rascon signed, and as he
did this, he faced Daniella, since she could read his
movements better than anyone else. She explained
when he finished. "He was only trying to say that
he went to the kitchen for a bite to eat when . . ."
she held up Ellen's notions-belt that Rascon had
passed to her, "he discovered this lying on the floor
next to the pantry door." But Ellen was nowhere
about. She watched the lad for a moment and then
grew alarmed as she told the rest, "He says Ellen
never goes anywhere without her 'belt'—it is right
beside her bed as she sleeps, too." Tears misted
Daniella's eyes as she asked them all, "What could
have happened? Rascon has looked everywhere!"

Master Landaker tapped his bottom lip with a
forefinger; then his face lit up but still he looked

none too pleased. "I have it. You may not like the sound of this, for I believe there is some foul play afoot. First, I must ask: What were you lads doing in this hall? And why is my prized suit of armor scattered thus?"

With deep voices, Sebastián and Juan chimed in unison: "I heard a noise, and got up from bed to investigate." Then the two younger men stared at each other and shrugged with a weak smile that said: "We could have killed each other . . . if one had gotten that sword before the other!"

"I think we were both headed for the sword at the same time," Sebastián went on, then shrugged, "and we both *got* there at the same time. I am terribly sorry about the suit, Gregory, and I shall have it repaired if it is damaged. Truly, I was only after the sword—and your silver 'knight' kept us both from reaching it."

"Thank God for that," Daniella said in a quiet voice. Then she slipped her hand in Sebastián's. "How are we going to find Ellen? I'm worried about her, Sebastián."

"I was just about to suggest something," Master Landaker said, his expression thoughtful. "No one has searched the secret passageways."

"How about outside, has anyone looked there?"

Robert the manservant entered just then with the stablehand, telling them that they had just made a thorough search of the immediate grounds. "There's no sign of her. I believe there is some formidable force behind all this."

Dame Charlotte came back downstairs to tell what she had found. "Nothing," she said. "Her room is just as she always leaves it, nothing has been disturbed, not one object."

No one returned to bed that night. Fires were lit in many of the rooms to ward off the chill that had invaded Tallrock during the wee hours, and Sophie, Daniella, and Rascon sat together with fluffy blankets and chairs pulled up to the fireplace. Dame Charlotte was too nervous and tense to sit still, so she roamed the silent house in search of some clue to explain the sudden disappearance of Ellen Congal.

Master Landaker had to brush tears away every so often, for Ellen was the oldest living link to his childhood; her parents had taken care of him when he was just a lad skipping about the grounds of Tallrock. Folks back then had often heard of some mischief he and Ellen had planned together. Ellen had seen Gregory marry his beautiful childhood sweetheart, Phoebe Trahern, and saw him sire three healthy sons and his daughter, kindhearted and lovely Eileena. She'd witnessed the deaths of so many, including Phoebe, who had died of a wasting disease that had swiftly claimed her life. Ellen herself had never married. And now with the woman so much on his mind, afraid of what disaster had befallen her, Gregory Landaker wondered why the gentle and sweet Ellen had never taken a husband, for many had requested her hand and many had been turned down.

"Ah Ellen," Gregory murmured now as he rested before the fire. "Where could you be at this time of night? Please be alive, my dear, for I know my days will be gray and cheerless without your lovely presence. Even my nights, when you wait upon me and bring me some warm libation to make my sleep easier." A tear slipped from his eye as he envisioned her dear, sweet face always hovering near, seeing to his comfort and that of others. "I pray you are safe wherever you are, Evelyn." He said her real name now, remembering how she became a little annoyed when one said it; Ellen was just her nickname that Mistress Phoebe had given her and she had loved it and it stuck. "My friend, I pray that you will be found to be alive and well, that your fate is not to be a tragic one. Even if you have been hurt, please take courage, for I shall nurse you back to health and keep you forever at my side."

Gregory Landaker's hands clenched as he continued. "Whoever has taken you away shall pay! And if that wicked Drake is behind this—again—our longtime enemy will surely find the end of his days has come at last!"

"Who are you talking to, my father-friend, is it someone I know?" Sebastián made sure his presence was known immediately so as not to startle the aging Landaker.

"Aye!" Gregory snarled. "I make a promise to my beloved Ellen to kill that evil bastard whose ancient ghosts and living blackguards haunt us still. The Black Prince . . . There were two of them, you know, one was good, the other"—Gregory shrugged—"not so many know of him, but he was Evil itself and his terrible aura wafts about this land even now." He looked up at his adopted son whose green-gold eyes were mysterious and glittering. "Ha, that wily devil is afraid of ghosts, as is his younger brother Robert. Perhaps we shall get them yet!"

Sebastián tapped his chin in deep thought, then he said, "Of course . . . we'll scare them to death."

"Splendid idea, lad," Gregory drawled as he came to his feet; he was quite energetic for a man in his midsixties. "My cousin's restless spirit will thank me for that, he who wanders about these halls, and at times you can even hear the heartbreaking cries of my cousin."

"You mean Lord Steven Landaker?" Sebastián questioned with raised eyebrow.

"Aye. The very same. You have donned his guise before. Do you think you could do it again?"

"What? Dress up as Steven Landaker?" Sebastián asked. "I could, but there is someone who would like to take my place in donning the guise of Lord Landaker."

"You have already discussed this matter with someone else?"

"I have."

"And has he agreed to put on the disguise?"

"He has."

"Who is he?"

Sebastián narrowed his eyes. "You shall see. Later. For now, let us concentrate on helping save Ellen. We might be able to get to her—"

He let it drop and Gregory's eyes shot upward. "What did you say? Am I to understand you have found her?"

"I believe so . . . *Wait!*" He put a restraining arm on the man's arm as Master Landaker made to step from the room. "Are you sure you can take what I am about to say?"

The older man placed an amazingly strong grip upon Sebastián's wrist, and growled, "I can take anything . . . if only Ellen is alive!"

"She is alive . . ." Sebastián groped for words and just then Daniella's slender form filled the doorway.

". . . but she is in dire and desperate trouble," Daniella declared in a soft voice. "She has been found at the ruined castle near Carn Bodawen . . ." Daniella could not find it in herself to go on. Tears pooled in her beautiful turquoise-gray eyes.

Sebastián took up, "She has fallen into a pit." He gritted his teeth hard. "Or she had been thrown into it and left for dead!"

"What?!" Gregory Landaker walked quickly from the room, not awaiting an answer but going swiftly to take up his cloak and gloves. Over his shoulder he tossed, "Let us be gone before the afternoon is wasted!" Quickly following that, "What is being done to get her out?"

"I have tried," Sebastián said, then explained that he had been about to be let down on an old rope when the thing broke and he almost tumbled in after her. "The pit is deep; we can hear her whimpering. She sounds to be in pain. There are men from the village gathered there now; I left to come and tell you. We have sent down sustenance but have no idea if she has touched it or not . . . she can only sob and whimper."

"Dear God!" Gregory exploded. "How do you even know it is she?!"

Sebastián thought for a moment and then he looked really worried, as he said, "We don't."

Dame Charlotte entered the bedchamber for the fifth time in a quarter of an hour, and she begged and pleaded with Daniella and Sophie again. "This is insane, I tell you. There is nothing a woman can do to help the men."

"Not *a* woman, Charlotte, but three of us," Sophie averred, placing a blue cloak about Eileena's shoulders.

Charlotte wrung her hands in her apron. "At least leave Eileena here. It is madness to bring her along. The seaswept cliffs are no place for an invalid . . . *Dear Lord!*"

Rascon peeped out from behind Eileena's pale-blue skirts; his eyes were round and frightened.

"Why . . ." Sophie blustered. "Look to the lad, he has more sense than all of you put together. See, he did not go along with the men!"

"True," Sophie said. "Juan demanded that the lad stay with us and—"

Charlotte interrupted, "Aye, you said it yourself: He demands that we all stay put here . . . What is the boy doing? Has he gone mad? Just look, he is jumping up and down . . . Calm down, lad, you know the men are doing all they can to help get Ellen out of that pit."

"Rascon . . ." Sophie gently admonished. "You must keep calm; you are frightening Eileena." She took a closer look; Eileena's eyes were darting wildly about the room as if expecting a ghost to appear at any moment. "You are right, Charlotte, we will not take Rascon and Eileena with us, they are too—*What was that?* Did you hear it?"

Just then Rascon grabbed Eileena's hand, trying to make her stand up, but she would not budge, she just kept staring around the room in a frightened fashion.

Daniella went to the door and stood listening into the hallway, her heart beginning to pound, her swallowing difficult. "Perhaps the men are returning." A trip to the window next told her that such was not the case. "The sun is swiftly vanishing. I wish they would come back." Gripping her shoulders, she hugged herself as if she were cold. Her eyes widened. "There is that strange sound again. It . . . it sounds like something . . . dragging against stone."

Now Dame Charlotte swallowed hard. "Stone stairs . . . in the secret passageways."

"Footsteps . . ." Sophie's voice died away.

Despite the shudder that went through her, Daniella tried calming everyone. "But the men searched the passageways and they could not find anything. At least not this morning, they couldn't."

Charlotte nodded. "Rats."

"What's that, Charlotte? Did you say *rats?*" The older woman nodded and Sophie agreed only half-heartedly. "P-perhaps."

Now Eileena stared in the direction of the marble fireplace; she seemed not to be breathing at all. Her hands were white and lifeless in her lap . . . and when she dared to turn her head slowly, she saw that Rascon had faded into the draperies . . . and then she saw him darting toward the door that would lead him to the main staircase. In her dazed and frightened mind, Eileena knew he was going to summon help. They would soon need all the help they could get . . . *they were coming for her again. She just knew it.*

Eileena's hand shot out taking hold of Sophie's skirt, and she gripped the silky material as if it were a lifeline and held on for dear life.

"Eileena," Sophie said with a nervous little laugh, "I know you are frightened; we all are." She lifted and patted the white hand. "It will be all right, for the men shall soon be returning and we pray that

Ellen will be along. Don't fret so, darling, it was probably only a mouse or a rat that we heard."

A very big rat, Daniella was thinking, to make that strong a scuffle. Her eyes were caught by a sudden movement and she was startled for a moment. "Dame Charlotte, where are you going? You should stay with us . . ." A look was exchanged between Daniella and Sophie. "Just in case . . . there is—"

Charlotte's shoulders straightened imperiously. "Now look who is warning whom. But I shall not be so foolish as to leave the house. Relax, I shall soon return with a hot spot of tea for all of us. Now where did that rascally lad go?" she asked herself as she walked from the room with ramrod-stiff back.

"Uh . . . uh . . . uh . . ."

Daniella and Sophie spun around at the same moment, and both stared in shock at Eileena!

It was Daniella who rushed to stand in front of Eileena and lifted her hands; they were like the hands of a corpse, dead and buried.

"Eileena . . ." Daniella began gently. "You said something. What did you say?"

Her hand lifted to point behind Daniella. *"Drayyy—!"*

I am afraid to look. Fear or no fear, Daniella jerked her head and looked . . . and before her eyes took in the devils, she felt the malevolent force.

They had been so quiet.

The youngest man bowed from the waist. "Good evening, Dany."

The voice was dearly familiar to Daniella. Perhaps, she thought as she turned slowly to see who else was there with him, perhaps *not so* dearly. She felt for and found Sophie's hand and held tight while they faced the men—three in all—and with their full skirts they endeavored to hide Eileena from view and Daniella fruitlessly dreamed of escape.

Come home now, Sebastián, come home . . . please . . . we need you!

Daniella finally found her voice. "Robert, I see you have come to . . ." She could not finish; for to do so would be to put Eileena in grave danger. She had been about to say, *You have come to Eileena to beg forgiveness.*"

"Yes, I have come," Robert drawled, putting emphasis on the last word. "But we must hurry, my darling. You see, we shan't be caught here when your gallant husband arrives, and I do believe they will be getting that silly housekeeper out of the pit. Ah! I have forgotten my manners. Daniella, this is my brother, Sir Lucian Drake." He lifted her hand and led her to stand before the tall, thin man attired all in black. "And Sir Lucian, this is the lady I've told you so much about. Daniella Wingate. Is she not beautiful?"

"Robert, I am not Win—" Daniella was cut off as Robert squeezed her fingers as in a vise.

"Ah," Sir Lucian purred in a deep and silken voice. "You are indeed like a velvet rose . . . the magnificence of a blushing rose." He bent to lift her hand and kissed the moist palm. "I see you are nervous," he laughed. "All women are nervous upon first making my acquaintance, my dear. But it shall pass when we come to know each other better. Ah . . ." He turned to Sophie. "And this lovely woman must be a Landaker bride?"

Sophie disliked the man at once. "That is correct.

402

And so is Daniella a Landaker now. Tell me, how is it that you have come to be in my bedroom uninvited? You are rude, Sir Lucian. You have entered through the wrong door."

Suddenly Sir Lucian's hand shot out and he slapped Sophie hard, making her head jerk from side to side. Then he cuffed her on her chin, causing blood to trickle down her throat. Sophie's dark burnished hair flew about and her chin came to rest upon her heaving chest; but her eyes were blazing hatred for the man who had dared treat a woman so roughly. Here was the wily devil who had kidnapped and almost murdered Eileena . . . *Eileena!*

Sophie's hand groped back to feel for Eileena's hand, but it was not there! When gentle-hearted Sophie at last opened her bruised eye, she witnessed the first of a series of scenes that would forever be imprinted cruelly upon her mind.

Eileena had already been trussed up like a turkey; and a strange man who Lucian Drake called Ivan held her before him and kept her from slumping to her knees by jerking on her arm every time Eileena fell into a swoon.

Daniella was being dragged from the room toward the secret passageway marked by a wood panel beside the marble fireplace. Robert Drake had Daniella by her long silken rope of hair, twisted about his wrist, while the fingers of his other hand dug mercilessly and brutally into the soft flesh of her shoulder.

"Robert, please, don't do this." Daniella tried to pull away as they entered the dark and dank passage that led to a set of long and steep stairs, going down, curving down into the dark void below, perhaps into hell. "Where are you taking us? Why are you doing this?"

Robert laughed satanically. "It is for your own good, my Dany Rose. You never really understood how much you meant to me. I am going to show you just how much different our love is going to be from now on."

Sophie squeaked as a large and furry creature halted on the stone step and then moved to scurry down fast as his tiny black legs could carry him. In the torchlight held aloft by Ivan, Daniella had seen the sharp, nasty teeth and the demon-red eyes; ever to imagine that rats had been housed in the walls of Tallrock as they slept made her skin crawl horribly.

Robert yanked Daniella closer. "You are going to be my prisoner of love, Dany. I'm never going to let you get away—not this time!"

Daniella's brow furrowed as she looked at her childhood playmate. "Robert, I allowed you to go free not long ago. Please, can you not do the same for me and the others? Eileena will not come out of this alive—she is already near the edge of death."

"I care not for others." Robert gave Daniella's arm a painful squeeze. "You and I are all who matter. And we have treasure, Dany—Landaker's treasure. You should see it; I told you it was here. We discovered the vast storehouse in the dried-out tunnel. The Landakers had it wrapped and stored."

"Oh Robert," Daniella said softly. "Those must be family treasures. How could you be so unfeeling?"

"It is easy to hold that emotion"—Sir Lucian hissed over his shoulder—"with hate, pretty lady."

Daniella ignored the evil, older man. "Those

jewels must have been put away for the future — or perhaps they are family heirlooms."

Robert's laughter was eerie in the cavern. "You said it — family jewels. There is gold. Silver. Pieces of old jewelry that must have come from India and ancient Rome and Spain! It is all ours now, Dany, we have transferred the Landaker treasures to Sir Lucian's ship. Now we shall never want for anything. Wealth and love and parties every night. You shall be my princess . . . *Watch out for that step, Dany! It is crumbling* . . . we shall wine and dine as the wicked ancient Romans. You will be dressed in creamy silks, shimmering satin, and golden chains, emeralds and rubies, sapphires and diamonds, all yours — and mine."

Daniella saw the sweat on Robert's brow. "You are mad!" She pulled back on the hurtful grip that held her soft upper arm. "I will never submit to such treachery against the Landakers, Robert, nor will I drape myself in stolen jewels and rich silks for your — your orgies!"

"Dany . . . beware!"

"Keep the blond wench still!" Lucian ordered as they finally came to the bottom and stood in a cavernlike corridor where seaward water trickled down and spongy sea-colored moss grew on lichenous walls.

Daniella told herself to keep talking to ensure the safety and peace of mind of the other women. "How did they keep the treasure dry and safe, I wonder."

Eileena kept looking to Daniella for assurance and confidence, but the most she could do was keep the conversation flowing and continue smiling at her friends while swallowing her own fear.

"I have already told you," Robert snapped coldly. "There is a dry tunnel down here—but it takes a long time to reach it. Besides, we have emptied it of all the valuables . . . unless you have a liking for old family portraits?"

Daniella shook her head, staring away from Robert's look of greed.

While they were waiting for Ivan and others, who had suddenly appeared at the cave's hidden entrance in the north wall and were in the process of busily removing the camouflage, Daniella sidled closer to Eileena and Sophie. They had to hold Eileena up, for she was growing weaker by the minute and she seemed to be colder than usual, even though they had draped her warmest cloak about her shoulders. For Daniella, there had been no time to grab a wrap, and Sophie shared hers whenever they were allowed next to each other—which was not often enough to put their heads together and make plans.

Sophie whispered carefully. "The two brothers are mad. They would kill merely for the pleasure it would give them."

Daniella looked away from Sophie, and down at the brown sand. "We have to do something about Eileena—she cannot go on much more. They have only bound her hands; not ours. Cruel."

"I see the undisguised hunger for you in the young man's eyes. Can you talk to him—this Robert?"

"He cares nothing for anyone, Sophie. My childhood friend has grown hard and cruel. Robert has lost his heart." *If he'd ever had one in the beginning.*

Sophie read Daniella's thoughts. "He never had

one, you mean. He is a handsome devil; too bad he is so evil. He is a Drake?"

"He is. An old family friend"—Daniella choked up here—"brought Robert to our home in the Carolinas years ago. I believe it was when Sir Lucian, the pirate, could not afford to care for his younger brother. Oh, Sophie . . ." Daniella shook her head. "Two of my beloved friends have gone bad. First Alain and now Robert."

"Daniella, they were *always* bad."

Daniella stared at Sophie for long moments before she spoke. "You are right." She sighed. "As Sebastián was also correct in warning me. It is ironic that Sebastián became my husband, since his aim was vengeance. He set out to use me as a pawn in this deadly cat-and-mouse game. And now . . ."

Sophie licked her dry lips. "I am sorry to have to say this, Daniella. When Sebastián finds you are gone, he will taste the pill of bitter regret. He will feel the guilt. He will pay the price for his quest for vengeance."

"I wish it were not so." Daniella bowed her fair head, saddened that their relationship might come to this sorrowful and tragic end. She would be swept away. There was no knowing what would happen to Eileena. And Sophie, dear Lord, she carried a child within her womb just as she herself did.

The sun had gone down, and outside the moon was a pale reflection of itself in the waters of the little cove.

When Robert came for her, she begged him to leave Eileena in the cave, but her words fell on deaf ears. Robert, in his greed and lust, had turned as evil as his older brother Lucian.

407

"Come, my fairest maid," Robert murmured with a hand about her waist as he helped her from the cave, since she was bound at the wrists, and into a waiting wagon. "We go to a friend's up the rugged coast and after we conduct our business, we shall board the *El Draque* and sail away into the savage sea." He laughed cruelly. "You'll never see that bastard husband of yours again. You will learn, Dany, when you know me more intimately, that this man can take care of his own."

Chapter Twenty-five

If I must die
I will encounter darkness as a bride,
And hug it in my arms.
                    — William Shakespeare

The breath of the horses and men steamed in the crisp autumnal air along the rocky coast as riders passed the ruins where once had stood the massive stone walls and battlements and towers of Lostwithiel Castle. Now there was no sign of life in the ancient ruins — not a mouse, not even a bird.

Sebastián stared around, his eyes icy green slits, devoid of their sunlit depths, devoid of any emotion whatsoever.

A shudder raced through his body as he relived the panicky black fright that had swept him when he'd discovered Daniella, Sophie, and Eileena were missing!

It seemed an eternity since Rascon had run to meet the rescue party coming up the sea road. Ellen had been bundled in front of Gregory Landaker on his huge Thoroughbred. As far back as Sebastián's memory served him in his tense and apprehensive state, he could not recall the lad ever being out of breath before. Rascon had tried desperately to speak, but the only sounds that had emerged were squawks and pitiful squeaks of urgency.

Finally Sebastián had grasped the truth: The women had been abducted during the time they'd been rescuing Ellen. The housekeeper had been used in a diversionary tactic to give the villains time to skip away with their captives. *Bastards!* For two days and nights now without much sleep, the men had hunted for the women with tireless effort.

Sebastián had called for silence as Dame Charlotte began to relate the events that had led to the abduction. After the telling, Sebastián had flung riders from the villages wide in search of his beloved wife, Sophie, and Eileena. *Ah, Eileena . . . Not again.* Would he ever see her alive again, he wondered?

Sebastián had mused on who could have been the treacherous one at Tallrock. Ah! Geraldina Gancho. Before she left she must have opened the seaward gate to give the villains entry into the passages of Tallrock! It must be, he'd thought. After questioning Gregory he discovered that the master of Tallrock had sought diversion with the willing redhead. With an old man's false pride and stupidity — as Gregory called it — he had "shown" Geraldina around, his tour including the dark passageways of the mansion. Gregory had not revealed the family heirlooms in the secret tunnel, but Geraldina had, nevertheless, been curious when he'd evaded her questions pertaining to the "dry" and "spacious" area between the dank passages . . .

Now Juan slowly rode his great-limbed brown horse. He'd been through indescribable horror in his mind and heart over what might have come to be Eileena's final fate.

The *Desdemona* had arrived the day before, twenty-four hours after the abduction. The captain

f that ship had answered that he'd spotted no
other ships heading out into the Atlantic. With an-
ger-bright eyes, Sebastián was realizing that the
Drakes must have gone up along the rock coast and
been moving like insidious snakes in the tall grass.
Soon, if not already, it would be too late!

There must be a ship waiting for the villains and
their captives . . . somewhere beneath the cliffs of
serpentine rock, in one of the wooded coves. *But
where?* Sebastián's mind screamed.

A new beard—amber in color—darkened the
bronzed jawline of Sebastián's face. He had become
thinner. If he would, even for a moment, allow his
mind to dwell on the fact that Daniella was with
child—and, of course, Sophie, too—he would be
rendered utterly incompetent to handle any situation requiring strong body and clear mind.

Kneeing his mount, Sebastián joined Juan in the
fork of the dusty road up ahead. He could make
out the mysterious bundle of clothes riding close to
Juan's lean hip in the saddlebag.

"Some sixth sense keeps telling me to return to
the old ruined castle site," Juan was saying.

"I am of the same mind," Sebastián agreed.
"Let's go then!"

The battering winds released unearthly howls
around the wild and mossy ruins, and stinging salt
spray reached those huddled together in a corner,
their colorful skirts tucked in at their ankles, en-
deavoring to keep warm.

Daniella and Sophie spoke in hushed tones while
taking turns at keeping Eileena warm. No matter
how valiant their efforts, Eileena kept shivering like

a leaf tossed in the wild ocean wind. Eileena had been walking on her own these last weeks, and at the moment they were grateful to Juan for his help in massaging her limbs to start them working, otherwise Eileena would have perished long ago.

Sophie rubbed Eileena's hands between hers. "What do you suppose they are planning for us now?" she asked Daniella.

Daniella kept her eyes trained on the young ruffian who was guarding the crumbled entrance to the pirates' hideaway. "They are moving the treasure to the ship anchored out in the cove. As soon as that is done, I believe they will bring us out to the ship. God only knows where, then." She ended in a deceptively calm voice.

A fleeting smile touched Sophie's lips and then evaporated seconds later. She'd been remembering the day Teague had asked her to become his wife and she'd responded with a definite "Yes, my love." For years they'd awaited a child to come along and add even more happiness to their already blessed marriage, since a child would crown it with perfection. Now Sophie was with child, but would she lose the babe now, she wondered sadly? Or would she be rescued by her wonderful husband and the handsome merchant captain who'd stood as best man at their wedding: Sebastián Landaker.

Daniella was having similar thoughts. Yet, *their* marriage had been a tumultuous one from the onset. She realized now that she always had an inkling in her deepest heart that Sebastián and Steven were one and the same. So it was not peculiar that she'd felt affection for both! For a while she'd worried that she had become a wanton, desiring her foppish husband one minute and falling into the arms of

412

the scoundrel captain the next.

The menacing pirates were almost finished loading their stolen booty, and every once in a while Robert Drake would show at the entrance to make certain the guard did his job and the women weren't sneaking away.

Daniella glanced up. Robert's eyes met hers and she shivered with distaste, realizing that Robert was no longer the harmless childhood playmate he'd once been to her. Robert would not care that she was carrying Sebastián's child, oh no. It might, however, be dangerous for him to learn of her pregnant state. Having come to comprehend Robert's true color — black — she doubted he had any heart at all.

Daniella reflected back to the day in the Carolinas when Robert had returned at long last. Oh, the lies he'd fashioned! Robert lived an imitation of life, revolving around preposterous lies. Robert had been more clever at cloaking his real self than Sebastián had been with costume, makeup, and wig!

Daniella clenched her fists in the gritty sand. "Damn him." She looked sideways at Sophie, but the kindhearted woman was hugging Eileena close and hadn't heard Daniella's curse. "Damn him to hell," even softer this time.

Now Sophie looked up, and Daniella could read the stark fear and helplessness in the woman's eyes. *If only there were some way to escape before the ship sailed — with them on it!* Daniella thought.

All of a sudden the clouds parted. Daniella saw a vision flash before her eyes, and in it Sebastián was atop a white war horse, a sword in his hand flashing for a second in the imaginary sun.

Daniella could feel it. She knew that Sebastián

413

was searching for them! He had to be, for his love burned as brightly and gloriously as that momentary sunburst she'd witnessed in the overcast sky. She pictured Rascon's impish little face then. The mute boy. He shall lead them. Like a candle in the night, showing the way.

Daniella's eyes burned. Sebastián might be on his way even now! The Drakes had hidden them in the trackless green forest for two days, and then they had brought them to these ruins. A rescue was in the making. She could feel it, feel his spirit reaching for her, almost feel his presence.

The moment was shattered.

"We are ready to take the women now."

Daniella heard Robert's confident voice and she despised him more than ever as he stood there lording his evil over helpless women. *What has become of you!* Daniella shouted inside herself. She glared at Robert with burning and reproachful eyes, wanting to scream at him: *Not yet! Not yet! Give it more time!*

Robert's dark eyes blazed down into hers as he came to give her his hand. "It is time to go now, Dany."

"Not yet. Please, we are tired. A little more time."

"Ah, Dany, I know what's on your mind. He has forgotten you already. Such a pity."

"No! It's not true!"

His laugh raked her nerves and she itched to slap him, hurt that once-beloved face from out of the past. Hurt Robert Drake in any way she could . . . He'd caused harm to many. So many, dear God.

Daniella spat her first words of hatred to him, in fact to anyone, ever. "I despise you, Robert. De-

414

spise you for bringing death into the Landaker family, for harming Eileena—and mostly for what you are about to do now!"

Robert bristled before his hand shot out, and he slapped her back and forth across her velvety cheeks, leaving a fiery imprint on either side. Then, in an action thoroughly repulsive to Daniella, he caught her to him close, letting her feel his lust, and sneered down into her smarting face. "You are mine now, bitch! You were always mine!"

A satanic voice sounded behind Robert: "And perhaps you shall be a little bit mine also."

Daniella gritted her teeth. "You will have to kill me first."

"Which one of us do you refer to, fair lady?" Lucian inquired, his dark eyes raking over listless Eileena with ill-disguised contempt. "Ah . . ." he sneered. "The wilted white flower." He gave his full attention back to the blond-tressed Daniella. "Ahh, I can see I shall have to prune this snowy rose. I love to break a woman's spirit and use her like a whore."

Lucian waved an arm as if dismissing them all from class. "Take the bitches to the ship—now!"

While the guard tied the helpless women with sun-bleached rope, Daniella hissed under her breath, "You, none of you, shall escape the Tiger's wrath."

Robert heard. "The Tiger. Hah! The tiger and the rose. A tragic romance, that. I am sorry, Dany, but I'm afraid you shall inherit the tempest for your bed partner . . . perhaps more than one. You'll never see your lover again. Not where we are going."

"And . . ." Daniella stood with her chin high as

her wrists were next in being tied. "Where the devil would that be?"

"To hell, my beautiful snowy rose."

Never again would he be Robert, her friend, her beloved childhood playmate . . . *never*. Daniella swallowed her terrible grief.

Wild determination to survive whatever the costs glowed within the sea-colored depths of Daniella's eyes.

"No, Robert, to pay well for your abominable acts, that is where *you* are going. It is where you belong." Her face clouded. "May the ghost of Tallrock send you there."

Robert stared at her and he could not repress the disquieting shivers that rippled his lean frame. *Ghost?* Not the rumored ghost of Steven Landaker. *No.* That apparition had not been seen around these parts for years. *Had it?*

Daniella's words had been like a shroud of death thrown over him. He looked up into the threatening dark sky . . .

Just then it began to rain.

Juan had learned how to kill when he was just a boy. To kill swiftly and without mercy, that is the way he'd been trained by his Portuguese cousins, soldiers in the formidable, death-dealing army. He was certain this day there would be no need for bloodshed when they caught up with the Drakes. There was a better, cleaner method than stabbing one with a dagger or lopping one's head clean off with a sword. *Deluding the unwary . . . and fear . . . is the beginning of all ends.* To come full circle with the evil brothers, the Drakes.

A rumble of thunder forced Sebastián to look up at the sky, making him unpleasantly aware that at any moment a torrent of rain would come bursting from the dismal blanket to make their going difficult.

"Dios mio!, I pray we reach them in time!" Juan shouted under the angrily muttering gray sky.

Sebastián bent his shoulders to the howling wind and lifted the cowl to his long black cloak. "We only have a feeling, Juan, my friend. How can we be certain that the bastards have returned to Carn Bodawen?"

"Our feelings are true, and pure, Sebastián — they will lead us to the place."

Only the aggressive shape of Sebastián's nose could be seen emerging from his cowled profile, and Juan looked at him now with the knowledge that his eagerness to dispose of the nuisances in their lives — namely Robert and his devil brother — was every bit as great as his own.

This gnawed their insides . . . ruthlessly.

Chapter Twenty-six

Rascon hid in the scrubby and gnarled bushes near the ruins, watching the dark, ruthless pirates stash the stolen treasure aboard the ship and then return to shore. But now Rascon's attention was held by the scene inside the old rock walls.

From his vantage point, Rascon had a clear view into the ruined place where a huge, uneven section of the old Norman castle had crumbled or been blown away from a warring ship that could have sailed into the cove hundreds of years before.

Hunkered down, Rascon peeked through the bushes watching the man he hated most in the whole world enter the ruins. Lucian Drake. For a time the pirates conferred, and Rascon wondered what was going to happen next.

Now the ruffians were binding the women's wrists to make doubly sure they wouldn't get far if they should try to make a run for it. *The evil, sneaking bastards, treating women in such a terrible bad way!* Rascon's lips were so tight they went almost purple.

The lad was nauseated with outraged fear and frustration. Helplessly he watched the guard manhandle Eileena — as if she were some pig or chicken he was trussing up! *Bastard!* After Eileena was secured tightly, the manhandling pirate gave her a shove that sent Eileena reeling against the ruined wall. Rascon stood and shook his fists at the pirate.

Gritting his teeth, Rascon balled his little hands into even tighter fists. From somewhere deep within his soul came the words: *I . . . I w-wish I w-was b-b-bigger. I . . . I'd l-lick y-your b-boots!"*

Rascon blinked and swallowed hard. *Was that me? Did I say those words?*

"I-I d-did!" He slapped his rump and jumped into the air, gasping between words spoken aloud, then hugged himself for joy. "I-I r-really *d-did!!"*

Rascon whooped, then slammed a hand over his mouth quickly. He could tell the others now!

Whirling about, Rascon ran as fast as his skinny legs would carry him to the little golden mare he'd left grazing not too far away. With luck he should be able to reach the men before they wandered too far in their search for the kidnapped ladies. As Rascon mounted, he decided to use the road to the other side of the forest—just in case he was being watched. It would be faster, too, and he could cut them off as he doubled back into the trees!

Rascon had not gone far when he caught sight of the two riders up ahead. They were coming straight for him! Rascon couldn't be sure they weren't enemies. Like some of Drake's men. He started to knee his mount toward the woods. From there he could make out the riders' identities as they rode by.

With unsheathed weapons in hand, Sebastián and Juan urged their mounts into a faster pace while setting out after the stranger they'd seen from afar coming down the road.

Juan leaned into his horse's mane as the sword in hand was held high over his dark head. "Let's get him. *Ayy!*"

"Juan . . . listen!" Sebastián shouted back, his mount now flanking the other's. "He might be one of ours!"

"We shall see, won't we?"

It was in the minds of both men that the rider who'd dashed off into the woods could be one who the villains had sent to ride guard around the perimeter of their hiding place. If that was true then they were close by; still, they had to proceed with caution lest they fall into an ambush!

Juan went one way, Sebastián the other. They'd silently agreed to flush him out, knowing that their prey hadn't gotten far yet, since the woods were like a tangled jungle in this remote area!

"There he is!!" Juan shouted as Sebastián broke through at the same time the small, pale rider did.

Sebastián and Juan came at him at right angles and the valiant lad slowed his mount to a stop, positioning his arms over his head as if in anticipation of a sudden blow.

Then his voice, loud and squeaky, cut into the rainswept air!

"I-It's me. D-d-don't h-hit me!" Rascon peeked up and saw who his attackers were. "S-Sebastián . . . Juan—d-don't you kn-know m-me?"

Juan's mouth fell wide.

"Dios!!" Sebastián shouted as he reined his startled mount abruptly and drew closer. "You spoke! *Rascon spoke!*"

"U-uh-huh!"

Whirling his mount, Juan joined them, seeing the strained look on the lad's face. "What is it, lad? You have something to tell us."

"A-aye!" Rascon directed a shaking finger back

420

n the direction from which he'd come just minutes
efore. "H-hurry! Th-they got th-the women. H-
urry! F-follow *me!*"

Fear pounded through Daniella in ever-deepening
vaves. The demonic ruthlessness of the Drakes had
truck clear home to her—and, dear God, Robert
vas a stranger to her now. He seemed to grow in-
reasingly mad and satanic with every moment that
assed. He had not heeded her pleas when she'd
mplored and begged mercy for Eileena. All this
eemed to do was force the guard to treat Eileena
ven worse—no doubt from Robert's command to
o so! For punishment!

Daniella raged at Robert Drake as she spun
bout. "Why will you not leave her be? Can't you
ee she cannot take much more?"

"Cease your rantings, Daniella, else I finish the
ood-for-nothing wench off now!"

When the guard passed by Daniella—while they
nade to usher them to the longboat—she whirled
bout and lifted his pistol. Just like that, *she had
t!* She held the weapon close to the man's head
vhile Robert stood gaping at her incredulously,
vondering how she'd turned the tables so fast on
hem!

Daniella's eyes had gone hard. "Untie Sophie and
ileena or else this man gets it—and you, too!" She
pun to put the nose of the pistol square in
Robert's face.

Daniella leaned forward to unsheathe the wary
nan's sword while he stood mesmerized and gaping
t the blond captive—who was not a captive any
onger—helplessly in awe of the strength and cun-

ning she had suddenly displayed.

Robert had not moved an inch. "And you, Miste
Drake—you will do exactly as I order or, as I said
you will get it, too! *Now move to help untie them!*

Robert snarled, showing his large white teeth. "
thought you had her tied up!" he yelled at the cow
ering guard. He dropped his cutlass and dagger, a
she ordered. "You crazy wench—you won't ge
away with this. Even now my brother is no doub
watching your foolish movements in his spy glass
Soon he will return to shore with the longboat an
then we shall see how brave you are—Daniell
Wingate!"

"Never!" Daniella hissed, waving the gleamin
sword in front of Robert's nose. "Never call me tha
again. I am not an unmarried woman as you
wormy brain seems to insist. I am Daniella Landa
ker and I carry Sebastián's child!"

Pain washed over Robert's features and h
seemed to turn gray as ashes right before her eyes
"What a foolish *bitch* you are," he murmured witl
a snarl. "You could have had everything with me!

Daniella tossed her head. "But Robert, I *do* hav
everything I'd ever want, right now. Sebastián is m
love—my life—and you, Robert Drake, are not
part of it any longer—not even a friend. You hav
done your evil deeds as if . . . as if others do no
count in this world. But now . . . now they must b
laid to rest."

Robert shrugged nonchalantly. "What do yo
mean to do?"

"First untie Eileena and Sophie as I ordered mo
ments ago. That bumbling oaf of a pirate seems t
have passed out cold. Do it—now! Then we wil
wait and see."

While untying the women, Robert sneered arrogantly, "My brother and his men will come ashore soon and he will seize you again."

Daniella waved the loaded pistol in front of Robert's nose. "Not with this in my possession, he won't!"

Paling considerably, suddenly sick to his stomach, Robert could do nothing more than glare at Daniella through narrowed eyes. *Oh, she is staying on her toes, with pistol in one hand and dagger in the other! Daring and bold and triumphantly beautiful she is. Hah! The heroine!* Dammit all to hell. He should have taken her body long ago in the misted woods and be damned by her temper instead of facing death at her lily-white hands! *The heroine? She hasn't won yet!*

"Ah well . . ." Robert began quietly while shaking in his boots! "You will tire long before I, wench. *Then* who will have the advantage?"

"Remember, my *old* friend, I have the pistol while you have nothing but your despicable words to toss at me."

Daniella then kicked the other weapons out of sight while waving the pistol in front of their noses. Then the guard broke and made a run for it and Daniella lifted the pistol to fire.

After several moments had gone by, the pistol was still fully loaded.

"Hah." Robert sneered into her frustrated face. "Daniella, little blond wench, why did you not shoot? A coward? Who would have ever thought it?"

Swiftly Daniella came back at Robert with the nose of her pistol. "Because, you see, I am saving this shot for you."

"My, you are smart Dany, to realize it is a single-shot pistol. Playing make-believe again, eh?"

Daniella lifted her chin. "You, Robert, are the one living on make-believe and wanton lies. You cheat. You dishonor. You steal . . . murder. You are half a man, Mister Drake."

Cocking an eyebrow, Robert looked her straight in the eye. *"Mister* Drake is it now?"

"Be still."

"I love you, Dany," Robert whispered huskily, his eyes like hot coals in his ruddy face.

Daniella sneered back. "Your honeyed words are cloaked in poison. Lies. Even if you did love me, Mister Drake, your life trudges on the borders of hell."

Robert waved a hand in the air. "You think I have lied to you, Dany?"

"Think?" Daniella scoffed. "I know your color now. You are black clear to your soul. You use helpless women for your evil ends."

Like sharp and black glittering glass, Robert's eyes roved Daniella's lithe and shapely form, coming to rest on the dangerous weapon she held in her hand. "I have never seen you as you are now, Dany."

"And . . ." She tossed her head. "You never will again."

With a mad gleam in his wild eyes, Robert said, "Have you not heard of the restless ghost that roams the cliffs and woods nearby? He is Lord Steven Landaker . . . Ah! Now I have your attention! Steven is one—of several—who my brother Lucian killed."

"Afraid, Robert? Of a ghost? I know this ghost quite well."

"What are you saying?"

Her misty eyes connected with Robert's wildnes. "Robert, why, didn't you know I married teven Landaker?"

"You cannot be serious! You married *Sebastián* andaker! My brother, I told you, did away with teven a long time ago. He is only a . . . a ghost hat some imagine roaming the moors at midight!"

"That might be true, but I say this and I say it rue: The man I married was Steven Landaker. The ame is on our marriage contract."

"It . . . it cannot be! Damn you, dark wench, ease your lying!"

From atop the cliff a deep voice fell down upon hem:

"She speaks the truth, Drake. Steven Landaker ives. A pity you do not believe that even now he valks the earth alive and well as you and I."

"You *lie!*" Robert shouted, shaking his fists. You both lie! Come down here. *You* . . . Sebasián Landaker—you are her husband! You cannot ool me." Robert laughed, a demonic sound rising o the dark misting sky. "I know you married her nd took her away from me!"

"I took the lovely flower away on my worthy vesel," he called down, "but it was Steven Landaker he wed—truly."

While Robert shook his balled fist, Eileena and ophie, huddled together in the back of the scrub, tared up at Sebastián, grateful to see him, knowing hat *now* there would be no further harm to fear.

Robert saw his chance and grabbed it. Daniella vas so engrossed in staring up at her beloved that he stood momentarily off guard. She saw the green-gold fire in her love's eyes . . .

"Daniella, *watch out!*" Sebastián called out.

But it was too late! Robert had charged Daniell: and snatched the pistol from her hand, giving he arm a painful wrench as he took it.

Green eyes gleamed with warning before Sebas tián gathered himself and leapt from the cliff t land in the soft sand below. *There he froze dead i his tracks!*

"Stay where you are, Tiger!" Robert warned, giv ing Daniella's arm a twist behind her back as h held the pistol against her forehead. "One mov and this bride of the restless phantom is dead."

Hugging Daniella around the waist, the pistol a her brain, Robert dragged her with him since he rubbery legs refused to move.

Sebastián called, "Lord Steven Landaker—com forth!"

With insanely wild eyes going from Sebastián t the rock ledge above, Robert suddenly froze when caped figure appeared. *What's this?* The dark appa rition threw the dark cowl back and Robert's mout! dropped agape, for there stood the dark phanton of his dreams, long black curling hair and all.

"S-Steven Landaker," Robert hissed. "M-m brother killed you. You are only a ghost—you can not hurt me!" Robert gave Daniella's arm anothe painful twist. "Stay where you are, phantom!"

"Steven" spoke in a shivery voice. "I am comin down."

Daniella swallowed, terror billowing through her *How can this be,* her mind kept asking her. *"How?* she said aloud.

Robert jerked his head around to Daniella "What did you say? I thought you married this—

426

this phantom?"

"I did," Daniella said with a soft gasp, then looked from Sebastián to the black-wigged figure. "But he . . ." Again she stared from the apparition on the cliff to her husband, her eyes full of fascination.

"He *is* a ghost," Sophie murmured, transfixed.

Eileena, too, had succumbed to wonder—a dreaded wonder, since the Landaker cousin had been dead these many years and she'd never seen Steven's ghost, not until now. She was beginning to see a lot of things in life she'd not beheld in years. Robert looked between the dazed faces, realizing that this could not be a trick they were playing on him. Those looks were too real to be pretend!

"Sebastián killed him," Daniella mumbled cryptically, her brain dazed and numb. In her terror-filled mind she began to believe that perhaps there truly was a restless phantom who roamed the clifftops and the grounds of Tallrock.

When will the poor soul be laid to rest?

Just then Eileena screamed and everything happened with lightning speed!

An eerie cry penetrated the tempest-charged air and then "Steven" Landaker was landing on his feet, light as a cat in the sand—not three feet from where Eileena and Sophie stood transfixed. Daniella struggled to free herself, but Robert held a relentless grip on her, still pointing the pistol to her brain.

Eileena stared into the dark cinnamon eyes. Lord Steven Landaker had jade eyes—just like Sebastián. This was not her dearly departed relative! Not the phantom who roamed the moors at midnight! *Who. . . ?*

427

Eileena's heart sang and she whispered one name—a name that no one else could hear, for she'd said it low. *Juan.*

Sophie was trying to pull Eileena back up the slope and away from danger, but Eileena would not budge. Sophie caught sight of the willowy figure darting from scrub brush to gnarled tree, and then he came running toward them, sliding home—behind Eileena's and Sophie's skirts.

"E-Eileena," he stammered. Seeing the joy alight in the girl's eyes, Rascon plunged on. "I—I can t-talk. I-I got the daylights scared outa m-me, 'cause I was a-fraid th-they were going to h-hurt you!"

Robert stared as if mesmerized by the lad's daring.

Eileena reached out a trembling hand to draw the rumpled head close to her bosom. Her face was warm and loving—and then she watched as her beloved Juan threw his cloak off and leapt nimbly into the air and dropped a lightning kick to Robert's arm. The pistol went spinning and Sebastián caught the thing in midair. Then he pointed it directly at Robert's head while Daniella came running to his side. Sebastián wrapped his free arm securely about her waist.

The phantom stepped back.

Sebastián waved the pistol. "We have some unfinished business, Robert Drake."

But Robert was staring with a mad light in his eyes, staring at the phantom as if he couldn't believe what was there before his eyes.

Daniella turned then as the dark phantom came up behind her. *He is grinning!* She found herself staring into cinnamon-dark eyes. *Juan!* For a moment she was startled out of her wits, then she

ealized that Juan had donned Sebastián's famous
lisguise—nothing more!

"I'm sorry to have fooled you, too, my love,"
Sebastián bent to whisper in her ear, "but it was the
only way."

Her heart was full of love. "I know, Sebastián."

Worshipful eyes dropped to the slight bulge under
her waistline. "Are you all right? Is the—?"

"We are fine, my darling."

Just then Robert let out a shriek of frustrated
rage and jealousy. He bent to sweep up a fallen
dagger and charged the cloaked figure. Juan's eyes
bulged in shock just as the blade entered his body
and then was removed as Robert wrenched back,
the bloody dagger dripping and red!

"N-n-no!" Eileena screamed, then fell into
Sophie's arms as she fainted dead away.

Unafraid of the mesmerized Robert Drake, Rascon scrambled to Eileena's side, cupping her pale
face in his trembling hands. "E-Eileena, w-wake
up!"

"She is all right, Rascon," Sophie said, her
frightened eyes returning to the desperate show-
down.

"Kill him, Sebastián!" Juan got out between
groans and grimaces of pain. "Do him in!"

Sebastián was torn between going to his best
friend Juan and going after Robert—who was
scrambling up the slope to escape. He still had the
dagger—but now he had Daniella also!

Threatening the blade at Daniella's throat, Robert
stood looking out over the cliff watching for signs
of his brother. "Dammit, where—?"

Sebastián's voice floated to Robert. "They have
already come ashore, Drake." His voice was closer

now.

Robert spun about to face the man he hated most. No, there were *two*. The phantom Steven Landaker was the other—he'd always hated ghosts. He laughed, staring down to where the cloaked figure lay, his blood spilling onto the ground. Robert swallowed hard. *Blood? Ghosts were not supposed to have blood!*

Sebastián caught Robert's attention and pointed to a spot on the beach where dead bodies were littered. "Your brother is one of the dead—my men caught them sneaking ashore while my brave wife was holding you with her stolen pistol. That is why you didn't see the fight, Robert Drake. Poor Robert, you always had eyes for the wrong woman—*my* woman. Daniella and I are like one . . . we are inseparable. We have proven our love and know each other's hearts and minds. I know her thoughts before she gives voice or action to them."

"Not this time!" Robert rushed to the edge of the cliff, taking Daniella with him. Her eyes were round and bright, and she seemed to be holding her breath as she looked over the side to the jagged tiers of gray rock.

Leaping toward Robert, Sebastián grabbed him by the throat, flinging Daniella toward the green sward where she would be safe. Now he turned on Robert, and the vicious movement caused Robert to lose his footing. He was falling, holding on to Sebastián, meaning to take him with him, but Sebastián yanked back. Now Robert was clinging to the edge, his grip holding tight to Sebastián's wrist.

"Come on, come with me to hell." Robert pulled hard as he could. "No one will have Daniella then."

430

He was panting with his exertion.

"You bastard!" Sebastián gritted into Robert's face. He unlocked Robert's grip . . . then their fingertips merely touched . . . now Robert was falling . . . *falling.*

Daniella did not look as Robert's body bounced onto the rocks, blood squirting from his skull. Then at last Robert Drake lay still at the bottom.

Daniella's gaze lifted to Sebastián, his eyes as ravaged as her own. He'd not wished Robert's death any more than Daniella had — but the Drake family had done so much harm to decent people.

Daniella's head lowered and she looked aside remaining slumped in the sand while the others made their way back to the house in the wagon that had been sent for.

What seemed hours later, someone came to gently place a heavy coat around her shoulders. Then she was alone again.

The body of her childhood playmate was taken away.

Someone again appeared at her feet. "You will take a chill. The day is darkening," the voice said with tender compassion for her bleeding heart.

Sebastián sighed when still she had not moved to rise. "He was not worth all this suffering, you know."

Daniella looked up into Sebastián's beautiful tiger eyes. "You were right. The Drakes had a taint in their blood."

"Thank God there were no children of the brothers."

Sebastián pulled Daniella up to stand in the warmth of his loving embrace. "Gone. They are all wiped from this earth. I am only sorry that Robert could not have been forced to ask Eileena's forgiveness. It might have done her some good. But whatever, Robert has paid enough."

"Yes . . ." Daniella walked beside her husband "Enough. His soul is laid to rest. At last."

In hell, Sebastián was thinking. *Abysmal darkness to him who evil thinks and lives.*

Chapter Twenty-seven

As we look back, the passage
seems like a walk through a mist,
taken so lightly.
— Johanna Salmi

Chill north winds sighed among the tumbled
stones and along the coastal grounds of Tallrock;
but it was cozy and toasty warm in Sebastián's bedchamber inside the huge house where Dany, wearing a midnight-blue velvet robe, lay with her head
upon her husband's shoulder. She had never felt
such peace as she did now.

All the way home from the ruins of Lostwithiel
Castle, Daniella had taken comfort in Sebastián's
nearness as they rode and she had dwelled in security . . . as she did now.

Daniella sighed happily and gazed up at Sebastián as he slumbered next to her. He would always
have the scars, but he was still handsome enough to
steal her breath away, she thought as her bluish-
gray eyes shone like stars and she drank in the comfort of his masculine nearness as she snuggled
closer.

The vibrant colors of the sun peeked over the
ledge of the window just then, and suddenly Daniella was endowed with new exuberance and energy.
She felt as if she could embrace the whole world!

She felt as if she would like to go for an exhilarating ride, in fact, with her cherished husband beside her. She rose swiftly from the soft, warm bed.

"Sebastián! Wake up!" She began to tickle and tease him and he opened his glorious green eyes with all the gold flecks swimming around in them and gazed up at her.

"What is it?" he asked, awakening to the sight of his beautiful bride bending over him, her shining blond hair spilt over her shoulders and the low-cut neckline of her nightgown and robe. "Mmm, you look good enough to eat, m'dear."

"Come on, Sebastián — rise up. I wish for you to look at the sunrise with me. It is a new day! And I have a thrilling eagerness to feel everything in it. Even the chill winds!"

He growled and, reaching out, he caught her by the ankle just as she was trying to get off the bed again. "And I want to feel everything in this bed — namely *you*."

"Sebastián!" she squealed, playfully and seductively pretending to escape him as she rolled and shifted and protested with muffled little shrieks. He caught a handful of her bottom and she squealed even louder, and then blushed hotly as she thought of the others in the house hearing her squeals.

His voice became husky as he ordered, "Come here, my little sun-haired wench. It seems a lifetime since I last held you in my arms, and I want to hold you now! Touch you! Caress you! Ravish you with wild loving until you are out of your mind with pleasure!"

"But what about last night?" Dany sneaked in playfully.

"Last night?" he countered in a tight voice. "That

was not the height of passion, Dany my love. The most intimate we got was to fall asleep in each other's arms with our legs entangled." His voice dipped to a more intimate pitch. "Now I want to slowly savor every inch of—

—your . . . beautiful . . . little . . . body." He sucked on the pearldrop of her earlobe.

"Hah," Daniella scoffed as he reached for her. "It will not be so small and dainty in a few months." She laughed. "Then try to get your arms around me, *El Tigre,* and see how far you get!"

Suddenly he looked very serious as he asked, "Is it all right for us to . . . ah . . . you know." He placed a gentle hand upon the slight tummy bulge. "Do you know what I am saying. He will not be hurt?"

"He?" Daniella giggled and screwed up her face. "You are so sure the babe is a 'he?' "

"Not really. A girl just like you would do just as fine." He grinned impishly. *"If* she looked just like you, my beautiful wench."

She brought his hand back to her belly after he had taken it away with a look of bewilderment on his handsome face. "Of course it is all right, Sebastián. I want you as much as you do me, and I assure you the babe will not be hurt." She grinned impishly. "Lord! It is not as if we were going to savagely tear into each other and make love!"

Sebastián bent his head and his lips found hers, and then the passion began, the magical passion they had always shared. Looking deeply into her eyes while kneading a breast through the nightgown, he murmured, "I love you . . . I love you . . . Love you *querida,* and cannot say it enough to express the height of my passion and love for you.

435

Dios, mere words are not enough," he ended with a passionate look in his eyes and a catch in his deep voice. *"Comprende?"*

"Sí." With a soft smile, Daniella gazed into his face. Tears misted her silken amber lashes and threatened to spill over them.

"This is not the first time," he said, kissing the lobes of her ears. "I will say it over and over, forever and ever, until death do us part. You are my passion flower and I cannot live without your sweet nectar; I am insatiable. I want to greedily feed on you until I am filled to overflowing and can take no more . . ." He grinned lazily. "For a while."

"You are my tawny tiger," she murmured, wrapping her arms about his shoulders as he kissed her throat, "and I cannot live without your strength."

She giggled.

"What is so funny?" He lifted his mouth from the column of her ivory throat where he had been lightly nibbling.

"Oh . . . I was just recalling a day gone by." She smiled in remembrance. "How you played your part so well . . . bending your wrist and posturing like a dandy in silk stockings."

"Think it is funny, do you? You do not know what it is like to have your face painted up like a foppish dandy . . . to wear a wig that probably had little creatures running around in it . . . to walk around with my nose in the air and striking leggy poses."

"But, oh Lord, you did!" Daniella bounded to her knees, pointing a coral-tipped finger at his handsome face. "I recall in our bridal chamber as you went to close the drapes against the invading moon . . . I couldn't believe what a catch I'd made."

He watched his wife closely in her playful mood. "What?"

"Once it had struck me, I made it a point to forever hold the sight in my memory. And *what* a memory is your mighty physique, my lord."

"Well then . . ." He shrugged. "If you knew the name of my game?"

"I did *not* know your game—not at the time. It was not long ago that I suddenly sat up in my bed, recalling that you had not strutted like the dandy on your way around the room and back to the bed." She looked at him with half-smiling lips, waiting for his reaction. "Instead you had swaggered like the endearing scoundrel that you are."

Sebastián pulled her back down to the bed and wrapped his arms about her as he rested his bristly chin upon the top of her silky soft head. Dany gazed up into his rugged profile as he spoke.

"Oh, my love, you do not know the half of it. The bitter pill of regret I tasted over the way I had treated you. When you were missing after being abducted by the Drakes, I wanted nothing more than to find you and tell you how deeply sorry I was to have caused you so much grief and unhappiness."

"But Sebastián, I was not *really* unhappy." She twirled her fingers in the hairs of his chest. " 'Tis true that I experienced some grief after my father died and you were so bad to me—"

He heaved a deep sigh. "I am sorry for that, too."

Daniella glanced aside to the rays of sun lying on the floor, then spoke softly. "Sebastián . . ."

"What is it, *querida?*" He brushed the top of her head with his chin as if deep in thought; but he was listening to every word she spoke, since every one was precious and to be treasured.

"You did not tell me who gave you the scars and the wound to your leg."

Her winged eyebrows rose in waiting.

"No?" When she shook her head, he went on. "Sir Lucian and I fought a duel on the *Emerald Tiger.* That was before he and his mean younger brother sent me on my way to the Tinto dungeons."

"Oh, no!"

"Oh, yes. Believe me. I don't know how Spider could have stood it all these years. We broke out of there; I could not have managed it without his inspiration and his help."

"Spider is a fine man; I spoke to him in the garden on several occasions of late." Her petal-pink lips flashed with a sudden smile. "He seems to spend an awful lot of time there." She turned her neck to glance up at her husband.

"That is what his tasks entail now, Dany. He is Tallrock's new gardener." Sebastián smiled. "Spider has a way with *roses,* a green thumb I guess you would say."

Silence reigned. The morning was glorious as the sun found and warmed them while dust motes floated, giving the room a smoky, romantic atmosphere. After a space, Daniella said, "It is getting entirely too hot in here."

"Ah, my darling wife, let me help you," he said as she began to remove her velvet robe. He grinned wickedly then. "How about if we remove the nightgown also." His eyebrows rose and she silently acquiesced. When she had done that, with his help, he said, "You take my breath away, Dany, for you are so incredibly lovely, like a misty, moonlit rose

438

just waiting for the gentle and tender kiss of midnight dew to fall upon its sweet, soft petals."

"Oh, Sebastián—you are so romantic." She turned in his arms and as he was already naked, there was no need for him to remove his clothes. Her voice emerged soft as a night's summer breeze. "I used to dream about you, long before we met. I had the same splendidly romantic dream, over and over. When we met in my dream and you kissed and held me, I was very confused and frightened, though I knew that at last I had met my handsome dream lover when you stood in the Blue Room to greet me the first time ever in the flesh."

"Dany, I cannot undo the things I spoke or did in the past. You must know by now that I was speaking of revenge, and I wanted to get back at the Drakes through you. My mind was . . . a delirious mind. I say delirious because I was in such a state upon meeting you. I could not believe that such a woman breathed and walked upon this earth."

"Sebastián." Her voice was soft and tender. "I understand fully now why you disguised yourself as Steven Landaker. A dead man. The phantom of Tallrock. It was a perfect disguise. No one knew what the real Steven looked like." She laughed. "At least not in the Carolinas. Though, what would you have accomplished, say, should the Drakes have confronted you in disguise?"

He chuckled softly. "I would have frightened Lucian to death *long* ago! Lucian fought with the English gentleman Steven—a duel—and killed him coldbloodedly before the amateur could even begin to parry and thrust. I also donned the disguise because I've always wished I'd been born with black hair. Most Spaniards are."

Daniella smiled. "I love you just the way you are, with your tawny mane and your fair eyebrows and unusual black lashes." She thought of his infamous father, Captain Kidd, and wondered if Sebastián ever felt bitter for never knowing the love of a father. "I would never wish you to be anyone else, Sebastián."

He flashed a tender smile her way. "Now we will speak of our future. What are we going to name the babe?"

"I thought Edward—if it is a boy."

"I like that," he said with a warm feeling in his chest. "And if it is a girl?" He played with her tangled locks and breathed in her delicate womanly scent, grateful to God for sending her to him to cherish and treasure for the rest of his days.

Shyly Daniella presented, "How about Rebecca?"

"That is nice. But I think it will be a boy."

She pressed her head against his ironbound chest to glance up at him. "A boy it is then."

He laughed. "You are very easy to persuade."

"Kiss me, Sebastián, kiss away the past. Embrace me, never let me go, my wonderful and eager tiger."

Suddenly he bent his head, and his mouth moved upon hers, and Daniella forgot everything—the past, the present, the future. He was all that mattered, and what he was doing to her heart, her soul, and, especially at the moment, her pliant body as his lips teased a rosy nipple and his fingers moved across her supple hips to seek the jeweled treasure within the valley.

"Dearest Sebastián . . ." Daniella squirmed as his strong embraces and gentle kisses touched her all over, gliding over every inch of her lithe, graceful body. "Tell me of your love! Display to me your glorious love, my darling—my tawny tiger."

He convinced her of the truth of his undying love as he began to move and she felt the delicious hardness between them. Enchanted hands wandered her tear-dampened cheeks and he sucked in his breath.

"Why are you weeping, m'love?"

"I know such overwhelming happiness, Sebastián. I am so full of love and perfect joy." She sighed and turned closer to him, wanting never to be too far away from him.

"I will not disappoint you, Dany, my love. You will receive everything your beautiful self is worthy of—and more."

With a patient labor of love he moved over her, his manliness musically reverberating through her womanhood, and she felt the giddy motion while ravenous desire gnawed at his loins and the passion of his ardor mounted like a raging fire out of control. She moved to lean down and kiss his forehead, smoothing the tawny curls back away from his deep-lined, handsome face.

The words were his:

"This is love, sacred and sweet, you are no longer my dark rose, but my passion, my fire. Your beautiful body was created for my fierce, cherished caress."

A cloud of her hair covered them like a vibrant, clinging mantle and the roaring fire spread between their bodies, consuming them in passion's forging flame.

There was now only the luxury of lovemaking and the loving, silken caress as their fervent bodies came together and Daniella's lithe frame arched toward him as he lowered closer and his soul told of his love for each part of her body, affording so much pleasure that she thought she would swoon where she lay.

"Please, *please!*" she begged, holding him as if he would disappear and never return, her mouth trembling against his own. She clung to him in absolute surrender, his strength hard and ready against her body.

With a smooth and swift thrust, her husband entered her and her thighs pressed wantonly around his hard hips. Sebastián's fingers ran through Dany's silky hair at her nape. Then he kissed her face all over as he moved. And moved. And moved!

"You are mine, we are one," Sebastián murmured, moving a little deeper into her.

"Oh yes, Sebastián!"

And then he moved all the way, harder and harder, longer and longer, until they were consumed in love's flaming glory, and he murmured, "I will love you always."

"Always," she echoed.

And their love stood still, captured forever like a fine-stemmed rose in glass.

Epilogue

Before Sebastián and Daniella left the beautiful, rugged coast of Cornwall for Braidwood in America, they shared the Yuletide with the Landakers. Presents were exchanged and the joy of the season was shared by one and all. Daniella's baby had come early, and he was a gorgeous baby boy who they had named Edward Wynne. He had soft blond hair like his mother, and the tawny-green tiger eyes of his father.

Lucian Drake had been the one to kill Lord Landaker in a duel, and now that his dark, evil flame had been crushed, the name Drake was wiped from the earth, never to be heard again. Steven Landaker's restless ghost finally had been laid to rest; no one would ever see — or *imagine* — the tall apparition haunting the grounds and cliffs of Tallrock.

Both Rascon and Eileena could voice their happy thoughts and joy of the season out loud and share their profound happiness with everyone. Eileena and Juan were a happily married pair now, and it was plain to see as they sat gazing raptly into each other's dreamy eyes with hands twined together tightly in Juan's lap that they were very much in love. She had finally been able to say, *"Yes now, my love,"* and Juan had been oh so ready to accommodate her.

Rascon stayed on at Tallrock, not being able to

tear himself away from his beloved Ellen who had taken him under her motherly wing and treated him as if he were her own son. And Gregory Landaker beamed, for he and Ellen had found a peaceful and tender kind of love to carry them joyfully into their golden years.

Teague and Sophie were blessed with their first child, a pink cherub of a girl who they aptly named Angeline. This Daniella learned in the letter she received after she and Sebastián and the babe had been home in the Carolinas for two weeks. Another surprise came not long after the letter from Cornwall, and Daniella was just handing her chuckling baby Edward over into the capable hands of Cook Vivien, who brought him into the cozy kitchen every morning for a bit of porridge and honey. Vivien winked over her shoulder as she went out of the room with the baby, who was reaching out a chubby fist to the couple standing in the hall like doting relatives. Bettina and Jaecko followed Vivien into the kitchen, Bettina's marriage ring winking boldly where her arm was folded behind Jaecko's back. It had been a nice wedding, and Jaecko had become Braidwood's gardener; he and Bettina had moved into the cottage out back that Daniella had given them as a wedding present.

Sebastián's home had been on the sea always when he was not staying at the Landakers', or a lonely inn somewhere, but now he lived with his wife at Braidwood and shared his wealth of merchant ships with her, as she shared everything of hers with him.

Now Sebastián brought her the fine piece of parchment bearing the imprint of the Wingate family coat of arms. She read her father's words:

"I am not long for this world, my darling Daniella Rose. I am at peace, though, knowing you will be cared for and loved. I know who he is; I suspected from the beginning, and I want you to understand your welfare and happiness in life took precedence over everything; that is why I did what I did when the sly dandy came to our door and requested your hand." Daniella's eyes were wet as she glanced up at her husband standing beside her. "For now I can go to my grave in peace and meet my reward when the good Lord comes for me. It was there alive in his eyes, Daniella Rose, my darling. He already does love you, the Tiger does."

Daniella's cheeks flushed a bright peach. With a blond twirl of hair resting on her shoulder, tickling her throat, she looked up as she felt a gentle yet firm squeeze to her shoulder. The words in the letter swam in her vision and her heart answered her father's endearing tidings. *I know, Father dear, believe me — I know.*

Author's Note

> When pirates were in the employ of
> kings . . .

At the turn of the eighteenth century, just as the
pirates were coming under heavy pressure from the
Royal Navy in American and Eastern waters, an
event in faroff Spain galvanized the attention of
every European maritime power—and for a while
gave the pirates assurance of gainful legal employ-
ment. The event was the death in November 1700
of King Charles II of Spain, whose disputed will
touched off the War of the Spanish Succession.
During that war, pirates turned legitimate and became privateers—more or less official naval auxilia-
ries whose job was to prey on the enemy's merchant
vessels.

Charles had died childless, leaving a vast empire
that included territories in Italy and the Netherlands, as well as New World holdings that stretched
from the West Indies to the Philippines. In his will,
he named as sole heir the grandson of France's
Louis XIV, who ascended the Spanish throne as
Philip V. But England and the Netherlands backed
a rival claimant to the throne, Archduke Charles of
Austria. Before long, practically all Europe was at
war: England, the Netherlands and Austria, together with Sweden, Denmark, Prussia and the Sa-

oy, in grand alliance against France, Spain, and Bavaria.

In May 1702, England's Queen Anne issued a proclamation authorizing private shipowners to seize enemy vessels. And a number of ships were immediately fitted out as privateers. Given such license to plunder, many pirates hastened to sign up. For one thing, by doing so they would be exempt from impressment into the exceedingly harsh life of the Royal Navy. For another, they stood a good chance of earning enlistment bonuses.

Between 1704 and 1707, a fleet of thirteen privateers operating out of the port of New York captured or destroyed thirty-six enemy vessels — with a huge profit of £60,000. This price was indeed high. Yet, by the end of 1707, the colony's privateering fleet had suffered the loss of two hundred sixty men in fights with French, Spanish, and other enemy ships. Even so, enthusiasm for privateering remained undiminished. This was especially true after 1708 — when Parliament renounced its ten percent claim to all prizes taken. In wartime, British and American colonial privateers captured more than two thousand prizes, most of them French.

Despite the heavy inroads made on enemy shipping by privateers, the war itself was decided on land in a series of bloody fights, commencing with the Battle of Blenheim, in which the Duke of Marlborough dealt France its first military defeat in forty years. Under the Peace Treaty of Utrecht in 1713, Philip V remained on the throne of Spain but lost his holdings in the Netherlands. France, its economy shattered, yielded the dominance of Europe to England. As for the privateers, the need for these semiofficial commerce raiders vanished as swiftly as it had arisen. Riding on toward the mid-eighteenth century, their crews promptly returned to villainy on the high seas. They performed the exact workings, but once again were outside the law . . .